PURPLE HEART

SEALS: *The Warrior Breed Book Two*

William H Keith, Jr
writing as
H Jay Riker

SAPERE
BOOKS

PURPLE HEART

Published by Sapere Books.

24 Trafalgar Road, Ilkley, LS29 8HH

saperebooks.com

ISBN: 978-0-85495-870-2

To the team...

AUTHOR'S NOTE

This is a work of fiction, but it is fiction based closely on various accounts of the actual events comprising the early years of the Underwater Demolition Teams of World War II. Readers who were actually there may recognize words and deeds transplanted to characters who are entirely the product of the author's imagination. This reworking of history was done in most cases for dramatic purposes and should in no way be construed as disrespect for the brave men, living and dead, who wrote the real saga of the UDT. This is especially true in the case of Lieutenant Commander Draper L. Kauffman — the real-life counterpart of David Coffer — the man who organized the UDTs, and whose exploits are legendary within the modern-day fraternity of the teams.

Any changes to the actual events, both deliberate and accidental, are entirely the responsibility of the author. Many of the episodes recounted in this book actually happened much as they've been described. In general, the more unbelievable an incident as depicted in this story, the more likely it is to be based solidly on fact. The men of the UDT — like their modern-day counterparts in the U.S. Navy SEALs — were remarkable men, true heroes in every sense of the word.

Truth, it seems, *is* stranger — and often more wonderful — than fiction.

— H. Jay Riker
May 1994

PROLOGUE

Thursday, 23 November 1961
Anteroom to the Oval Office

"What the hell am I doing here?"

Lieutenant Steven Vincent Tangretti sank back into the leather sofa, trying to force himself to relax, but in another five seconds he was on his feet once again, restlessly pacing the floor. The Secret Service man standing guard outside the door to the Oval Office watched impassively, arms folded across the front of the jacket of his sharply tailored gray suit.

Captain Michael T. Waverly looked up from the copy of *Life* magazine that he'd pulled from a rack next to his overstuffed chair. "Take it easy, Gator, or you're gonna burn out a bearing," Waverly said, grinning.

Tangretti shot Waverly a hard look. "Easy for you to say, Captain. You've met the guy. Me, I think I'd rather be swimming up to an enemy beach. In daylight. With a target painted on my chest."

"Hey, look, what's the worst that can happen? He cashiers you, takes away your pretty medals, and you end up penniless on the street."

"He could shoot me."

"Nah. That's only in wartime. We're not at war, right? So you have nothing to worry about."

The cover of the two-month-old magazine Waverly was reading, however, carried the headline "A CITY DIVIDED: CRISIS IN BERLIN." The Soviet-built wall across Berlin had brought East-West tensions to a fever pitch in August; in

April, it had been the Bay of Pigs. And according to the reports Tangretti had seen, things were heating up in a god-forsaken corner of Southeast Asia called Vietnam. Christ, if there wasn't a war now, there could be one at any moment. The world was coming apart at the seams, and Tangretti stood a good chance of being smack in the middle of it when it blew.

"Nothing to worry about, huh?" Tangretti eyed the Secret Service agent watching them from across the room. "That gentleman over there looks like he'd as soon shoot us as talk to us."

"Ah, he's just there in case the Russians decide to storm the White House. Relax, Gator. It's not like you're trying to get in uninvited. Don't forget, *he* asked to talk to *you*."

"That's what's worrying me. The President of the United States of America does not talk to lieutenants. Especially shaggy *old* lieutenants who are never going to make lieutenant commander."

"Screw that. You're not old."

"Old enough. Forty-three. And twenty-five years in."

"Well, it's slower going up the ol' ladder for mustangs. Especially in peacetime."

That was true enough. Tangretti had first met Waverly early in 1945, when they'd both been assigned to UDT-21. Tangretti had been a gunner's mate first class at the time, while Waverly had been a young lieutenant. Eighteen years later, Waverly was a captain, solidly on the waiting list for rear admiral and head of a newly formed Navy special operations branch reporting to the CNO himself. Tangretti, who'd been commissioned from the ranks during the Korean War, was now a rather senior lieutenant … and the Executive Officer of none other than UDT-21.

"I sometimes think I should've stayed a white hat," Tangretti growled. "Damned chiefs and petty officers run the Navy anyway. I don't know why I let them talk me into a commission in the first place."

Another door to the anteroom opened, and a White House usher in formal dress walked in, followed closely by a second Navy captain, who in turn was trailed by a yeoman first class in immaculate dress blues and carrying a briefcase. Tangretti was already standing; Waverly rose from his sofa.

"Hello, Joe," Waverly said, smiling. "Thought you were going to miss the show."

"Not this show," the captain, said with a half-smile as he advanced to shake Waverly's hand. His eyes riveted on Tangretti, masking the hint of a twinkle. "Good morning, Lieutenant. It's good to see you again."

"I take it you know Captain Galloway," Waverly said, turning to Tangretti. "Assistant Chief of Staff to Arleigh Burke?"

"We've met," Tangretti replied. Galloway thrust out one blunt paw and Tangretti took it, squeezing hard. "It's been a goddamned long time, sir."

"It has indeed, Lieutenant. I've been hearing a lot about you lately."

"Uh, I gather lots of people have, sir," Tangretti said. He nodded toward the door behind the emotionless Secret Service man. "Including *him*."

Waverly chuckled. "I think our two-striper friend here is having an attack of nerves, Joe. He's convinced himself that he's going to be flogged and keelhauled in there."

"Ah, don't sweat it," Galloway said, grinning. "I don't think he's keelhauled more than eight or ten guys in all since he was skipper of the 109."

"What about the flogging, sir?"

The others laughed.

Damn, how long *had* it been? You couldn't be in the Navy for twenty-five years without your path crossing and recrossing that of other old hands time and time again, but it had still been quite a while. The first time Tangretti had met Galloway, it had been *Lieutenant* Galloway, and Tangretti had been a GM1 and a member of the infant Underwater Demolition Teams. Funny how things worked out. Back then, early in 1944, Galloway had been a Pentagon liaison officer, on the staff of Admiral Ernest J. King, the Chief of Naval Operations. Now, here he was a captain … and on the staff of the current CNO, Arleigh Burke.

Maybe some things never changed.

Other things did, though. At that meeting, Tangretti and Richardson had just come from Kwajalein, the first UDT operation in the Pacific. They hadn't known it, yet, but they'd been on their way halfway around the world, to England, and then to Omaha Beach. The UDTs in the Pacific, the CDUs in Normandy … the very beginnings of the modern Underwater Demolition Teams. Back then, the powers-that-were still hadn't had a clear idea of what to do with these men whom one admiral at the time had characterized as "half fish, half crazy."

"Lieutenant," Captain Galloway said. "You've been with the teams from the start, haven't you?"

The question startled Tangretti. Damn, had the man been reading his mind? "Just about, sir."

"What class?"

"NCDU One-E, sir. August, forty-three."

Galloway pursed his lips and gave a low whistle. "That *was* one of the first. And, as I recall, you got shipped to the Pacific after that. With that wild buddy of yours. What was his name?"

"Richardson, sir. Henry E. Richardson. But everybody called him 'Snake.'"

"I remember you two in my office in Washington. After Kwajalein. You had a good-luck piece with you. A bullet you'd caught underwater while swimming off the beach."

Tangretti grinned, relaxing somewhat. He still had that bullet. Years ago he'd had a metal smith drill a hole through the base, and he wore it now on a chain around his neck, with his dog tags. He could feel it pressing cold and hard against his skin beneath his T-shirt.

"I remember, sir. You told Snake his promotion to lieutenant had come through and gave him his railroad tracks."

"Really? I'd forgotten that."

He was talking as though he was having trouble bringing the meeting to mind after so many years. Tangretti had the feeling, though, that Galloway wasn't having to work to remember at all, that his conversation was a ploy to get Tangretti's mind off this morning's meeting. Galloway's mind was sharp, as finely honed as a razor, and incapable of forgetting anything. Eighteen years ago, Joseph Galloway had been assigned as a liaison officer, a go-between for the CNO and then-Lieutenant Commander David L. Coffer and the UDTs. Tangretti was pretty sure that Galloway not only remembered Snake Richardson, he remembered exactly what had happened to him.

Tangretti couldn't forget, that was for damned sure.

Galloway selected one of the room's stuffed chairs and sank into it. The yeoman remained standing at formal parade rest near the door they'd come in, while Waverly went back to his sofa. Reluctantly, Tangretti found a chair as well, but he perched on the edge of it, as though ready to leap to his feet in an instant.

"You believe in the teams, don't you, Gator?" Galloway said.

"Huh? Sure! Wouldn't of stuck it eighteen years if I didn't."

He exchanged a meaningful glance with Waverly. "And, as I recall, you were pretty hot on the UDTs being able to do things that, strictly speaking, just weren't on their résumé. Am I right?"

"Like going up on the beach? Beyond the highwater mark? Yeah, sure."

"Why?"

Tangretti shook his head. "Sir, one thing combat ain't is nice and neat. I don't care what some son of a bitch sitting in a nice, comfortable office back Stateside says, what the *rulebook* says. When people start shooting at each other, there are times when the rules and regs have to go by the board.

"And I'll tell you something else. People today are scared of nuclear weapons, what they call the push-button war. There's nothing new in that. The scientists were telling us about push-button war a long time before any of us had ever heard of Trinity or the Manhattan Project … or Hiroshima. And one thing I learned in the war was that a man is more important than a machine. He's more flexible, sneakier, harder to fool, more observant, and just plain damn smarter than any machine or weapon you could make."

"I'd have to agree with all of that. So what's your point?"

"The point is, Captain, that nowadays we need *men*, and the things men can do in war, more than ever. The UDTs could do a lot more than chart beaches and blow up obstacles. To tell you the truth, they've been doing more than that ever since we got started."

"Reconnaissance inland," Waverly suggested. "Raids and ambushes. Intelligence gathering."

"All that and more," Tangretti said, nodding. "But hell, why are we going over this? It was all in that report you asked me to write."

Galloway nodded toward the Secret Service man … and the door at the man's back. "*He's* read that report, Gator."

Tangretti knew that Galloway was not referring to the agent.

"He has, huh?" Tangretti licked his lips nervously. "What'd he think? Did he say anything to you?"

"I imagine that's what he wants to talk to you about this morning. But let me tell you this much. The President feels very much the way you do about the need for small, highly trained teams of men, unconventional forces, trained for unconventional warfare. He's been pushing for that in all of the services. He's been taking a keen interest in the army's Special Forces and their ability to fight guerrilla wars. Now he's looking into the possibility of doing the same thing with the U.S. Navy."

"No … shit." Tangretti took a deep breath.

"No shit. When he calls us in there, Lieutenant, he's going to ask you some questions about the teams, about what you think the UDT could do with an expanded role, especially in the low-intensity conflict and guerrilla wars we're seeing today. He'll probably ask you about your personal experiences, about the thinking behind that report of yours. Give him straight answers, tell him what you think."

Tangretti was thoughtful for a moment, staring at the door. The man in the office beyond had been in combat. He knew the score.

"You know, Captain," he said slowly, "if we'd known at Omaha Beach and Okinawa some of what we know now…"

"What?" Galloway asked. "What would've been different?"

"Well, for one thing, a lot of damned good men wouldn't have been thrown away, fighting battles they were never trained or equipped to fight in the first place."

"Maybe battles like Omaha and Okinawa were necessary," Waverly said. "They taught us how *not* to do things."

"Assuming we're bright enough to learn the lesson." Tangretti shook his head. "Sometimes, sir, I don't think we're all that smart. We never seem to learn, do we?"

Galloway smiled. "Oh, I don't know about that. There are men like you, and quite a few others, who've been talking for some time about the need for a new kind of warrior. And there are men like *him*, a few, who are willing to listen ... and who are in a position to do something about it. Maybe things do change, with time."

"Time," Tangretti said. "And lives. That's the real problem, isn't it, sir? The people we lose while we're learning those lessons in the first place, stumbling around in the dark."

Or crawling up a sandy beach under a hail of machine gun and mortar fire, he added to himself. At that, though, there were things a damn sight worse than being under fire.

There was that rainy morning in Weymouth, for instance, over seventeen years before...

CHAPTER 1

Tuesday, 13 June 1944
Weymouth, England

As though by divine providence, the raging Channel storm that had threatened to delay the D day landings for yet another month until moon and tides were again right had lifted just a few scant hours before the largest invasion force in history had been scheduled to go ashore on the Normandy beaches. Now, one week after D day, the meteorological forecasts were calling for a return of the storm but, so far, all there'd been in southwestern England was a long, monotonous drizzle.

Gunner's Mate First Class Steve "Gator" Tangretti climbed painfully out of the taxi, paid the driver his fare, then stood on the curb for a long moment, leaning on his cane as he stared at the neat, white-painted house behind its picket fence and rose trellis across the street as the rain trickled down his face and the back of his neck and dripped off the brim of his white hat.

Damn, he wasn't looking forward to this, not one bit. Facing German machine guns at Omaha had been nothing compared with what he felt he had to do now.

The house appeared nonthreatening enough, but he found he was having trouble making himself take the first step. His leg ... God, his leg was killing him. The bandages were wet, and he could feel the sutures tugging at his skin.

Well, he could stand here and drown ... or he could go on and get it over with. Somehow mustering the last shreds of his courage, Tangretti slopped through the puddles across the street, leaning heavily on the cane as he pushed through the swinging white gate beneath its arched trellis, then started up that long, long brick path to the front door of the house. A Mrs. Wollington lived here, he gathered, a woman whose husband had died in an air raid during the Blitz, whose son had died in Crete. Rather than selling the house in Weymouth, she'd rented out the upstairs, a means of stretching her small pension from the government.

Standing on the top step, he hesitated a moment longer, then knocked on the door.

There was a long wait, during which Tangretti heard the drone of a large formation of aircraft passing overhead, masked by the drizzling overcast. They were headed south. Toward France. *Everything* was headed toward France these days. Except, of course, for men like Tangretti, who'd already fought there and come back wounded.

Or who'd been shipped back in a box. Actually, most of the dead had been buried over there, buried in the six-foot plot of French soil they'd purchased with their lives.

He was reaching up to knock again when the door opened a crack and a small, birdlike woman peered out. "Yes?"

"Mrs. Wollington? I wonder if I might see Mrs. Richardson. Your lodger."

Her eyes raked him suspiciously up and down through the crack in the door. "Who should I say is calling?"

"Steve Tangretti. I'm a … I was a friend of her husband's."

The woman hesitated only a moment. Then the door swept open, and Mrs. Wollington stood before him, wiping her hands on an apron. She was small and neat and worn by the years, perhaps fifty years old, though her silver hair gave her the spinsterish air of someone much older.

"Oh, do come in out of the rain, sir. What was I thinking of, keeping you out on such a day as this!"

"Perfectly all right, ma'am," Tangretti said, gratefully stepping inside. The house was cheery and warm; from the front hallway, he could see into a parlor beyond, and up a flight of stairs.

"Here, let me take your wet things. Is Mrs. Richardson expecting you?"

"I ... no. No, she's not." He pulled off his sopping raincoat and white hat and handed them to her. "But she'll remember me."

"Were you ... there?" she asked, shaking out his coat and hanging it up on a standing rack in the hallway. "At Normandy, I mean."

"Yes, ma'am. I was there."

Hellfire sweeping that narrow shelf of a beach. Men struggling ashore among the geysering spouts of water from the furious gunfire sweeping down from the heights overlooking the coast. Everywhere, struggling, desperate, pathetic knots of men, separated from their units, huddling in the imaginary shelter of the German beach defenses, as the demolitioneers moved among them, trying to get the men to move so that they could plant and fire the explosives that would clear the obstacles.

"Well, come on into the parlor and make yourself warm. I'll go up and tell Mrs. Richardson that you're here. Would you like tea?"

"Well, if Mrs. Richardson wants to see me, that would be nice. Thank you." He looked around the parlor, uncertain of himself. He was wearing his dress blues, and the wool was damp despite the raincoat he'd worn over it. He didn't want to sit on any of the soft and perfect-looking chairs and cushions that filled the small room. He felt out of place, and not a little clumsy. A small fireplace opened beneath a heavy mantel, the fire laid but not set. Photographs cluttered the mantel top, most of them of a kind-looking, fiftyish man in a suit and tie and wearing horn-rim glasses, or of a brash and jaunty-looking youth in the uniform of a British Army leftenant. An open case, velvet-lined, displayed a military medal, a stark silver cross with a rider engraved at the center with the words "for gallantry," hanging from a plain blue ribbon.

The British George Cross.

Tangretti had the feeling that that mantel was a kind of private shrine, an altar to fallen loved ones, and he kept a respectful distance.

"Oh, she'll want to see you, sir," Mrs. Wollington assured him as he turned stiffly on his cane to face her. "I have no doubt of that. The ... well, the telegram, you see, didn't say that much."

"No, ma'am," Tangretti replied. "They don't, usually."

We regret to inform you that your husband, Lieutenant Henry E. Richardson, was killed in the line of duty during the recent fighting on Omaha Beach. His death was in the best traditions of the United States Navy...

One hundred seventy-five Navy CDU personnel had been at Omaha Beach. Thirty-one of them had been killed, another sixty wounded, for a casualty rate of fifty-two percent. Hell, there'd been talk going into D day about how the CDUs could lose ninety percent or better, so maybe they'd gotten off light.

That didn't help the fifty-two percent, though ... or the friends and family and wives and kids and girlfriends they'd left behind.

Damn, why did it have to be Snake?

The two of them had been buddies since the very first day of NCDU training, when their instructor had had them count off, pairing the ones with the twos and telling the men that the guy beside them was their partner ... a relationship that ultimately had been proven to be as close or closer than marriage in some ways.

That had been last August, when Tangretti and Richardson had gone through one of the very first of the new Navy Combat Demolition Unit classes at Fort Pierce. Tangretti hadn't liked Richardson much, at first. Tangretti, a former Navy Seabee, considered himself to be a smooth operator, a cumshaw king, a guy who could materialize any needed item, however strange or unlikely, in the unlikeliest of places. He'd been an enlisted man, a white hat ... a guy who *worked* for his living, and, God help him, he wouldn't take an officer's commission if they handed him one on a silver platter. Richardson, on the other hand, had been a former civil engineer with a big shot father who'd wangled him a commission. He'd been an ensign when Tangretti first met him. He'd also been hot stuff with the ladies, a real Don Juan who liked to brag about his sexual exploits, whether they involved a comely barmaid or an admiral's daughter.

Somehow, and despite their differences, the two had eventually hit it off, becoming inseparable. That was one thing about Fort Pierce: if it didn't break you, it forged you into a part of a team and made the other survivors of the course closer to you than brothers. After graduating from the Naval Combat Demolition course, Tangretti and Richardson, "Gator" and "Snake," had volunteered for duty with a new unit just then forming up in the Pacific, the brand-new Underwater Demolition Teams.

At Kwajalein, in January of 1944, they'd taken part in the Navy's first UDT operation, swimming up to the Japanese-held island and even crawling out onto the beach, carrying out a reconnaissance that, among other things, told the brass waiting aboard the invasion fleet how deep the water was over the coral reef sheltering the island and its lagoon, whether or not the sand was firmly packed enough for tracked vehicles, and what kind of obstacles the Japanese had put in place to stop the expected waves of Marine landing craft and amtracks.

After Kwajalein, Tangretti and Richardson had been flown back to Washington, where they'd reported to Lieutenant Galloway at the Pentagon, answering his questions about the UDT operation and the endless litany of unforeseen problems that had accompanied it. And after that, it had been back to the NCDUs, now referred to as the CDUs, which were gathering in England for the long-anticipated invasion of France. Snake and Gator had been sent to England specifically to pass on some of the experience they'd won in the Pacific.

Hell, they might as well have stayed in the Pacific for all the relevance their experience had had to the European Theater of Operations. In the Pacific, the idea of sending in boatloads of men to check out beach approaches had swiftly been streamlined by the men themselves to fit the circumstances. A man stripped down to swimming trunks had a far better chance of getting close to a hostile beach than an LCI full of guys in fatigues and helmets and life jackets. The Fort Pierce training had never emphasized swimming, interestingly enough. In the Pacific, though, long-distance swimming reconnaissance of enemy-held beaches had already proven to be one of the most important and innovative developments of the early UDTs. Tangretti had heard that the UDTs were now required to swim a mile at sea to qualify for combat deployment.

In the ETO, however, things were quite different. Preliminary beach reconnaissance had been handled by Navy/Marine Scouts and Raiders and by British forces who'd slipped ashore from submarines to investigate the Normandy beaches and their approaches. The biggest threat to the invasion was thought to be the miles and miles of beach defenses, the "dragon's teeth" and "Belgian Gates," the ramps and traps and hedgehogs and roadblocks designed to pin an invading force on the beach while the machine guns and mortars and artillery implanted in the hills beyond ground it to a bloody pulp.

Knowing that the success of the invasion depended on getting through the obstacles and off the beach as rapidly as possible, the architects of D day had decided that the Navy CDUs would be best employed clearing lanes through the static defenses for the incoming landing craft. As they'd arrived from America, the CDUs had been folded into teams of Navy demo men and Army engineers, thirteen-man "Gap Assault Teams" that would go ashore ahead of the first wave to take out the German beach obstacles. The savage naval and air bombardments that would precede the landings would so stun and disorient the defenders, it was predicted, that the GATs should have no trouble deploying along the beach and blowing wide, buoy-marked passages through the literal forest of concrete and steel and high explosives that marked the outermost wall of *Festung Europa's* defenses.

Well, that had been the idea, anyway.

"Hello, Steve."

He turned slowly, leaning heavily on his cane. Veronica Richardson was standing in the doorway. Small, with lustrous black hair pulled back in a bun, she was wearing her WAC uniform without the olive-drab jacket and hat — brown shoes under a khaki skirt and blouse and tie. She was a tiny, perfectly formed woman whose head barely came up to the lanky Tangretti's chest. He would have thought of her as delicate if he hadn't seen her once in a barroom brawl, smashing a chair over a soldier's head. God … had that been only four months ago?

"Mrs. Richardson."

Her face looked tight and drawn, but she managed half a smile. "I think we know one another well enough for you to call me Veronica. Don't you?"

"Sure … Veronica. I, well … He gestured down at his right leg. "They just now let me out of the hospital. I … I wanted to come. To see how you were."

"You were there? With him?"

Tangretti managed a nod.

"Please. Sit down. Is your leg very bad?"

His right leg was throbbing like someone was taking a hammer to it, just above the knee, but he wasn't about to admit that. The truth of it was, they hadn't exactly "let him out of the hospital." Last night, sick of the inactivity and knowing that he *had* to make this call, he'd found an orderly willing to be bribed with a quart of whiskey and had forged a doctor's illegible signature on the release papers the guy had been able to steal from the nurses' station.

"It's okay, really," he told her. "I'm a bit wet, still. I don't want to ruin any of the furniture…"

"Nonsense. This furniture's seen worse. Sit here. Let me pull up the ottoman for your leg. There. Is that okay?"

He settled back, feeling the overstuffed chair enveloping him. "Wonderful, thanks." He sighed. "I may never be able to get up again."

She drew up a ladder-backed chair and sat down, facing him from a few feet away.

"Your leg's not broken, is it? I mean, you wouldn't be up and about if it were."

He grinned. "Well, I sure thought it was at the time, but the doctors tell me the bullet just kind of nicked the bone a bit. It hurt bad, and I was bleeding a lot, but actually I was lucky." His smile faded. Had he just said exactly the wrong thing? It was important to Tangretti that this lovely young woman, who'd already been hurt so badly by the war, wasn't hurt even more by his clumsiness. "I was real lucky," he finished awkwardly. "I just … I just wish Snake could've come out of it okay too."

"Maybe you could tell me about it. All of it."

Veronica Richardson, he reminded himself, was just twenty-one years old, the daughter of a Milwaukee brewery worker. She seemed awfully damned steady right now, though whether that was from maturity or shock he couldn't tell.

"You sure?"

She nodded. "I *have* to know, Steve. All the telegram said was that he was killed. Not where. Not when. Not why."

"You're with First Division G-2," he told her. "I'd think you'd know a hell of a lot more than me."

"*Shit,*" she said, the bitter word shocking on her lips. "Do you think they tell us a goddamned thing? It's all troop deployments and beachheads and reconnaissance in force. It's not *real!*"

Her hands were clenched into tight, tiny fists in her lap. Her eyes had the haunted look of someone who'd been crying a lot but was determined not to let the barriers down in front of others.

Veronica had been married to Snake … how long? Damn, less than two months. With a jolt, he realized it would have been just two months this coming Friday. They'd been married on April 16, six days after all leaves had been canceled and all military personnel confined to base.

Happy goddamned anniversary…

"Well," he started lamely, "you know the CDUs were organized to clear the German beach obstacles out of the way, so that the landing craft could get ashore. We were supposed to be the very first guys to hit the beach."

"The Demolitioneers," she said, using the CDUs' unofficial name for themselves.

"Yeah, except they split us up, put us in with Army engineering platoons called GATs, Gap Assault Teams. In theory, you see, us Navy guys would take out the obstacles below the water line while the Army got the ones above. On paper it looked great, everybody with a job to do, a place to be, y'know? They put Snake in GAT-5. I was in GAT-4.

"Well, a lot of things started going wrong right from the start. In fact, I guess if something could go wrong that morning, it did. The landing waves got tangled up going into the beach. Lots of people were coming ashore at the wrong spot. The fire, God, the fire from the shore was awful, *awful*. The first men ashore were stopped at the water line. Lots of them were taking cover behind the beach obstacles there. The GATs, well, some arrived late and some made it ashore but lost all their explosives and gear in the water. Lots of the officers were dead, no one knew where they were. Those teams that had their gear, well, they had to deal with the soldiers hiding behind the obstacles they were supposed to be blowing up…"

He'd expected Veronica to stop him with questions, but as he began describing what had happened that fire-swept morning a week before, she simply sat there and listened, her eyes restlessly searching his face as though seeking something more, something beyond the words he was giving her. Mrs. Wollington came in after a while, carrying a lacquered tray with a teapot, cups, and a plate of scones. Setting the tray on a small table nearby, she went over to the fireplace and used a long match to light the paper crumpled beneath the logs. With the fire going, she came back and sat down near the tea service, leaning forward and listening to his story with the same intensity as Veronica, as though wanting to experience what he'd seen and felt.

Wanting to be a part of it, wanting to *know*.

Ten minutes later, he was still describing the horror that had been Omaha on the sixth of June. Both women had read accounts in the newspapers, of course, but lurid headlines like "BLOODY OMAHA" had rapidly given way to more optimistic articles, with glowing accounts of "OUR BOYS HEROICALLY FORGING INLAND" and "KRAUTS SURRENDER IN DROVES." Newspaper stories from the front, radio broadcasts over the BBC, none of them carried the reality, the feel of what it was to be in battle, the noise, the stench, the knee-weakening terror felt by every man from lowest private to highest general.

"Well, there was this ravine, a wide gap in the cliffs above the beach," he told them. "Kind of a natural, funnel-shaped exit leading up off the beach and onto the bluffs beyond. The Germans had blocked it off, you see, with barbed wire and a big concrete wall. Snake and a bunch of other guys from GAT-5 had made it clear to the mouth of that ravine, see, and had to blow that wall."

He'd already explained how early on he'd become separated from GAT-4 and come ashore alone, his gear lost, without even a rifle.

"I saw some guys doing demo work down the beach," he explained, "and I wandered over to join them, to sort of feel less lonely, y'know? On the way, I found some Hagensen

Packs and a Bangalore Torpedo in a knocked-out DUKW and dragged them along."

Hagensen Packs were satchels filled with up to forty pounds of C-2 high explosive. Bangalore Torpedoes were lengths of pipe designed to be screwed together, one ahead of the next, each section containing C-2 and a connecting length of primacord. They were designed to be laid across barbed wire or a mine field and detonated, blowing a wide swath through the obstacle.

"Anyway," he went on, "it turned out to be GAT-5, and Snake was there with them. They were looking for a way to blow that wall, and I'd happened to find just what they needed."

"You were always good at that, Gator," Veronica said, surprising him with his nickname. "Hank … Snake, I mean, he always said you could find anything, anywhere."

"Maybe if I hadn't found that stuff," Tangretti said slowly, "Snake would still be here. I don't know. I keep replaying it in my head, trying to see how it could have been different."

Tears were spilling down Veronica's cheeks, leaving faint trails in the light dusting of face powder on her skin. Hurriedly, then, Tangretti pushed ahead.

"We had to take out the wire before we could get to the wall," he said. "We tried to use the torpedo to blow a hole through the wire, but when we hooked up the detonator and battery and cranked it up, nothing happened. I guess an exploding shell must've severed the detonator wire before we could touch it off. Anyway, one of us had to go back to the near end of the torpedo and use a fuse igniter to light the primacord. I went. Snake wanted to go, but I wouldn't let him. I made it to the torpedo all right. I'd cut the fuse for two minutes, and I hooked it up to the primacord and lit it. I was hotfooting it back down the draw to where the other guys were waiting when a Kraut machine gun hit me in the legs. Snake … Snake, he came running in after me. Dropped over top of me just before the torpedo went off. I was kind of fuzzy after that, but I gather Snake dragged me partway down the draw, then another guy came out and the two of them carried me the rest of the way back to the beach."

Tears were wetting Tangretti's face now. As he talked, it was as though he was reliving that hell on the beach. His leg was hurting worse now, and he reached down to massage the stiff muscles just above the bandaging that still encased his leg beneath his blue woolen trousers.

"I came to back behind the sea wall. Snake was down. He'd been hit in the side going in after me, but he'd kept on going anyway. Told me he was worried about me, that he couldn't let me go in alone. He said we were partners. Then he just closed his eyes and he was gone."

Anxiously, Tangretti searched Veronica's face for some hurt or disappointment beyond the savage pain she must be feeling already. He'd spent a fair part of the trip out from the hospital wondering if he should lie to her, to make up some appropriate last words that might let her know Snake had been thinking about her at the end. The fact of the matter was, Snake hadn't said a thing about Veronica. Despite what the movies might claim, men rarely talked about wives and loved ones on battlefields.

Maybe because it just hurt too damned much.

In any case, he'd made his final decision only moments before. He would be honest with her, tell her exactly what had happened, without embellishment. Veronica had always impressed him as a sharp girl, smart and intuitive. If she guessed that he was spinning stories for her benefit…

"You said you got hit in both legs?" Veronica asked him.

"Aw, just a scratch on the left," he said. "And, like I said, just nicked the bone on the right. It'll be right as rain before y'know it."

"I'm glad." She paused, then drew a deep breath. "Gator, I've got to know."

"Yeah?"

"Did he — I mean, was it fast? Did he suffer very much? I've heard stories…"

"Well, you know, guys don't usually feel very much right after they're hit. Snake, well, I swear, Veronica, he was more worried about me than he was about himself. I'm not even sure he knew he was hit. He just, well, kind of collapsed after a few minutes. And … and that was it I don't think he hurt much at all."

And thank God for that, anyway. Some guys did hurt, and Tangretti didn't think he'd ever be able to get their screams out of his brain.

"I see. Thanks, Gator. I believe you."

"He … he was my best friend, Veronica." The tears were coming faster now, and unashamedly. "What are we going to do without him?"

Veronica rose from her chair, then gently kneeled beside Tangretti's chair, laying her head against his chest. At a loss for words, Tangretti folded his arms around her as she sobbed quietly against his blue jumper. His eyes met those of Mrs. Wollington, and for a moment he thought she was going to say something, to protest this not-very-seemly tableau.

But her eyes were moist as well, he saw, and after a moment, she nodded to him, then very, very quietly stood up and slipped out of the room, closing the door to the parlor behind her. The tea and scones were left, untouched, on the table.

"I wish I could have died instead of him," Gator told the crying girl. "I wish —"

"Don't … Gator," she said, her voice muffled against his chest. "There's no way you could outguess a bullet. He's dead and we have to … have to live with that."

"I miss him, Veronica. *God,* I miss him."

"We both will, Gator. I don't think we'll ever stop missing him."

He held her tight against him and knew that she was right.

CHAPTER 2

Wednesday, 14 June 1944
U.S.S. *Gilmer*
Off Saipan

It was early morning, with a dazzling tropical sun hanging just above the island in a sparkling blue sky studded with puffy white clouds. The picturesque cone of Mount Tapotchau, an extinct volcano, loomed above the scrubby trees and palm plantations lining Saipan's western coast.

Saipan, Tinian, Rota, and Guam were the four largest and southernmost of the islands among the straggling chain of coral reefs, atolls, and fifteen larger islands called the Marianas, isolated in the vastness of the Pacific halfway between the Solomons and New Guinea to the south, and the Japanese home islands to the north, between lonely Wake Island to the east and the Philippines to the west.

Operation Forager, the American invasion of the Marianas, was expected to open a whole new chapter in the bitter warfare against the Japanese Empire. All of the islands save Guam had belonged to Japan since World War I, and the Japanese considered the Marianas to be part of their homeland. In Tokyo, General Tojo had proclaimed Saipan to be the southernmost anchor of the Empire, a bastion that the Americans would never pass. Saipan was thirteen miles long, north to south, and the town Garapan on its west coast, often described as the capital of Japan's central Pacific empire, had a population of nearly ten thousand. There was concern that many of the civilians might join the Imperial military forces based there in a desperate, to-the-death struggle.

The Marines had never faced an objective quite like this one.

Under the overall command of Vice Admiral Raymond A. Spruance, Vice Admiral Richmond Kelly Turner had assembled a joint expeditionary force similar in size to the one that had invaded North Africa twenty months before, 535 ships and 127,571 troops, including the 1st, 2nd, and 3rd Marine Divisions, with two Army divisions, the 27th and the 77th, in reserve. He was supported by TF-58, the fast carrier task force commanded by Vice Admiral Marc A. Mitscher.

Since June 11, carrier aircraft had been pounding the Marianas. This morning, two bombardment groups, including seven battleships and eleven cruisers, with eight escort carriers in support, had taken up position off Saipan and neighboring Tinian and begun hammering away at the islands at close range, a thundering, slamming fury of noise and flame that raked the islands from end to end, paying special attention to eight beaches that stretched along four miles of Saipan's southwestern coast.

Lieutenant Michael T. Waverly stood on the forward deck of the U.S.S. *Gilmer*, an aging, flush-deck destroyer that had been converted into a troop-carrying APD, a high-speed transport. Just three hundred and fourteen feet long and thirty-one feet abeam, the *Gilmer* was rolling slightly in the two-foot swell that had kicked up under a strong offshore breeze. Waverly steadied himself on the deck with one hand on a stanchion, pressing a pair of binoculars to his eyes as he slowly scanned the coastline a few thousand yards to the east. He could see the beaches, low and narrow, backed by drifts of sandy soil and masses of tropical forest interspersed with the orderly rows of plantation palm groves. Here and there, the fire-brilliant vermilion of a tropical flame tree showed through the tangle of trees and scrub. Explosions flashed and rumbled among those trees, adding flickers of real flame to the scene. The island was so large, however, that it appeared to be absorbing the salvos of shells with very little to show for it.

Offshore, surf flashed white above the coral reef that walled off Saipan's lagoon. North, the broad, flat coral reef, nearly two hundred feet wide, paralleled the coast a full mile from the beach, studded every few hundred yards by buoys flying brightly colored pennants — presumably planted there by the Japanese as range markers for their mortar and artillery crews. South, the lagoon narrowed to the length of a football field. Midway down the objective area, the beaches were broken by a rocky promontory called Susupe Point. Beyond, part of a luxuriant green-clad spine running the length of the island, Mount Tapotchau towered fifteen hundred feet above the surrounding sea, somehow serene despite the drifting patches of hazy smoke rising from the preliminary bombardment. The *Gilmer* was making her way gradually closer to the reefs off the northern beaches.

"Mike?" a voice said at his back. "How's it going?"

Lowering the binoculars, Waverly turned to face the man behind him. "Oh, good morning, Commander. Just having a peek at the target."

Lieutenant Commander David L. Coffer was UDT-5's skipper. Tall, lean, and angular, nearsighted to the point of needing thick glasses, he was already a legend within the teams as the man who had almost single-handedly pieced together the Navy's demolition training course at Fort Pierce, the school that for the past year had been feeding hundreds of men to the CDUs in Europe and the UDTs here in the Pacific.

Most of the members of Team Five had served under Coffer when he'd been running Fort Pierce, and morale in the unit was sky-high as a result. Coffer had a reputation for caring for his men, and his men had responded with genuine affection. The stories circulating about his past — and about his legendary tussles with Washington — only added to the aura of the legend.

"Just making the rounds, Mike," Coffer told him, coming up and leaning against the safety rail. His eyes were on the beach and on the white curl of surf marking the offshore reefs. "Well. Are you ready for this?"

"Yes, sir," Waverly replied. He looked Coffer up and down, then glanced down at himself with a wry grin. "I'm ready. I'm not sure the Japanese are, though."

Neither Coffer nor Waverly was immediately recognizable as an officer of the United States Navy at the moment. Like most of the UDT men awaiting the orders to board their landing craft, both men were wearing nothing but swim trunks, waterproof watches, knives in black scabbards, and canvas shoes. Their entire bodies had been painted a camouflage blue, and black stripes had been marked along the entire length of their torsos, legs, and arms, a thick stripe every foot, with thinner stripes at every half foot. It gave the men a strange and atavistic look, as though the UDT combat swimmers had assumed the guise of striped fish or seagoing reptiles. The paint had been Coffer's idea, one with highly practical applications beyond the suggestion now making the rounds aboard the *Gilmer*, that the paint jobs were intended to frighten to death any Japanese soldiers who happened to see them. Arguably the strangest part of the costume was the men's shoes. Necessary to keep them from slicing open their feet on the razor-sharp coral, the shoes had originally been bright white, but Coffer had ordered them dyed blue to match the men's skin paint. Somehow, the dye hadn't come out quite right, and now most of the men were wearing shoes that were colored a darling baby blue.

"Well, I'd still just as soon the Japanese never see us in the first place," Coffer said. Shading his eyes, he squinted above the shadow of Mount Tapotchau at the rising morning sun. Thunder rolled across the water as the U.S.S. *California*, half a mile beyond the *Gilmer*, cut loose with her main batteries. Seconds later, pillars of dust rose behind the beach and the trees like hazy poplars, but with little noticeable effect.

Waverly knew precisely what must be going through Coffer's mind at this moment. He could read it in the man's eyes, in the disapproving, downward quirk of his mouth.

In April, just before their departure from the new UDT base on Maui, Coffer had been called into Admiral Turner's office and told he was to take his men into the beach at Saipan at 0900 hours — nine o'clock in the morning — on D minus one, the day before the invasion was scheduled to begin. UDT-5 and UDT-7 were to carry out a detailed and protracted reconnaissance of the Saipan landing beaches, including a hydrographic survey. The men would have to get as close to the shore as they could, mapping underwater obstacles, noting water depths along a precisely measured course leading from the reef to the beach, checking surf conditions, plotting the locations of gun batteries ashore, marking mines, and, as if that weren't enough, blowing up all of the obstacles in the beach approaches.

According to Waverly's informant, there'd been a near confrontation between the lanky UDT officer and the vice admiral, with Coffer insisting that men did *not* simply swim up to someone else's beach in broad daylight.

"You do," Turner had replied with characteristic bluntness, and that had terminated the interview. Mere lieutenant commanders did not argue strategy, tactics, or policy with vice admirals.

Now, almost two months later, Coffer was still chafing against an order that he saw as nonsensical ... and a damned waste of lives. Hell, the teams could do nearly everything Turner wanted with a dark-of-the-moon reconnaissance at night. Why was the invasion command insisting on a recon in broad daylight? Coffer, Waverly knew, was certain that casualties among the teams might run as high as fifty percent.

In Turner's defense, the plan called for a savage bombardment of the island, one that would leave the defenders so dazed and confused that an army could swim up to its beaches without attracting much, if any, enemy fire at all. But Waverly had noticed that lots of senior people in this war tended to put more trust in preliminary air and sea bombardments than results so far had been able to justify. A massive bombardment was supposed to have softened up Tarawa, for instance, and look at what a bloody shambles *that* had been! And the news from England suggested that the Normandy landings had run into much the same problem on D day, especially at Omaha Beach. Damn it, all you had to do was look at that island, at that deceptively peaceful slope of Mount Tapotchau, and know that there was just too much territory over there to guarantee that every square yard would get a decent going-over from the battlewagons offshore. The Japanese could be hiding anything in there, buried away in caves or hidden in concrete bombproofs. Turner's ships and Mitscher's planes could pound away at Saipan until doomsday and not have a damned thing to show for it.

"Don't worry, Skipper," Waverly told his worried commanding officer. "It's next to impossible to even see a guy bobbing around in the ocean all by his lonesome. With these Halloween costumes we're wearing, I'll bet the bastards don't even come close."

Coffer glanced at Waverly and managed a small grin. "I hope you're right, Lieutenant. But just in case you're not, you have your list memorized?"

"Uh … yes, sir. One: Lieutenant Commander Coffer. Two: Lieutenant —"

"That's okay, Mike." Coffer sounded tired. "Save it. I believe you."

Every enlisted man and officer in Coffer's team had memorized Five's chain of command, a numbered list of the team's fifteen officers in their order of precedence. If they did suffer fifty percent casualties, there could be a lot of confusion if officers were killed and the men didn't know who was in charge at a critical moment. It was a precautionary measure that the men joked about — the fast-track promotion list, they called it — but it added a grim touch to the preparations for the day's activities.

Behind them, another salvo bellowed forth from *California's* forward fourteen-and-a-half-inch guns, the orange flash doubled by the reflections in the water below. The concussion of the big guns was a palpable thing, flattening the water around the old battlewagon and still strong enough across almost a thousand yards of open water to slap at Waverly's bare skin. The sound of those shells hurtling over the *Gilmer* on their way to the island sounded — no, *felt* — like the passage of a freight train.

"No reply yet from the beach," Waverly said. He squinted at the shoreline, now, he estimated, about a mile away. Surf flashed and rolled on the reef north of Susupe Point, about halfway between the ship and the shore. "Think maybe they're all asleep in there?"

"More likely they don't want to give away their positions." Coffer glanced at his watch. "Almost Roger Hour," he said. "We'd better get moving."

"Aye, aye, sir."

As Coffer walked aft toward the bridge past the 20-mm mount on *Gilmer's* foredeck, Gunner's Mate First Class Tom Davies came up behind Waverly. His black-and-blue paint job glistened in the morning light. "The Old Man looks worried," he said in an offhand way.

Waverly turned back to face the beach. "Damn straight. I would be, too, wouldn't you?"

Davies made a face, a scowl turned grotesque by the blue paint. "Shit, he should've thought of that before deciding to leave his nice, cushy desk and come out here and play with us roughnecks. It's not the same out here as being instructor at a—"

Waverly spun, glaring at Davies. "Stow it, mister!"

"Huh? I just meant —"

"*Stow* that crap! You don't know that guy's story, and until you do you don't have the right to comment on it, got it?"

"Sure! Sure!" Davies raised his hands. "Hey, I didn't mean anything by that, sir!"

Waverly tried to make himself relax, forcing down the anger. Davies, he reminded himself, was one of the few men in Five who hadn't come aboard from Fort Pierce ... and therefore he didn't know about the Old Man, not firsthand, at any rate. Davies had been a first-class diver, a hard hat working at Pearl who claimed he'd gotten bored mucking about in the mud at the bottom of the harbor and put in for hazardous duty instead. His request had dropped him in with Team Five, newly arrived from the States.

"Let me tell you something about the skipper," Waverly said. "He graduated from Annapolis, but at first they wouldn't give him a commission. Weak eyes. So he served a stint in London during the Blitz, working in UXB."

"Disarming unexploded bombs?" Davies said, eyes widening. "No shit?"

"No shit. Served as a sublieutenant with the Royal Navy Volunteer Reserve. You should hear some of the stories. Hang around in this outfit long enough and you probably will. After that, he got his commission and a job organizing the Navy's bomb disposal school. And he was at Pearl right after December seventh, disarming unexploded Japanese bombs."

"You're tellin' me the guy has nerve," Davies said. "I'll buy that."

"After that," Waverly went on, relentless, "Washington put him in charge of forming this unit. He did it, did it all, starting with the training program at Fort Pierce. Almost from the beginning, though, Coffer was bombarding Washington with requests for transfer to combat duty. According to one piece of scuttlebutt I heard, he was chewed out a few months ago by some admiral in Washington who simultaneously received *two* requests that Coffer be assigned to amphibious force operations, one from Admiral Kirk in England, the other from Admiral Turner in the Pacific.

"Only trouble was, both 'requests' had the same wording, exactly."

Davies chuckled. "Oops."

"Yeah, oops. And that should give you an idea of how hard the skipper's been working to get out here and join us."

"So how did he get out here?"

Waverly shrugged. "The word is that Turner really did ask to have him sent out here at about the same time the skipper was sending out those requests. Hell, I wonder if the Pentagon didn't finally decide to reassign him just to get him out of their hair. But whatever happened, now he's here, CO of Team Five and senior UDT officer for this whole damned shooting match, and I can't think of one damned man in this whole, damned, man's Navy who I'd rather follow." Waverly reached out and for emphasis tapped his blue-stained forefinger three times squarely against the black, four-foot ring where it crossed Davies's chest. "And you, mister, had better learn to keep your trap shut until you know what you're talking about. And *who* you're talking about."

Davies swallowed. "Aye, aye, sir. Sorry, sir."

Relaxing suddenly, Waverly grinned. "Aw, forget it. Just a friendly piece of advice, okay?"

"Sure, Lieutenant. And … thanks."

Waverly wasn't sure whether he'd come down too hard on the guy, but he was worried that Davies wasn't fitting in with the rest of the team. Five was a close-knit bunch, thanks to their shared experience at Fort Pierce and thanks, too, to the near hero worship they felt for Coffer. The handful of guys like Davies who'd joined the team in Hawaii were still outsiders, kept at arm's length until they'd proven themselves.

It was a hell of a note that they were going to have to prove themselves in the crucible off Saipan. Fifty percent casualties? Waverly wondered if the skipper hadn't underestimated, if ninety percent might not be a more realistic figure. The real question was how many of the men would actually force themselves to press ahead, despite what was certain to be heavy fire from the shore, to carry out their orders and get as close to the beach as possible. How close would they get before deciding that swimming any closer would be nothing short of suicide, and turn back? Two hundred yards? One hundred? Would they even make it past the reef and its ominously flagged range marker buoys?

"Now hear this, now hear this" blared from a Tannoy speaker set on *Gilmer's* bridge superstructure. "Beach reconnaissance party, lay to the boat deck and man your boats."

"That's us," Waverly told Davies with a sigh. "Let's go earn our pay."

Like other APDs, *Gilmer* carried four LCP(R)s amidships, slung from davits, one on either side of the transport's stacks, and another pair immediately aft. The Landing Craft, Personnel (Ramped) — also known as a Higgins boat — was thirty-five feet, ten inches long, with a ten-foot-nine-inch beam. Fully loaded — with either thirty-six troops or four tons of cargo, it drew three and a half feet of water aft. They were no-frills craft, completely lacking a superstructure. Twin gunner's cockpits were built into the hull forward, seven feet abaft of the narrow bow ramp, but the .30-caliber machine guns normally mounted there had been removed from *Gilmer's* four boats. They would have to rely on speed this morning — they could manage a blistering nine knots when fully loaded — rather than offensive armament.

UDT-5 numbered eighty-five men and fifteen officers, one hundred men tasked with surveying the landing beaches north of Susupe Point. Each of *Gilmer's* LCPs had been assigned a seven-hundred-yard stretch of beach, with seven pairs of swimmers responsible for each beach. After going over the LCP(R)s side, they would be led in by twelve men on six "flying mattresses," two-man rafts equipped with electric motors and orders to guide the swimmers in. Officers on flying mattresses at each beach were assigned to coordinate the swimmers, to encourage them, and if need be, to rescue them. Coffer, his glasses now taped to his head, was going to be on one of the mattresses; Waverly would be on another.

The entire team was gathering on the boat deck as crewmen swung the LCPs out over *Gilmer's* sides and gentled them down to the water. Each was piled high with several small, black rubber rafts aft of the big, mid-deck engine housing, and several UDT men rode the boat into the water. The rest waited on deck to go down the cargo nets already draped over the sides. They were a weird-looking crowd in their blue camouflage paint and black stripes. By now, most had donned the rest of their improbable outfits. Some wore kneepads, and all wore or carried heavy canvas work gloves to protect them from the coral. They wore steel helmets and also carried the new, glass-front face masks that one of the men in Five had ordered from a sports shop in Hawaii. Balsa floats for marking mines, three-inch-by-ten-inch plastic slates for recording depths and obstacles, and pencils for writing underwater all dangled from their belts. In addition, one man in each swim pair carried a reel of fishing line, measured off with cloth knots at twenty-five-yard intervals. Some of the officers held bulky handie-talkie radios, theoretically waterproofed. They would use them to talk to the team members who stayed behind in the LCPs, coordinating naval gunfire and the pickup of the team at the end.

A mile to the south right now, UDT-7 would be deploying off a second APD, the aging four-piper *Brooks*, for a similar reconnaissance.

As Waverly approached the waiting men, he heard a familiar, raw-throated *whoop-whoop-whoop* and the thud of canvas sneakers on the deck. Torpedoman Second Class Charles

Foglio was doing an war dance, as a circle of his buddies laughed and thumped out a tom-tom beat on their slates.

"Get it out of your system, Blondie," Waverly called. "When we get in to the beach, we're supposed to be quiet!"

Foglio stopped his dance and grinned, his teeth startlingly white through the paint. "No sweat, Lieutenant. I just figured with all this war paint, y'know?…"

"Blondie" had not received his nickname from the color of his hair. Small, wiry, the son of a third-generation Italian family from Philadelphia, he was dark-skinned and black-haired. No, Foglio had been "Foggy" until he'd won the new nickname during the cruise from San Diego to Hawaii in April. The ship had been a passenger liner converted to troop-carrying duties, and packed aboard along with the men on their way from Fort Pierce to join UDT-5 at Maui had been — wonder of wonders! — the first regiment of Army WACs to be shipped to the Pacific.

A memorable cruise … and all the more so because of the raw material it had provided for the tales the men told one another during the late-night bull sessions that were one of the enlisted man's primary forms of entertainment at sea. "Tail tales" were always the most popular stories, naturally enough, even though there was rarely any sure means of verifying whether the accounts were true or the products of their tellers' overheated imaginations. Aboard ship, especially, the chances for privacy were damned few and far between.

In Foglio's case, though, Waverly tended to believe everything he'd heard. The man claimed to have been screwing three different WACs just during the passage between San Diego and Pearl, using one of the lifeboats for a bedroom. He had trophies to prove it, too — three pairs of women's panties, two white, one black, the elastic waistbands stretched to three different sizes. Foglio insisted he liked blondes best, and that talking them out of their panties first was his way of proving that they really *were* blondes.

Hence, the nickname "Blondie." On Maui, the son of a bitch had actually been charging other enlisted men a dollar apiece for the chance to inhale the fragrance of his trophies; one buck, one hit. Despite his mercenary streak, Blondie was popular with the rest of the team and a good, steady man.

He would also be Waverly's partner for the swim in to the beach this morning.

"Hold 'er aft!" a voice called from a nearby working party of seamen in white hats and dungarees. A burly chief boatswain's mate bossed the lines of men holding the boat falls with a voice like rattling gravel. "Hold 'er for'ard! Steady … now lower away!"

The last of the boats were in the water alongside the *Gilmer*. UDT men already in the boats cast off the davit falls, and the LCPs were secured only by painters at bow and stern. Another salvo boomed from the *California* and was echoed by the cruisers and other battleships in the northern bombardment group. They were hammering now at the beaches themselves and at the lines of trees just beyond. *Hit 'em*, Waverly said to himself, a heartfelt prayer. *Hit the bastards, by God!*

It seemed incredible, but the Japanese still hadn't replied. If, in spite of all of Waverly's doubts, the naval bombardment could shellac the coastal defenses hard enough, this cockeyed plan might actually have a chance of succeeding. Maybe it *was* succeeding. His heart was hammering inside his chest so hard right now he thought the men standing nearby must surely be able to hear it, despite the thunder in the background.

The men were lined up, their joking and bantering over. Without a word, they began throwing their legs over the ship's side and starting down the cargo nets, as other men already in the boats leaned out, holding the improvised ladders taut. Waverly had been assigned to Boat Four, the southernmost LCP in Team Five. His team would be the one surveying the beach immediately to the north of Susupe Point, which everybody agreed was likely to be a hot spot. *Please, God, let them give Susupe the most God-awful pasting —*

A geyser of water exploded up out of the sea, thirty yards to seaward of the *Gilmer*, the concussion hammering at the soles of Waverly's feet through the steel deck. A second later, two more geysers erupted, neatly straddling the APD, one just to port, the other to starboard. Waverly heard a high-pitched *ping*, and one of the sailors on the boat falls crumpled up, selected at random by a chunk of hurtling shrapnel. Water cascaded across the deck.

"Oh, Christ," someone yelled. A half mile farther out to sea, waterspouts splashed playfully along the *California's* port side. A flash and a puff of smoke snapped off the battleship's control tower, just above her bridge. A hit! More shells howled in from the island, striking the sea around the *Gilmer* in savage bursts of spray and foam.

"Into the boats!" Coffer yelled above the sudden crowd noise and the agonized cries of the wounded sailor. "Everybody, into your boats!" The lines of UDT men shuffled along faster, vanishing over the side.

Waverly scrambled down the net with the island at his back, feeling stark naked against the APD's hull and expecting another round to come crashing in at any second. He let go of the net and dropped the last five feet, landing with a heavy thud in the bottom of the pitching boat. The engine was already running, the UDT coxswain standing at the wheel wearing dungarees and helmet and life jacket instead of the paint and survey gear sported by the others.

Another shell howled in, falling short, hurling spray into the blue sky that fell in a cold, salty rain across the men huddled in the bottom of the landing craft.

Suddenly, it looked like this was going to be as rough as Coffer had predicted.

One: Lieutenant Commander Coffer, Waverly thought to himself, reciting the chain of command with all the heartfelt fervor of a magical incantation. *Two...*

CHAPTER 3

Wednesday, 14 June 1944
UDT-5, Boat Four
Off Susupe Point, Saipan

The shells kept coming.

The boat raced toward the coral reef, now eight hundred yards distant, and the Japanese guns ashore followed the LCP(R) all the way. The coxswain was zigzagging in an attempt to make the enemy gunners' jobs as difficult as possible; before long, Waverly found his initial fear and feeling of vulnerability had evaporated somewhat The enemy gunners might have the reef carefully pegged out with range marker buoys, but their fire wasn't all that accurate at any distance out to sea. Mortar bursts kept falling in astern, sending up thundering columns of spray in the landing craft's wake ... but always where the boat had been a few seconds before, never *quite* where it was at the moment.

Even so, both the *Gilmer* and the *California* were both rapidly drawing off now, putting a few thousand more yards between themselves and the Japanese shore batteries.

Which left those guns with no targets save the four Higgins boats now bouncing across the swell toward the reef.

"So, Lieutenant," Blondie said, shouting to make himself heard above the roar of the LCP(R)'s engine. "What d'you think? Did that flyer do our job for us?"

Waverly grinned back. "Won't know till we get there, I guess." He paused as another mortar went off with a dull, teeth-rattling *thump* astern, and salty rain drizzled on the men in the boat. "Hell, he didn't do our job for us. He just gave us more to do!"

The day before, a Navy Avenger off one of the carriers, flying over the island at three thousand feet, had been hit by antiaircraft fire. Two crewmen had been killed outright, but the pilot, a Lieutenant Martin, had been blown clear over the eastern coast of Saipan. His chute, shredded by the explosion, had failed to deploy completely, but miraculously Martin had hit four feet of water at an angle, smacked into a sandy bottom, and somehow survived, shaken and bruised but otherwise unhurt.

His splashdown inside the lagoon one hundred yards north of Susupe Point and a hundred yards from the beach had not gone unnoticed, however. In fact, he'd attracted the undivided attention of every Japanese sniper on the shore. Gathering up his chute, Martin had splashed across the lagoon as bullets hit the water around him. Still under fire, he'd reached the reef and run across the coral, then dove into the open sea beyond. There, he'd inflated his seat cushion life raft, rigged a piece of his parachute as a sail, and managed to get far enough out to sea that a PBY Catalina on search-and-rescue had been able to set down and pick him up.

Later that same afternoon, Martin's report had been radioed to the *Gilmer*. Turner's operations center wanted the report verified. According to Martin, the water in the lagoon was only four to six feet deep, while the water over the coral was only about one and a half feet deep. As the group assigned to that particular stretch of beach, Boat Four was ordered to check the numbers ... and to locate and mark the crashed Avenger.

The closer the Higgins boat drew to the seaward side of the reef, the heavier the volume of fire from the shore.

Raising his head above the LCP(R)'s bulwark, Waverly studied the evil-looking thrust of Susupe Point, now just a few hundred yards off the landing craft's starboard quarter. There *had* to be Japanese mortar and gun positions among those rocks and trees, but he couldn't see any flashes or smoke. Mortar bursts were flowering astern now one after another in a savage, sustained barrage. Some rounds were falling short, and when they hit the barely submerged coral of the reef, they sent up spinning fragments of rock with the spray. Waverly had thought it a silly idea to go swimming wearing a steel helmet ... but watching the coral splinters rain from the sky, he was glad now for the extra protection.

"I think the fire from our ships has let up a bit," Mineman First Class Howard Perkins yelled above the roar. "It ain't time for the planes yet, is it?"

According to the operations plan, the shore bombardment would lift at 1000 hours — almost an hour from now — to allow aircraft from Mitscher's baby flattops to come in and give the Japanese defenders a close-up pounding.

"Nah," Blondie yelled back. "Our ships're just pulling farther out to sea, gettin' the hell outa range of those guns. Assholes couldn't hit fuckin' Australia at that range."

"Shit," a machinist's mate second, a kid from Brooklyn named Horwitz, replied. "I just hope they don't drop any short. The Japanese're bad enough without help from our guys, know what I'm sayin'?"

Lieutenant j.g. Ralph Dobson had been detailed to stay with the LCP, so he wore fatigues and a life jacket instead of the stripes of the other team members. "Hey, maybe if they drop some rounds on us," he said nervously, "the Japanese'll think we're on their side!"

Despite the gallows humor, the men in Boat Four were remarkably steady, Waverly noticed. *He* didn't feel up to cracking jokes. Maybe, he thought, it was just that everybody had a different way of handling the waiting.

"Hey, Blondie!" Davies called back from his position on a bench ten feet forward.

"Yeah?"

"You got your trophies with ya?"

"Hell, no!" Blondie shot back. "You think I wanna risk giving 'em a wash? No, I got 'em stowed safe and sound back aboard ship."

"Too bad," Davies replied. "It'd be nice to have a whiff and remember why we're out here, about now."

"I'll give you a whiff," Davies's swim partner said, raising his elbow. "Here."

A mortar round thundered close aboard, less than ten yards astern and to port. The boat shuddered and tipped, the bow coming down with a splash, then rising again in a cascade of white spray.

"Soon as we get back, Davies!" Blondie yelled. "I promise! And for free!"

Fifty yards off the seaward edge of the reef, the boat's coxswain spun the wheel and turned the boat parallel to the beach, heading north, away from Susupe Point. Mortar fire and artillery shells continued to splash and boom around the LCP(R), and now the men could hear the hammering chatter of machine gun fire as well.

"Mr. Waverly?" the coxswain yelled. "I don't think we can get in much closer than this! They've got the reef pretty well pegged!"

Japanese fire was lashing the water between the LCP and the reef to white froth, punctuated steadily by the thump and

51

splash of towering columns of water. Suddenly, an explosion banged loud and hard in the air high above the boat, and Waverly heard the *ping* of ricocheting shell fragments. Several men in the boat dropped to their hands and knees, and Waverly thought for a moment they'd been hit … until he saw Horwitz laugh and rise again, juggling a hot and twisted bit of metal from hand to hand. Bits of shrapnel were highly prized as souvenirs.

The coxswain slowed the boat to a crawl, still parallel to the reef. "Okay, men!" Waverly yelled. "Get the mattresses over the side!"

Working together, the men heaved the first of the inflated two-man rafts over the side. Clutching their gear, Waverly and Blondie scrambled over the LCP's gunwale and dropped into the raft, which bobbed wildly beneath their weight. The mortar rounds that had been following the landing craft walked closer, and Dobson began signaling frantically, pumping his fist up and down. "Go! Go! Go! Get the fucking lead out!"

Waverly laughed, the sound just a bit shrill. He didn't know whether Dobson was swearing at him or at the LCP(R)'s coxswain, but the obscenity was uncharacteristic of the young man, who'd come from a rich Providence, Rhode Island, family, had attended Yale, and had a reputation of being a quiet, studious sort. With the Higgins boat's engine idling, the craft wallowed unpleasantly in the swell, and all the while the Japanese gunners were narrowing down the range, each miss closer than the one before.

Blondie positioned himself in the rear half of the rubber boat and got the motor started, as men aboard the LCP(R) handed Waverly their gear, a waterproof walkie-talkie, a bundle of float markers, a couple of face masks. The engine buzzed to life, and Waverly cast off the raft's bow line. Crouching low, little showing above the swell save their heads and shoulders, they steered the unwieldy little craft clear of the slow-moving Higgins boat.

Without warning, the feeling of vulnerability Waverly had experienced earlier returned. He and Blondie were all alone in a tiny raft, steering deliberately for the Japanese-held island to the east.

The morning sun was well above the volcano cone symmetry of Mount Tapotchau now, making Waverly feel about as exposed as a large beetle crawling across an empty dinner plate.

It was not a comfortable feeling.

While Waverly and Blondie were clambering onto their flying mattress, other members of the team dropped a second raft into the water, securing it fore and aft to the LCP(R)'s port side, the side away from the beach. A mortar round exploded twenty yards to starboard.

"Get this bucket moving, Chief!" Dobson yelled at the coxswain, slapping the back of the man's helmet. The coxswain pushed the boat's throttle forward, and the LCP(R) began picking up speed again, leaving Waverly and Blondie bobbing toward the reef in their tiny raft.

"Lamb!" Dobson called. "Davies! You guys're up!"

Engineman Second Class Peter Lamb and GM1 Tom Davies, the first two combat swimmers in line, clambered over the LCP's gunwale as the craft sped north through the water, lying down side by side in the rubber boat.

Pete Lamb had struggled for a long time with his surname. He'd been teased mercilessly about it in school, when he was a kid growing up back on Chicago's west side. He'd been teased about it in boot camp, at the Great Lakes Naval Training Center, and again when he'd gone to engineman school. Fort

Pierce had been the worst, but he'd earned some respect from the others after winning a couple of fights that mixed his tough-kid street rough-and-tumble with the commando hand-to-hand techniques they'd been learning at the NCDU school. When Davies had joined Five at Maui, Lamb had thought he was going to have to start the routine all over again when the guy had cracked a smile on hearing his name, but Davies had just shaken his hand and said, "Good to meet you, Lamb. I'm Davies, and if you ask me where Goliath is, I'll flatten you."

Lamb decided he liked Davies on the spot, even though the guy hadn't gone through Fort Pierce and didn't seem to mesh with the rest of the guys, probably for that reason. Lamb, who stood just five-six and was as solidly packed as a boxer, had taken the skinny, six-one Davies figuratively under his wing, despite the difference in their ranks. They'd trained together at Maui, and now they were teamed for the swim to Saipan.

Lamb just hoped the guy had what it took. Hard hat diving was one thing; swimming a mile into a hot beach under fire was something else.

Clinging to the front of the raft, Lamb lay with his head less than a foot above the water. The LCP(R) was up to full speed again, and the wake curling aft past the bow slapped and thumped at him through the thin fabric bottom of the raft and exploded into his face. It felt as if they were going much faster than nine knots, though he knew the sensation of speed was largely illusion. He kept his eyes on Lieutenant Dobson, watching the man as the officer checked bearings off the shore. Suddenly, Dobson raised his right hand up beside his head, finger extended, then brought it down again sharply, pointing at the two men.

"Go!"

Together they rolled off the raft, hitting the water with a splash and surfacing a moment later in the speeding boat's wake.

According to the reconnaissance plan drawn up by Commander Coffer, seven pairs of swimmers were to be dropped into the water from each LCP(R) at one-hundred-yard intervals parallel to the beach. Each team consisted of a lineman and a searcher. The lineman was to anchor his fishing line to a buoy on the reef, then unreel it as he swam to the shore. Every twenty-five yards, as marked by the cloth tags knotted into the line, he was to stop and measure the depth of the water, using his own painted body as a yardstick and recording the depth on his slate. His partner was to zigzag back and forth all the way in, looking for mines or dangerous coral heads to mark with his balsa wood floats. In this swim team, Davies was the lineman, Lamb the searcher.

Some of the teams had additional orders. Those swimmers closest to Susupe Point, where the enemy fire was expected to be the heaviest, were supposed to split up halfway into shore, with one swimmer pressing on as far as he could — as close as fifty yards off the beach if possible — while the other man stayed behind to insure that the information they'd gathered to that point would make it back to the fleet.

The two men had already tossed a coin to decide who would have the privilege of going on ahead and who would have to wait behind. Lamb would be the stay-at-home, and he envied Davies his luck. Going in would prove he had what it took to be in Team Five, once and for all. As they pressed their masks over their faces, however, and started swimming clumsily toward the reef fifty yards away, he could feel the throb and shudder of explosions transmitted through the water.

Damn, suppose this *was* a suicide mission, like the scuttlebutt said?

Well, maybe the two of them would end up proving that they both had what it took to be UDT ... posthumously.

Crouching in the roughly wallowing flying mattress, Waverly found that he didn't have nearly as good a view of the island and its reef as he'd had aboard the Higgins boat. His head was literally only two or three feet off the water, and when the rubber raft slid into the trough between each swell, he found he couldn't see much of anything except green water on all sides. Blondie held the tiller on the little electric outboard tightly, though, and they motored steadily toward the shore, cutting toward the reef at an angle that gradually took them farther from the threatening loom of Susupe Point. Rounds continued to whine overhead, striking the water with thunderous impacts, but much to his relief, Waverly found that most of the shells were following the LCP(R). The Japanese were paying little attention to the flying mattresses, at least for the moment.

Picking up the walkie-talkie, Waverly extended the aerial and switched the radio on. "Doghouse, this is Dog-one," he said, pressing the transmit switch. "Doghouse, Dog-one. Do you read me? Over!"

There was a hiss of static, and then Dobson's voice sounded, tinny in his ear. "Dog-one, this is Doghouse. I read you!"

"Nice to hear a friendly voice, Doghouse." As the next wave carried his raft higher, Waverly stared north, picking out the low, gray hull of the LCP, now about four hundred yards away. "We're starting toward the reef now. Over."

"Roger, Dog-one. We've got two more pairs of swimmers to go, then we'll head for the standoff point. We'll be here if you need us. Good luck!"

"Thanks, Doghouse. You too. Dog-one, out."

Leaning over the side of his raft, Waverly could see the coral reef rising to meet him through the crystal water. Visibility underwater looked good, despite the silt stirred up in broad, spreading patches by the bombardment. He could see perhaps twenty or thirty feet down, and the seaward side of the coral reef looked like the side of a pale, blue-green mountain.

"Crossing the reef now," he called to Blondie. He reached for his slate to start making a map.

The mortar burst struck twenty yards away, a shattering crash of raw noise, followed by a surging wave of water and a drenching spray. "Shit, Lieutenant!" Blondie called. "I think they spotted us!"

Another geyser of water exploded from the sea on the other side, and Waverly had to grab for the side of the raft to keep from being pitched clear.

"I think you're right!"

Machine gun fire yammered from Susupe Point. Waverly twisted in the raft, trying to get a fix on just where they were. The mattress had just crossed over the reef line. They were about three hundred yards from the point, perhaps five hundred yards from the beach. At that range, the Japanese couldn't be too sure about what it was they were shooting at, but they'd sure decided they'd spotted *something* worth shooting at bobbing around in the surf.

Turning about in the opposite direction, Waverly tried to spot the swimmers, who should be moving toward the shore now. Damn ... where were they? He really couldn't see a thing, and the constant *thud-whoosh* of mortar explosions in the sea around them wasn't making things any easier. Carefully, bracing himself on the rubber raft's sides to keep from tipping it over, Waverly levered himself higher, searching the surface of the water along the reef toward the north. He could still see the LCP(R), now making a fast turn away from the beach as shell bursts continued to walk up its wake, but he couldn't make out the swimmers.

God, he thought. *Have they been wiped out already?*

They say you never hear the one that hits you. Waverly was caught totally unprepared by the explosion, which blasted from the sea just a few yards to his right. With the other incoming rounds, he'd heard the eerie, high-pitched whistle of the falling shell, but this one detonated without a shred of warning, picking up the little mattress and spinning it end over end through the air. Waverly hit the water flat on his back, and for a moment his world was filled with a cold, white avalanche of water that made him think of being trapped beneath the hammering spill of a waterfall.

Sputtering, he got his feet under him, feeling the rough grate of coral beneath his canvas shoes, but he stayed in a water-hugging crouch, certain that if he stood up he'd present an easy target for snipers or machine guns ashore. "Blondie!" he called. "Christ, Blondie! Where are you?"

"Here, Lieutenant!" a voice called from behind him. Turning, he saw the raft, floating upside down, and Blondie clinging to its side.

"You okay?"

"Yeah … think so. Had the wind knocked out of me. Shit, that was fuckin' close!"

"A miss is as good as a mile. Let's get the raft turned over."

Together, they struggled to right the flying mattress, but each time they lifted one side, it skittered away from them like a balky horse. To get any kind of leverage on the overturned raft, they would have to stand up … and there were those Japanese snipers ashore.

"Shit, Lieutenant," Blondie said, panting. "I think we should leave the fucker and swim for it."

"Damn it, Blondie, that's not the plan," Waverly replied. Half rising from the water, he reached across the raft's bottom, trying to pull the far side toward him, up and over. "C'mon! We can right this thing. Now lend a hand!"

Gouts of water, each easily two feet high, splashed across the surface, racing toward the two men in a ragged, zigzagging line.

"Duck!" Blondie yelled, and the two men dove for cover.

The water was about two feet deep here, and murky with the suspended coral sand and silt stirred up by the explosion. Waverly could hear the bullets striking the water close by with sharp, piercing chirps. The waves passing over the coral nudged him forward, and he felt a painful sting in his knee. Damn … a coral cut. Maybe he should have worn kneepads, like some of the other UDT men. But damn it all, he'd not expected to have to go swimming!

Raising his head above water, he swallowed a gulp of air. His mask was still dangling by its rubber strap around his neck, but his helmet was gone. When had he lost it? Probably during the explosion. Blondie surfaced nearby.

"C'mon! Help me with the mattress!"

"No can do, Lieutenant," Blondie replied. "Look."

"Ah, *shit*… "

The raft, still upside-down, was slowly collapsing into a limp blanket of black rubber, floating on the swell.

"It's okay, Lieutenant," Blondie told him. "When we flipped, we lost the motor and battery, too, and I'll be damned if I was going to paddle that thing all the way in to the beach with my hands!"

Another mortar round struck the water, but farther off. Even so, Waverly felt the concussion, amplified in the thicker medium of the water, pound at his chest and belly like a muffled hammer blow.

"Okay," he said. "We swim." He wasn't entirely sure what the two of them could accomplish, but they had slates and pencils and balsa markers. Maybe they could map the approaches to the beach north of Susupe even though they didn't have any fishing line, or replace some of the information lost if one of the other swim pairs was hit. And there was that downed Avenger to look for.

Waverly adjusted his mask, pressing it over his face and inhaling through his nose so that the outside pressure molded the rim tightly against his skin. Diving underwater again, he swam back and forth, searching the bottom until he spotted his radio. He wasn't sure if it was still working after the beating it had just taken, but he decided to hang on to it anyway, a symbol of his last remaining link to Dobson and the rest of the fleet. The coral beneath his hands was rough, in places as sharp as a razor. He paused long enough to pull his work gloves from his belt and put them on. Surfacing again, he signaled to Blondie, and the two men started across the reef toward the beach, half swimming, half crawling in water that varied from one and a half to two feet in depth.

The gunfire from shore seemed to be increasing, and Waverly wondered if it really was, or if he was letting the fear get to him.

Shit, it didn't really matter, did it? Dead was dead, and he had a job to do. Grimly, he pushed ahead over the reef, as the water grew shallower and the surf broke wildly about his body.

CHAPTER 4

Wednesday, 14 June 1944
UDT-5
Swimmer Team Dog-seven
Off Susupe Point

Tom Davies pushed his way forward over the rugged surface of the reef. It was more like walking than swimming; the water was less than two feet deep in places, just like that downed Avenger pilot had said, and with a surf breaking on top of the reef, swimming was almost impossible.

But he found that by lying flat in the water he could kick his way along the reef with his feet, using one gloved hand to keep his bare torso off the coral, the other to hang on to the condensed milk can that served as a spool for his fishing line. He reached a tag of cloth knotted into the line, and crouched motionless in the water as he noted the measurements on his slate: "75YD — 1/2'."

He'd expected to be scared stiff once he hit the water, but he found now that it wasn't as bad as he'd been anticipating back when he was squatting in the bottom of the LCP(R) with nothing to do but count the mortar splashes astern. As he concentrated on the work he had to do, the Japanese fire became little more than a distant and sometimes annoying background noise. He was having more trouble with the surf breaking over the shallow parts of the reef than he was with enemy shells or bullets, and the waves crashing around him actually gave him a weird sense of security. Four or five hundred yards offshore, he doubted that the Japanese could even see him, much less deliberately take aim and hit him.

He continued moving across the reef, reeling out the fishing line behind him as he went.

Lamb splashed up to within twenty-five yards, the separation swim partners were supposed to maintain for safety. "Hey!" he shouted. "Catch anything yet?"

Davies held up the makeshift reel, which had been assembled from three four-inch milk tins welded end to end and made bulky by the seemingly endless length of fishing line and knotted tags wrapped around it. "Damn," he called back. "Not a nibble. Think we're using the right bait?"

The fishing jokes had been circulating through the UDTs for a couple of months now. Navy supply personnel in Hawaii had been mystified by three requisitions for fifty-five *miles* of fishing line. One UDT officer had been asked point-blank how long he'd been in the war zone, with the assumption that he was suffering from combat fatigue; another, when asked what he was fishing for with fifty miles of line, had simply grinned and replied, "Japanese. Big ones."

But few people outside the teams knew what the UDT was, or what they did. Their make-do enthusiasm often resulted in strange requests, made all the stranger when Admiral Turner's headquarters backed the UDT requisitions with a curt, give-'em-whatever-they-want attitude. Face masks? There were damned few of those things, used only by a handful of sport divers and spear fishermen in Hawaii and on the West Coast. Hundreds of empty milk tins? Miles of fishing line? Strangest of all was the UDT's insatiable appetite for condoms. First the CDUs in the Atlantic and then the UDTs in the Pacific had taken to ordering case after case of rubber prophylactics, until all someone had to do was mention that he was "in demolition" to get an odd look or two from the harried supply personnel ashore.

Naturally, the UDT men took great pride in *not* admitting what all those rubbers were for.

But a condom was absolutely the best thing to use to keep an M-1 fuse igniter dry even in heavy surf. And since adapting condoms to that purpose, inventive UDT men had found plenty of other ways to use them as well, from encasing supposedly waterproof watches and compasses as protection from the corrosive effects of salt water, to inflating them and tying them off with a bit of fishing line for use as floating marker buoys.

A mortar round thumped into the reef a hundred feet off. "Let's move," Lamb suggested, and Davies heartily agreed. Their best defense right now appeared to be to keep moving.

About seven hundred yards from the beach, the coral reef ended abruptly, giving way to the crystal-clear water of the lagoon. Davies was relieved to finally get off the coral and away from the pounding surf that had threatened with each shoreward surge to drag his body across the jagged surface of the reef.

Ducking his head beneath the surface and looking around through his mask, Davies found that the bottom was only about three feet deep here, a bit shallower than the report by Lieutenant Martin had suggested. Noting the spot and the depth on his slate, he started swimming toward the shore, staying underwater for as long as he could hold his breath, surfacing briefly only when he couldn't hold it any longer. Lamb, meanwhile, swam off to the left, carrying out his part of the survey, searching for obstacles or mines. So far, Davies hadn't seen any beach approach defenses at all — save, of course, for the vigorous gunfire from the shore.

He'd found that the glass-faced mask gave him a truly remarkable clarity of vision underwater. The glass and the water together magnified things slightly; Davies had perfect twenty-twenty vision, but the effect was what he imagined it must be like to be nearsighted and don a pair of prescription glasses for the first time. He could see Lamb's painted body — underwater the paint looked silver-gray and black — kicking away from him to the left, seemingly close enough to touch, though he had to be at least five yards away. The surface seen from under water had a mirror-bright quality where it caught the light from the sky, shifting and gleaming like liquid mercury.

The visibility made it easy to check for obstacles. He estimated he could see for maybe fifteen yards before details became lost in the gray-green murk in the distance.

Surface … breathe … dive again.

One thing he didn't like about this way of doing things was this damned helmet. The brim kept bumping on his face mask, threatening to dislodge it every time he dove under water, and its weight made him feel sluggish, even a little trapped. Too, now that he'd been in the salt water for almost an hour, he found that the helmet's inside straps were starting to chafe uncomfortably at his forehead. A little more of this and he'd be rubbed raw, and God alone knew what kind of jungle rot you could pick up in a tropical island lagoon.

Surface … breathe. He unbuckled the helmet and let it sink to the bottom. He felt another flag slip off the reel beneath his fingers, so he stretched out full-length on the bottom, dropped his elbow to the coral sand bottom, forearm extended straight up, and estimated that the water here was twice as deep as his forearm was long, still about three feet, close enough. He marked the depth on the slate, then surfaced again for air.

They were more than halfway to the beach now from the drop-off point beyond the reef. When Lamb surfaced nearby a moment later, Davies waved. "About time to split up, don't you think?"

Lamb scanned the beach, then looked south, shading his eyes as he studied Susupe Point, now only a couple of hundred yards away. "Aw, shit, Davies," he replied. "The Japanese can't hit a damned thing. You could steer the *Gilmer* into this lagoon and they wouldn't be able to hit her. I think we can both make it all the way in."

The explosions of mortar fire, the bursts of machine gun fire from the shore, were continuing unabated. Not all that much of the fire seemed to be aimed directly at them … but the Japanese were sure as hell shooting at something.

Or somebody.

Davies shook his head. "Negative, buddy. We'd better play it by the book. You stay here. I'll take a quick sneak-and-peek and be right back. Let's see your slate."

They compared slates to make sure that both had the same information scrawled on their surfaces. Then, still unreeling the measuring line, Davies ducked back under water and started swimming.

Suddenly, it was very lonely, without a swim partner somewhere close by. He wondered how the rest of the team was getting on … how many casualties they'd taken already. The fire wasn't too bad, at least, not yet … but it was bound to get worse when the swimmers got within easy rifle shot of the land.

Skimming midway between the sandy bottom and the brightly shifting quicksilver of the surface, Davies kept swimming.

*

Swimming with that damned crackerbox walkie-talkie, Waverly decided, was going to kill him quicker than enemy gunfire. The water here was only four feet deep, but the thing dragged at him like an anchor. Pulling his feet beneath him, Waverly stood up, keeping himself crouched to present a small target to enemy marksmen. Extending the radio's antenna, he pressed the transmit switch. "Doghouse, Doghouse," he said. "This is Dog-one. Do you read, over?"

He released the talk button and listened, squeezing the speaker against his right ear while he jammed a forefinger into his left, trying to hear. Shit … he wasn't even sure he could hear static on the thing. Maybe the so-called waterproofing wasn't, and the radio had shorted out in the salt water.

Screw it. He discarded the radio, letting it sink to the bottom.

A mortar round landed twenty-five yards away, the concussion sweeping his feet out from under him and ducking him in the water. He surfaced again as the spray drizzled across the lagoon. He could clearly hear the yammer of a machine gun coming from the point, but he couldn't see where the fire was aimed.

Foglio broke the surface beside him, gasping for air after a particularly long underwater swim. "I think … I've got it," Foglio said, blowing and panting.

"Got what, Blondie?" He had to shout as three more rounds crashed into the reef a hundred yards behind them.

"The idea behind this whole damned UDT operation. See, the brass sends us out today, in broad daylight, and the Japanese use up all their ammo taking potshots at us. Tomorrow, when the jarheads come ashore, the Japanese'll be out of ammo and they'll all surrender!"

"Makes sense to me. Maybe —"

Machine gun fire searched for the two swimmers, probing from the scrubby trees along the northern side of Susupe Point. This time, Waverly thought he saw the sparkle of the gun's muzzle flash as the gunner aimed at him. Water splashed thirty feet away.

"Duck!"

Waverly bent double and submerged, then swam as hard as he could, surfacing yards away. Blondie came up nearby, spitting water.

Gunfire skipped and spattered across the surface again, behind him this time. The enemy was using short bursts, rather than a long and wasteful salvo, and they seemed to be having trouble finding the range. Floating low in the water, he quickly made a sketch on the corner of his slate, marking the gun's position in relation to some prominent and distinctive boulders and trees. Probably it was a couple of Japanese in a foxhole with a Nambu ... but it might be a well-camouflaged pillbox, positioned in just the right spot to lay down a devastating enfilading fire on any Marines struggling ashore across this part of the lagoon.

"Hey, Lieutenant," Blondie called. "Notice anything about our fire support?"

Waverly turned to face the ocean. The bombardment group was about three miles offshore now, a line of gray hulls along the horizon beyond the reef. Turning again, he faced the shore. Shells were still slamming into the jungle and the hills half a mile behind the beach, but the beach itself and the treeline beyond it were quiet, almost peaceful.

"Fire's slackening," Waverly replied. "And they're moving it inland." Raising his left hand, he looked at his watch, reading the dial through the tightly stretched transparency of the condom he'd tied over the watch's casing to waterproof it.

"Ten hundred hours," he told Blondie. "Time for our air support."

The ops plan called for the naval gunfire to move inland at 1000 hours, giving the bombardment aircraft a clear shot at the beach ... and also lessening the chance of hitting the combat swimmers with short rounds as they neared the shore.

Treading water, the two swimmers looked up, searching the sky overhead, but the heavens remained a glorious — and empty — cloud-spotted blue.

"Where the hell are our planes?" Foglio growled.

"They'll be here, Blondie," Waverly replied. The machine gun ashore let off another burst, sending a scurrying line of waterspouts chopping toward the two swimmers.

"They'd damn well better!" Foglio yelled, and then he plunged under the water.

Waverly gulped down a deep breath and followed.

Lieutenant Commander Coffer had gone in on the second boat north of Susupe Point, scrambling out onto a flying mattress along with a seaman named Paige. Mortar fire plunged and thundered, aiming primarily at the four tempting LCP(R)s as they made their runs parallel to the coast to drop off their swim pairs. Coffer and Paige made it through the surf and across the reef; once inside the lagoon, though, the LCP(R)s had pulled back out of mortar range, and the fire shifted to the flying mattresses that were guiding the swimmers in toward the beach.

Round after round exploded along the reef, showering the UDT men with spray and fragments of coral. At first he'd assumed that the rounds were from the Navy ships offshore, falling short, but when he radioed his Exec aboard one of the LCPs, he learned that the explosions crashing along the reef weren't short … but long. The explosions came faster and thicker the farther in the men went, until it seemed to Coffer that they would never be able to carry out their survey in the teeth of that kind of fire. One round landed fifteen yards from his raft, but the two men rode out the swell and kept steering for the shore. Three hundred yards from land, he and Paige finally anchored the raft and then rolled off into the water. They would be less conspicuous swimming than bobbing about on the waves in the vulnerable little raft.

Coffer was having considerable trouble seeing much of anything but a vast, noisy blur. His glasses were still taped to his head, but they'd quickly become frosted with a thin layer of salt. Paige helped him; back aboard the *Gilmer*, the men had joked about the seaman being the skipper's seeing-eye dog, since he was farsighted and would be able to see detail at a distance. By the time they'd swum and waded to within one hundred yards of the shore, however, even with his nearsightedness, Coffer could see Japanese troops moving at the edge of the treeline behind the beach. The fire from the sea had slackened; aircraft were supposed to be bombing and strafing the enemy positions to cover the UDT, but the sky remained ominously vacant. In fact, the enemy soldiers were taking advantage of the seeming lull in the bombardment to stand up in their trenches or to walk down to the edge of the water, firing at the dozens of heads bobbing in the waters of the lagoon.

Crouching in four feet of water, Coffer took the radio he'd carried with him from the mattress, pulled out the antenna, and pressed the transmit key. "Charlie Horse, Charlie Horse," he called. "This is Charlie-One. Do you read? Over."

Static hissed from the receiver.

Paige, floating in the water nearby, looked back toward the reef. "Maybe nobody's home, Skipper."

"You know how it is, Paige. They get bored, decide to take in a movie…" He tried again. "Charlie Horse, this is Charlie-One. Do you read me? We need air cover! Over."

Gunfire whined overhead, then chopped bright splashes into the surface a few yards away.

"Skipper?" Paige called. "I think they see the radio!"

"Charlie Horse, Charlie-One. Do you read me? Over." He could hear something over the radio now, but he couldn't make out the words.

"Charlie Horse!" he yelled. "We need air cover! Where are our aircraft? Over!"

A trio of rounds slapped into the water less than five feet away, and both men ducked beneath the waves. When they rose again, he tried once more, this time calling the other radio-equipped officers in the lagoon. The fire from the shore was heavier than even he had anticipated, and it seemed senseless now to have the men try to keep pushing to the fifty-yard mark.

But he couldn't raise anyone and finally decided that the radio had been damaged by the water or by rough handling. He might be getting through, but he couldn't hear the replies. Dropping the radio, he tried to signal other team leaders to the left and right but succeeded only in drawing more enemy fire.

Besides, it looked to him as though most of the men had already passed the one-hundred-yard line and were moving in closer, despite the fire. *God*, these were good men!

Too good to waste. "Come on, Paige."

"Where we going, sir?"

"Back to the mattress. Some of these boys are going to need help getting out of there, and I want to be able to offer them a ride."

Together, they started swimming back toward the center of the lagoon.

Davies broke the surface, gasping for breath. *Damn*, this was hard work … and if the skipper hadn't insisted that every man in the Team qualify for swimming one mile last month, he probably never would have lasted this long. It helped that nowhere was the lagoon so deep that he couldn't stand. Unless the fire was really heavy, he could always call a halt and simply float there with his shoes dragging on the bottom while he caught his breath.

Still, he was starting to get tired. Davies considered himself to be in pretty good shape. Maybe he hadn't had the weeks of tough physical training that nearly everybody else in Team Five had undergone at Fort Pierce, but it took muscles and, even more, it took *endurance* to work for hour upon hour inside a stiff canvas suit, weighed down by the ponderous mass of a hard hat diving rig, the lead weights, the Frankenstein boots as you clumped around on a muddy bottom beneath the keel of some Navy ship. Davies was sure he had what it took.

Even so, he was tiring fast now, and that was worrisome. He'd swum nearly one mile in toward the Saipan beach, but he still had a mile to swim to get back to the pickup point. He'd heard Coffer had instituted the one-mile qualifying swims after learning the men would have to swim a mile in to shore. What was the idea … that the men would wait there for the Marines to pick them up? Or that sheer adrenaline would give them the boost they'd need to manage that second mile back to the LCP(R)?

Time for another depth check. The bottom was shoaling now as he got in closer to the beach ... two feet, barely enough to hide in stretched out on his belly. Raising his head above the surface, he estimated that he was twenty-five to thirty yards away from the beach and about fifty yards from where the coastline took a right-angle turn out to sea from the coast, forming the base of Susupe Point. It was quiet in here, almost peaceful, though the mortars were still hammering away at the reef half a mile behind him, and naval artillery fire continued to howl overhead, hurtling across the beach and slamming into the hills inland.

Damn ... where were the Navy planes that had been promised? It was nearly 1030 hours now. They ought to be swarming all over this beach, bombing and strafing anything that moved. Hell, he could *see* the Japanese back there, moving among the trees. It looked like they had a line of trenches dug into the sandy soil about ten yards above the water line, just about where the trees ended and the open beach began.

Only then did it strike Davies just how close he'd come to the Japanese lines. The orders were to get to fifty yards from the beach; some guys back aboard the *Gilmer* had been taking bets about how close the swimmers would actually be able to get before the enemy fire got so heavy they would have to turn back. Not even Coffer, he'd heard, expected them to get as close as a hundred yards ... and here he was, GM1 Tom Davies, sitting sweet and pretty just twenty-five yards off the beach!

He wasn't going in any closer, that was for damned sure. The Japanese were moving through the woods in a pack; he could see their khaki uniforms flashing in the patches of sunlight filtering down through the trees. Gunfire banged and shattered from the shore, and there was a heavy haze of gun smoke drifting among the trees. As he watched, he saw the running troops jumping into a waist-deep trench, as an officer waved his sword toward the lagoon. Others were standing up and banging away with their rifles at some target behind Davies and to his left, though from his vantage point in the water he couldn't see what they were shooting at.

At least none of the shots were coming his way. Davies didn't think they'd seen him yet, but if he went much closer they would have to be blind not to.

He hesitated, thinking things through. Now how the hell was he going to prove to the other guys in Five that he had made it this far? He could just imagine the bragging that would be going on among the guys who made it back to the *Gilmer*, Blondie, for instance. The way he talked up his sexual escapades, he'd probably be telling stories about how he'd gone ashore and laid half the female population of the island.

Well, now … there just might be a way.

Thirty yards to his left, a small buoy rode the swell just beyond the point where it broke on the shoaling bottom and spilled into a low, hissing surf. It looked like the same sort of range marker the Japanese had used on the reef and farther out in the lagoon — an anchored, rusty brown can with an upright mast and a small orange pennant fixed to the top of it.

Davies dropped his makeshift spool of measuring line. He'd taken it as far in as he could, and he damned sure wasn't going to take it back, reeling in all those hundreds of yards of fishing line as he went. Gently, he breast-stroked through the water, swimming parallel to the beach until he could reach out and grab a cleat fixed to the top of the rust-streaked buoy. Pulling off his mask, he unbuckled the strap, then refastened it around the buoy's mast.

There. *That* should prove to the unbelievers that Davies had been here!

Water gouted five feet to the left. An instant later, something struck the buoy with a sound like a clashing gong, and Davies ducked under water and began swimming as hard as he could away from the beach. Surfacing for air, he turned and looked back over his shoulder. Oh … *shit*! At least a dozen Japanese soldiers had spilled down out of their trench beyond the treeline and were spreading out along the beach. An officer was with them, and at a distance of less than one hundred feet, Davies could see details like the man's round rimmed glasses and the flash of sunlight off his long, slightly curved sword. He was pointing that sword at Davies and screaming at the troops at the top of his lungs. "*Isoge*! *Isoge*! *Utsu*!"

Gunfire cracked and banged, and spouts of water splashed around Davies. He took a deep breath and went under water again. The gunshots continued, their sound muffled, and he realized that the Japanese must be able to see him easily beneath the clear water of the lagoon. Bullets hissed and shrieked as they chopped into the water. Even without his face mask, Davies could see the arrow-straight lines of bubbles they drew through the water when they hit nearby. After traveling only a couple of feet, though, the bullets lost all velocity and fluttered like leaves to the bottom.

The water grew deeper with distance from the beach. Three feet now … almost four. A bullet chirped into the water just ahead of him, slowed, then drifted toward the bottom. Davies reached out and caught it as it fell. Bernie Horwitz might have grabbed that hot piece of shrapnel from the bottom of the LCP, but what a souvenir *this* would make! He didn't have any pockets in his swim trunks, so he tucked the spent bullet into his mouth.

His lungs bursting, he surfaced, porpoising into the air, dragging in a quick breath, then submerging again. The next time he surfaced, almost forty seconds later, he took a quick look around and realized that he'd just covered a hell of a lot of distance. Not bad for someone who'd been as tired as he'd been after a one-mile swim.

Amazing what a charge of adrenaline could do for your body, even when you were exhausted.

The party of Japanese soldiers on the beach had stopped shooting at him, but bullets were still snapping in from the south. Somebody on Susupe Point had spotted him and was trying to pick him off. He changed direction slightly, swimming northwest now to put some distance between himself and both the beach and the point.

Too late, he realized that he'd lost track of his fishing line during his wild swim from the buoy, and that without it his chances of finding his way back to the waiting Lamb were pretty damned slim.

Well, there was nothing to be done about that now. Maybe they would spot each other when he reached the reef. A machine gun opened up from the point, and the bullets snapped into the water inches above his body.

Forget about that shit, man, he told himself. *Swim, God damn it, swim!*

CHAPTER 5

Wednesday, 14 June 1944
UDT-5
Dog-one

"Lieutenant! Lieutenant! I found it!"

Waverly reared up out of the water high enough to spot Blondie Foglio's waving arm. They'd split up twenty minutes ago to cover more ground, and now it looked as though that strategy might have paid off.

Swimming toward Foglio, Waverly checked their position — about eighty yards from the beach and about two hundred yards from the north side of the point.

"Whatcha got?" he asked, drawing close to the bobbing Foglio.

"Come on down and see." Foglio jack-knifed and went under. Waverly followed.

The water here was considerably deeper than the areas they'd surveyed earlier, as much as six to eight feet in places. As soon as he submerged, Waverly saw what his partner had been so excited about.

The wreckage was spread out on the sand like the parts of an enormous three-dimensional puzzle. Most of it was jagged and anonymous, but some was recognizable. He saw the rounded outer half of a wing, painted a dark blue-gray with the American star roundel clearly visible. Nearby was the Avenger's gun turret, seemingly intact, like a huge silver marble lying on the bottom, not far from one of the landing gear struts with the tire still attached. Blondie was floating beside the Avenger's engine cowling and prop. It looked like the plane's nose had half buried itself in the sand. The engine block, nakedly exposed, stuck up to within a foot of the surface, as did one of the long black arms of the aircraft's propeller.

Carefully, Waverly searched along the front rim of the cowling until he spotted what he was looking for, a long number stamped into a metal strip mounted on the engine block itself, visible through the intake. Quickly, he noted the serial number on his slate. If it checked with the records for Lieutenant Martin's Avenger — and Waverly was certain now that it would — that would be proof of Martin's incredible tale about crashing here in the lagoon and walking away from it.

Not all of the aircraft was here. From the look of it, it must have disintegrated in midair. The tail and main body should be around here somewhere, though.

Waverly and Foglio surfaced together.

"What do we do now?" Foglio asked.

"We'd better mark it," Waverly replied. "Damn thing's a menace to navigation." When small boats and amphibious vehicles started plying this lagoon tomorrow, that engine block could tear the belly out of an unsuspecting small craft. "You have any floats?"

"Nah. They were getting in the way."

Waverly made a face. Quite a while ago, it had been clear that there weren't any mines or submerged beach obstacles to buoy, and they'd discarded the clumsy balsa wood floats. Now, when they needed them...

"Hang on a sec, Lieutenant," Foglio said. He smirked, reaching under water as though rummaging about for something. "Here ya go. I never go anywhere without a few spares."

From a small cloth pouch tied to his belt, Foglio produced a rubber condom, still in its tinfoil pack. Tearing the pack open, Waverly shook the condom out, then blew into the open end. "Got some string?"

"Right here." Foglio used his knife to cut off a length of fishing line, also carried in the bag. Waverly tied the mouth of the condom shut, then dove back under water, paying out the line, then tying it off on a loosened rivet protruding from the torn-open cowling of the Avenger. When he surfaced, the inflated condom bobbed on top of the water, the receptacle in the tip pointing at the sky like a warning finger.

Shells exploded nearby. Waverly checked the sky. Still no planes. Somebody had screwed up somewhere.

Foglio noted the direction of his gaze and grinned. "Snafu, Lieutenant. Situation normal: all fucked up."

"You got that right, Blondie. Let's get the hell out of here. I think we earned our pay for today."

"I'm with you, sir."

The shellfire followed them, or seemed to, as they swam back toward the reef. Behind them, their improvised marker balloon continued to bob and twist with the passing waves.

Pete Lamb was worried. Davies had been gone for a long time … longer than he should have needed to swim in to the fifty-yard line and swim back again. Something had happened to the hard hat diver. Shit, shit, *shit!*

It was 1040 hours, and the pickup rendezvous was set for 1100, fifty yards outside the reef. If he left right now, he might just about make it.

But Lamb couldn't leave without Davies. If he'd gotten himself shot in there…

Grimly, Lamb grabbed hold of the fishing line and began pulling himself along hand-over-hand. Follow the line, and he ought to find Davies. He figured he wasn't really disobeying orders; he would just go far enough into the lagoon to have a good look ... maybe halfway in, then right back. There shouldn't be any harm in that, and he'd still be able to get his all-important slate of beach survey information back to the *Gilmer*.

Machine gun fire spat and snapped, stirring up the water ahead. Too far ahead for them to be shooting at him. What the hell were the Japanese shooting at? He started swimming faster.

The explosion came out of nowhere, an avalanche of raw power and noise that lifted the stunned Lamb clean out of the water and hurled him into the air. He had a dazed instant's impression of sky alternating with water as he tumbled over and over ... and then the feeling of falling ... falling...

He hit the water as the splash from the mortar explosion crashed around him, a solid wall of white water, and then everything went thunderously black.

Davies was swimming for the reef, staying under water for as long as he could, surfacing for a brief gasp of air, then submerging once more. He found he could move a lot faster now without the burden of the reel and fishing line.

Dumb idea ... anyway, he thought, pulling himself along with a powerful breaststroke. *Just as easy ... guess the range ... by eye...*

The less gear the team had to carry with it on these swims, the better, so far as he was concerned.

Where the hell was Lamb?

Surfacing again, he saw movement to his right. For a chilling instant, he thought the Japanese had launched a boat and come after him, but then he glimpsed two blue-painted, black-striped bodies lying in the raft and recognized Lieutenant Commander Coffer and Seaman Paige.

"Davies!" Coffer yelled at him across the water. "You need a hand?"

"I can't find Lamb, Skipper!" he called back. "I left him here somewhere, this side of the reef."

Coffer rose higher in the raft, balancing himself with his hands on the sides as he scanned the lagoon in all directions.

"I don't see him," Coffer called back. "Why don't you —"

Twin mortar bursts erupted nearby, drowning out the rest of Coffer's words. The machine gun on the point had opened up again too, probing toward the bobbing mattress.

"Listen, sir!" Davies yelled. "If it's all the same to you, would you get that damned thing out of here? It's drawing fire!"

Coffer's teeth flashed in his painted face. "Understood, Davies. See you at the rendezvous!"

"I'll be there!"

But where the hell was Lamb? Judging by the angle of Point Susupe, measured off the thrust of Mount Tapotchau, this ought to be the right area. He checked his watch. There was still some time left, if he stretched it. He started swimming again, this time in a spiraling circle that got bigger and bigger as he moved out from the center.

Ten minutes later, he found Lamb sitting on the coral on the lagoon side of the reef as breakers splashed and surged around him. "Lamb!" The man seemed dazed. When Davies shouted, he looked at him with a blank, unrecognizing gaze. "Lamb! Lamb, are you okay?"

He swam up to the man and took him by the arm. There was blood trickling from the corner of his mouth, but he seemed to focus on Davies for the first time. "D-Davies?"

"Yeah, buddy. I'm here. What happened?"

"Don't … know. Hurts…"

He sagged then, and Davies caught him. It didn't look like he'd been shot. When Davies pressed a hand against Lamb's left side, though, he thought he felt something give with a crackling pop. "You've lost a couple ribs, boy," he told Lamb, not sure whether the man heard him or not. "C'mon. I'll get you to the pickup."

Two by two, the men of UDT-5 were returning to the seaward side of the reef. Most had discarded their helmets. All had left marker buoys and fishing line in the lagoon. But every man still had his precious waterproof slate and the tightly scribbled columns of all-important numbers they bore.

The four LCP(R)s were back, right on time, circling in the choppy waters off the reef. Their coxswains had learned earlier, during the drop-off run, that speed and maneuverability gave them an edge against the Japanese gunners. But they were running into considerable trouble now with the pickup.

Back at Maui, they'd practiced various techniques for retrieving swimmers from the water, but so far the easiest method was to simply have the LCP(R) pull up to a swimmer, reverse its engines, and loiter in one spot while other team members aboard the Higgins boat bodily hauled the man out of the water. That had worked fine at Maui, but the coxswains had definitely gotten nervous about the incoming fire from the island earlier, and things were far worse now as the Japanese brought more and more of their weapons into play. South of Susupe Point, where fire from the shore was even heavier than it had been to the north, one of Team Seven's boat officers, Lieutenant j.g. Sidney Robbins, invented an alternate means of getting men back aboard … tossing them a life ring attached to a line as the boat thundered past without stopping. The man in the water would grab hold of the life ring, and his buddies aboard would haul him in. It was a laborious and time-consuming method, and more than once a tired swimmer would let go of the ring, forcing the boat to circle back for another try.

There *had* to be a better way…

"Come on, Lamb! Don't you die on me! Not now!"

It was 1125 hours, almost thirty minutes past the time when the men were supposed to rendezvous for pickup. The trip across the reef had been sheer hell, dragging the unconscious Lamb along a few painful steps at a time. With the tide ebbing, the water was too shallow now for swimming, but the mortar and sniper fire continued unabated.

And as the water grew shallower, the surf actually grew rougher, crashing around the two men like a savage, living thing that tried every few seconds to sweep them back the way they'd come, thundering and hissing past them, dragging at their bodies, then reversing its pull in a long, steady tug toward the open sea.

Davies took advantage of the outgoing currents, making most of his scrambling gains in the intervals between incoming waves, then hunkering down for the explosion of surf as it rushed past him, heading back toward the lagoon. Both of his knees were bloody from the coral, and he had an ugly gash down the inside of his left forearm where a wave had knocked him against the reef. He wondered if there were sharks circling in the water offshore, sharks attracted by the scent of blood in the water.

At last, though, he reached the seaward side of the reef, and without hesitation plunged in, his left arm thrown across

Lamb's shoulder and chest in a lifesaver's carry as he stroked with his right. He could see one of the LCP(R)s now, circling beyond the reef. Oh God, oh God, don't decide to leave now...

The Higgins boat was turning away. Christ ... no! Come back!

No ... it was stopping again. There was another swimmer out there, and the Higgins boat was stopping so that the UDT men already aboard could haul him out of the sea. Shells splashed nearby, but the coxswain held the little craft steady until the men were safely aboard.

The very last flickers of energy propelled Davies on. Stroke ... stroke ... stroke... He'd *never* been this tired, even after a six-straight-hour shift in a hard hat rig at Pearl. He was getting weaker by the moment, and he knew that he wouldn't last long if the guys in that boat didn't see him.

Then the LCP(R) turned and was moving toward him, the white mustache of its bow wave grinning at him like a demented smile. Vaguely, he was aware of the crash and whoosh of shells falling in the sea nearby, but he scarcely noticed them. It was all he could do to keep Lamb's head above water. The boat slowed and he stopped swimming, treading water as the landing craft's gray hull drifted closer. Hands reached out to grab him — he couldn't see whose. Somebody jumped in beside him and helped support Lamb.

"He's wounded..." Davies gasped out. "Chest ... his ribs busted, I think."

Someone dropped a rubber raft into the water alongside the boat and made it fast. Together, Davies and the other UDT swimmer hauled Lamb into the rubber boat, where other men could reach down and gently drag him the rest of the way aboard.

He didn't even remember being pulled aboard himself. The next thing he was fully aware of was somebody offering him a cigarette as the Higgins boat picked up speed.

Away from Saipan.

"Ya did good, Davies," Dobson said, slapping him on the back. "Lamb's got a couple of dinged ribs, but I think he's going to be okay. Let's see those cuts of yours, now."

"Hey, Davies," Horwitz said as Dobson began swabbing at his knees with iodine. "The skipper's sure gonna be sore when he sees you lost your mask and helmet!"

"What happened there, Davies?" Lieutenant Waverly asked from the other side of the boat. "You sell your gear to the natives?"

"Man oh man, that's government property," Blondie added, laughing. "They're gonna take it out of your pay, buddy!"

At that, Davies managed a grin. "Yeah, but just wait till you guys get a load of where I left my mask!"

When he told them, they whooped with delight, and Perkins bet him ten dollars that the mask wouldn't be there after the invasion force hit the beach in the morning.

Davies smiled. Fort Pierce or no Fort Pierce, he *belonged*.

Coffer and Paige had already been picked up by another boat by the time Davies and Lamb made it back to their LCP(R). After tallying up the totals, Coffer learned that of the one hundred officers and men who'd gone in the water off the north beach, just one was known to have been killed, while two more remained missing. He hardly dared believe that; he'd experienced the heavy fire himself, had seen the Japanese troops standing in their trenches as they blazed away at the swimmers in the lagoon.

Ensign Adams's boat continued to patrol back and forth off the beach, looking for those missing men, until Coffer at last ordered Adams to take his boat back to the *Gilmer*. Even then, he'd not wanted to give up the search himself. Gunner's Mates Root and Heil were almost certainly dead ... but Coffer didn't want to abandon them if there was even the slightest chance that they might still be alive.

Returning to the *Gilmer* to offload the UDT men, Coffer had then returned to the reef in a boat with four volunteers. By 1230 hours he was almost ready to give up the search, when a radio call from a cruiser in the bombardment group passed the word that one of her lookouts had spotted what looked like a couple of men clinging to a Japanese buoy anchored just beyond the reef.

Checking the report, Coffer dove into the sea once more, swimming all the way to the buoy in question before he found that what the cruiser's lookout had spotted was a coral head sticking up above the water.

But when the LCP(R) made the run back in close to the reef to pick Coffer up, there were six UDT men aboard, not four. The boat had spotted Root and Heil clinging to another buoy and had picked them up before circling back to retrieve Coffer.

As snipers' bullets chopped into the water nearby, Coffer had swum for the boat and been dragged aboard. There he found out that Heil had been hit in the leg going in. Root had used a first-aid kit to bandage the wound, then left him on the reef while he made the reconnaissance swim in to the beach and back, as ordered. On the way out, he picked up his buddy and towed him across the reef and out to another buoy, anchored on the seaward side of the reef.

Later, aboard the *Gilmer*, Coffer had learned that only two men had been killed with Burke's Team Seven. Things had been a bit rougher on the southern beaches, with several of the boats pretty badly shot up and several men wounded. A general meeting by the assembled team officers began pooling the information acquired during the swims.

Most of the news was good. Neither UDT-5 nor UDT-7 had spotted any underwater mines or obstacles, and both groups had managed to get men to within a very few yards of the beach. The coral reef would block boats from the lagoon, of course, but nowhere would it be a serious obstacle for LVTs — the Marine Landing Vehicles, Tracked, more popularly known as amtracks or alligators.

One discovery made by the teams had ominous implications for the landing by the Second Marine Division on the beaches north of Susupe Point. Ensign Adams was already conferring with the Second Marine Division's tank commander about that problem. Possibly, a last-minute change in the Second Marine Division's deployment would avoid the difficulty …

The UDT officers also began compiling observations about the reconnaissance, observations that would be applied to future missions. Clearly, and mercifully, casualties had not been as severe as expected, though none of the men in the compartment that afternoon was willing to suggest yet that daylight swims off enemy-held beaches might become routine. After experiencing the enemy fire for themselves, they still felt the idea was suicidal … and all the more so when it was realized that a communications foul-up had stopped the deployment of the carrier aircraft at 1000 hours. Most of the officers agreed that helmets were more of a nuisance than a help, that the masks were a superb idea for searching for underwater obstacles, and that the fishing line probably wasn't necessary. Team Seven had used neither the line nor Coffer's painted-swimmer idea, and, though they'd not returned as many depth readings as had Team Five, the men of Seven agreed that they'd had no difficulty estimating the distance they'd swum, as opposed to having to measure it off of a reel.

Possibly, in future, UDT swims could be made with less encumbering gear.

The buddy system had clearly proven itself. Lamb and Davies, Heil and Root, those teams and others had demonstrated that the men stood a better chance of surviving if they carried out their mission in pairs. Team swimming would be emphasized in the future.

Finally, a better way had to be found to recover swimmers off an enemy beach. All eight LCP(R)s engaged in the operation this day had been lucky; sooner or later, a Japanese mortar was going to nail one of the boats while it was backing down to retrieve a swimmer, and twenty men could die. Robbins's idea with the life ring showed promise. Maybe something could be done with that.

H hour was scheduled for 0830 hours the next day, and the UDTs still had a lot of work to do, organizing the mounds of data acquired in the lagoon into a form that the invasion's planners could use.

But the word had already been flashed to Rear Admiral Hill, commanding the attack force which was scheduled to arrive off Saipan in the predawn hours of the next morning.

Mission accomplished: the LVTs can land unimpeded.

Coffer's men kept working far into the night.

CHAPTER 6

Thursday, 15 June 1944
U.S.S. *Rocky Mount*

"Request permission to come aboard, sir," Waverly recited, saluting the Officer of the Deck.

"Granted."

The sun was not yet up, though the eastern sky was aglow with the promise of sunrise at 0530 hours. The sky was clear, the air deliciously cool. Waverly was too tired to appreciate it, however. Together with every other officer in UDT-5 and UDT-7, he'd been up nearly the entire night, going over the mountain of data accumulated during the beach reconnaissance the morning before, transferring literally hundreds of depth soundings on the men's slates to standard charts of the lagoons and reef approaches, double-checking every entry, questioning the men, getting their impressions.

The end result was a stack of charts and notes that the UDT officers had brought with them from the *Gilmer* to the Amphibious Force flagship.

The U.S.S. *Rocky Mount* was a big ship, 135 feet longer than the *Gilmer* and displacing over twelve thousand tons. Originally commissioned as a Combined Operation HQ Ship, she'd since been fitted out as the flagship for the chiefs of combined forces — in this case Admirals Spruance and Turner. Despite the tonnage of brass on board, as Waverly and the other officers of both UDT-5 and UDT-7 gathered on the Rocky Mount's quarterdeck that morning, they expected that their debriefings would be carried out by relatively junior officers.

The last of the officers climbed the long metal ladder leading up the *Rocky Mount's* side and in the age-old ceremony saluted the ship's ensign, saluted the Officer of the Deck, and requested permission to come aboard. With permission granted, the OOD, a young commander in meticulously pressed, spotless blues, turned and addressed the entire group of thirty naval officers. "Gentlemen? If you would follow me."

The OOD led them aft, up an outside ladder, and then into the ship's superstructure. "Mr. Coffer," the OOD said. "If you would come with me, please. The rest of you, through there, if you will."

"Through there" led to a large compartment with the traditional gray-painted bulkheads and low, pipe-cluttered overheads of all naval vessels. The spartan furnishings included folding wooden chairs and a large table. The men had just found seats for themselves when someone at the back of the compartment leaped to his feet. "Attention on deck!"

With a clatter of wooden chairs scraping on steel, the men rose to attention. Two men in khaki uniforms with stars pinned to the collars strode into the compartment. Waverly recognized one of the men right off. The one in the lead with weather-battered face and receding white hair was none other than Vice Admiral Turner himself. The second man in line was a Marine lieutenant general, and they were followed by several Navy and Marine aides.

"Gentlemen," Admiral Turner began. "Be seated." As the UDT officers resumed their chairs, Turner's normally dour features twisted into an unaccustomed grin. "By God, men," he said, "I'm proud of you all…"

Their debriefing with the invasion's senior officers took almost an hour.

*

Coffer's debriefing was carried out personally by Rear Admiral Hill, who'd come aboard the *Rocky Mount* earlier that morning. He'd already delivered his report on the success of yesterday's reconnaissance to Admiral Oldendorf aboard the cruiser *Louisville* the previous afternoon, and Oldendorf in turn had radioed the information to Hill, so the debriefing now was almost a formality, especially since the real work of getting the charts of the reef and lagoon areas to the amphibious task force commanders was being handled by the team's junior officers.

"So," Hill said as the interview began winding down. "Your report said only three men lost in all?"

"Yes, sir." Coffer nodded, feeling again the irrational mingling of emotions, the sadness over the losses mixed with the sheer, heady joy that so few had been lost. "One from Five, one from Seven, and one sailor off the *Brooks* who was in one of Seven's boats."

"And only one of those was lost in the water?"

"Yes, sir. One man in Team Five. One of my best, a popular guy."

"Wounded?"

"Eleven. Five by enemy fire, six from concussion. Those mortar rounds pack a hell of a punch under water."

"You know, Commander, it could've been a hell of a lot worse."

"Yes, Admiral. I'm well aware of that."

"It could be that we've underestimated how hard it is for soldiers ashore to see and hit something as small as the head of a man swimming a hundred yards or more out at sea."

"Possibly, sir." Coffer still disagreed with the idea of sending men up to a hostile beach in broad daylight, but this wasn't the time to go into that. He spread his hands. "Admiral, these are the best damned men in the service. I've never seen anything like the bravery, the dedication, the plain, simple guts displayed by those boys off that beach yesterday. When I wrote out their orders, I didn't expect any of them to get closer to that beach than a hundred yards. I thought we'd be lucky if half of the men made it that far. Do you know, every team made it at least to the twenty-yard line, and some went in even closer than that. One hundred percent, Admiral! One hundred percent of those men gave me everything they had.

"But every damned one of them went in, calmly and slowly making his search, measuring out his line, noting depths on his slate, and with high explosives dropping all around them all the while. I quite simply have never seen anything like it in my life.".

There was a sharp rap on the compartment door. "Enter," Hill snapped.

A Marine major stuck his head in. "Excuse me, Admiral, but when you're finished with Mr. Coffer, General Watson wants a word with him."

"Very well, Major." Hill turned back to Coffer. "I think we've about covered everything. Commander?"

"I'd say so, sir."

"I appreciate your filling me in on what went on in there yesterday. I would have to say that I agree with your assessment about your men. They did a splendid job."

"Thank you, sir."

"Dismissed."

"Aye, aye, sir."

Ten minutes later, Coffer found himself being ushered into another of the office compartments that seemed to occupy most of the labyrinth of the *Rocky Mount's* interior spaces. This compartment had been reserved for Major General Watson, the commander of the Second Marine Division.

The moment he stepped into the office, Coffer knew that this interview was going to be considerably different in tenor from the last one.

"Coffer!" Watson roared from behind his desk, his face dark with anger. "What the hell do you think you and your people are playing at?"

"Sir? If you are referring to the reconnaissance yesterday —"

"You're damn right I'm talking about your reconnaissance. What in the blue blazes were you thinking of, taking your people in that close to an enemy-held beach! Don't you *ever* try that again, not unless you actually want to lose half of your men!"

Coffer considered several possible answers … including an explanation that it was Admiral Turner who'd ordered the daylight reconnaissance in the first place.

But any excuse he made would sound like exactly that — an excuse. Nor would an attempt to pass blame to a superior officer be well received by another superior. Coffer had been in the Navy long enough to understand that rule very well indeed. So he stood at attention, focused his gaze on a nondescript patch of gray bulkhead behind Watson's right shoulder, and said, "Yes, sir."

"Damn it, man, even the Japanese can hit a man at thirty yards!"

"Yes, sir."

"Aw, cut the Annapolis crap." Watson relaxed slightly. "I'm not mad about that. Your people did a splendid job." Then the general's face darkened again. "But I am mad, mad as hell, about this!"

The flat of his hand came down on a sheaf of papers lying on his desk. Coffer couldn't see what was written on the top sheet, so he remained at attention. No doubt, Watson would get around to telling him what he was angry about in time.

Glowering, the general picked up the report and waved it, inches from Coffer's nose. "Are *you* the man who's been ordering my tanks around? Who the hell's tanks do you think they are?"

Ah. That was it. The team's Marine liaison officer had delivered Coffer's report to the Second Division commander, and the report included a suggested change in Second Division's invasion deployment.

"General, the battle plan calls for the Second Marine Division's tanks to go ashore on the left flank. That's the northern end of the beachhead."

"I can read a map, Commander," Watson growled, picking up a chart from his desk and unrolling it. "Especially when it's *my* goddamn map and *my* goddamn operations plan!"

Coffer leaned forward, indicating the two-mile strip of beaches north of Point Susupe. "We found the water in the lagoon up here on the north side to be deeper than anticipated, sir. Five to six feet, in places. Not three to four, as the original charts suggested."

"How do you explain that discrepancy?"

"Well, sir, those original depths were estimates based on aerial reconnaissance, and from twenty-year-old charts. The new depth readings are based on measurements taken by my boys in the lagoon yesterday morning."

"And you're confident of these readings?"

"Yes, sir. Completely confident." Dragging his finger across the chart, Coffer indicated the planned approach route for Watson's armor. "Your tanks would make it across the reef in here fine, but once they dropped into the lagoon, they'd drown."

The invasion plan called for Watson's Second Division to assault the beaches north of Susupe Point, while the Fourth Marine Division went ashore on the beaches to the south. Marine amtracks — tracked, amphibious troop carriers — would swim in from the sea, wade across both the reef and the lagoon, and land troops directly onto the shore. In the north, Second Division's assault would be supported by tanks offloaded from LCTs and LCMs directly onto the seaward side of the reef. But tanks were delicate creatures when it came to seawater. If the water reached higher than their rear decks, their engines would be quite literally flooded.

Watson grunted. "Your damned report says you've found another way across the lagoon."

"Yes, sir. It's a strip of shallow water, never more than three feet deep, running diagonally across the southern end of the lagoon, about here. My report suggested that you might wish to consider shifting your tanks to the south end of the Second Division's beaches, here, just north of Susupe Point."

"Commander," Watson said, his voice taking on a patient tone, as though he were explaining the obvious to a particularly obtuse child, "have you ever managed an amphibious landing? Planned one? Do you have any idea how complex an operation an undertaking the size of a division-strength deployment against a contested beachhead actually is?"

"No, sir." Actually, he thought he had a pretty fair idea. A typical Marine division numbered over seventeen thousand men, the population of a fair-sized town. Feeding, equipping, arming, and transporting a force of that size was a titanic logistical operation; getting them ashore in the face of determined enemy resistance without having the entire force dissolve into complete chaos was nothing short of astonishing.

But he had the distinct feeling that he'd be wise not to suggest that he knew a division general's job as well as Watson did.

"I didn't think so. Do you have any idea how difficult it is to change an operation of this complexity ... *two goddamn hours before the troops are set to hit the beach?*"

Coffer glanced at a clock mounted on the bulkhead. It was 0618. H hour for the landings this morning was 0830.

"You don't just shift all of the tanks from the left flank to the right with no warning, no preparation," Watson roared.

"Of course not, sir."

"That sort of thing could cause incredible confusion on the beach."

"Yes, sir."

"Now just how the hell did you figure my tanks could find their way along this safe passage of yours?"

Coffer blinked at the change in Watson's thinking.

"Well, sir, I figured me and some of my people could lead your tanks ashore in a couple of LVTs. We'd go in first, planting marker buoys along the way. Your tanks offload on the reef, about here, then follow in line behind us."

Watson stared at the map a moment longer, then slowly nodded. "Okay. By God, we'll do it." He raised his eyes then, pinning Coffer with a gaze that mingled fire with ice. "But let me tell you something, Commander. If every one of my tanks isn't ashore by twelve hundred hours, if even one tank drowns out on this underwater highway of yours across the lagoon, then by the Lord Harry there is one certain UDT lieutenant commander who is going to be either court-martialed or shot!

I'll decide which when I see how bad the damage is. You hear me?"

Coffer swallowed. "Yes, sir. Loud and clear."

"Then get out of my sight."

"Aye, aye, sir." He turned to go.

"Oh, and Coffer?"

"Sir?"

"Damned good work. I think you've got something here with this UDT outfit of yours."

Coffer left the compartment shaking his head.

The invasion of Saipan proper began behind a savage final bombardment from the sea, while twenty-four LCI-G gunboats edged as close to the reef as possible and unleashed howling swarms of rockets and hammering salvos of 40-mm gunfire into the beaches. The lead wave of LVTs went in behind the rockets ... and this time, dozens of carrier aircraft roared in low above the lagoon, bombing and strafing the beaches just one hundred feet ahead of the advancing Marine amtracks. There were ninety-six amtracks in the first wave, supported by sixty-eight LVT(A)s — tracked, armored monsters, each bearing a squat turret mounting a single sawed-off 75-mm howitzer. The fire from the island was savage and unrelenting, reminding many of the Second Division's old hands of Tarawa.

This time, however, the majority of the men weren't forced to wade across hundreds of yards of open lagoon under fire but were delivered aboard their steel transports straight to the enemy's trenches ashore. The LVTs took heavy losses crossing the ranged-in reef and lagoon, but the survivors hit the beach at 0843 hours, growling, steel-hulled beasts that rose dripping from the water like fantastic, green-mottled amphibious dinosaurs. Their rear ramps came down, and the Marines charged out onto the beach, twenty-four men spilling from each amtrack, their shouts and roaring battle cries sounding above the incessant chatter of machine guns and the thud and boom of mortar fire.

The second wave was on the way across the reef before the last LVTs of the first wave were ashore.

"So the general went along with the change?" Waverly asked Coffer. The unarmored, open-topped LVT lurched heavily as it clambered up the seaward side of the reef, forcing him to grab a handy bulwark for support. As its tracks crunched into coral, the improbable-looking vehicle began grinding ponderously across the reef toward the lagoon. Another amtrack, with Ensign Adams and several UDT men inside, led the way. Astern, the sea was filled with ships and landing craft, many still circling at their line of departure, others already churning across an impossibly blue sea toward the island. All around them was the wreckage left behind by the advance of the leading waves, amtracks crumpled, broken, and set ablaze by direct hits, or standing empty and abandoned after a disabling near miss. Marines who had abandoned knocked-out tracks were everywhere, wading across the shallow water toward the beach, rifles held above their heads to keep them dry. Twenty minutes after the first troops had landed, all eight thousand Marines were already ashore, fighting from the moment their boots hit the sand. Enemy fire continued to shriek and thunder across the lagoon, raising great pillars of white water among the ugly black stains of smoke from burning vehicles.

Coffer clung to his own section of the gunwale. Mortar bursts exploded to either side, sending a shudder through the thin hull. The LVT's interior was crowded with marker buoys, each attached to several feet of white line and a small mushroom anchor.

"Well," Coffer replied, shouting to be heard above the thunder of the explosions and the roar of the amtrack's Cadillac V-8 engines, "let's just say he wasn't thrilled with the idea, but he decided to give us a chance."

Lurching and rumbling, the amtrack navigated across the shallow surf atop the reef, through which the men of UDT-5 had crawled and swum the morning before, then bumped off the coral and into the shallow water of the lagoon beyond. Astern, the first LCM plowed through the water, angling toward the spot where the guide LVTs had first grounded on the reef.

"Uh, oh," Waverly said, staring aft at the oncoming LCM. "He's coming in too fast."

"He must want to make sure he gets far enough onto the reef," Coffer said. "I think—"

Then the LCM rammed the reef at full speed, plowing up and onto the coral for fully half of its fifty-foot length, stranding itself high in the surf. Its ramp came down, however, and the single M4A3 Sherman tank aboard emerged, engine gunning as it rumbled into the shallow water atop the reef and pivoted right to follow the guiding amtracks.

"Here we go," Coffer said. "I hope those guys can steer."

Together, Waverly, Coffer, and the UDT personnel aboard the amtrack grabbed marker buoys and anchors, tossing them over the side at intervals to mark the safe route across the lagoon. Japanese mortar fire was heavy, but except for a near miss or two — and a scramble by the boat's enlisted crew for scalding-hot scraps of shrapnel that had clattered into the amtrack's cockpit — they made it into the shallow water just off the beach safely.

By that time, the Second Division's tanks were wading across the lagoon in line-ahead, like a string of baby ducklings following one after the other. Japanese shells exploded in geysering pillars of white to left and right of the path, but the tanks kept coming, breaking into the shallow water off the beach and spreading out, grinding up past the lead amtracks on the beach and into the woods beyond. The sounds of battle, the gunfire, the crump and thunder of mortars, the sharper barks of the M4s' 75-mm cannon, seemed to double and redouble in volume, as a pall of smoke blanketed the shoreline.

Every tank was ashore before noon. Not one blundered into deep water and drowned. On the north end of the landing beaches, where the tanks had originally been scheduled to land, a foul-up in navigation had put the Sixth and Eighth Marine Battalions ashore nine hundred yards too far to the north, and the Marines came ashore into a ®ring fire that stopped them cold ... and would have been suicidal for tanks even if they'd managed to swim across the deeper waters of the lagoon in that area.

The UDT's change of the Second Marine Division's battle plans had proven to be justified ... and a complete success.

After leading the tanks ashore, Coffer ordered the amtrack to head back across the lagoon to check on the grounded LCM. From the reef, the UDT officers could see two men still aboard. Two of the landing craft's four-man crew, it turned out, had jumped overboard and swum for a UDT Higgins boat circling nearby. The others, however, frightened of the pounding surf, refused to leave the LCM despite the Japanese shells crashing about nearby on the reef.

The amtrack carrying Coffer and Waverly pulled up alongside the circling LCP® and the two officers transferred to the boat. Lieutenant j.g. Dobson helped them aboard. "How are we going to get those people off?" Waverly asked him.

"Perkins has an idea," Dobson replied. As they watched, the blue-painted UDT man dove over the side, trailing behind him a length of white line.

Waverly thought the man was going to tie the line to the LCM so that the LCP could pull the larger craft off the reef ... a dubious idea at best since by now the LCM was high and dry, and the line was far too slender to take that kind of strain.

Perkins clambered up the LCM's transom, however, and could be seen talking to the sailors. There was an argument of some sort, and then Perkins was tying the line around both of the men's waists. He signaled, and the LCP's coxswain gunned the engine, taking up the slack on the line. A moment later, the two sailors were dragged off the LCM's stern and into the water. Perkins dove in after them, following them back to the boat.

"Seems a bit extreme, doesn't it?" Waverly asked. "I hope those two can swim!"

But a few minutes later, the men were hauled dripping aboard the LCP, terrified but safe.

"Commander Coffer?"

"Yeah?"

A sailor handed him the receiver for the LCP®'s radio. "Somebody on the horn for you!"

Waverly stood by as Coffer held the handset to his ear. "This is Coffer. Yes, sir." There was a long pause. "Yes, sir. I understand." And another pause. "Aye, aye, sir. We'll be ashore as fast as we can."

"What was that all about, sir?"

"That was the beachmaster. Halverson. He heard there were some of those crazy demo people in the area and he wants to see us."

"What, he wants us to blow up Japanese? That's supposed to be the Marines' job now."

Coffer chuckled. "Not quite. He wants to talk to us about blowing a small channel through the reef. If we can open a hole through from the sea to the lagoon, they'll be able to take boatloads of supplies all the way in to the beach, instead of having to offload it at sea onto amtracks."

"Makes sense."

"C'mon. Let's grab us a cab."

The "cab" turned out to be another shore-bound LCT grinding across the reef, this one loaded with twenty-four Marines and their gear. Hailed by Coffer, the driver stopped long enough to take the two hitchhikers aboard. "Christ," one Marine said as the two UDT officers dropped into the amtrack's well deck. "What is this, Halloween?"

Waverly looked down at himself. Like Coffer, he was wearing nothing but his blue swim trunks and baby-blue canvas shoes, and the paint he'd acquired for the reconnaissance the day before was still very much in evidence, a kind of dusky, smeared blue that covered him from head to toe, interrupted here and there by a smudged remnant of one of the black measuring stripes.

Minutes later, the amtrack growled onto dry sand, the rear ramp creaked down, and the Marines, followed by Waverly and Coffer, scrambled out. Coffer had learned that the beachmaster ought to be up *that* way, somewhere…

Shells were shrieking in over the trees to explode on the beach or out in the lagoon. Hundreds of Marines were crouched along the top of the beach, where sand gave way to soil, where trees and the shattered stumps of trees gave some small shelter from the gunfire chattering away from farther back in the woods. It sounded as though the heavy fighting was taking place several hundred yards farther in, but bullets clipped the palm fronds overhead repeatedly, and none of the Marines seemed anxious to get up and move around in the open.

As the two UDT men approached, one grizzled-looking Marine sergeant rose partway from the hole he was occupying, reached up to tip the brim of his helmet back, then spat a brown wad of tobacco juice into the sand. "By *God*!" he exclaimed incredulously, looking Coffer and Waverly up and down. "Now I've fuckin' seen everything! The fuckin' tourists are here and we ain't even *got* the damned beach yet!"

It took a while to find the beachmaster. It proved hard to get the Marines to take them seriously enough to answer their questions.

CHAPTER 7

Lieutenant Alexander Hamilton Forsythe III paused just inside the door of the O Club and studied the room with a casual, careless gaze. The crowd was sparse tonight, and the babble of conversation was subdued.

A young man in a crisp Army officer's uniform caught his eye from a table on the far side of the room and waved vigorously. Forsythe answered the gesture with a languid motion of his hand. He had to dodge a waiter and a pair of young ensigns who looked like they were already three sheets to the wind before he reached the table.

"Pull up a chair, Alex, and help me drown my sorrows." Dr. Christian Lambertson took a sip from his drink as if to emphasize his words. His tone was bitter.

"The meeting didn't go well, huh, Doc?" Forsythe said, settling into the chair across from Lambertson and summoning a waiter with an impatient gesture.

"There's a great understatement! It seems, Lieutenant, that the esteemed General MacArthur doesn't want our kind in his ravell of operations. Evidently he doesn't approve of unconventional operations."

Forsythe shrugged. "We've been called worse, Doc." He turned his head as the waiter bustled up. "Get me a martini, boy, and don't take all night."

"Yessir," the man replied, bobbing his head. Forsythe watched him hurry off and thought about Lambertson's news.

Forsythe had graduated third in his class from Harvard in the summer of '36 and had been pursuing a promising legal career in his father's Boston law firm when the attack on Pearl Harbor changed everything in his life. Not long afterward, he had done his patriotic duty and joined the Navy. He had found military life a bore until his uncle, a captain on the staff of Fleet Admiral King in Washington, had pulled a few strings to land him a slot with the newly formed Office of Strategic Services when it was created — at least officially, after a shadowy existence Forsythe had only heard rumors about — in June of 1942.

The OSS was the brainchild of General William Donovan. "Wild Bill," as he was usually called, had won the Medal of Honor in World War I and had been a successful lawyer between the wars. Fascinated by the possibilities of intelligence gathering and unconventional warfare, Donovan had convinced President Roosevelt to let him try out his ideas. The organization had recruited officers from all the military services and set them to exploring unusual and unorthodox methods of fighting the Axis powers.

But Donovan and his OSS weren't universally popular, by any means. J. Edgar Hoover had perceived the new organization as a threat to his own power base in the FBI. He had arranged, for instance, to have South America declared off-limits for OSS operations. And because the organization had drawn more than its share of officers with wealthy Ivy League backgrounds — such as Forsythe — it had come under fire as a haven for the privileged and the elite. "Oh So Social" and "teacup spies" were some of the milder epithets applied to the OSS, though anyone who knew the organization at all knew that the Ivy Leaguers were only part of the picture. Forsythe had met everything from fellow Harvard socialites to thugs and jailbirds in the two years since he'd joined Wild Bill's team.

Lambertson was a good example of the unusual characters attracted by the OSS. Before the war he'd been a student at the University of Pennsylvania Medical School with a particular interest in the human respiratory system. Lambertson had invented a self-contained underwater breathing device he had christened the Lambertson Amphibious Respiration Unit, or LARU. One of his teachers, a British physiology professor, had heard that his embattled countrymen were looking for just such a system to outfit commandos for covert operations along enemy-held coasts.

By that time Lambertson had graduated and started his residency in Philadelphia, and from what Forsythe had heard, his contacts with the British had been bizarre to say the least. As a junior resident, Lambertson hadn't even had an office for holding meetings. Instead, Lambertson and his distinguished visitors from across the Pond had discussed the secrets of developing underwater respiration for commando operations while sitting in the maternity ward waiting room among the expectant fathers. And between meetings Lambertson had borrowed a sewing machine, normally used for repairing hospital gowns, to stitch together prototype breathing devices from canvas.

The Brits had been impressed by the LARU and adopted it for use with their manned torpedoes, called chariots, which had seen extensive use in the Mediterranean. In the meantime America had joined the war and Lambertson, who held a reserve commission as a captain in the U.S. Army, had been called up to active duty. He'd done his best to convince

American authorities of the usefulness of his breathing device. But his efforts had met with little success. The Navy had studied the LARU for salvage diving but turned it down. Then the Naval Combat Demolitions people at Fort Pierce had tried out some prototypes — along with masks, swim fins, and other diving gear — but their tests had run into problems and the training program hadn't been that concerned with underwater swimming anyway. At Fort Pierce they were training with canvas antigas suits, boots, and other heavy gear with an emphasis on demolitions work carried out from landing craft rather than using chariots or swimmers to infiltrate a beach. That was the way the Demolitioneers had gone ashore at Normandy.

Growing discouraged by the Navy's lack of interest, Lambertson had been surprised when the OSS had approached him to help in the creation of a unit of "operational swimmers." Unlike the Navy, Donovan's people were impressed by the possibilities of the LARU, an oxygen rebreather that left no trace of the underwater swimmer's passing to attract attention from the surface. The new OSS Maritime Unit had consisted of a hundred men divided into three teams of about thirty each. They trained at Camp Pendleton in California and on the island of Nassau in conjunction with their British counterparts, and became quite proficient at underwater commando operations. Forsythe, who'd been captain of the swim team at Harvard, had been funneled into the new program and had first met Lambertson on Nassau. Because his swimming had impressed his superiors, Forsythe had wound up working closely with the Army doctor on the training program there.

Then came the new orders. Donovan had arranged to have one of the Maritime Unit teams assigned to the Pacific Theater of Operations, and Admiral Chester Nimitz had agreed that they could play a useful role in the war against Japan. So Lambertson, Forsythe, and the rest of their unit had packed up and moved from Nassau to Maui. They'd arrived only a few days earlier, but Lambertson had been quick to start exploring the possibilities of convincing PTO staffers of the usefulness of his team and his methods.

Apparently it hadn't gone well.

The waiter returned with Forsythe's drink. "I thought Nimitz was interested in us," he said, taking a sip. "What happened?"

Lambertson shrugged. "Like I said, MacArthur has other ideas. And he, Nimitz, and Halsey have joint authority. I guess he's putting his foot down on letting the Maritime Unit operate on its own."

"So what are we doing? Training? Did they want the LARU for the Navy divers?"

"No way," the doctor said with a sour expression. "No, they have their own training program and they don't want to change it now. Hell, they've decided they don't even want me hanging around and nagging them!"

"What do you mean, Doc?"

"They're transferring me to Burma. About as far away as they can send me and still keep me in the war."

"Transferring *you*. What about the team?"

"The rest of you boys aren't going to be operating as OSS anymore. They're putting you into one of the new UDTs. Team Ten, I think they said."

"A UDT? Great." Forsythe stared into his drink, not bothering to hide his gloom. "So we'll have to toe their line now, huh? Don't they realize the OSS has spent a lot of time and money just to get us to where we are now? What a waste!"

"Well, like I told 'em earlier, it's not much of a surprise. Who's going to use his stealth weapon when his cruisers are in shape, huh? At least you'll be where the action is. Burma's mostly a British show. I'll probably be an instructor again. And I'll be lucky if I ever see any Americans to pitch the LARU to again. The Brits already use them, for Pete's sake! Talk about a dead end!"

Forsythe looked away. Damn it, he was *proud* to be a part of the OSS and tired of being treated as a second-class citizen in the war effort. Maybe he'd put in for a transfer. The OSS was doing good work in every other ravell of the war, and maybe in another slot he'd have a chance to do a job that mattered instead of getting submerged in the Navy's UDT program.

After all, if he'd wanted to go UDT he could have volunteered for Fort Pierce instead of joining Donovan's organization. The Demolitioneers were mostly salvage divers and civil engineers, not his kind at all. He belonged in the OSS...

Forsythe finished his drink and made his excuses to Lambertson. He needed some time alone to think.

"Listen up, men! My name is Chief Howard Schroeder, and I will be one of your instructors for the next six weeks of your UDT training."

Forsythe studied the big, beefy man with the bushy red beard as he paced back and forth in front of the formation drawn up on the lava-strewn field behind the ragged tent city that was the UDT training center. The men of the Maritime Unit had been flown out to Maui from Pearl the day before and had spent the night under canvas. Now, already hot and sweaty under the glare of the morning sun, they were lined up together with a crowd of sailors someone had identified as Navy demo men.

So far, Forsythe thought, he didn't find his new assignment very impressive.

He'd fired off a half dozen telegrams, to Uncle Donald and to various influential family friends in Navy posts from the Pentagon to the Pacific Fleet, asking them to see what they could do to expedite the official transfer papers he'd spent Sunday morning filling out. But of course even with pull back in the States it would take time for a transfer request to work its way through channels, so he was resigned to facing the UDT training.

Now that he'd seen the living conditions they were expected to put up with for six weeks, he hoped that transfer wouldn't be long in coming through. Even the exile to Burma Lambertson had drawn sounded better than this makeshift excuse for a naval base.

"The officer in charge of training here at Kamaole is the Exec, Lieutenant Commander Chapman, and he'll be taking an active interest in your work," Schroeder continued. "But I don't expect any of you lot to go disturbing the Exec with your troubles unless you've seen me first. You got me?"

"Yes, sir!" Most of the responses came from the demo men. The OSS Maritime Unit wasn't nearly as hung up on formal military conventions as the regular Navy, and Forsythe, along with the other OSS men, didn't see much reason to start playing toy soldier now.

Schroeder regarded the OSS contingent with a sour expression for a moment but didn't say anything about their less than enthusiastic response. "All right, here's the drill. A UDT Team is made up of fourteen officers and eighty-six enlisteds, a hundred men. Now most of you are from the

Combat Demolition School at Fort Pierce … Class 6A, correct?"

"Yes, sir!" A few voices made the response promptly.

"Well, you lot get a special bonus, not because you've earned it but because you happened to turn up in the right place at the right time." The tone of Schroeder's voice made it clear just how little he thought of the "special bonus" he was describing. "We're going to put you together with a draft of men from a special swimming commando unit of the Office of Strategic Services, the OSS. These guys have had a lot of specialized training as combat swimmers, so they've got a lot on the ball."

At Schroeder's words something like a groan, more felt than heard, seemed to rise from the demo contingent. Forsythe darted a look at them. Surely the rank and file Navy hadn't heard enough about the secret doings of the OSS to know anything about Donovan's organization or the derision that was so often directed their way. What was making them react that way?

The chief paused, then plowed ahead as if nothing had happened. "You've been designated Underwater Demolition Team Ten. The senior officer from your two groups is Lieutenant Coates of the Maritime Unit. Mr. Chapman has designated you as CO of Team Ten, Lieutenant. Do you have anything to say?"

Coates, standing beside Forsythe, took a step forward. "Thank you, Chief," he said quietly. "Men, I'm sure that all of us are going to have to make some adjustments. I've heard a lot about you Fort Pierce graduates, all of it good. You probably don't know much about the Maritime Unit, because a lot of what we've been trained for is classified, but I can assure you that our swimmers are some of the best and we've been trained for every contingency you can think of. We've got a lot to learn from each other, and I'll expect all of you, OSS men as well as Demolitioneers, to chip in, do your jobs, and make this team work."

As Coates finished and stepped back into place beside Forsythe the red-bearded CPO spoke up again. "All right, then. Let me add a few more things. For the duration of your training Mr. Chapman, myself, and the other instructors here will be in charge of all your activities. Some of you Fort Pierce boys are going to be pretty damned surprised at what they didn't tell you back in the swamps. UDT training stresses swimming long distances and doing beach survey work, stuff you didn't need to know back in demolition training. And in case any of you are thinking of pulling the same line on me that some smart-ass from the last class tried, about how you've all been trained by Commander Coffer's course and you know everything there is to know about your job already, you might chew on this. Commander Coffer was one of the first people through our little school here, and let me tell you he swam, he learned survey technique, and he sweated under me and my boys right alongside his men. So don't go getting any ideas about how Fort Pierce men know everything."

Forsythe took a step forward. "Chief?"

Chief Schroeder raised one bushy eyebrow. "Lieutenant, ah…"

"Forsythe, Chief. The Maritime Unit's had extensive training in long-distance swimming already and in beach reconnaissance work too. We've even been trained to use underwater breathing gear, which I understand the UDT doesn't have and doesn't want. So why do we have to go through all this?"

"Well, Lieutenant," Schroeder answered in a low, dangerous voice, "I might say it's because we want to verify your capabilities, since you OSS guys are a little bit of an unknown quantity in these parts. Or I might say it's because you might not know all the specific procedures we use in the UDT. Beach survey work out here requires some very specific training so you know the kinds of things the Marines are looking for when they're getting ready to hit the beach. But mostly, Mr. Forsythe, you have to go through all this because that's what the Navy says you have to do, so I'm afraid, sir, that you'll just have to go along with us for the next six weeks. Is that reason enough, Mr. Forsythe?"

"Er ... yes, Chief. I guess it is." Forsythe felt himself blushing. He thought he could hear some more muttering among the demo men.

"Nice going, Alex," Coates said softly. "Here I go preaching cooperation and togetherness and *you* have to go and stir the regular boys up all over again. Thanks a lot."

"Sorry, Art," Forsythe answered, blushing all over again. "It's just I hate to see the unit thrown away like this. We're getting dragged down to their level instead of getting to use the skills we've been training for all this time, and I just don't like to see it."

"Well, keep your attitude to yourself. It's going to be hard enough getting our boys to mix in with theirs without having my officers making things worse. You read me, mister?"

"Aye aye, sir," Forsythe answered. It was the first time in weeks he'd actually addressed another OSS man so formally.

Schroeder was still talking. "Okay, last thing. This base has come a long way since we started it back in April, but it doesn't exactly have a lot in the way of amenities. You'll each be given a tent assignment, six enlisted or three officers to a tent. This field here doubles as a parade ground, a training area, and, when you're off duty, the official sports field. Watch out for the lava outcroppings. They can be pretty damned treacherous. You'll be doing most of your drills down on the beach, and you're encouraged to swim on your own time as well. It's good practice, and good recreation too — about the best you'll find around here. There's a rec hall, but it still doesn't have any furnishings. And we should have the mess hall back in shape in a few more days. It burned down last month and we've been eating outside ever since." He paused. "Oh, yeah. One more thing. The new CO has a very firm no-smoking rule. We store a lot of explosives around here, and we don't much want to lose the mess hall again now that we've just got it back up. So the smoking lamp is out, permanently."

The muttering this time came from both groups in ranks. Sure, Forsythe thought irritably, it was smart to take precautions around areas where explosives were stored. But didn't they have them set aside somewhere safe? What kind of slipshod outfit was this UDT bunch, anyway?

He wasn't sure he wanted to find out.

"All right, you apes, time to see how you do in the water! We're gonna do this by the numbers, two at a time, and see what kind of swimmers we've really got. Forsythe! White! You're first!"

Forsythe turned to look up at Schroeder, who was standing on a low rise to one side of the beach where he could see everything that went on. Lieutenant Commander Chapman and several other instructors were behind him, looking on, presumably ready to take the measure of Team Ten before the training got serious.

After the team's official formation the day before, Forsythe had spent most of the afternoon supervising work details storing the gear the OSS contingent had brought from Nassau and getting the outfit settled in. Coates had been careful to divide up the Maritime Unit so that most tents were a mix between OSS and NCDU men. Forsythe had drawn two tentmates from the Fort Pierce contingent, Lieutenant j.g. Culver and Ensign Hall, neither of whom seemed any happier with the arrangement than he was.

This morning they'd been rooted out of their tents at an ungodly hour and put through Physical Training exercises in swim trunks and canvas shoes before being allowed to eat breakfast, an experience almost as challenging, as far as Forsythe was concerned, as any mere regimen of push-ups and jumping jacks. With the mess hall still being finished, the meal was prepared in a field kitchen and eaten in the open air, where flies and sand seemed to get into everything.

They'd gone straight from breakfast down to the beach. Forsythe hadn't been expecting to swim yet, since though they were in trunks they hadn't been ordered to break out any of their other swim gear. All the OSS men had brought their personal equipment with them, as well as the heavier supplies that belonged to the Maritime Unit as a whole. Forsythe had left his mask, fins, and diving knife in a canvas bag under the cot in his tent.

"Ah, Chief…"

"What is it this time, Mr. Forsythe?" Schroeder asked with a frown.

"I was just wondering … what about our gear?"

"Gear? What gear? You're swimmers, not salvage divers."

"Our masks and fins, Chief. What about them?" He knew the UDT wanted no part of the LARUs the Maritime Unit had brought, but Forsythe couldn't imagine long-distance swimming without the basic diving equipment they'd been using for months back on Nassau.

"Masks ... yeah." Schroeder shrugged. "Yeah, some of the boys used masks at Kwajalein, and they're going to be standard issue when we can get a reliable source of supply. We damn near cleaned the islands out equipping the teams for Saipan and Guam, and we can't issue any more right now."

"Some of us have our own, Chief," Forsythe said. "Our own fins, too."

"Fins! You OSS boys actually mess around with those goddamned things? You guys have a lot more to learn than I thought."

"What are you talking about, Chief?" Forsythe demanded. "I thought you people were serious about long-range swimming here."

"We are. And I've never seen anybody swim with those silly web things on his feet and last more than a few minutes. Then it's leg cramps and fatigue and no end of grief. No way we're using swim fins in this outfit!"

"I can outswim the best man you've got, Chief, if I've got my fins on. Faster *and* farther." Forsythe realized, too late, that he'd done it again. Once again his big mouth had set him up to bear the brunt of Schroeder's acid tongue.

But Chapman leaned forward and said something in Schroeder's ear, and the chief nodded with seeming reluctance. "Okay, Lieutenant, put your money where your mouth is. You've got yourself a race. Crenshaw! Fetch the lieutenant's swim gear. On the double!" One of the OSS men broke ranks and headed for the tents at a trot.

"Er ... Chief, who am I swimming against?" He had a feeling he knew the answer even as he spoke.

Schroeder's evil grin confirmed his fears. "That would be me, Lieutenant."

"And may God have mercy upon your soul," somebody behind Forsythe said in a stage whisper.

The enlisted man returned in minutes carrying Forsythe's kit bag. Schroeder, who had moved down to the water's edge, looked on impatiently as Forsythe prepared himself. He kicked off his canvas shoes and pulled on the fins, then slid the strap of the diving mask over his head, leaving it up off his face for the time being. Then he walked down to join the chief, his gait a little awkward in the fins as he crossed the sandy beach. A few of the NCDU men laughed. "Lookit the frog!" someone said.

"Rules are simple, Lieutenant," Schroeder told him. "Just start circling the lagoon. First one to head on in is the loser."

"You got it, Chief," Forsythe answered. He pulled down his mask and settled it over his eyes and nose, then strode out through the gentle surf until the water was deep enough to let him swim. With practiced ease he pushed off, hard enough to propel him under the surface. Then he started to swim, using a strong but economical breaststroke to cut through the water.

It felt strange to be swimming near the surface, without the LARU to let him stay under, but he didn't let it throw him off his steady pace. At first Schroeder kept a little way ahead of him, but Forsythe soon caught up and then passed the chief by.

Time stretched out, and he kept on swimming, around and around the small lagoon. After a time he began to tire, but he knew that Schroeder, for all the man's sheer raw strength, would be feeling the fatigue worse. A swimmer who knew how to use his fins could get a lot of power from an easy, gentle kick, and that would make all the difference where endurance was concerned.

Plainly whatever they had seen of fins before had failed to impress the UDT men. Forsythe knew that fins weren't that common outside of a few narrow special interest sports, so it was likely the men who'd passed judgment on them for the Navy hadn't known how to use them properly. And until the swimmer learned the knack for using fins they would tire a man out faster than swimming with bare feet or even shoes, and they could indeed cause painful cramps.

Forsythe couldn't help but feel smug. Maybe this would convince the UDT people that the Maritime Unit knew their stuff after all…

At length he heard Schroeder's booming voice calling to him as he raised his face out of the water to breathe, and Forsythe stopped where he was. Treading water, he turned to look at the beach. Schroeder was kneeling in the sand, breathing hard, water streaming from his beard and down his hairy chest. "All right, Lieutenant," he called, pausing for breath again. "All right, you've made your point."

As he headed back to the beach Forsythe was grinning. Yes, maybe he'd just struck a blow for the OSS Maritime Unit after all.

CHAPTER 8

Sunday, 25 June 1944
Red Beach, Saipan

"Damn it, sir," Coffer said, exasperated. "I'm not going to see my people used as combat infantrymen. You've got to help me keep the Marines off my back."

"Good luck to you on that," the beachmaster said with a squeaky laugh. "Some of these Marine platoon commanders've been down here scrounging anything on two legs. They've been after my boys since the day we came ashore."

Captain Theodore Halverson — better known as "Mouse" to the people working for him because of his almost comical, high-pitched voice — was beachmaster of the Saipan landings, the man in charge of which boats went where, which cargos got unloaded when, and which way the incessant traffic jam of vehicles — of tanks, jeeps, trucks, and amtracks — went to get off the beach. Just over five feet tall but muscular and barrel-chested, he was also known as "Five-by-Five," and his voice, magnified over the loudspeakers set up along the shore, could be heard shrilling across every part of the beach.

Ever since the landing, Coffer and the UDTs had been working almost nonstop under Mouse Halverson's iron command. They'd started by blasting new channels through the coral reef, allowing larger landing craft — LCMs and LCIs and the big, tank-carrying LSTs more popularly known as Large, Slow Targets — to come all the way up to the beach to unload their cargos. Next they'd begun clearing some of the wrecked landing craft from the beach approaches — a delicate job requiring a delicate touch, since too large an explosive charge could spray more shrapnel than a Japanese mortar burst. After that they'd completed a detailed hydrographic chart of the entire beach area, then charted a boat pool off Green Beach 3.

After ten days, the demolition men were exhausted. Mouse seemed tireless, moving rapidly from beach to beach, always there to chivvy the men on ... or to land hard on some Marine or sailor with a stalled vehicle with a burst of invective and the command to "get that goddamned piece of junk off my goddamned beach."

Halverson cut a distinctive figure on the beach, with dungarees torn off at the knees, a vest hanging open over his broad, bare chest, and a dirty ball cap on his unruly hair. He looked up at Coffer and cocked his head. "Speaking of Marines, Commander," he said, "there's one hunting for you this morning. A major, no less. Told him I hadn't seen hide nor hair of you, but he'll be sniffing around the beach lookin' for you, I expect."

"He say what he want?" Coffer asked ... but he had a sinking feeling that he already knew the answer.

"Couldn't say. But the Marines must be having a time of it if they're tryin' to draft anybody with two legs they think can hold a rifle!"

Coffer groaned. Almost from the moment they'd come ashore, the three UDTs working on the beach had looked like God's gift to the Marines ... a full company's worth of men who could be issued with rifles and sent up to the line. The fighting on Saipan had been fierce and unrelenting. The Army had finally cleared out the southern half of the island, but the Marines had run into savage, almost fanatical resistance on the slopes of Mount Tapotchau. If Coffer's anticipated fifty

119

percent casualties to his teams had not materialized, Marine losses ashore had been unexpectedly severe. It was no wonder some Marine officers had been trying to draft Navy personnel who didn't appear to be doing anything at all … except blowing things up in the lagoon.

Two days earlier, four men from UDT-5 had vanished, failing to show up for an evening work detail muster. Waverly was carrying them on the books right now as AWOL, but Coffer wondered if they might not have been grabbed by the Marines. Hell, knowing the men involved…

MM2 Horwitz and MN1 Perkins had been good, steady men. Coffer had had his eye on the other two, however. GM1 Davies was not a regular Fort Pierce demo man, and there was a story going about that he'd disobeyed orders during the beach reconnaissance to swim to within a few feet of the shore, where he'd left his swim mask on a Japanese buoy. And as for TM2 Foglio, well, the man's reputation for tall stories had been sure to lead him into trouble someday when he tried to live up to them. Now, possibly, that was just what had happened.

Possibly the men had gone inshore on some kind of lark or a dare. With Davies and Foglio, that was distinctly possible. Then, too, they could have been snagged by a Marine press gang … or they could have been shot. Coffer's men had come under sniper fire several times during the past days. But it did seem unlikely that four men from the same unit would all vanish at once, without even leaving bodies to bury.

Bodies had been very much on Coffer's mind these past few days. As Marine casualties had increased, there'd been a steady line of wounded Marines coming down out of the island's interior … and a silent stream of bodies as well. Marine and Army burial teams had been working around the clock to bury the men killed during the past week, but still the air tasted more and more of that sick-sweet, throat-clutching stink of death.

"Maybe I should talk to that major," Coffer told Halverson after a time. "I keep wondering if one of them made off with my four guys."

"Could be, Commander," Halverson replied. "You know it wouldn't be the first time … uh oh."

"What?"

"Well, well," Halverson said, looking past Coffer's shoulder and up toward the edge of the jungle. "Speak of the devil and up he pops."

Coffer turned and saw a Marine officer walking toward him across the sand. The man looked gaunt, almost haggard, with several days' growth of beard and a shirt with one sleeve nearly torn away.

And walking behind him, equally gaunt and dirty, were the four missing UDT men.

"You're Mr. Coffer?" the Marine asked, coming closer.

"Yes, Major," Coffer said. "What have you found there?"

The major gave a tired smile. "Commander, I've got to tell you. These four men have been with my battalion for two days. They have done an excellent job and I'm proud to have had them with my unit, but I'm sending them back. Either I'm going to get into trouble, or they will."

Coffer gave the men a cold stare. Horwitz and Perkins were staring at their canvas shoes. Foglio and Davies met Coffer's glare, but only Davies didn't seem particularly concerned.

"Well, thanks for bringing them back, Major."

"Thanks for the loan, Commander. They were damned useful."

As the major walked away, Coffer turned to Halverson. "Captain? Would you excuse me and my men for a minute please?"

Halverson grinned. "Hey, take two minutes, Commander. I see some dumb bastard down there cluttering up *my* beach." The diminutive beachmaster strode off, already shouting shrill imprecations.

Coffer turned back to the four men. Thanks for the '*loan*'!"

"Uh, well, sir," Foglio said. "It's like this…"

"We sort of volunteered, sir," Davies said. "The Marines needed some demo work done in the jungle, and…"

"Yeah," Horwitz put in. "We thought we could help. We didn't know we was gonna be gone two days."

"We tried to get word back to the team," Foglio said. "But communications are kind of chancy back there."

"Perkins?" Coffer asked. "What do you have to say?"

"No excuse, sir," Perkins said woodenly.

"What the *hell* were you people doing in there, anyway?"

"The Marines had a pillbox that needed blowing, sir," Davies said. "And one thing kind of led to another…"

"'And one thing kind of led to another,'" Coffer mimicked. "You run off into the jungle, you don't tell anybody where you're going … there's a word for that in this man's Navy, people. It's AWOL — absent without leave!"

"We're ready to accept whatever punishment you think appropriate, sir," Perkins said.

"Look, we're sorry for the trouble, Skipper," Foglio added. The others nodded agreement

"Unfortunately," Coffer replied, "sorry just doesn't cut it. This is the *Navy*, damn it. You can't just up and run away to do whatever you damn well please whenever you damn well want to!"

Coffer stared at the men. He was angry, as angry as he'd ever been in his life. For ten days now he'd been trying to keep the Marines from stealing his men … and these four had gone off on their own and joined them. They had to be disciplined. But how?

That was the kicker. Up until now, there had been one and only one punishment for men who broke the rules in the teams … and that was to be kicked out of the UDT — "sent back to the fleet," as the men liked to say. But these four were good men, four of his best. He didn't want to summarily kick them out; damn it, he *needed* them. The UDTs' work on Saipan was almost done, but soon they would be swimming ashore at Tinian or Guam or some other god-forsaken coral speck in the Pacific.

But if he didn't punish them, the men might get the idea that they could go off skylarking any time they took the idea into their heads. Discipline would vanish … and with it, morale. They *had* to be punished…

He had an idea.

"Okay, men," he said after thinking the problem through. "As you know, the only real punishment we have in the teams is to send you back to the fleet."

"Sir!" Horwitz said, shocked. "Please don't —"

"Quiet!" Coffer barked. "You had your chance. It's my turn now. You men hear me?"

There was a mumbled chorus of "Yes, sirs."

"Okay," Coffer went on. "This is the way it is. I'm giving you each a choice. Back to the fleet … or you can volunteer for a burial detail."

"B-burial detail?" Foglio said, his eyes wide.

Coffer jerked a thumb over his shoulder, indicating the line of corpses on the beach. "The graves people need help. I've had a couple of requests already … which I couldn't answer because one of my teams was four men short. But we've learned to get along shorthanded just fine, thank you, so if you want to stay with the teams, you'll volunteer for special duty with the burial detail. Five days!" He looked from man to man. "Well? It's your choice. What'll it be?"

Davies drew himself up straighter. "Sir! I volunteer for the special detail!"

"Me too," Foglio said.

"Yes, sir."

"Me too, sir."

Coffer kept his calculated scowl in place, but something stirred inside. He'd just offered these men a choice between leaving the UDT and accepting five days of the most unpleasant duty imaginable … and they'd chosen to stay with the teams.

He was proud.

"Oh, *Christ*," Foglio said, stopping and laying his head down on the handle of his shovel. "I don't know if I can take any more of this!"

"Three days," Horwitz said. "Three stinking days…"

"You have quite a way with words, Bernie," Davies said.

"Hey, Blondie," Perkins said. "You ain't quittin', are you?"

Foglio raised his head and stared at Perkins for a long moment. All four men wore dungarees and helmets, with strips of cloth tied over their mouths and noses. That effort to keep out the smell and the taste of tropic-rotted flesh was all but useless, however. The stench hung heavy in the air, clinging to the earth, to their clothes, to their very skins. They'd told one another at the beginning that they would grow used to the smell, that after a day or so they wouldn't even notice it … but it seemed that the conventional wisdom simply didn't hold true this time. Foglio was convinced now he was going to be inhaling that distinctive odor of death until his own dying day.

It had gone on and on, the men rotating with other members of the burial party as they dug trenches in the soft ground, wrapped bodies and parts of bodies in blankets or tarps or whatever was available and lowered them into the earth, recorded the position and the name and number of the dog tags ... when those could even be found.

Foglio looked down at the body they were burying now. The kid's face looked almost peaceful, despite the blackened skin and the stomach bloated by gas. If only the kid's legs had still been attached, maybe it wouldn't have seemed quite so horrible...

"I'm sorry, guys," he told the others. Tears were rolling down his cheeks. "I ... just ... can't ... *take* ... this."

"Hey, easy, Blondie," Davies said. "You want to take a break?"

"No, man. *Nothing* is worth this! I can't take another two days of this. I can't take another hour! I'm for chucking it."

"Blondie, I ain't never seen you shook like this," Horwitz said.

"Look, I don't want to talk about it, okay? You guys stay if you want. But I'm gonna find the skipper and tell him I'm quittin'."

Perkins emptied the shovel of earth he was holding. "I'm with Blondie."

"I don't want to leave the teams," Davies said slowly.

"Then stay."

Davies shook his head. "Nah. We're in this together. Let's go find the skipper..."

"I'm with you," Horwitz said. "Shipmates, right?"

"...*after* we finish here," Davies added. "We owe it to these boys, right?" He dug the spade into the trench, removing another shovelful of earth.

After a moment, the others joined in.

Their excursion with the Marines had seemed harmless enough at the time. Mouse Halverson had been working them like slaves, and it was grueling, tedious work, too, not the sort of romantic excitement that all of them had pictured when they'd volunteered for demolitions. Going off with the Marines had been Foglio's idea, but the others had agreed readily enough. Anything for a little excitement, after a week of boredom and backbreaking work.

And what had it gotten them? More backbreaking work ... with a generous helping of nightmare thrown in. Foglio had been sick more times than he could remember these past three days. The worst of it, for him, was thinking about Pete, his younger brother.

Pete, who'd been shipped off to a place much like this one, called Guadalcanal, and never come back...

That evening, the four UDT men approached Coffer and, sadly, told him that they could not continue for two more days, that they were requesting transfers back to the fleet. Coffer had simply looked them up and down, told them to go get showers and to report for duty at 0700 hours the next morning.

That night, back aboard ship in the crew's mess, someone asked Foglio to tell the story about the WACs aboard the transport. Normally, Foglio was only too happy to oblige. He liked being the center of attention, liked having the guys listen to what he had to say, even if half of them didn't believe him.

For the first time, though, Foglio had shaken his head and left the compartment. Somehow, he didn't care now whether anyone believed him or not.

The war, suddenly, seemed a lot bigger — and, paradoxically, more *personal* — than it had before.

And he wasn't sure how he was going to deal with it.

"Ah, so this is the hiding place of that notorious outlaw, the Tan Gator! I was wondering if I'd ever catch up with you!" Though the voice was familiar, Tangretti couldn't place it against the babble that filled the crowded ward.

He winced as he shifted his weight and turned over in the bed, silently cursing the pain in his leg. But he almost forgot the discomfort as he caught sight of his visitor. "Chief! Chief Wallace!" His eyes went to the new insignia on his collar. "Excuse me. *Lieutenant* Wallace! What are you doing here?"

William M. Wallace shook Tangretti's hand. "Good to see you again, Gator." He paused. "Sorry about the Snake. I know how close you two guys were."

Tangretti's welcoming smile faded. "Yeah. A damned waste..."

"The ward nurse told me you were out once, and now you're back in," Wallace said. "What gives, Gator?"

Tangretti shrugged. He knew now that he'd pulled a pretty stupid stunt a couple of weeks earlier, when he'd gone AWOL in order to visit Veronica. He'd made it back to the hospital that evening — barely — with two of the stitches pulled out and his leg hurting worse than it had after he'd been hit. They still hadn't figured out that he'd signed himself out of the hospital by forging an illegible doctor's signature; things were so confused with the flood of wounded coming back across the English Channel from France by that time that it was simply assumed that he'd been the victim of some sort of administrative mix-up ... but he had gotten a stern lecture from the head nurse on his ward about trying to do too much too soon.

"Er, yeah, well…" Tangretti mustered a smile. "I guess I pushed things a little. Now the damned leg's infected and the docs say I'll be laid up for weeks. Of all the stupid —"

"That's what you get for thinking you can run Nature the way you run the Navy, Gator," the brawny lieutenant told him. "Sometimes you just can't cheat, know what I mean?"

Tangretti thought of Richardson, dead on Omaha … and of Veronica. "Yeah. I'm finding that out." He looked away for a moment, trying to keep his face from betraying his emotion. "I guess I did manage to finesse my way out of the next op, though. Can't clear the beaches in the south of France flat on my back in bed, can I?"

"I guess you didn't hear yet. Our boys didn't draw the next one. Force U got the job."

"Aw, you're shitting me, right? Who's had the most experience with Kraut obstacles?"

"Maybe somebody figured the boys in Force O deserved a break," Wallace said gently.

The Demolitioneers in the D day invasion had been divided into two forces, designated O and U after their assignments to Omaha and Utah beaches, respectively. From what Tangretti had heard, Force U hadn't faced anything like the hellfire of Omaha. "Even so, I never figured Commander Gilbert would stand still for that!"

"He didn't," Wallace said. "The way I heard it Henderson just assumed he'd be taking Force U in on Anvil because us Omaha guys had been hit so hard, but Gilbert wouldn't have it. They finally ended up flipping a coin for it."

"They *flipped* for it?"

"Yeah. You think Eisenhower knows how the Cos of the combat demolition outfits are deciding invasion logistics? Anyway, Henderson and his Force U bullyboys get to see the Riviera, while we're going to be shipped home to the States."

"And then what?"

Wallace shrugged. "Probably the Pacific. I hear they can't get enough Fort Pierce men out there. You'll probably end up right back where you started from, dodging bullets with the UDT."

"Guess so." The words reminded him of Richardson again. They'd been so eager to get out of the Pacific back in the days when the brass out there didn't seem to know how to use the Demolitioneers effectively, and they'd welcomed the string of lucky breaks that brought them into Overlord and the chance to be in on the kill in Europe.

If they had stayed with UDT-1, maybe Hank Richardson would still be alive...

He shoved the thought away and changed the subject. "You sure seem to know all the skinny. But then you're one of the brass hats now, aren't you? What's the story? How'd a confirmed chief like you end up getting fitted for gold braid, huh?"

Wallace chuckled. "Not my fault. I did what everybody else did on Omaha, did the job, you know? Got scratched up a bit, but not near as bad as you. I thought it was a real waste, though, us doing all that work on the beach and then not getting a chance to see it through. We were trained for demolitions work, and it's pretty damned silly to limit us to the high water mark. So I grabbed a couple of packs of demo gear and hitched a ride inland with some of the dogfaces. Spent a few days helping them push back the Krauts, blowing up obstacles until I ran out of charges. By the time I got a billet on a boat heading back across the Channel, these new orders had come through. Lieutenant j.g., of all things! You could've knocked me over with a string of primacord! But there wasn't a hell of a lot I could do about it, so I gave 'em my best grin and promised I'd be an officer and a gentleman."

"So what're you doing here, anyhow?"

"The powers that be tagged me for a special assignment. You know, everybody left their gear, all the stuff they didn't actually need for the invasion, back in the assembly area barracks. A lot of guys were wounded and shipped to hospitals wherever there was room for 'em. If we let the bureaucrats try to get the gear and the men back together, they'll still be working on it when our grandkids are in the Navy. So me and Chief Fields have been traveling around with a truck full of stuff and a list of who ended up where."

Tangretti shook his head. "Hell. That seems like a dumb way to utilize the skills of a highly trained Demolitioneer. I thought they had personnel services to do make-work shit like that?"

"Well, you know the Navy. You've got an empty billet…"

"You need a warm body to fill it," Tangretti completed the line. Wallace laughed, and Tangretti joined in, the first time he'd laughed in a long time.

"God damn it, Gator," Wallace said, "I'm sure glad I found you. When you get back on your feet, I want you to do something for me, would you?"

"Anything, man. Anything. Even if it takes Ike's signature to get it done!"

"Nothing like that, you petty forger! No, I'm going to need myself a best man. Alice and I are getting hitched before the orders come through to ship us all Stateside." Alice Pascoe was a local girl Wallace had met in Falmouth. Tangretti had never met her, but he'd heard plenty in the weeks before D day.

He couldn't keep his reaction from showing on his face. "What's the matter, Gator?" Wallace asked.

Tangretti shook his head glumly. "Look, Lieutenant, maybe it's none of my business, but you're making a big mistake. Just like Snake did. A Demolitioneer shouldn't get married. Never. It's not fair to the girl, and it's not fair to you, and it sure as hell ain't fair to the buddy who has to go and tell her when you buy the farm on some god-forsaken stretch of beach!"

Wallace looked uncomfortable. "I ... sorry you feel that way, Gator. I was really hoping you'd stand up with me, prop me up at the altar and all..."

"Not this sailor! I was Snake's best man, remember? Pulled every string and made every deal I knew how to let him and Veronica get hitched, and for what? So he could go off and get himself killed after just one night with her? No thanks, Lieutenant. I'll always love you like a brother the way I would any Demolitioneer, but I won't help you make the worst mistake of your life!"

He could see Wallace fighting to control his anger. "I ... I see. I'm sorry, Gator. But Alice and I are getting married, whatever you think. I wouldn't marry her before Overlord, because I thought I might buy it and I didn't have the guts to make the kind of commitment Hank Richardson did. But he was the one who made the right choice, Gator. Maybe he and Veronica didn't get the chance to spend much time together, but by God he made the best of the time he had. I won't make the mistake of pushing Alice away again."

Tangretti closed his eyes. "You'll do what you want to, of course, Lieutenant. I really hope everything works out for you, for Alice ... but don't expect any cheers from me. Cause I think you're making one hell of a mistake."

He was suddenly very tired.

CHAPTER 9

Friday, 30 June 1944
Naval Combat Demolitions Unit
Training Center
Fort Pierce, Florida

Boatswain's Mate First Class Frank Rand set his seabag down and mopped his face with a handkerchief. He had almost forgotten just how oppressive the heat and humidity of a southern Florida afternoon could be. As he tucked the sweat-soaked cloth back into the top of the blouse of his undress white uniform he looked up at the ominous thunderhead building up over the Atlantic. They'd have one of those notorious Fort Pierce downpours before the afternoon was over, he decided.

There wasn't much activity going on around him. The NCDU school was a tent city that straggled across Hutchinson Island, one of two swampy, low-lying barrier islands protecting the little resort harbor of Fort Pierce. The Demolitioneers had been latecomers to the Amphibious Base and found the Navy and the Coast Guard had already divided up the choice sites — including hotels and a casino — to house the various aspects of the military presence here. So the NCDU base was small and makeshift, with a couple of unfinished-looking buildings and a lot of canvas. Rand supposed that most of the NCDU trainees were out in the swamps on training exercises this afternoon, leaving the base itself almost empty.

"Frank! Good God, man, what are you doing back in this damned swamp?"

Rand recognized the deep, chesty voice and turned just as a meaty hand thumped him on the shoulder. "I missed your ugly face, Gunny," he said with a grin. "Not to mention the heat, the humidity, the snakes, the gators, the mosquitoes, and living in tents! Send me to a real war zone, I told 'em, and sure enough they shipped me back from Normandy to this hellhole."

Gunnery Sergeant Drake's answering smile looked more than a little bit forced. He was a big man, hard, lean, and competent, with the anchor-and-globe Marine emblem tattooed on one thick biceps. Despite the heat and humidity his T-shirt looked fresh and clean. From his expression Rand could tell the man was jealous of anyone who had gotten a chance to see the war firsthand. "Did you get in on the fighting?" the Marine asked, managing to sound almost wistful.

Rand nodded somberly. "Yeah. I was on Omaha." He looked away, trying to shut out the images that came flooding back unbidden of the bloody beaches of the D day invasion. "But now that we're in France there ain't much use for Scouts and Raiders."

"So you're coming back to be an instructor again?" Drake flashed another smile, more convincing this time. Though he was an NCO in the Marine Corps, Drake was also part of the Navy/Marine Scouts and Raiders, specialists in scouting enemy coasts prior to an invasion. Some of them, Drake and Rand included, had been assigned to the NCDU school at Fort Pierce when it had first been established to help set up a training program based on the S&R course. But it wasn't exactly the work they signed on to do, and Rand had managed to get a combat assignment soon after the first few NCDU classes had graduated. With other S&R men, Rand had helped guide the landing boats in to Omaha Beach and ended up on shore in the middle of some of the heaviest action of D day.

Rand shook his head. "Not me. I put in for a transfer to the Demolitioneers. I'm a student this time, not a teacher."

"You — a demolition man?" Drake looked scandalized. "What happened to Raider Rand, the one-man invasion force? I thought Scouts and Raiders was your whole life!"

"Things change," Rand said shortly, unwilling to say anything more. He had joined the Scouts and Raiders in search of a role that would let him live up to his father's heroic World War I record, and at every turn he'd tried to push himself to the very edge. At Normandy Rand had finally found the chance to prove himself, leading a squad of American soldiers up a path he'd found to knock out a pillbox that had the Army pinned down on the beach.

But in the course of the battle he'd learned something about heroism, watching the deeds of a small band of Naval Combat Demolitions men who had fought and died not for glory, not for recognition, but *just to get the job done.*

Rand had helped train some of those men the last time he'd been posted to Fort Pierce. Now he had returned, determined to join the ranks of the men who had so impressed him on the beaches of Normandy.

Drake seemed to sense his reluctance to talk about the invasion. "Well, it's good to see you back, Raider, even if you are one of the victims now." The Marine gave him an evil grin. "Nothing personal, you know. We'll just be doing our jobs."

"Yeah, right," Rand said. "And the fact that your job's going to be riding us all until we give up —"

"Hey, Frankie, all part of the service!" Drake laughed. "You wouldn't want us to go soft on you now, would you? Not the rough, tough Normandy man who took on Hitler all by himself!"

"Never saw him," Rand said, mustering a faint smile. "He must've been off visiting Eva or something. But he left one hell of a reception committee, I'll tell you that much." In his mind's eye he could see again the pair of Germans who had stumbled out of a shattered pillbox in front of him, trying to surrender, only to be cut down by submachine gun fire. And the little NCDU man who had dragged his buddy out of a withering crossfire and then died there on the beach. Once Rand had thought of war as glory and honor and adventure. He knew better now, after Normandy.

Picking up his seabag again and slinging it over his shoulder, he changed the subject. "So, how's it been here in mosquitoland? How many others from the old gang are here?"

Drake shook his head. "Not many, I'll tell you. You know old Bill Wallace shipped out to England ... yeah, that was before you left. And the Old Man got himself a combat assignment out in the PTO a couple months back."

"Coffer? Man, I don't think I could even imagine this place without him at the helm!"

"It's been hectic, that's sure enough. Lieutenant Culver went to the Pacific with Class 6A last month. Harrison shipped out, too. Hell, we don't even have the Mad Russian around here anymore."

"Well, shit, man, it sounds like this place is gonna be dull as dishwater. What do you do for fun around here if you can't place bets on what the Mad Russian's gonna do next?" George Kistiakowsky had been a civilian scientist co-opted by the NCDU to work on experimental explosive devices. Eccentric and irrepressible, Kistiakowsky had been famous for careening around the compound in a tank, among other exploits, and had been a favorite source of jokes among the staff of the training base. "So where'd he go?"

Drake shrugged. "No one knows. One day he was here, then he was gone. I heard some scuttlebutt that somebody showed up in the middle of the night flashing government credentials and orders to have him released immediately, but nobody knows anything for sure. I figure he got drafted for some top secret project, you know, Buck Rogers stuff."

"Either that or they got sick of him playing with tanks and threw him in Leavenworth," Rand suggested with a grin.

Drake laughed again, then glanced at his watch. "Look, man, I gotta go. Big meeting with the brass at fourteen hundred … another complaint about supplies missing from the S&R stocks. Somebody seems to think some of our boys are involved!"

Rand chuckled, remembering the way the early NCDU classes had liberated everything from boat paddles to cook's stores without ever having any of their thefts proved. "How *could* they think such a thing? Well, don't let me keep you back, Gunny. I still have to get checked in. Maybe I'll see you over the weekend, huh?"

"Don't bet on it," Drake said. "They're keeping us pretty damned busy around here these days. Ever since the Old Man left it seems like we've been falling further behind every day."

As the big Marine hurried off Rand turned away and started toward the ramshackle building that served as the administrative hub of the NCDU school. He found himself wondering if he had made the right decision, coming back here for training as a Demolitioneer. Once he had thought that Scouts and Raiders was the ideal outfit for him, but in the end the work had left him feeling empty. Would he do any better on this new team? Or was he doomed to always search for the end of the rainbow without ever realizing it couldn't be found?

"Dress right... *Dress!* Eyes front! Atten-*HUT!*"

Rand drew himself to rigid attention and stared straight ahead as Drake paced back and forth in front of the trainees lined up on the parade ground under the dim light of dawn. It was strange to be on the receiving end of one of these bellowed indoctrination speeches after having seen so many from an instructor's point of view.

"I am Gunnery Sergeant Drake, but for the next few weeks, as far as you're concerned, I am God and all his Saints rolled into one! In case you apes aren't sure what it is you signed up for, I'll remind you. This is the Naval Combat Demolitions Unit Training Course, where we turn screwups and goofballs into Combat Demolitioneers!" Drake gestured at a short line of tough-looking men behind him, strangers to Rand. No, on second thought one of them did look familiar ... Grover, that was it. He'd been in one of the early NCDU classes Rand had helped train. He was wearing chief's stripes now. "These men are your other instructors. You will obey them, as you will obey me, without question or hesitation. Some of the training you will receive will involve live explosives and hazardous situations, and by God I won't have any man, officer or enlisted, putting other people at risk by second-guessing or sounding off out of turn."

The Marine stopped pacing and faced the trainees squarely. "The basis for successful Combat Demolitions is teamwork. By the time this course is through you will learn to be team players or you will be out on your ass. Everything you do, from this day forward, is not for yourself, not for the Navy, not for

137

your country or for the girl back home, but for the *team*." His eyes seemed to be resting on Rand as he said it.

Was Drake still thinking about "Raider Rand," the lone wolf? Rand had won a Silver Star in Sicily for going alone in a small boat into one of the beaches and setting up a light right under an enemy-held pillbox, but his CO had given him a thorough chewing-out along with the recommendation for the medal. Frank Rand had never been much of a team player, until that moment on Omaha when he had forced himself to ignore another German strong point in favor of going back to bring explosives and a squad of soldiers up the cliff path it guarded.

He believed in the value of teamwork now ... didn't he? Or would "Raider Rand" start to reassert himself the next time there was an opportunity to play the hero?

"From the right," Drake bellowed. "Sound off by twos!"

"One!" "Two!" "One!" "Two!" The calls went down the line.

When the last "Two!" had rung out, Drake took a step back. "All right, you apes. Each of you ones is paired up with the two on your left. You men are partners ... swim buddies. The man you're teamed up with is going to be your brother and tentmate and best friend all rolled into one. You married guys are gonna get to know your swim buddy better'n you know the missus. Screw up, and your buddy goes down with you. Get something right, and it's his success just as much as yours. From here on out, you and your swim buddy are a team, and it's as a team that we're gonna put you through your paces."

Rand studied the man next to him who was supposed to be his partner. He was a tough-looking little fireplug of a man with dark hair and thoughtful eyes, his uniform identifying him as a second class gunner's mate. His stocky frame gave an impression of strength and physical endurance, but those eyes made it clear he was more than just some muscle-bound tough. The shorter man looked up as he returned Rand's scrutiny.

Drake didn't give them much time to examine their partners. "I can't repeat often enough the importance of learning to work as a unit. For the duration of the training there will be no distinction between officers and enlisted men. You will share equally in the work, in the training, and in the exhaustion, and woe be unto the man who tries to take refuge behind rank or time in service or anything else to get special treatment either from the rest of the class or from any of the instructors.

"One of the things that makes a Demolitioneer special is the knowledge that he's a part of a genuine team. Each and every one of you who makes it through NCDU training will share a very special kind of bond. Around these parts, that bond is called 'Hell Week', even though the brass prefers a politer term, 'Indoctrination Week.' But ask anyone who's been through it. Hell Week it's been since the very beginning, and Hell Week it'll be for you."

There were some scattered groans from the ranks, but Rand knew there wasn't a man there who really understood just what the gunnery sergeant meant. He did, though. He had helped refine the week-long torture the men called Hell Week back when he'd been one of the S&R instructors. They had taken the eight-week training course the Scouts and Raiders went through and distilled it into a single intensive week of sheer physical agony. The man who survived Hell Week was supposed to be able to survive anything.

"Those of you who make it through — and it won't be many, I'll tell you that much right now — you'll always know that your buddies in Demolitions have been through what you've been through. You'll know you can function as a part of the team come hell or high water. And you'll know your

139

buddies'll never let you down either, 'cause they've been through it too." Drake paused. "We're going to give you a privilege earlier classes didn't get … fifteen minutes of free time before the official start of Hell Week. You might spend it getting to know your new swim buddy … unless you'd like to say a few prayers instead. You're gonna need all the help you can get, here on Earth and from Heaven too. But you can be sure we'll supply all the Hell you'll be needing. Fifteen minutes, people. Fall out!"

The formation broke up in little knots of chattering men. Rand wanted a cigarette and a few moments to gather his thoughts, but he found his partner following close on his heels as he started to wander away from the center of the field.

"Name's Kowalski," he said. "Stan Kowalski, from Chicago."

"Rand," he answered shortly.

"Rand? Frank Rand?" Kowalski's voice wavered a little. "I heard about you. Scuttlebutt says you were at Omaha. I heard you scouted out the beaches all alone, before the invasion, and then led a commando attack when the Army hit the beach."

"Don't believe everything you hear, sailor," Rand told him. "Yeah, I did some scouting. Mostly stayed offshore, taking bearings and getting the lay of the land. Never did get up on the beaches, but a couple of my buddies did so the brass could get samples of the sand. As for leading commandos in…"

"Well? What about it?"

"Let's just say it's gained a little in the telling, okay? Fact is, I was supposed to be guiding landing boats in, but my own boat got sunk and I waded ashore cause I didn't know what else to do. Then I got lucky and spotted a path up a cliff, and some crazy colonel told me I was a second lieutenant in the Army and gave me a patrol to lead up to the top. After the battle there was one hell of a fight over whether or not a Navy boatswain's mate could also be an Army lieutenant, but they finally decided the colonel didn't have that kind of authority and I was back in the Navy again."

Kowalski chuckled. "Sounds typical. You see much fighting?" His voice held an edge that sounded familiar to Rand. Where had he heard that anxious enthusiasm before?

"Only one day ... but it was one hell of a day, Ski. One hell of a day."

"Damn, you were sure one lucky bastard. Wonder if I'll ever get a chance like that?"

And then Rand knew where he'd heard that tone before.

In his own voice, when he'd dreamed of nothing but the glories of war.

CHAPTER 10

Thursday, 6 July 1944
UDT School, Amphibious Training Base
Kamaole, Maui, Hawaii

The voice that answered Alex Forsythe's cautious knock was querulous. "Enter!"

It was one of only a handful of real buildings at the UDT school, a makeshift wood building that housed staff offices and a shared reception area where a pair of overworked yeomen tried to keep up with the demands of keeping the whole operation running. The walls were unpainted and already showing damage from too much moisture and too little care, and the furnishings, even in the offices, were meager at best.

Forsythe opened the door to Commander Chapman's inner sanctum and went inside, wondering what had prompted the summons. Chapman had recently moved up from Exec and training officer to the CO of the UDT training center, though he still carried out most of his previous jobs as well. It was never good when a senior officer took too much notice of one of the trainees…

"Lieutenant Forsythe, reporting as ordered, sir," he said formally.

"Take it easy, Lieutenant," Chapman told him, looking up from his desk. "You're not being called on the carpet. Not this time, at least, eh, Chief?" He exchanged a wry look with Chief Schroeder, who was standing in front of him, managing to look like a red-bearded pirate despite his neat, crisply pressed uniform.

The only chair in the room, aside from Chapman's, was occupied by Lieutenant Coates, Team Ten's CO. Despite Chapman's words, Forsythe couldn't help but feel nervous at facing these three together.

Although he'd gotten off to a rocky start with Team Ten, Forsythe had felt things were getting better. After the race with Schroeder in the lagoon swim fins had suddenly become all the rage at the training center. Chapman himself had endorsed the use of fins for all UDT men and ordered the OSS team members to start training their Fort Pierce comrades in their use. At first all they had were the fins they'd brought as personal gear from Nassau, but Chapman and Chief Schroeder, who had a reputation as a scrounge going back to the time he and a UDT man named Tangretti had collected tuna fish killed during a training exercise with explosives and traded them for two cases of Scotch, had pulled strings and scoured the islands until they found a source to supply the extra swim fins they needed.

Because Forsythe had shown a special flair for training, he had ended up as more instructor than student, a role that suited him just fine. But he knew that his teammates still weren't ready to accept him fully, and that knowledge still rankled.

Damn the Fort Pierce men and their misplaced elitism! They were convinced, it seemed, that only someone who had gone through the training in Florida could be relied upon, and despite the best efforts of all the higher-ups they were still reluctant to open up to the former OSS men in the outfit. It made things difficult, to say the least.

But at least, Forsythe thought, he'd be out of the mess soon enough. All he had to do was get by until a transfer came through. Meanwhile, the swim fin training at least made things tolerable while he waited for his request to make its way through channels.

"How'd you like to wrap up your training early, Alex?" Coates asked him.

"Early?" He raised an eyebrow. "I thought the whole team finished together. Or are you saying... He trailed off. It was still too early for a transfer to have come through, he was sure. Had they decided they didn't want him in the UDT anymore?

Somehow the thought that the UDT might not think he was worthy of them overrode his earlier determination to look for a better slot.

"Here's the deal, Lieutenant," Chapman said. "Intelligence is looking for qualified swimmers for a special mission. They wanted to tap UDT, but none of the teams is close enough to detach trained men for the job. So we thought some of your OSS people might be ideal for the job — Coates here tells me that what they're looking for is pretty close to the kind of stuff you guys trained for. And your name came up as someone qualified to command the detachment. Interested?"

"Yes, *sir*," Forsythe said, more eagerly than he'd intended. "I'd be glad to see some action for a change."

Coates chuckled, and even Chapman cracked a smile. "Well, sorry we couldn't challenge you enough here, Mr. Forsythe. Maybe this'll be what you need." He glanced down at an open file folder on his desk. "Coates recommends White, O'Leary, Crenshaw, and Barker as the rest of your team. You have any problems with that?"

"No, sir. They're all good men."

"Good. Then the five of you should pack and be ready to catch the boat over to Pearl tonight. You too, Chief."

Forsythe looked at Schroeder. "The Chief's coming too?"

144

"Yes, he is, though God only knows how I'm supposed to replace him here. Chief Schroeder's done some damned good work all the way back to UDT-one days, and the powers that be asked for him specifically." Chapman looked at him with a quizzical expression. "Is there some problem, Lieutenant?"

Of course everyone at the training center knew about the history of friction between Forsythe and Schroeder. "No, sir," Forsythe said. "Not on my side."

"Good. That's settled then. This mission is classified, so it is not to be discussed with anyone who isn't involved. Am I understood? Good. Dismissed."

Forsythe was smiling as he followed Coates and Schroeder out of the office. This was better than a transfer, a chance to get back to exactly the kind of work he'd been trained to do. Maybe Lambertson's fears had been exaggerated after all. A successful OSS-style op might lead the brass to change their views, MacArthur or no MacArthur.

And meanwhile he'd be free of the uncomfortable atmosphere that prevailed in Team Ten. And even if Schroeder was along, away from the training center he was just another CPO, a subordinate. That meant Alexander Forsythe would have his chance to shine!

The contingent from Maui had crossed over to Oahu aboard an LCP, reaching their destination just before sunset. Waimanalo, located on the other side of the Koolau mountains from Honolulu and just down the coast from Bellows Field, was the center of operations for the Pacific Fleet's amphibious arm. According to Schroeder it was the original home to the UDTs as well, but after Kwajalein, when the need for further training and a vast expansion of the teams had become obvious even to the most stubborn of the brass hats in PTO,

Chapman had been directed to set up shop on Maui.

But Waimanalo continued to serve most other elements of the amphibious forces in Hawaii.

Forsythe found himself regretting the UDT move to Kamaole. Not only was Waimanalo a breathtakingly beautiful setting, set under the lush green bulk of three-thousand-foot-high Konahuanui, but it was also close enough to the fleshpots of Honolulu for an enterprising young officer to enjoy himself now and again. Maui had a few bars and clubs, but it wasn't exactly a haven for sophisticated nightlife.

He had resisted the temptation to go in to town that first night, knowing he had meetings set for Friday morning. Instead he promised himself a night or two to remember before he left Oahu, and turned in early instead.

Now he and Schroeder were facing Rear Admiral Paulus P. Powell in his office near the hub of the Waimanalo base. Powell was Chief of Staff to Third Amphibious Force, commanded by Vice Admiral Wilkinson, the unit tasked with operations in the central Pacific. Looking harassed and impatient, Powell had waved them into his office with an imperious gesture as soon as the Marine sentry announced the pair and had started talking without preamble.

"Third Force has drawn the assignment of invading the western Carolines," he was saying, jabbing a blunt finger at the map spread out on his desk. "Specifically Peleliu and Yap. General MacArthur wants them neutralized to secure his flanks when he moves against the Philippines. Trouble is, the Carolines are too damned close to the main Japanese bases in the Philippines for comfort. They know MacArthur wants to liberate Manila, so they have good reason to be watching for us. Our aerial and sub recon has spotted them putting in some kind of underwater obstructions around the islands, and we need to survey them before we can send in the troops."

"You mean before we even commit to the invasion, Admiral?" Forsythe asked, frowning. Standard UDT practice, as Schroeder and others had been pounding it into his head these past weeks, called for survey and clearing work to be done immediately prior to the actual invasion.

"That's exactly right, Lieutenant." Powell nodded. "We have to decide if an invasion's worth the cost, and the only way to do that is some kind of assessment of the actual defenses. We don't need them cleared, just checked over by experts who can tell us whether or not Peleliu and Yap are vulnerable. We can mount an ordinary clearing operation once we decide to give the invasions a green light."

"And it's essential we do it with a minimum of exposure to our people." Lieutenant Commander Charles Edward Fitzgerald spoke up from the corner of the office where he had listened to the admiral with folded arms and a disapproving expression. Fitzgerald had been introduced as the CO of the special mission the UDT men had volunteered for, an officer on loan from the Waipio Amphibious Operating Base, which was located just down the coast from the UDT facility on Maui. He looked like a living recruiting poster, with square jaw and blond hair and a neatly tailored, carefully pressed uniform. A fastidious dresser ravellf, Forsythe had nothing against an officer who took care of his appearance, but there was something almost cardboard about the Amphibious Operations man that bothered him. "If the Japanese get the idea that we're interested in those islands, they'll pump troops in there until we don't have a chance to take them. So any recon work has to be done in secret. That's where your experts come in, Lieutenant."

Powell nodded again. "That's right. We've done everything we can from airplanes and sub periscopes. Now we need swimmers to get right in there and check the approaches out. It's a little outside of normal UDT work, but your OSS Maritime Unit has had the kind of training we think you'll need to do the job."

"Pretty tall order for six men, Admiral," Schroeder commented. "And it's a long, long swim from Saipan to Yap!"

"Ten men," Fitzgerald corrected him. "We'll have four of my specialists from Waipio in the unit as well."

"As for transportation," Powell added, "the submarine *Burrfish* will be responsible for delivering your team. You'll deploy off the sub to scout the islands. We figure she can slip in and out right under the noses of the Japanese so we don't call too much attention to our interest in that area. She'll only surface at night, so you can make your approaches under cover of darkness."

Forsythe looked from Fitzgerald to Powell, not sure which one's words disturbed him most. The Maritime Unit had trained in operating from subs, but he was wary of any op that involved too many lines of authority. After the reactions the OSS had faced so many times in the past, he couldn't help but wonder if regular Navy types would really know how to use the assets they were deploying so casually. And the notion of not just reporting to Fitzgerald but actually mixing with some of his men, of unknown qualifications or experience, reinforced his discomfort.

He finally focused on Powell. "If I may ask, Admiral, just who is in charge of the actual operation?"

Powell exchanged a glance with Fitzgerald. "Captain Aiken commands the *Burrfish* and is in charge of getting you in and out. But Commander Fitzgerald is responsible for the actual missions. You and your swimmers report to him. You, Lieutenant, are responsible for managing the individual ops, under his direction. Is that clear enough?"

"Yes, sir," he answered crisply. Inwardly he was suppressing a groan. He would have been happier to hear that Schroeder was getting a field commission and being put in command of everything. At least Schroeder understood what it was like to do a swim.

That brought a smile to his lips. Maybe the Fort Pierce people with their misplaced esprit de corps had a point after all. Men who shared the same training could at least rely on each other … and their Cos. Could the swimmers rely on Fitzgerald when they got out on the firing line?

"*Burrfish* is under orders to sail on Sunday. That doesn't give you much time to get ready." The admiral stood up, and the others followed suit. "I won't disguise the fact that this isn't exactly a dream assignment. You'll be deep in enemy waters, and even a top-notch crew doesn't always come back. Not to mention the dangers of your recon work. You'll be crammed aboard the *Burrfish* with eleven extra men in a space that's already too small, and you'll be out of touch with land for weeks or even months. Thoroughly unpleasant and dangerous work from first to last. Do you want out now, or do you still want to volunteer?"

Schroeder gave him a broad grin. Forsythe, despite his doubts, wasn't about to back out either. "I'm game, sir."

Powell extended a hand first to Forsythe, then to Schroeder, his handshake hearty. "I knew I could count on the UDT. You men are a credit to the uniform. Good luck!"

"Come on, Alex, you can tell me. You keep dropping all these hints about shipping out, but every time I ask about it you change the subject. Why are you being so mysterious? Do I look like a Japanese spy to you?"

Alex Forsythe studied the girl in the flickering light of the campfire. She was tall, with golden hair cascading over her shoulders and a figure that looked good even in the drab WAVE uniform she wore. No, she didn't look anything like a Japanese spy to him. But as usual a touch of mystery about his life was working perfectly, piquing her interest while his careful seduction plan unfolded. He wondered idly just how many women he'd ensnared with this approach over the past two years. Forsythe had never blatantly revealed anything about the OSS or his work with the Maritime Unit to any of them, but somehow the right mix of hints and knowing looks had always paid off.

"I bet you're really Tokyo Rose on vacation," he told her with a grin. "And you're probably just waiting for me to turn my back while you drug my champagne and carry me back to Japan so Tojo can pump me for all my secrets."

She laughed, a musical sound against the counterpoint of the crackling fire and the distant, booming surf. Her name was Maggie something-or-other, and she worked in Administration at the base hospital in Pearl. That was all he knew about her, all he needed to know for tonight.

And after tonight? That didn't matter. Tomorrow he'd be neck-deep in the preparations for Powell's mission, and Sunday *Burrfish* was due to sail. Who knew when the mission would be wrapped up? And then it would be on to other stations, other jobs … other girls.

Forsythe had gone into Honolulu in search of some fun after the meeting in Powell's office, getting an early start for his chance to party before *Burrfish* sailed. According to the written orders they'd been handed after the conference, they were to report on board the sub late on Saturday and sail before dawn Sunday morning. That left tonight for fun. If he was going to be shut up inside some sardine can of an overcrowded submarine for weeks or months on end, Forsythe reasoned, he deserved a good send-off first. He'd made the rounds of some of the better nightclubs in Honolulu, spending his money freely as he tried to drink, dance, and romance his way across town.

Maggie hadn't even been his first choice for the night. She was a little too straitlaced for his taste, the kind of girl who made seduction a job instead of a game. There had been another girl, a little redhead he'd started talking to over drinks at a hotel lounge downtown. She'd been all primed to accept his invitation to move the party to more private surroundings in one of the rooms upstairs, but she'd left in a huff after he'd asked Maggie for a dance while the redhead was off freshening up. Not that it really mattered. If the first gal had been the possessive type, he was better off without her.

Eventually he'd persuaded Maggie to leave the lounge, but she hadn't taken the bait from his hints about a private party upstairs. So he'd played another card that rarely failed him, the romantic moonlight walk on the beach ploy. A friend serving on Admiral Turner's staff had told him about this tiny, secluded cove in a letter written long before Forsythe had known he'd be posted to Hawaii, and the addition of a roaring fire, a pair of wineglasses, and a bottle of vintage Dom Perignon was all he'd needed to make the excursion perfect…

"Come on, darling, have another glass." He held up the bottle, nearly empty now. "We can't let good wine like this go to waste."

"Don't you want it?" she asked. "I don't want to be greedy…"

"It is yours, my lady," he said with an air of exaggerated gallantry. Forsythe filled her glass before she could protest and tossed the empty bottle away. Although he'd been out on the town for hours he'd been careful not to drink more than he needed to get a good buzz. The champagne had been for Maggie, to loosen her up.

She took a sip. "It's so quiet here," she said. "So peaceful. You can almost pretend there isn't a war out there on a night like this…"

Forsythe murmured a reply without really hearing her. He hadn't needed this much time to seduce a woman since his freshman year at Harvard, when some of his friends had set him up with that shy little virgin and took bets on whether or not he'd make it with her. She'd finally succumbed to his charms, of course … although her attack of conscience the next day had cost his father a pretty penny to keep things quiet.

"Alex? Did you hear me?" Her voice had taken on a harder edge, and he realized she'd asked him something that hadn't registered at all.

Thinking fast, he looked at her as if seeing her for the first time. "What? Oh, Maggie … I'm sorry, darling. I was just thinking … about being away from you. They say these sub patrols are long. Lonely…"

"A sub patrol?" Her eyes widened, and her voice quavered a little. "You didn't say you were in submarines."

"It's a … new assignment." Forsythe could see the sadness in her eyes. "What's wrong, Maggie? What is it?"

"It's just … my brother … he was on the *Wahoo* when she went out on her last patrol…"

"Sunk?" He tried hard to put the right note of sympathy in his voice.

She shrugged. "The boat just … never came back. The Japanese never claimed to have sunk her. It's like they just sailed off the edge of the world or something. I think I could handle it better if I knew for sure that Sam was dead, but *not knowing*, that's the worst." A tear trickled down her cheek.

He reached out and brushed it away. "I'm sorry," Forsythe said quietly, the sympathy sincere this time. For a moment he struggled to find something he could say that might comfort her, but he couldn't find the right words.

She shook her head. "No … no, Alex, I'm the one who should be sorry. Here you are about to go off on a patrol, and I'm talking about … about … not coming back. The last thing you want to be thinking about tonight is … what could happen."

He gave her his best reluctant hero smile. "The Japanese'll have a hard time taking me out of the game," he said, back on ground he knew. A little sympathy, a little sadness, a little worry for the brave sailor off to fight the war … all the right ingredients. Just like the time with that nurse in San Diego, the one who'd given him her patriotic all the weekend before he shipped out to the Atlantic. Well, to Nassau, to be exact…

Now was the time to move things along. "You know what I really need now?" he asked suddenly, standing up.

She looked up at him uncertainly, then shook her head. He could almost see her inward struggle in her blue eyes.

Forsythe grinned. "I need a swim, that's what. Between the wine and the moonlight and the surf, I'm going to fall asleep. A quick dip in the ocean's just the thing to wake me up again!" His fingers were undoing the buttons of his jacket as he spoke.

"What are you *doing*!" she asked, standing up. It was hard to tell in the firelight, but he thought she was blushing. "Are you nuts?"

"What's the matter, Maggie? You never saw a man go swimming before? Why don't you join me?"

"I couldn't ... I mean, I don't have a suit..."

"Neither do I. Haven't you ever gone skinny-dipping? Come on, you'll love it!" He turned away as if to preserve his modesty as he took off his pants and shorts, then ran to the water's edge and dove in cleanly. The water was cool, bracing. "Come on, Maggie, don't be afraid," he called out as he started treading water a few yards from the beach. "Look, I'll turn my back if you're shy. And once you're in the water I won't see anything. Come on ... it'll be fun. The water's really great!"

She hesitated only a moment longer. He doubted that she'd had enough wine to make her really drunk, but by now her barriers were down and it wouldn't take much to get her to agree. "You have to promise not to look," she said, and this time he was sure she was blushing. Her hand went to the top button of her blouse and hovered there, as if she was still not sure she was doing the right thing.

"I promise," he reassured her, turning away. "See, this is me not looking." He took a breath and jack-knifed in the water, diving down to the bottom and striking out away from the beach. He knew she was hooked now. No need to rush...

Still, no need to pass up an opportunity, either, he thought as he started for the surface once more. He turned in the water on his way up, and his head broke the surface as quietly as if he was doing a recce on an enemy-held beach. She was down to her bra and panties now, standing so that she was in profile, the flames highlighting her creamy skin and golden mane. As she unsnapped the bra and let it fall she suddenly seemed to sense his eyes on her, but he dove under again before she could turn and catch him watching. The view of her full breasts illuminated by the flickering firelight excited him despite the inhibiting effects of the cool water.

When he surfaced again, he heard splashing nearby. She was waist-deep and wading away from the beach, looking back and forth as she searched for him. He angled toward the girl, moving quietly through the water. He approached her from behind and slipped his arms around her, enjoying the feel of her bare skin against his. She squealed and wriggled free. "Alex!" she protested, but her giggle gave the lie to the mock severity of her tone. "If you're going to play games like *that* I'm getting out of the water now!"

He made a face and splashed her. "Okay, how about a race?" Forsythe flashed her a challenging grin. "Out to that rock and back. What do you say?"

She nodded. "Okay. But I warn you, I'm a pretty good swimmer…"

"I'll risk it. Ready… Go!" He struck out, holding nothing back, and pulled ahead of her quickly. He reached the small rock he'd pointed out and was already starting back before she'd covered half the outward distance.

When Forsythe reached the shallow water where they'd started he didn't even pause, but stood up and ran through the surf up onto the sandy beach. By the time Maggie finished the return leg he'd arranged everything neatly. He was sitting near the water's edge with his legs drawn up to his chest, an almost modest pose. All of their clothing was carefully piled beside him.

She crossed her arms over her breasts and stood there in the waist-deep water. "You win," she called, breathing hard from the exertion of the swim. "You win. Now turn around so I can come out and get dressed, okay?"

He shook his head slowly and gave her a broad, leering smile. "I really don't think so, darling," he drawled. "I mean, to the victor goes the spoils, and all that."

"Come on, Alex…"

"Come on yourself. You want your clothes back, you have to give me a little show first. Come on out, honey…"

She hesitated, but when it was clear he wouldn't relent she came up out of the water slowly, dropping one hand in a vain effort to preserve a shred of modesty.

As she walked toward him with the firelight caressing her naked skin Forsythe surged to his feet and advanced to meet her. She didn't fight when he took her in his arms and kissed her. After a moment's resistance she melted into his embrace, and they sank down to the sand as one.

Another beachhead captured, he thought, savoring the feel of her body against his.

Forsythe wondered, idly, if he'd ever see her again.

CHAPTER 11

Saturday, 8 July 1944
NCDU Training Center
Fort Pierce, Florida

The first week of training lived up to the name Hell Week, and the last day was the worst of all. It was called "So Solly Day," and it was the culmination of a week of sheer agony for everyone in the training class.

They had started with forty-eight men, but by So Solly Day only twenty-seven remained. Most of the others had simply given up and left the program, Dropped on Request — "DOR" in Fort Pierce parlance. There had also been two men injured in the training, one hospitalized after being bitten by a cottonmouth during a boat drill in one of Hutchinson Island's interminable swamps, the other a victim of a broken leg suffered during a grueling cross-country march.

But the casualties, wounded and DOR alike, did nothing to slacken the pace of Hell Week. The trainees had sweated out exercises; forced marches with heavy packs; boat drills where six-man teams had to carry inflatable boats overland, deploy them in the water, then paddle tremendous distances only to repeat the whole process again and then one more time. The instructors rode them hard from before dawn to long after dark, and they lived on K rations and too little sleep. But even as some of their number fell by the wayside, the others had found themselves drawing more and more closely together as the days passed.

They spent their scant free time trading yarns and life histories. Rand learned that Stan Kowalski had been born and raised in Cicero, just outside of Chicago, where his father owned a mom-and-pop grocery store. Kowalski had worked in a construction firm that was widely reputed to have Mob connections, and after getting a nasty cut across one cheek from a tree branch that had slipped out of someone's hands during a morning march, the rest of the boat team had hung the nickname "Scarface" on him in honor of Al Capone. He seemed to prefer it to Ski, but not by much.

Kowalski had served for a time with the Seabees after joining the Navy, but he'd been quick to seize the chance to volunteer for Combat Demolition. As Rand had suspected on the first day, he was eager for action, adventure, the glory of war, and nothing Rand said could shake his enthusiasm. From time to time Rand found himself hoping that Kowalski would wash out in the training. He liked the youngster, but he couldn't help picturing him meeting the horrors of a real battle firsthand … like the NCDU men on Omaha Beach.

The rest of his team, the ones who lasted through Hell Week, were a mixed bag. Ensign Larry Jones, the leader of the boat team, was an easy-going young officer with a considerable flair for games of chance. Even after a hard day's training he frequently tried to muster interest in cards or dice. Chief Charles "Stoky" Stark was a Texan who had come out of Supply and had quickly earned a reputation as an operator. Rand couldn't help but compare him to Gator Tangretti, one of the early Demolitioneers, a man who had shown a true genius as a scrounge. It seemed some things never changed. And then there was Shipfitter Second Class Matthew Jennings, a scrawny, underweight kid from Georgia. Jennings was cursed with clumsiness and a steady streak of bad luck — his nickname in the team was "Jinx" — but he met the challenges of Hell Week with a kind of stubborn dedication that wouldn't admit defeat.

They were the survivors from their boat team, one of the original eight six-man groups, who lasted to see So Solly Day. There had been times along the way when each of them, even Rand, had considered dropping out of the training course, but none of them had opted to DOR. And they'd learned the value of working together, whether it was humping a seven-man inflatable boat and a heavy pack through the mud or helping each other overcome the challenges of a devilish obstacle course.

Rand himself had worked extra hard, trying to assist his teammates any way he could, determined not to fall back into the lone wolf habit that had defined him for so long. When Jennings had run into trouble making the two-hundred-yard qualifying swim that everyone had to pass as a basic part of the training, Rand had been there. The kid had suffered a bad leg cramp the first time he tried out, and Rand had gone in to help, then wheedled Drake to give Jennings another chance. The second time around he'd made it, barely. Luckily, Rand knew, the Fort Pierce training didn't really emphasize swimming skills. The NCDU program envisioned Demolitioneers hitting the beaches from landing craft just ahead of the first wave of an invasion, and you needed only enough swimming skill to stay out of trouble.

Then there had been the time Stark had gotten sick on the march after drinking from a pool of brackish water. Rand had carried his pack along with his own until the big chief had recovered enough to pull his own weight. They were a team, after all, Jones's Jaguars, and Rand was determined to see that they made it all the way through training as a team. Even the sixth member of their party, a first class named Skinner, hadn't been dropped yet. He'd been shifted to another crew on the memorable day when three of the six men in Miller's Mosquitoes had DORed together, to help fill in the gaps in the team's shrunken ranks.

For the trainees, So Solly Day began before dawn. They embarked aboard several Higgins boats to stage a mock landing on Hutchinson Island's eastern beach. Wallowing through the rolling Atlantic surf, the boats lurched and bobbed, and there were several trainees who looked distinctly seasick. It all reminded Rand of the opening minutes of the attack on Omaha…

The landing craft dropped their bow ramps a few yards from the shore, and in that same moment the beach ahead erupted in fire and thunder as instructors watching the exercise set off a string of heavy demolition charges. The sudden rippling of explosions made trainees cringe and hesitate, but they weren't allowed to hold back long.

"Go! Go! Go!" Gunnery Sergeant Drake, perched in the port-side gun tub of Rand's Higgins boat, bellowed loud enough to be heard over the last few explosions on the beach. "Come on, you slugs! Let's move it!"

Rand was the first one out of the boat, with Kowalski and Chief Stark close on his heels. The other trainees followed suit, more reluctantly.

As he ran through the shallow water and up on the hard-packed sand Rand was thinking back to his days on the other side of this exercise. So Solly Day was carefully prepared to expose the trainees to conditions as close to real combat as the Fort Pierce staff could make it, with constant harassment by explosives and booby traps that would weed out any man who couldn't deal with the noise or the dangers posed by demolitions. In theory the explosives were never detonated close enough to the men to put them in any real danger, but it was often hard to guarantee they'd be completely safe in practice.

And despite the best efforts of the people who had created this whole drill, Rand himself included, he knew now it was a far cry from the real thing. Omaha had taught him the true face of war, and no matter how frightening or realistic this exercise was, it could never truly represent what men faced when they hit an enemy-held beach.

But it was the closest the trainees would come to actual combat conditions until they faced the enemy on a genuine beachhead, he told himself grimly.

Drake followed them ashore, still shouting and pointing inland. The ground behind the landing area was a tangle of dense vegetation, and the instructors urged the men on into the difficult terrain with curses, threats, and half-pound improvised TNT hand grenades thrown judiciously to herd them in the appropriate direction. As Rand remembered it, they were supposed to lob those tiny bombs no less than ten feet away from any of the trainees, but he also knew that it didn't always work out that way. It kept everyone on their toes as they plunged into the undergrowth.

And so it proceeded, hour after hour on the day everyone agreed was the toughest time short of a real beach-clearing op any Demolitioneer would face. The terrain varied, from jungle growth to marsh muck to sand and surf to pits of slimy, clinging mud, but the pressure and the noise were constants. As they pressed through tangled mangrove swamps they set off tripwires tied to explosive booby traps, and they had to watch constantly even on relatively open trails for the telltale signs of wires tied to demo charges in the trees nearby. As they waded through waist-deep pools of mud and water heavy twenty-pound charges were set off around them, sending gouts of water and debris far overhead to rain down muck and grime on them all. And men who tried to stay still, to keep from moving into danger, soon found that danger had a way of moving to them. The instructors and their grenades were never far behind, and they didn't hesitate to bend the rules about safe blast zones a little if they thought a trainee needed particular encouragement.

Rand remembered when Commander Coffer had first been designing the So Solly Day exercises. "If a man can keep his wits about him when everything around him is falling apart," the lanky bomb expert had said one time, "then it just may be that he's steady enough for this job." The idea was to weed out anyone with an inherent fear of explosives, so that the men who were left could be sure of counting on their teammates when they went into action for real.

Although he'd seen plenty of classes going through the course and had done his share of encouraging reluctant boat crews to keep moving through the deadly training ground, Rand was developing a new respect for the men who'd gone through it before him. No wonder those Demolitioneers evolved such a bond of comradeship. Any man who went through this hell, like any man who went through the hell of a real battle and didn't break and run, deserved that respect.

The day's climax came with the trainees hemmed in to a small perimeter, crouching in foxholes. For an hour, one charge after another was set off around them, the almost continuous noise of detonations filling their world to the exclusion of all else. A few men broke down under the constant strain and were quickly ushered out of the exercise, but Rand was proud to note that not a single member of Jones's Jaguars was among those who couldn't take the heat.

And then, suddenly, the noise stopped. For a long moment Rand couldn't believe just how unnerving total silence could be.

Chief Grover appeared at the lip of the foxhole where Rand and Kowalski had taken refuge from the blasting. Somehow the man was still neatly dressed, hardly even sweating from the hot, humid Florida afternoon. His dungarees showed few traces of the mud and filth that literally covered the trainees from head to toe.

He blew a whistle. "Men, you've made it through So Solly Day and through Indoctrination Week. You've proven that each of you has the fiber to be a Demolitioneer, that you can handle stress and physical exertion and exhaustion and more noise than you've probably ever heard in your lives before." Grover grinned down at Rand and Kowalski. The chief pipefitter had been one of Rand's earliest NCDU victims back in the old days, and no doubt he was enjoying the role reversal. "Don't ever doubt that you're prepared for what's out there on the beaches. Any Fort Pierce man can hold his own on any stretch of sand from here to Tokyo Bay. From here on out your training will focus on the technical side of what we do. You'll learn demolitions techniques, hand-to hand combat, and everything else we feel you'll need to get the job done ... but now you'll be able to learn at a pace that isn't calculated to drive you to a DOR. So let me give you, formally, the words you've been waiting to hear. Trainees ... secure from Hell Week!"

The submarine was even more cramped than Forsythe had imagined, so oppressively close that he was already wondering how he was going to stand being cooped up aboard for months on end. The eleven men of the recon mission put a severe strain on the already overcrowded facilities of the sub, and it was clear that her skipper wasn't at all pleased with what he described as "running a goddamned taxi service."

Still, they'd been assigned quarters, the enlisted men berthing in the forward torpedo room while Forsythe ended up sharing a tiny cabin with two of the sub's junior officers on a rotation schedule that made legal briefs look simple by comparison. They hadn't even sailed yet, but Forsythe was already wondering whether the whole complex dance would hold up once they actually put out to sea.

They had the whole of Saturday afternoon to get settled in, making sure their equipment was properly stowed while Fitzgerald went over the mission plans with Commander Aiken and his Exec. The two separate groups in the recon team, the Waipio men and the UDT detachment, had split up their responsibilities, with Chief Ballard and his Amphibious Operations men getting personal effects in their proper places while Forsythe and Schroeder supervised the Team Ten work party in checking over the inventory of unit gear in the storage locker set aside for their use deep in the bowels of the submarine. As he checked off each item of equipment on his clipboard, Forsythe's thoughts drifted back to the night before, to the beach and the firelight and the girl … what was her name again? Maggie, that was it. That had been one beachhead recon mission to remember, he told himself with an inward grin. Despite her blushing virgin act, the girl had proved an eager, energetic lover. It was really too bad he couldn't arrange a repeat performance for tonight…

"Mr. Forsythe?" His blissful musings were cut short by a painfully young sailor who had appeared in the corridor outside the storage locker that had been assigned to the team. "Mr. Forsythe, Commander Fitzgerald's compliments and would the members of Team Ten please assemble in the wardroom? Right away, he said, sir."

"Right. We're on our way." He turned. "Well, you heard the word from on high. Crenshaw, White, secure that gear. Looks like we'll have to finish up here later."

Chief Schroeder and the four ratings followed him forward to the sub's cramped wardroom, where they gathered around the table and waited. After about five minutes, Fitzgerald came in, followed closely by Lieutenant Commander Chapman, Forsythe's erstwhile base commander.

"As you were," Chapman said hastily, to save them from having to make even an effort to come to attention inside the tiny compartment. "I couldn't let you Team Ten men sail without seeing you off."

He sat down at the head of the table. "I won't keep you long, men. Admiral Powell asked me to give you a final briefing before you left port. Not about the mission. There'll be plenty of time for that after you're at sea, and Commander Fitzgerald has all the details of what you'll need to look for. But the work you'll be doing out there is something completely new, and the admiral wanted me to make sure you understood what's going to be expected of you. The Waipio men have already had their chance to hear some of this from Commander Fitzgerald, but I thought it was best if you heard this from an old UDT hand. I was with the UDT right back to the very beginning, and I remember what it was like back then when *everything* we did was brand-new.

"The normal UDT operation uses a hundred men working in close conjunction with an invasion fleet. On this mission, *Burrfish* will be alone, and you men and Commander

Fitzgerald's contingent will carry the whole weight of the operation on your shoulders. You may have to make a few things up as you go along because you can't count on being able to go by the book — what you do in the next few weeks may very well end up *being* the book the next time we need to launch a mission like this one. I've seen you Team Ten men in training, so I know what you're capable of from firsthand experience. And I know that Commander Fitzgerald hand-picked his contingent because he knew they were the best men for the job."

Chapman looked around the table from one face to another. "Improvising, writing the book as we go along, that's been a central part of what we do ever since we started the UDT. When we first got moving we didn't even have plans to put swimmers in the water, until some bright boys in the teams figured out that the best way to get the info we needed at Kwajalein was to strip down and dive in. And Commander Coffer, the man who first put naval demolitions on the map, never believed in swimming at all until he came out here. It wasn't needed in Europe, and the Fort Pierce school still doesn't stress swimming except for basic qualifications. So when he first heard that Admiral Turner expected his men in Team Five to swim a mile into the beaches for Saipan, he realized he had to rethink everything his men were prepared for. They still tell the story of what happened then every time two UDT men sit down to swap war stories over a beer, don't they, Chief?"

The UDT officer smiled as Chief Schroeder grinned and nodded. "Coffer and Lieutenant Burke, from Team Seven, were at the O Club over at Puunene Air Base one night. They started betting on who could swim the farthest, wagering cases of beer on the challenge and getting the men from both teams so caught up in the excitement that it went from a personal match between the Cos to a contest between the two teams. Those guys worked like sons of bitches for that beer, and in the process they found out just how well they really could swim … for the right incentive."

The men around the table chuckled. "The point is this," Chapman went on. "This is a dangerous mission, and one that'll require creativity as well as courage and commitment. If you don't feel comfortable working outside the rules, speak up now. No one will think less of you if you opt out now."

"Hell, Skipper, you know me," Chief Schroeder drawled. "I don't feel comfortable working *inside* the rules."

That brought a fresh round of laughter. Chapman smiled. "Thanks, Chief. You're one thing we can always count on in this man's Navy." His grin faded. "One last thing I've got to say, though it's distasteful to talk about. If all goes well you'll be in and out of Japanese waters without their ever knowing you were there. But if something goes wrong and you're captured, well… Look, nobody can give you orders to conduct yourself a certain way under interrogation. If they squeeze hard enough, they can make a man talk, and anyone who says otherwise is a fool, plain and simple. But on the other hand, the less the Japanese know about the UDT and how we operate, the better. If you can hold out and keep from telling them anything, you might be helping your buddies the next time *they* have to hit the beach. Or you can try feeding 'em a line. Hell, sailors can sling the bull when they're picking up girls, so surely you can put one over on the Japanese!" He stood up slowly. "That's all I have to say … except, good luck to you all."

Chapman left a stir of conversation in the wardroom as he left, but Forsythe remained aloof from the chatter. He sat staring at the seat where the UDT man had been, lost in thought.

For the first time, he was realizing just what he had volunteered to do…

Even though the Fort Pierce trainees were coming off the grueling pace of So Solly Day and Hell Week, it was a well-established tradition for the survivors to hit a few of the bars in town at the end of it all to celebrate. Rand remembered stories of some of the early classes, the ones he'd helped teach, and their exploits. It seemed that even Hell Week couldn't completely tire out Demolitioneers hyped up on adrenaline and relief that the worst of their training was over.

He had almost opted to stay ®n camp instead of joining the rest of the Jaguars coming into town, but Kowalski had finally prevailed on him. Rand really wanted to catch up on his sleep, recalling the first rule of combat he'd learned with the Scouts and Raiders long since, that sack time was more precious than gold. But he'd felt like he'd be letting the others down, so he'd finally agreed to join them for a few beers at One-Eyed Jack's, one of the favorite hangouts for demolition men on liberty. They'd come into town together, hitching a ride on one of the same Higgins boats the trainees had deployed from in the morning exercises. Though a causeway connected Hutchinson Island to the town of Fort Pierce proper, spanning the brackish waters of the Indian River, taking one of the regular ferry runs back and forth was a little faster, and most Navy men preferred to keep up appearances by coming into town by boat anyway.

The bar was crowded tonight, with the usual mix of NCDU, Scouts and Raiders, Marines, Coast Guard men, and locals, male and female. It was inevitable that the latter would draw almost instant attention from any group of sailors, and the Jaguars were no exception. Sitting around a table in the middle of the smoke-filled, crowded, noisy room, where conversation had to be shouted over the combination of background chatter and Glenn Miller music coming from the radio behind the bar, Jaguars speculated loudly on which of the women were the best prospects and how they could be pried loose from their current companions.

Most of the talk was focused on Jinx Jennings, though. In a slip of the tongue a few days earlier the young sailor had revealed the fact that he'd never been with a woman before, and Kowalski and Stark were determined to change that state of affairs before the night was out. "Come on, kid," Stark was saying. "You've been to Hell and back this week, and you took everything they could throw at you and then some. Don't tell me you're scared of a little woman!"

"Go easy on the kid, Stoky," Rand told him abruptly. "If he wants to get laid, he'll get laid. But you'll just mess up his head if you keep pushing him like that."

"The Raider's right, Chief," Ensign Jones said quietly. "If you're so hot for some action, get some for yourself. But you shouldn't sit there and hassle the kid." The tone and the words were equally mild, and no one at the table took them as an attempt to pull rank. That was another NCDU tradition, that there were few distinctions between officers and men. Except for the tiny rank insignia on his collar Jones showed no sign of his officer's status and rarely asserted himself outside the strict call of duty.

Stark seemed willing enough to drop the matter. He signaled the waitress for another pitcher of beer and leaned back in his seat to contemplate the view of a trio of women sitting alone near the door.

"How 'bout you, Raider?" Kowalski said. "What kind of women do you go for, huh?"

"Yeah," Stark said. "I don't think you ever said anything about your … your combat experience over in England. Those Brit broads as hot as everybody says?"

Rand shrugged. "I wouldn't know. I've got a girl waiting for me back home in Michigan, and I don't go shopping around."

"Another great icon falls," Jones commented with a smile. "See, Jennings, even the great ones have their weaknesses. Who'd've thought the mighty Raider Rand was some dull one-woman stay-at-home?"

As the others laughed Rand looked away. He hadn't told the whole truth. Before taking up his instructor's post at Fort Pierce the previous year, he had gone through an emotional crisis when his mother died in an auto accident and his father, embittered and old beyond his years, had accused Rand of being the cause of the disaster. Nancy Brown, his high school sweetheart, had helped him weather the storm during a short leave at home, and before he'd left he had promised to marry her after the war was over.

They'd exchanged letters almost daily for a time, but after his posting to England their contacts had fallen off. Caught up in the intense preparations for Operation Overlord, and reluctant to share his innermost thoughts and feelings with the military censors who went through every serviceman's mail, Rand had gradually cut back until he was writing to Nancy only sporadically. He'd last written her just after getting his orders to report to Fort Pierce … the same night, in fact, that he'd sought out companionship with a prostitute in Soho.

It had been a moment's weakness, a reaction to the feelings stirred up by the Omaha landings. Rand had been desperate for a human touch…

But since then his feelings about Nancy had been bothering him more and more. Hell Week had certainly helped him put aside his personal doubts for a while, but they were still there in the back of his mind, unresolved, nagging at him. He'd genuinely believed he was in love with Nancy, and the thought of her still haunted his dreams, but it seemed he couldn't really commit himself to her after all. First he'd stopped writing, then he'd betrayed her trust...

He wasn't sure how he felt about Nancy Brown anymore. And if there was still a spark of love there, did he deserve a second chance?

And there was a deeper concern, too. If he couldn't give himself, body and soul, to the woman who loved him, could he hope to keep the commitment to teamwork that he owed to the other men around the table? Together they'd made it through Hell Week. But how long would Rand hold to his promise to himself to put the needs of the team ahead of his own selfish desires?

CHAPTER 12

Monday, July 10 1944
U.S.S. *Rocky Mount*
Magicienne Bay, Saipan

Only yesterday, Admiral Turner had declared the island of Saipan secure. Likely there were still Japanese troops hiding out in the mountainous interior of the island, but organized resistance had collapsed. Among the enemy dead were the Japanese commander, General Saito, and the commander of the non-existent Imperial Central Pacific Area Fleet, Vice Admiral Chuichi Nagumo, both at their own hands. Nagumo's suicide in an island cave carried special significance for the victorious Americans; it was Nagumo who'd led the raid on Pearl Harbor two and a half years before.

The battle for the island had taken a bloody three and a half weeks. The bill had been high: 3,426 Americans killed — three times the number killed at Tarawa — and just over 13,000 wounded. Enemy dead had been estimated at well over 32,000. The suicidal banzai charge that had terminated Japanese resistance had been bad enough; Americans on Saipan were still trying to deal with the astonishing spectacle of hundreds of Japanese civilians leaping to their deaths from Marpi Point at the extreme northern tip of the island.

The idea of war against such an enemy, where even the civilians would rather die than surrender, was unsettling to most American military personnel. Most dealt with it by dehumanizing the enemy — a process deliberately aided both by official propaganda and by the press at home. It was a lot easier to think of the Japanese as subhuman, as evil caricatures of *real* humans who lacked such human values as respect for life ... even their own.

The ravellen on everyone's mind now, though, was a disturbing one. If the Japanese had fought this hard for Saipan, the first bit of territory invaded by the Americans so far that they considered part of their homeland, what would it be like once the Americans reached the home islands of Japan?

Anchored now in Magicienne Bay with a large portion of the American amphibious fleet, the headquarters ship *Rocky Mount* was again serving as the planning and briefing center for the reconnaissance teams. Magicienne Bay — promptly rechristened "Magazine Bay" by the troops and naval personnel stationed there, was a large, deep anchorage located on Saipan's southeastern coast, just north of Nafutan Point. Three miles to the southwest of Nafutan, just across the narrow Saipan Channel, lay the second largest island in the Saipan-to-Guam cluster at the south end of the Marianas: Tinian.

Twelve miles long, five miles across at its widest, Tinian promised to be another Saipan, with tough and determined Japanese troops dug into its hills and barricaded in its towns. The invasion of Tinian would be different from other amphibious operations in the Pacific so far in that the objective was so close to land already occupied by friendly forces. With Ushi Point, Tinian's northern tip, only three miles from Saipan, Marine amtracks and landing craft would be able to cross directly from one island to the other, and Saipan's airfields would offer convenient bases for Marine and Navy aircraft operating throughout the area.

Tinian was an important part of the Navy-Marine operational plan for the central Pacific. Less mountainous than Saipan, it possessed three excellent airfields, one of which — Ushi, just south of Ushi Point — was already large enough to handle Army B-29s ... and close enough to Japan that raids could be launched from there against the home islands. The first such raid, carried out by the 20th Air Force, based in China, had been launched just three weeks earlier, and with marginal success. Island air strips like Ushi would allow the superfortresses to begin pounding Japan with the same relentless persistence that RAF and American bombers had been using in Europe for two years.

So Tinian was slated for invasion, with "Jig day" — not all invasion dates were identified as "D days," at least partly for security reasons — scheduled for July 24. The major problem now, two weeks before the landings were to be made, was to select the area where the Marines would actually come ashore.

Lieutenant Waverly and Lieutenant Commander Coffer had been summoned aboard the U.S.S. *Rocky Mount* earlier that morning for a final briefing before the evening's planned reconnaissance of Tinian's beaches. The operations briefing center was crowded with brass, most of the officers members of the staffs of Admiral Turner, Admiral Hill, or Lieutenant General Holland Smith. Waverly felt out of place with all of the flag officers present, until he spotted one Marine captain — whose rank corresponded to that of a lowly Navy lieutenant. The man was Captain James L. Jones, and he was skipper of the Fifth Amphibious Corps Reconnaissance Battalion. Teams Five and Seven had been working closely with Jones's group for several days now, and Waverly had — grudgingly — come to respect both Jones and his men, despite the interservice rivalry that bedeviled both groups.

"Our chief difficulty," Admiral Turner was telling the assembled officers, "is going to be the terrain. There is simply not much to choose from, and the Japanese are as aware of the limitations in the geography as we are."

Waverly, with the other men crowded about the table, studied the chart, which showed all of both Tinian and nearby Saipan. Turner pointed to the island that was the Marine objective. "While the interior of Tinian isn't as mountainous as Saipan was, it is high. Most of the island sits behind sheer cliffs, ranging from bluffs eight or ten feet high up here at Ushi, to some real monsters in the south, a hundred feet high or more. All together, we have just four possible areas on the whole damned island to choose from. The principal objective of the operation tonight will be to determine which of the beaches is our best bet."

The choice was going to be a rough one. The largest potential landing area, and perhaps the most obvious one, was the 2,500-yard-long reef-barricaded lagoon immediately in front of Tinian Town, the island's capital, on the southwest coast. The landing beaches in that area had been tagged as the Red, Green, and Blue beaches.

On the eastern shore was Asiga Bay, which had a good beach and which — according to air reconnaissance photos — was covered by a nasty-looking chain of Japanese pillboxes and gun emplacements. That landing area had been named Yellow Beach.

On the northwestern coast, just below Ushi Airfield, were two beaches that the high command had lumped together as White Beach. They were unlikely landing areas at best; aerial reconnaissance photos had showed no sign of pillboxes or shore fortifications, but there were indications that the beaches themselves might be heavily mined, and the bluffs behind them were heavily wooded. Anything could have been hidden there. Most damning of all, perhaps, was the size of the beaches.

White 1, to the north, was only 60 yards across, wide enough to accommodate perhaps eight LTVs at a time. White 2, 1,200 yards to the south, was 160 yards wide, and it was thought that the coral offshore might make the approaches too narrow.

The fourth potential landing area, dubbed Orange Beach, was located on the west coast halfway between White Beach and Tinian Town. It, too, showed no sign of having been fortified. Coffer himself had discovered Orange Beach during a personal reconnaissance of the island ten days ago in a low-flying Navy Avenger torpedo plane. Every time the island had been surveyed before, dense fog had obscured Orange, but from what he'd seen from the air, Coffer had already decided that it offered the invaders their best chance of getting a solid beachhead established before the Japanese could shift their defending forces away from Tinian Town and Asiga.

"We've pretty well narrowed our choice down to these two," General Smith said when Turner had stopped speaking. He used a pencil to indicate Yellow Beach in the northeast, and White 1 and 2 in the northwest. "The lagoon at Tinian Town is simply too heavily fortified. It's obvious that that's exactly where the Japanese expect us to come ashore, and I, for one, would like to disappoint them." He straightened, slipping the pencil back into the pocket of his khaki shirt. "Besides, if we land there, my boys are going to be fighting house-to-house the moment they come ashore. The Japanese could turn that place into Stalingrad. I'm not throwing my boys away in street fighting where every building becomes a fort.

"Now, in the north, Yellow Beach would clearly be the best from a logistical standpoint. The question is whether or not the Japanese have fortified Asiga as strongly as they have Tinian Town. We have these photos of pillboxes, but there's no indication of mines or offshore obstacles.

"And as for White Beach, well ... it has the advantage that it's actually close enough for our artillery on Saipan to offer some fire support during the landings. It also gives us immediate access to the airstrip at Ushi. If the Japanese are convinced that the beaches themselves are too narrow to be worth bothering about, then they just might be what we're looking for."

"Tinian's back door," a Marine colonel suggested.

"Exactly. Unfortunately, even if White One and Two aren't defended now, if the Japanese get even a hint that we're sniffing around that area, it won't take much effort on their part to wall it off. If we can keep from alerting them, I think we can catch the bastards with their pants down and get a hell of a lot more ashore than they think is possible."

"The disadvantage," Turner pointed out, "besides the obvious one of how damned narrow those two beaches are, is that we can't tell from the air anything at all about the exits off the beach. The bluffs behind the waterline appear to be about eight, maybe ten feet high. We can't see any roads or other direct access through the bluffs because of the tree cover there."

Smith shook his head. "If the Japanese have fortified the area at all, we can't even consider that route."

"So," Turner said. "Yellow Beach or White Beach. Comments, anyone?"

"Sir," Coffer said. "I'm still curious as to why you are overlooking Orange Beach. The Japanese seem to have neglected its defenses too, and it's a lot wider than either of the White beaches. It seems to offer the advantages of both Asiga and White, without the pillboxes at Asiga or the narrow approaches at White."

Smith glowered, and Waverly saw the storm coming an instant before it broke. "Howling Mad" Smith, he remembered, had won that nickname because of his short temper. His firing of an Army general under his temporary command early in the Saipan operation had ignited a political firestorm back in the States, one that still hadn't been resolved and had inflamed the longstanding ill feeling between the Army and the Marines.

"You," Smith said, jabbing a forefinger at Coffer, "do the reconnaissance and the reporting. *We'll* make the tactical decisions!"

"Unfortunately, Commander," Turner said more gently, "Orange Beach also has some of the disadvantages of White Beach. It's wider, but not by much. And the approaches behind the beach aren't good. While Holland's Marines are still trying to break through the sand dunes behind the beach, the Japanese at Tinian Town could swing shut on them like a gate."

"Besides," Smith growled, "it's out of range of our artillery in Saipan. My vote is for White One and White Two. I say we storm in there and kick ass."

Turner nodded. "I would go along with that, if — and these are big 'ifs' — if they are not fortified, if the sea is not rough at the time of the invasion, and if we can get some people in there secretly just before J day to confirm conditions." He glanced up at Coffer. "That's where your UDTs will come in, Commander. If we can use those beaches, this amphibious group will be able to accomplish something that is very rare in modern warfare, and even rarer out here in the Pacific. *Tactical surprise.*" His gaze swept the crowded compartment. "Are there any other comments? Questions?"

Perhaps because of Smith's blast at Coffer, there were none.

"Very well," he continued after a moment. "Let's go over tonight's planned reconnaissance."

Both White beaches and Asiga Bay were to be explored that evening. The reconnaissance teams would include members from UDT-5 at White Beach and UDT-7 at Asiga — a double-header, as the op planning boys had ravelle it. Both parties would include Marines from the Fifth Amphibious Corps Reconnaissance Battalion. The plan called for the Navy swimmers to check the coral reefs and offshore defenses, while the Marines slipped ashore, scouted the approaches behind the beaches, and reported on Japanese fortifications and positions. A special UDT detail would also go ashore to verify whether or not White 1 and White 2 had been mined.

In both cases, the approach would be made by men in rubber rafts towed astern of LCP®s modified with muffled underwater exhausts. Off White Beach, the U.S.S. *Gilmer* would serve as radar boat, while off Asiga, the guide ship would be the APD U.S.S. *Stringham*. The radar ships would maintain bearings on both the target beaches and the rafts, guiding the reconnaissance teams by radio. On each side of the island, eight UDT men and twenty Marines would make the approach in four seven-man rafts. Four men from each group would stay with the rafts after the rest of the men swam in and would serve as communications relays with the mother ships.

On the White Beach side of Tinian, the boat groups would be divided between the two beaches. Commander Coffer would lead the UDT reconnaissance of White 2, to the south, while Waverly took White 1.

The operational planning group began by discussing the approaches to the White beaches.

"Which way is the current running?" Coffer wanted to know.

The intelligence briefing officer, a Navy lieutenant, dragged his finger along the chart. "North to south," he said, moving his finger along the chart. "And it's not very strong. A half knot, at the most."

"And the met boys are sure of their forecast?" Coffer asked, a bit sharply.

The briefing officer nodded. "Yes, sir. Overcast and light winds. No fog."

"With a full moon tonight," Coffer said, "if you're wrong and we have clear skies, this could get as hairy as a beach survey in broad daylight."

Waverly glanced up at Admiral Turner, wondering if that gentle dig would raise a response. It didn't.

"What concerns me, Commander Coffer," Turner said, "is that dry run of yours last night. What have you done to iron out the mistakes?"

Coffer grinned. "It was a bit wet for a 'dry run,' Admiral." The others in the compartment chuckled.

"As we expected," Coffer continued, "most of the problems had to do with the fact that my boys and the Marines have different operating styles, different ways of doing things. There's also a certain amount of them-against-us. Only natural, of course. The Marines have their own customs and traditions, while we have ours. We'll have to work together more before we get all of the problems worked out."

"I'd have to agree with Mr. Coffer," Captain Jones said. "The frogmen are good, damned good." He paused for effect. "Of course, they're not as good as *Marines*."

The officers crowded into the compartment, Navy and Marine, laughed. "Watch it with that 'frogmen' stuff, Captain," Waverly added, and the others laughed again.

He meant it lightly, though the term — heard increasingly among Marines, the non-UDT Navy, and in the news stories about the UDT that had begun appearing in Stateside papers — was never employed by members of the teams. Frogmen might be something employed by other countries — the Italian "charioteers," for instance, who'd mined two British battleships and a tanker in Alexandria Harbor late in 1941 — but not in the U.S. Navy. The distinction had become a minor mark of pride in the UDT. Men asked what they did tended to reply, "I'm in demolitions," or, if pressed, might admit to being in "the teams."

"The, ah, operation last night," Coffer continued, "was a valuable lesson. I've spent several hours already going over our techniques point by point with Captain Jones, here. I don't think we'll be making any of the same mistakes twice."

God help us if we do. Waverly thought.

The rehearsal had been set up here in Magicienne Bay, with Marines ashore given the assignment of play-acting their Japanese counterparts at White Beach and Asiga. Engineers had placed disarmed mines on the beach, to see if the UDT men could locate them. Techniques practiced had included joint Marine-Navy operations in rubber boats, the use of radar to guide the boats to their targets, and the use of penlights, waterproofed by wrapping them up inside the ubiquitous rubber condoms, for signaling.

Everything had gone wrong. For a start, the Marine recon men made their approach to a hostile beach in seven-man rubber rafts, taking them in to within five hundred yards of the beach before rolling over the side and swimming the rest of the way. This had the obvious advantage of letting the men save their strength for the actual work close in to shore, rather than tiring them out with a mile-long swim first. It had the disadvantage, however, of bunching up any problems with the navigation.

With the UDT method of surveying a beach, individual swimmer teams knew where they were when they left the landing craft and started toward the shore. If one or two of the teams got lost on the way, their mistake would be covered by others in the boat platoon who got to where they were supposed to be. It was extraordinarily unlikely that *everybody* in the team would make the same mistakes in navigation.

With the Marine method, however, if the guy navigating the rubber boat full of reconnaissance swimmers went wrong after they cast off their tow from the landing craft, then every man in the boat would start his swim from the wrong spot.

That's what had happened last night. Stronger-than-expected winds and currents had scattered the landing team rafts after they'd cast off from the LCP®s that had towed them in. *Gilmer's* radar had not been working right, and then her radio had gone down, increasing the confusion. The rubber boats had tried to make it in, but none had come ashore where they were supposed to. The UDT beach party had missed the mines because they'd landed too far to the north. The recovery had been even worse, with many of the swimmers unable to find where they'd parked their rafts. The rehearsal had begun at midnight, but it was dawn before the last of the widely scattered swimmers had finally been recovered.

Finding something as small as a man in the ocean at night, even when he was carrying a waterproof flashlight, had proven to be a daunting challenge.

The reconnaissance tonight would be the real thing. The problems encountered last night had been discussed endlessly, and ways of overcoming them agreed upon.

But Waverly was concerned. His approach to this kind of operation, increasingly, called for a rigid adherence to a detailed plan, a plan that ought to cover all possible contingencies. Unfortunately, it had been his experience so far that no matter how many contingencies were allowed for, there was always something new. He remembered kneeling on the coral reef off Susupe Point trying to turn that damned flying mattress over with Blondie. What was going to go wrong *this* time?

"I'm particularly worried about the recovery phase," Admiral Hill said. "It seems to me that we still haven't adequately allowed for problems with swimmers finding their rafts, or making it back to the LCPs in the dark. We can track rafts with radar, but I'm damned if we can track a swimming man."

"The waterproofed flashlights ought to help there, Admiral," Waverly said. "They worked well enough in the rehearsal last night."

"Assuming the swimmers can get back to the ships. Those penlights aren't visible across more than a few hundred yards, and the ocean is god-awful big, especially at night."

"That won't be a problem," Coffer said. "If, of course, the information on weather and currents is accurate."

"Possibly," Hill said. "Even so, I'm going to pass the word to my people to stand by for an all-out search and-rescue if some of your people turn up missing. We'll need a coded means of keeping track over the TBS of how many men have been picked up and how many are still missing."

TBS — Talk Between Ships — was the ship-to-ship radio channels that would be used to coordinate the operation. For some reason, at that moment, Waverly was reminded of his swim buddy at Saipan, Blondie. "Blondes," he said.

"I beg your pardon?" Admiral Turner said.

"Uh, sorry, sir. I said 'blondes.' That will be our code on the TBS. Swimmers who have been recovered will be blondes. Swimmers still in the water are brunettes."

"What?" Jones said. "They get a bleach job when they're picked up?" The others at the table laughed.

"I like it." Hill chuckled. "And I will be 'pin-up.' Captain Jones, Commander Coffer, I'm not going to rest easy until your girls are all safe and sound back aboard ship. This strikes me as a damned desperate operation."

"Desperate," Turner said, "but absolutely necessary. We can't even consider using this back door unless we know the Japanese have left it open."

"We'll find out if it's unlocked, Admiral," Coffer said.

"Leave it to the Marines and the UDT!"

But Waverly had the gnawing feeling that there were some aspects of this complex mission that could still go wrong.

CHAPTER 13

Monday, 10 July 1944

Off White Beach

The *Gilmer* and the *Stringham* slipped out of Magicienne Bay at 2030 hours that night. Almost immediately, the *Gilmer* had come right, rounding Nafutan Point and entering Saipan Channel, leaving the *Stringham* to continue on her own toward the south. One hour later, *Gilmer* was in position three miles off White Beach 2. Two LCP®s were swung over the side, care being taken to keep the operation silent, lest sounds, carrying across the open water, should alert Japanese sentries ashore.

Quietly, on muffled engines, the LCP®s moved toward the objective beaches, each towing two rafts astern. The promised overcast had never materialized. Instead, the full moon was intermittently obscured by drifting patches of cloud.

It was then that things started to go wrong.

Coffer held the waterproofed radio to his ear, trying to block out the sounds of lapping water and the rumbling from the LCP's muffled engine. Under tow, the seven-man raft tended to bob and jerk unpredictably on the Higgins boat's wake, and it was hard to hold the radio steady.

"Say again, Golf One. Over."

The voice of Lieutenant Jack Sylvester, aboard the *Gilmer*, *came* back, clearer this time. "Mercury Leader, Golf One. Radar out, repeat, radar is out. We're having a little trouble here. Over."

"I read you, Golf One." *Damn*! Without *Gilmer's* radar, could they find the objective beaches in the dark? Maybe it was a good thing the sky hadn't turned up overcast after all. They might still be able to navigate by the uncertain light of the moon. "We are proceeding to the drop-off point. Mercury out."

There was really little else to be done. The loss of *Gilmer's* radar was a complication, but not serious enough to end the mission. The LCPs should get the rafts in to within a mile or less of the shore, and from there the rafts would have no trouble paddling in to the swimmer drop point. The coxswains aboard the LCPs had already been alerted that the north-to-south current would require them to pull just a bit to the north. The radar would have been nice as a verification, but both the UDT and the Marine amphib recon unit had practiced this sort of nighttime navigation countless times before.

Minutes passed, and at last Coffer felt the LCP making a turn toward the left.

"There's our signal, Commander," a Marine squeezed in beside him in the crowded raft, Gunnery Sergeant Kyle, whispered near his ear. Looking up, he saw the wink of a pencil-light flash from above the LCP®'s transom. Kyle replied with two flashes of his own, and the Marine at the raft's bow cast off the line. Marines and UDT swimmers broke out the paddles and started leaning over the raft's sides, stroking vigorously and steadily toward the island.

Everyone in the reconnaissance teams that night wore light-colored swim trunks or shorts, canvas shoes, face masks, and pull-ring inflatable life vests worn over their necks and fastened at their waists. In addition, each man had coated himself head to toe with aluminum grease paint, which gave his body the silver-white sheen that had suggested their radio call sign, Mercury. Over their heads, they wore gray rubber hoods to make the outlines of their heads a little less recognizably human, in case they were glimpsed briefly against the night sky. The camouflage, it was hoped, would blend in with the white coral sand of the beach, just as the blue paint a month before had helped the UDT men lose themselves against the blue waters of the lagoon off Saipan. It gave them the eerie look of monk-cowled ghosts, gleaming slightly in the uncertain moonlight. No one was entirely sure the crude camouflage would work as advertised, but at least it carried with it a certain psychological boost for the man wearing it.

On an enemy beach at night, with no weapon save a diving knife, he would need every psychological edge he could get.

Odd. Coffer was having trouble seeing the island … and the increasing murkiness had nothing to do with his eyes. With a partly clear sky and a brilliant moon high in the east, the island ought to stand out stark and black and bold, but as the minutes passed, he realized that the visibility was becoming increasingly limited.

"Fog," he said quietly.

"Are we going to be able to find the beach in this, Skipper?" Davies asked.

"Should be able to, Tom," he replied. Reaching into the pocket of his shorts, he extracted a compass, flipped up the top, and checked their heading. Zero-eight-five … a bit north of due east, compensating for the current. "As long as we keep this course." He was worried, though. Two rafts, with fourteen men between them, were detailed to check out White 2, but Coffer could no longer see the other raft. It had been right there, five yards to the left, but he could see nothing now but drifting tatters of fog against the night.

Still, they'd been paddling long enough that they must be nearly to the swim point. He turned to Kyle. "Gunny? We ought to be about there."

"Yes, sir," the Marine replied. He was peering ahead into the fog, which was growing thicker moment by moment. "I'd guess we're about five hundred yards out now. Hear the surf?"

Coffer could hear the hiss of breakers in the distance.

"Yeah."

"The fog could be a blessing in disguise, Commander," Horwitz pointed out. "The Japanese won't be able to see a thing."

"Assuming we find the beach. Okay, this looks like the place. Let's get wet."

While one Marine waited in the raft, trying to keep position with one of the paddles, the other six men pressed their masks tight against their faces and rolled over the side and into the water.

Almost immediately, Coffer found himself to be alone.

Waverly and the six other men in his raft could hear the surf ahead. Since the fog had closed in half an hour ago, he hadn't been able to see more than a few yards across the water. Still, the Marines in the raft were sure of their position, five hundred yards off White 1. Waverly tapped Blondie's arm and signaled. "Ready to go?"

"Yeah, Lieutenant. Listen, ain't I about due for some shore leave about now?"

"We heard about you demo men and liberty," one of the Marines said with a chuckle.

"You can buy us a beer back at Magazine Bay," Waverly replied, "and we'll tell you about it."

"It's a date, Navy."

"Okay, Blondie. Let's find us a beach."

Like silver-gleaming fish, the swimmers rolled over the side and into the water. Waverly started kicking toward the shore but almost immediately realized that he couldn't see any of the others. The idea had been for the swimming parties to stick close together, but in the darkness and fog, that was clearly impossible. With only his head above water, Waverly could see the moon like a great, ghostly beacon high ®n the sky, but his immediate surroundings were completely cloaked in a thick and clinging gray mist.

Waverly could hear the surf ahead, however, louder than before, even though he couldn't see anything of the island. It was eerie, probing ahead in the darkness like this. Several times he stopped, treading water while he checked his compass and while he listened for the sounds made by other swimmers.

He heard nothing but the hiss and crash of water on rock, however, and decided that any sounds his teammates were making were being drowned by the surf.

His right foot struck sand. The bottom was shoaling. God, why couldn't he see the island? The fog was worse than the darkness itself, clinging low to the water and obscuring even a glimpse of the island, which ought to be looming up before him now like a solid black wall.

And then it was.

The island's materialization was so sudden that it startled him, setting his heart to pounding in his chest. What's more, that was no beach he was facing, but a sheer cliff at least thirty feet high. The surf flashed white where it crashed against the boulders spilled at the base of the cliff.

Okay ... so he'd missed the beach. *Think this through, Waverly,* he told himself. *Reason it out.*

The current was flowing north to south. Even with their attempts to compensate on the approach by steering a little to the north, it was still possible that the current had dragged them all to the south as they'd paddled ahead in the raft, and dragged him farther south still during the course of a five-hundred-meter swim. The damned beach was so narrow — only sixty yards — that it would be easy to miss. There was a cliff between White 1 and White 2; that wall of black rock in front of him must be that cliff.

So ... if the current had shoved him to the south of White 1, all he needed to do was swim north along the shore and he would find it. Likely he would find Perkins and Blondie and the others as well, no doubt with something to say about officers who didn't know how to navigate on the open ocean at night.

Moving closer to the shore, he found the bottom shoaling swiftly. Soon, the water was only a foot and a half deep. He could make the best time, he found, by floating on the surface and pulling himself along on the bottom hand over hand.

White 1 couldn't be more than a couple of hundred yards to the north.

Davies swam steadily, trying to maintain an even pace and keeping the loudest crash of surf directly ahead. He kept his mask up off his face; so long as his head was above water, he found he could see better that way. There was nothing to be seen underwater in any case, and the haze-blurred moonlight was comforting.

There! Seemingly out of nowhere, the island materialized less than fifty yards ahead. He could see the white sand of the beach, see the cliffs walling it in to either side. At about the same time, he felt his shoe bump against coral. Taking out his penlight, carefully sealed inside its tightly knotted condom, he lowered his mask, squeezed it over his face, and submerged. The penlight's illumination wasn't much, but it cast enough of a beam to show him the shadowy outline of a huge, spreading coral head, about five feet beneath the surface.

Flicking off the light, he surfaced for air. There was something floating in the water about ten yards ahead ... a piece of wood or flotsam off the island, possibly.

Or perhaps it was a half-submerged beach obstacle. He started moving toward it to check it out.

Then he saw a splash and realized that the shape in the water was another swimmer ... and he was coming toward Davies, away from the beach.

The UDT men had speculated a lot about the possibility of encountering Japanese frogmen. Not much was known about their combat swimmers, but everyone assumed they had them. How hard was it to give a guy a knife and tell him to go kill enemy swimmers? The Japanese had had a long, good look at Team Five and Team Seven working off Saipan. If they were smart, they would be anticipating a swimmer recon of Tinian and have swimmers of their own on alert.

Reaching to his waist, Davies slipped his dive knife from its scabbard, hesitating as he tried to decide if the other guy was circling left or coming straight on.

Straight on. Holding the knife in front of him, Davies started forward.

Suddenly, the other swimmer reared back in the water, as though surprised. Hell, maybe the guy hadn't seen Davies to begin with, had simply been patrolling off the beach. Well, the guy had seen him now. Davies caught the flash of silver moonlight off a drawn knife. Cautiously now, like two dancers, the men began to circle one another, knives drawn, Davies moving to the left, his opponent moving right, each obviously waiting for the other to make the first move. Circling closer, they were nearly within touching distance now…

"Aw, *shit!*"

At the other swimmer's exclamation, Davies realized that the "enemy" swimmer was Horwitz. This close, he could see the silver paint now, though in the pale moonlight and from a distance it hadn't been obvious.

"Damn, Bernie!" he whispered harshly. His mouth was dry with fear. "I thought you were coming off the damned beach!"

"I wasn't comin' anywhere!" Horwitz exclaimed. "I was circlin' around, tryin' to get a readin' off my compass!"

"Come on, Bernie. Let's get ashore."

Coffer saw the splash ahead and assumed it was another swimmer. He'd left his glasses behind this time, since he was going to have to wear his mask, and all he could really see was a blur, but the shape looked like a man swimming toward the shore. Coffer could just make out the beach now, a smear of white between darker masses that must be the cliffs to either side. He started swimming harder, hoping to catch up with the other man in the water, desperate, suddenly, for the simple fact of companionship.

Where was he? The man had vanished … probably under water. Coffer brought his feet beneath him, felt the bottom under his shoes. Maybe the other swimmer —

The attack was sudden and terrifying, a cold weight pressed against Coffer's back, a slender wire biting into his neck. Coffer tried to twist around and the pressure on his throat increased. God, the man was garotting him!

"Oh, shit! Sorry, sir!"

Turning, rubbing his bruised throat, Coffer squinted at the other man's white-painted face, just recognizable now as Gunnery Sergeant Kyle's. "S'okay, Kyle," he said, his voice breaking a bit as he spoke. "The countersign, by the way, is 'Betty Grable, Rita Hayworth.'"

"I know, sir. I really thought you were the enemy."

"C'mon, Gunny. Let's get onto the beach."

He was making good progress ... surprisingly good, gliding smoothly along the shore with scarcely any effort at all. The shoreline kept curving away to the right, as measured by the position of the moon, and Waverly kept following it, expecting each bend in the coast to be the opening to the cove sheltering White 1.

He'd ravelled, he estimated, about three hundred yards to the north of where he'd encountered the coast when he decided that this was all wrong. He *couldn't* have missed the objective beach by *this* much. If the LCP's navigation had been off by even a little, perhaps he'd missed White 1 to the north instead of the south. He decided to turn around and check in that direction. Otherwise, he was liable to find himself following the shoreline all the way around Ushi Point.

Reversing direction so that the cliff was on his left, Waverly began crawling south ... but now the going was a lot tougher. He didn't seem to be making as good a speed, and he began to suspect that another mistake had been made that night.

The current was stronger than expected ... and it was flowing in the wrong direction.

Cautiously, Coffer crawled out onto the white beach, feeling the grittiness of the sand beneath his palms and his knees. Reaching the spot where Kyle was already stretched out on the sand, he pressed himself flat, as though trying to make himself part of the beach. The surf rumbled behind them and to either side. Ahead, the beach rose steadily to a line of sand dunes and trees, a blur of grays and shadows to Coffer. Aside from the pounding surf, the night was silent.

There was something wrong here … something seriously wrong. Even without his glasses, he could see enough to know that this beach wasn't nearly wide enough to be White 2. Inching slowly forward, he tried to get a better look at the heights behind the beach, tried to imagine what they would look like in daylight, and from the air. He'd flown over both White 1 and White 2 ten days ago, and thought he was familiar with them both.

Everything looked different at night, and cliffs that altitude had flattened out to a low rise seemed to tower above him. Still, this whole beach couldn't be more than about sixty yards wide, and that told Coffer that this couldn't be White 2. It had to be White 1, which meant that he'd been off course by a good twelve hundred yards to the north. The only way that was possible was if there'd been a stiff offshore current, one flowing from south to north.

"We're on the wrong beach," he whispered to Kyle, and then he realized that he was alone. The Marine, as silent as a shadow, had slipped away to begin his reconnaissance.

Lying there in the sand, Coffer shook his head. Clearly, the weakest link in the UDT's operational chain now was in intelligence, which included not only assessments of enemy activity in a target area but also such mundane but vitally necessary information as meteorological reports and hydrographic data. No one else had arrived yet, which meant his swimmers must be scattered over half of the ocean out there, trying to find their beaches.

He felt a sharp pang of worry for his men. If he'd hit the shore this far north of White 2, where were the men assigned to explore White 1?

A current in the ocean can be a subtle thing, unseen, unfelt, unnoticed save by its end effect on boats or swimmers. If the current had reversed itself, then the attempt by the LCP to correct for a north-to-south current had compounded the error, putting Waverly and the other White Beach 1 reconnaissance swimmers far to the north.

To make matters worse, the moon was fully out from behind the clouds now, touching the waves around him with liquid silver. A Japanese sentry atop those cliffs might easily see him in the water below, despite his protective coloration, and Waverly remembered what Turner and Smith had said that morning aboard the *Rocky Mount*. Even if the Japanese hadn't fortified White 1 and White 2, if they spotted UDT swimmers in these waters, they would assume the Americans had a particular interest in this area and would fortify it accordingly.

It was well past 2300 hours. He tried standing up in order to see better across the water, hoping desperately to spot one of the other swimmers, but as far as he could see he was completely alone. Worried that watchers on the clifftop above him might see him, he lowered himself again into the water, then, reluctantly, began to swim out to sea.

Fighting the current was impossible and served only to tire him more. He couldn't see any of the boats, but he reasoned that if he could get farther out to sea he had a better chance of spotting the *Gilmer*, or one of the LCP®s. And at the worst … well, at least he wouldn't be spotted by sentries ashore and give away Admiral Turner's surprise.

*

"Betty Grable," Coffer whispered.

"Rita Hayworth," came the countersign. A moment later, Horwitz and Davies were with him on the sand halfway up the beach.

"Damn, Skipper," Horwitz said. "You look like you seen a ghost. All white, like."

"Very funny. We're on the wrong beach."

Davies nodded. "I thought so coming through the surf. This is too narrow. We must've hit White 1 somehow."

"Then we're s'posed to be off that way," Horwitz whispered, nodding toward the right. "What'll we do, Skipper? Stay put or go there?"

"Stay here," Coffer decided. "It won't make any sense wandering around lost in the dark. Besides, we don't know if any of the White 1 people will make it in okay. We're here, we'll check this beach."

"Great." Davies sounded relieved. "We'll start checking for mines, Skipper. Maybe you can start looking for obstacles in the water."

Coffer had the feeling that the men were trying to shelter him from the more dangerous work, but this was no time to argue. The two UDT men knew what they were here for. It was best to let them do it. "Go to it, boys." He checked his watch. "Almost twenty-four-hundred hours. We don't have much time."

Together, they began their reconnaissance of White 1.

Waverly was tired. It was as though the sea itself was fast sapping his strength, leeching it away with the very heat of his body. Reaching up, he grasped the pull ring on his inflatable vest and gave it a tug. With a hiss, its CO_2 cartridge inflated the vest around him, buoying up his shoulders and head.

That was better. It was easier to … just drift, to float with the current and try not to worry about where it was taking him. Hell, with luck, maybe he'd end up back in Saipan … though that island was canted far enough to the east of Tinian that that possibility seemed unlikely at best.

He tried not to think about sharks.

Michael T. Waverly had been born and raised in Norfolk, Virginia, the son of a Navy family, raised in a Navy town. His father had been a captain, had served aboard a cruiser in World War I, though he'd never seen action. A grandfather had been a midshipman aboard the U.S.S. *Kearsarge*. A great-grandfather had served aboard the U.S.S. *Constitution*, chasing slavers off the Ivory Coast in the 1840s.

Tradition.

Honor.

Duty.

And always the need for order, the need to have things rigidly laid out and regulation-square. That had been his father's doing. The Captain had held white-glove inspections at home every evening, and he'd run his family with the same adherence to formula and discipline as he'd run the quarterdeck of a ship.

What do you think of your son now, Father? he asked the star-studded sky overhead. The moon was blinding in all that black, sparkling immensity.

He'd not realized just how much he'd hated his father until he'd joined the Navy himself, seven years ago. The times the Captain had beaten his mother…

That, he thought, was why he'd never married … the fear that he would turn out to be like his own father. Waverly knew he had a temper, one that he always kept rigidly in check. There'd been a girl, once … but fear and shame and a kind of nameless disgust had made him break off the relationship before things had gotten too serious.

Waverly had joined the Navy because it had been expected of him. It was tradition, after all, that Waverlys go to sea. Eventually, though, he found freedom in deliberately separating his career path as much as possible from that of his father. His father had been a line officer, on the path of command. Waverly had deliberately volunteered for hazardous duty — first for mine disposal, and then for Combat Demolition Units — precisely because these were not command-oriented assignments.

He'd been UDT for six months now and had not regretted a minute of it.

The one trouble he still had, though, was in bending enough to meet the situation. He was learning that regulations didn't necessarily cover every situation … just as the manual describing fuse mechanisms on a German mine didn't necessarily take into account the possibility of booby traps, or a broken timing screw.

He thought about the girl. Her name was Cindy Johnson and she'd let him kiss her in the front seat of his father's Packard. He'd quit seeing her when she'd started talking about children … and marriage.

Damn, why couldn't he have married her and gone on to become a … what? All his life, his entire life had been focused on the fact that one day he would continue the family tradition and go to sea.

Shit.

He was going to sea now, drifting with the current, and it didn't look like he was going to get a chance to come back

CHAPTER 14

Tuesday, 11 July 1944
U.S.S. *Rocky Mount*
Magicienne Bay, Saipan

It was 0200 hours, and the fog that had settled in over the area was showing no sign of lifting. Rear Admiral Hill was spending that sleepless night alternating between the lookout wings of the command ship's bridge to stare up at the sky and the communications shack.

From the rags and tatters of radio traffic coming in from *Stringham* and *Gilmer*, it was clear by now that the reconnaissance operation was a shambles, particularly off the White Beach area. The UDT men off Yellow Beach had gotten well into Asiga Bay before hearing shots fired in the darkness ahead. Mindful of their orders to avoid alerting the Japanese to the fact that reconnaissance swimmers were working off their beaches, the Team Seven men had turned back. Unfortunately, as near as could be determined, the Marine element of the Yellow Beach force had kept on going. Some had already been picked up, but others were still in the water.

And off White Beach, a picture was very gradually beginning to appear as more and more Marines and UDT men made it back to the LCP(R)s waiting off the coast. Most of the swimmers had not been able to find the beach at all. Others, some of the men from the White 2 group, including Coffer, had hit the wrong beach, landing on the island twelve hundred yards too far to the north. Some had not even reached the island but, realizing they were lost, had turned back in the

199

darkness. Reports of a strong north-bound current suggested that some of the men might have been swept past the island, into the Saipan Channel.

About half of the men were back aboard the LCPs now, but the rest were still lost. Striding into *Rocky Mount's* communications shack, Hill demanded the microphone from one of the harried radiomen. "This the *Gilmer's* frequency?"

"Yes, sir."

Hill pressed the transmit switch. "Golf One, Golf One, this is Pin-up. Do you read me, over?"

"Pin-up, this is Golf One. We read you. Over."

"Golf One, this is Pin-up himself. How many blondes? How many brunettes? Over!"

"Ah, Pin-up, we have sixteen blondes at this time, and twelve brunettes. Over."

Twelve men still unaccounted for.

"Golf One, Pin-up. You will exercise every means at your disposal to recover those men."

"Roger, Pin-up. Wilco."

"Pin-up, out!"

The worst part of it was being here on the command ship, helpless to do a damned thing.

"The word is out?" he asked the lieutenant in charge of the ship's radio shack. "Other ships in the area are looking?"

"Yes, sir," the lieutenant replied. "They've all got the word. Still…"

"What?"

"Well, Admiral, it's a hell of a big ocean."

"I know it is, Lieutenant. And we're going to comb every inch of it until those boys are found!"

He was well aware of just how long the odds against finding them all were.

What was that? The farther out to sea Waverly got, the higher the ocean swells grew. The waves gave him a fairly good view for a long distance when he rode them to the top, but most of the time he found himself in the troughs or halfway up or down the sides, and then all he could see was water. He waited until the surge carried him to the next crest, watching carefully to the north. He'd thought … yes! A ship! Jet-black against the moon-silvered ocean. It wasn't the *Gilmer*. It looked smaller, and the silhouette of the superstructure was different.

For a moment, he wondered if it was Japanese.

No, the last report he'd seen, there were no Japanese ships anywhere in the area. Three weeks ago, a big Japanese task force had been on the way from the Philippines to relieve the Marianas, but there'd been a major battle — the Navy aviators were calling that engagement the "Marianas Turkey Shoot," so many enemy planes had been shot down. In the course of a three-day battle, from June 18 to June 20, the Japanese had lost three carriers, two of them to submarines, and their task force had been turned back.

He lost sight of the darkened ship as he slid into the next wave trough but spotted her again on his next rise. Quickly, he fumbled in the pocket of his shorts for his penlight. He wasn't sure the light would carry well across the five hundred yards distance he estimated separated him from the ship, but he could sure give it a try. Aiming the light, he flicked it on…

Nothing.

Angry now, Waverly shook the offending light, then studied it by the moon's illumination. He could just make out the pinhole in the stretched rubber of the condom, which had stretched a bit to accommodate the thimbleful of seawater inside.

Damn! Seawater and batteries didn't mix, and the flashlight was completely dead. Now what was he supposed to do?

The ship was heading west, probably coming out of the Saipan Channel.

There had to be another way. There *had* to be.

Resourceful or innovative thinking had never been Waverly's strong point. Damn it all, that's what contingency plans were for … to handle the unexpected.

But how could you draw up plans to face the unexpected? The paradox struck him funny, and he started laughing, a wild, desperate sound in the middle of the ocean.

And then he had an idea.

Reaching up, he pulled his face mask off, turning it in his hands until the moon flashed from the glass front. The mask was fairly reflective; he made it more so by smearing some of the greasepaint from his face around on the inside of the glass. Holding it like an emergency signaling mirror, he tried to flash the moon's reflection toward the ship.

Nothing. The ship kept moving, and Waverly almost despaired as he slid from the crest of a wave into its trough. As he ascended to the next crest, however, he tried again, holding the swim mask in now-trembling hands and trying to angle it so that it would catch the moonlight coming in over his shoulder. The ship continued to pass…

And then, as if by a miracle, the ship was slowing, was coming about. In another few minutes, he could make out the paravanes stowed along her sides. She was an American minesweeper, and she'd seen him, and was closing now to pick him up.

He checked his watch. It was nearly 0430 hours, less than an hour before dawn.

*

Coffer and Captain Jones stood in front of the chart table with Admiral Turner, Admiral Hill, and General Smith, analyzing the near-disastrous reconnaissance. "In short, Commander," Turner was saying quietly, "none of your men ever reached White 2 at all."

"No, sir," Coffer replied. He felt the failure sharply. It was like a rebuke. Against his men. Against *him*.

Turner glanced at Hill. "Were they all picked up?"

"Yes, sir," Hill replied. "No losses."

"But damned little gain, either," Captain Jones said. He had been with the Marine party at Asiga. Like Coffer, he still had streaks of the silver-white paint on his face, though he'd changed into his khakis after returning aboard ship.

"What was your assessment of Yellow Beach, Captain?"

"It's tough, sir," Jones replied. "I think we've got some serious problems on that side of the island."

"My men were sure they'd been spotted," Coffer added. "But I gather all of your people got ashore?"

Coffer had already spoken with the UDT-7 men who'd accompanied Jones's recon Marines into the bay. They were still convinced that they'd heard gunfire and assumed that they'd been spotted by sentries on the beach.

"Yes, sir," Jones replied. He pointed to the spot where the twenty Marines had gone ashore, on the north side of Asiga Bay. "We heard explosions too, like your men, but they didn't sound like gunfire so we proceeded to the objective. When we reached the beach, we realized that there were Japanese work parties there. I think the blasts we heard were demolition charges of some kind. It looked to us like the Japanese were working on strengthening the fortifications."

"That's bad," General Smith said. "They already have those pillboxes behind the beach."

"Sir," Jones said, "in my opinion, Yellow Beach is out of the running. We saw large numbers of Japanese on the beach and behind it, preparing the fortifications. We ran into barbed wire here … and here. Tank obstacles. Ditches. And in the water offshore there were mines and more obstacles."

"Which brings us smack back to White Beach," Turner said. "Your assessment, Commander?"

"As I've already explained, sir, we were only able to examine White 1. That beach is quite narrow. However, the Marines who made it ashore gave the approaches in the bluffs behind the beach a good going over. They report reasonably easy access onto the heights back here, and a dirt road that appears to head straight in to Ushi Airfield. Some of my people checked White 1 thoroughly and found no sign of mines or any other obstacles. No pillboxes. No signs of any Japanese activity at all. I'd have to say that, if the Japanese know about White 1, they must not consider it a threat."

"As we thought," Smith said. "Admiral, it looks like the back door is standing open."

"I'm still concerned about White 2, though," Turner said, scowling at the chart. "It's larger, and the Japanese may have toughened it up. We'll need both beaches to get everything ashore we need on J day. White 1 by itself just won't support the logistical load."

"Um." Smith studied the map a moment more before nailing Coffer with a hard stare. "Commander, now that we've seen what's waiting for us on Yellow Beach, I'm more determined than ever to use the White Beach option. But I'm not going to commit to that until we know exactly what's waiting for us down there. Will you take some men back to White 2 tonight and check it out?"

Coffer could feel the exhaustion dragging at his shoulders like a lead weight, but he nodded. "Absolutely, sir. I'll pass the word to my men."

"Good. Let's hope the technical difficulties have been ironed out this time."

"They'd better be," Coffer said with feeling. "They'd damned well better be!"

Davies waited for a moment in the surf, scanning the beach carefully, then dashed forward, keeping low to the ground to avoid throwing a large and moving shadow. Halfway up the beach, he dropped flat. Seconds later, Blondie Foglio joined him. Other shapes, silvery-gray in the moonlight, moved past the two UDT men and melted into the shadows at the top of the beach.

"Made, it," Foglio said softly. "Looks clear. This part, anyway."

"Yeah," Davies replied. "Piece of cake. Let's get to the treeline up there."

This time, every part of the operation had gone off perfectly. *Gilmer's* radar had guided the team in to the beach with absolute precision. This was definitely White 2, almost three times wider than White 1, and with higher cliffs to either side. The survey team this time consisted of twelve UDT and six Marines; another team was paying a second visit to White 1 as well. Most of the UDT men were still offshore, checking the coral reef and looking for obstacles. Some of the Navy men, however, had crawled onto the beach and were searching for mines.

"Hey, Davies?"

"What is it, Blondie?"

"Have a look."

Crawling over to where Blondie was lying in the sand, Davies followed the shielded beam of the man's pencil flash.

"What do you make of those?" Blondie asked. In front of him was a circular hole in the sand, a foot wide and several feet deep. Beyond, parallel to the shore, was another … then another and another beyond that.

"Looks like holes for pilings. Maybe the Japanese were planning on putting a jetty or a boardwalk or something in here."

"Maybe. This'd be a great place to offload supplies for Ushi, wouldn't it? What I'm thinking, though, is that those holes might look like something else from the air."

"Like land mines, maybe," Davies said. "Or holes for planting them in."

"Yeah."

"Could be. Let's keep checking the beach, though. Just because we haven't found any on this side —"

"Sst!" Blondie laid a warning hand on Davies's arm. The pencil flash winked out.

A moment later, Davies heard what Blondie had heard a moment before: voices … *Japanese* voices. He wondered if they had time to make it back to the water, but then a bobbing gleam of light appeared among the trees at the top of the beach. Seconds later, several men could be seen approaching, some of them with lanterns, while others carried tools or weapons of some kind.

They were coming directly toward the two UDT men, their lanterns casting a vivid glow against the night. Davies reached down and slipped his knife free. Blondie did the same.

"*A tsukareta*" one of the approaching men said, his voice high and nasal, almost a whine. It sounded like a complaint.

"*Naruhodo!*" someone else replied in a matter-of-fact tone. "*De wa … hayaku oki-nasai.*"

"*Hai,*" a third man said. "*Koko wa yoroin ja arimasen!*"

The others laughed, and Davies wondered what the joke was.

Turning, most of the figures spread out along the top of the dunes behind the beach and appeared to be working there with their tools among the low, scrubby weeds and other vegetation that held the landward side of the dunes together. One of the men, though, came down the dunes and started across the beach, walking slowly toward the water. When he was twenty feet away, Davies could see that he was a member of the Japanese naval infantry, a counterpart of the U.S. Marines. He carried an Arisaka rifle slung over his shoulder, and held an oil lantern in his right hand.

He ouldd see the two Americans any moment now…

His boots squeaking in the sand, the Japanese soldier came to within five feet of Davies's position, walking past without a stop. Davies felt enormous, as big as a beached whale, despite his white-paint camouflage and hood. The soldier came to a stop perhaps fifteen feet away, set the oil lamp down, then pulled a cigarette from a tunic pocket and lit it.

Davies and Blondie were lying side by side just outside the circle of yellowish illumination cast by the lamp, knives drawn, ready to attack if they were discovered. Davies could not imagine why the soldier hadn't seen them — he'd thought for a moment that the man had looked directly at them as he passed — but as he thought about it, he decided that carrying the lamp had ruined his night vision. Quite possibly he couldn't see anything now, except for the light and what was directly in front of him.

The soldier continued to stand there for a time, smoking his cigarette and staring out across the moon-silvered sea. At last, he flicked the butt out into the surf, a red spark spinning across the night, then stooped and picked up the lamp and began walking slowly south along the beach.

Blondie started to move, but Davies laid a hand on his arm, waiting … waiting… There was a terrible danger that someone else with the working party might come down onto the beach, but Davies wanted to wait until the soldier was well out of sight before moving. At last, he tapped Blondie's shoulder twice and pointed down the shelf of the beach. Side by side, like a pair of sea turtles making their ungainly way back to the ocean, they crawled slowly toward the surf, slipped into the tumble of incoming water, and vanished into its depths.

"Then it will be White Beach," Admiral Turner said, straightening above the chart table. For the past hour, the two men had been going over in detail the corrected charts presented to them by the men of UDTs Five and Seven. More reconnaissance work had already been planned for the near future, but for now there was more than enough for the American high command to begin planning for the invasion.

"Absolutely," General Smith replied. He set aside a now-empty coffee cup bearing the globe and anchor of the U.S.M.C. "The most disturbing part of this new information is that the reef off White Two is going to create a bottleneck in front of the beach only seventy yards wide. That's enough for free passage for only sixteen LTVs coming in line-abreast. And White One's only wide enough for eight. But it looks as though the Japanese have genuinely neglected to defend these areas."

"My staff is working on a plan for a diversion in front of Tinian Town and the lagoon," Turner said. "We may employ the UDT there, too, blowing holes in the reef, blowing up obstacles, that sort of thing. A strong demonstration on J day might pin the Japanese defenses in place."

"That sounds good. Do you believe the swimmers' reports about no mines?"

"Shouldn't I? It seemed pretty straightforward to me."

"Well, my staff people still don't believe there can't be land mines on that beach. The holes are quite clear from the air, and they say they must be where the Japanese are mining the beach. Still, the rest of the report seems conclusive enough. We *can* land on White One and White Two, mines or no mines, and I think we have a fair chance of snatching Ushi Airfield right out from under the bastards' noses, probably by J-plus-two. I'll have my people in Tinian Town by J-plus-seven."

"That may be a bit optimistic, General, given how hard they fought for Saipan."

"Maybe. But on Saipan we didn't come galloping down on their rear. Tinian is going to be different; I can feel it."

"I hope you're right, General." A knock sounded on the compartment door. "Come."

An aide stepped inside. "Admiral? Lieutenant Commander Coffer."

"Good. Holland? Would you excuse me?"

"Of course."

"Send him in."

Coffer stepped over the door's combing. "Lieutenant Commander Coffer, reporting to the Admiral as ordered, sir."

"Hello, David. Thanks for coming. I know you must be running a bit shy on sleep lately."

"No problem, sir. What did you want to see me about?"

Turner walked across the compartment to a desk in the corner and picked up a sheet of paper. "Commander, I'm putting through the paperwork to award decorations to those of your men who swam up to enemy beaches — in some cases who actually went up on the beaches — in the Saipan and Tinian operations. I thought you would like to see the order."

"Thank you, sir."

"Do you have any particular recommendations?"

Coffer accepted the paper but did not start to read it immediately. "Well, sir, you've seen my reports, and the reports of Lieutenant Waverly and the other officers on the teams. Every man in Five and Seven did an absolutely fantastic job. Especially the boys who went in against the Japanese mortars at Saipan."

"I agree."

Coffer began reading the citation. "Sir … this isn't right," he said, looking up after a moment.

"What do you mean? What's wrong?"

"Sir, you're directing that every enlisted man in Teams Five and Seven receive the Bronze Star. But that every officer will get the Silver Star."

"That's right. Except for you, of course. I've put you in for a gold star in lieu of a second Navy Cross."

"Congratulations, Commander," General Smith said.

"I don't know if you know this, General," Turner told Smith, "but our young friend here picked up his first Navy Cross doing bomb disposal work at Pearl right after the Japanese attack."

"Impressive."

"Sir …" Coffer began.

Turner sighed. He thought he knew what was coming.

"Spit it out, Commander."

Coffer handed the paper back to Turner. "Thank you very much, sir. But it's still not right. If it's all the same to you, I suggest that everyone get the Bronze Star. Officers *and* enlisted."

Turner frowned. "Well, it is *not* all the same to me, Commander. My directive stands."

"Sir, every man in those teams took equal chances and faced the same danger. The officers were no more heroic than the enlisted personnel ... and no better, either. If I might suggest, perhaps a unit citation of some sort would be more —"

"Negative, Commander," Turner snapped. "This is the Navy, and a certain form and protocol, a certain decorum, must be maintained. End of discussion."

"Yes, sir. Aye, aye, sir."

"That is all."

Coffer turned on his heel and strode from the room. He did not look happy.

"You know what you have there, Rich?" Smith said from the corner where he'd been sitting during the brief interview.

"No. What?"

"A revolutionary."

"I don't follow."

"Coffer's Reserve, isn't he?"

"Yes, he is. Why?"

"It's just that he's not your typical career naval officer. He's flexible. Bright. Innovative. Give him three good ways to do something and the son-of-a-gun'll find a fourth way, a better way. And he doesn't give a damn for doing things the way they've always been done, not if the old way is inefficient ... or if it's going to cost lives. He's going to make waves everywhere he goes in this man's Navy, that one is."

"I daresay you're right, Holland. Maybe people like him are the ones who ought to be running this war, eh? Not old-timers like you and me."

"Speak for yourself with that 'old-timer' garbage. What's next on the agenda?"

"Planning," Turner said, "just how we can get two Marine divisions ashore on these two beaches in anything like combat order and in anything less than two days."

The two men returned to the chart.

CHAPTER 15

Thursday, 20 July 1944
Guam

Four days before the scheduled invasion of Tinian, the Navy and Marine forces prepared to assault yet another of the Japanese bastions in the southern Marianas. The island of Guam had been an American possession until three days after Pearl Harbor, when it had fallen to the Japanese. Now, two and a half years later, the Americans were about to return.

As at Saipan and as at Tinian, the Navy UDT led the way with surveys of the enemy beaches. Ship and air softening of the island — the heaviest such bombardment so far in history — had been proceeding since July 8 and would continue until W day, July 21.

With Teams Five and Seven both occupied with the invasion of Tinian, the beach reconnaissance of Guam fell to Team Three, Team Four, and Team Six, which had sat out the Saipan operation as the operational reserve. The first nighttime reconnaissance of Guam's beaches began on the night of July 14; the first daylight recon was the next morning. UDT operations continued steadily throughout the next week, as teams surveyed beaches and reefs, charted depths, and began blowing up obstacles already planted offshore. Lessons hard-won at Saipan and Tinian were passed on to the Guam units; nevertheless, there were casualties.

The final reconnaissance took place on the night of July 20, the day before the scheduled American landings on Guam. Their bodies smeared white as camouflage on the sand, a number of UDT men slipped ashore out of the crashing surf on the beach just below the town of Agat. Except for the stealthily moving UDT swimmers, the beach was deserted.

After carrying out their assigned reconnaissance, four of the men began erecting a peculiar construction.

Throughout the Marianas operation, there'd been considerable good-natured friction between the UDT and the Marines. The Marines, after all, had the reputation of always being first ashore on a hostile beach, and the UDT men were laying claim to Marine tradition.

At Guam, that night, Team Four set the record straight … and also started a UDT tradition that would continue throughout the war, despite official attempts to stop it as a breach of security. When the U.S. Marines of the First Provisional Brigade waded ashore on Guam early the next morning, the first thing they saw as they stepped onto the beach was a plywood sign, five feet long by two feet wide, erected in the sand and facing the sea:

WELCOME MARINES
AGAT USO TWO BLOCKS
COURTESY UDT-4

This time, the teams could prove that they, indeed, had been first.

CHAPTER 16

Thursday, 3 August 1944
Wardroom, U.S.S. *Burrfish*
South of Peleliu, Palau Island Group

"Ballard."

"And I'll take Barker," Alexander Forsythe said, ticking off the name on the list in front of him.

"O'Leary looks good," Chief Schroeder commented. "I was impressed with his swimming back at Kamaole. A good man."

"He is," Forsythe replied.

"Then I'll take him, too."

"Right. O'Leary to you. And I'll take Crenshaw."

They were sitting at the wardroom table, going over the roster of the recon unit and dividing the men up into two groups. They had already agreed to alternate the two parties in carrying out the actual scouting swims, with Forsythe commanding one team and Schroeder the other. The process of assigning the rest of the men to their respective groups reminded Forsythe of choosing up sides in a schoolyard baseball game, but it seemed to be working out well enough. By the time they were done, Schroeder had two ex-OSS swimmers and two Waipio men, while Forsythe had Crenshaw and Barker of Team Ten plus two Amphibious Operations men.

"Okay, Chief," he said when they were done. "That takes care of who's who. Now we just have to decide which team pulls the first op tonight."

"Tell you what, Lieutenant," Schroeder said with a smile. "I've got just the way to handle that one fairly sitting in my seabag. If I can go get it…?"

"Well, I *could* just pull rank and say I'm taking my boys in…" Forsythe caught the look in Schroeder's eyes and held up a hand. "Whoa, there, Chief, just commenting. By all means, if you've got a better idea, we'll look it over."

Schroeder left the wardroom in a hurry, leaving Forsythe to study the roster again and muse over the ins and outs of the scouting mission.

The submarine was lying at the bottom of the ocean a few miles south of the island of Peleliu, waiting for nightfall and the chance to close in to launch the first recon effort.

Burrfish had left Pearl Harbor on schedule, making a good start. She'd ould on the surface for three days and nights, averaging seventeen knots, but on the morning of the fourth day she'd submerged to begin the difficult task of slipping into enemy waters. Their progress had slowed. Moving underwater by day, the sub had been forced to surface each night to recharge batteries, and the time had begun to hang heavy on the men cooped up inside the narrow confines of her hull.

Finally, a few days ago, they'd reached the operating area around Peleliu and Yap. They'd had a bad omen of sorts almost immediately. The sub's air-conditioning system had broken down, and conditions aboard had rapidly become intolerable. No one on the crew seemed to know what was wrong, but White, one of the ex-OSS men in the recon team, had come up with the answer. He'd seen something similar happen during training for sub ops in Nassau and suggested that the fault was in one of the sea valves on the outside of the hull. White had gone over the side that night and fixed the problem, but he had barely had time to get back up on deck when radar picked up an approaching ship and everyone on deck had been forced to scramble below before *Burrfish* made an emergency dive. They spent the remainder of that night playing cat and mouse with a Japanese subchaser, evading depth charge attacks and sonar searches. Throughout the next day the hunt had continued, with the Japs sending out search planes armed with depth bombs to support the ship. It wasn't until the next night that they finally broke contact.

At least the UDT contingent had come out of the whole situation with a little more respect from the boat's crew than they'd enjoyed before. No one knew about their OSS backgrounds or their past experience working off submarines, so White's unexpected knowledge had added to the mystique Forsythe had already encountered clinging to the Navy swimmers. Even Chief Schroeder, who knew the truth, had been complimentary.

They had reached the waters south of Peleliu earlier this morning and spent the day in hiding. Forsythe and Schroeder were spending the time finalizing the details of the operation, and he was finding the red-bearded chief a lot more friendly and easy to get along with than their early history at Kamaole had suggested. He was a quick-witted, competent man with a colorful past — he'd been a China hand before the war — as well as a broad sense of humor and an absolute dedication to the UDT concept. As they'd worked together in close quarters through the voyage out from Pearl, Forsythe had developed a considerable respect for the man, and he was beginning to feel that Schroeder, though he'd never admit it, felt the same way about him.

The chief reappeared at the wardroom door, grinning. "Here you go, Lieutenant. One genuine Guidance System, Random

Decision, Navy Personnel, For the Use Of." He set a deck of cards on the table and sat down across from Forsythe.

"You want to decide who tackles the Japanese tonight with a deck of *cards*?"

"Sure. High card gets the op."

Forsythe chuckled. "Only in the UDT," he said. "Okay, Chief, you're on." He shuffled the deck and gave it to Schroeder, who cut. Forsythe drew the nine of diamonds and laid it beside the deck. Then Schroeder drew his card and set it down with a triumphant flourish. It was the jack of clubs.

"Well, looks like you get it, Red," Forsythe said. "And I get the next one. Unless you want to go best two out of three…"

"I'm happy with this one, Lieutenant," Schroeder said. "Let's leave it alone."

"Yeah, you're probably right. Anyway, knowing you, the deck's probably rigged some way. Okay, Chief, I know when I'm beat."

"Wise man, Lieutenant," Schroeder told him, gathering in the cards.

"Anything else we need to discuss?"

"I'm still not too happy with the mission specs, Lieutenant. Are you sure we can't get some leeway?"

Forsythe shook his head. "I know exactly how you feel, Chief," he said. "But Fitzgerald won't budge. Our responsibility is to check out the underwater obstacles. Nothing else."

It had been a point of contention between Fitzgerald and the UDT men from the very beginning. The official specifications for the mission were to study the underwater obstacles the aerial recon photos had spotted. Schroeder and Forsythe had argued that they should also investigate the beach defenses and the lay of the land ashore. While the UDT policy was to stick to the water, most beach surveys also examined the ould e and made maps of obvious terrain features and potential defensive positions that dominated the beaches they were charting. But Fitzgerald had been very specific in limiting the scope of the swimmers' operations. While the recon parties were checking for underwater obstacles, the sub would continue routine periscope sweeps of the shoreline, and that was supposed to be all that was necessary.

Forsythe knew that there were limits to what could be picked up by a periscope sweep. But Fitzgerald had remained adamant.

He leaned back in his chair. "Look, Chief, as an official officer and gentleman of the United States Navy I'm telling you to accept the lawful directives of our commanding officer, Commander Fitzgerald." He grinned. "But as a fellow UDT scoundrel, Red, I suggest you do whatever survey work you think you need to carry out. For the good of the team, and all that."

Schroeder's eyes twinkled as he stroked his red beard. "I hear and obey, Lieutenant." He paused. "And thanks. I was wrong about you back on Maui. You'll make a good UDT man after all."

"Damn it, what the hell's keeping them?"

Forsythe looked across the chart table at Fitzgerald. The commander was tapping a pencil on the top of the table irritably, his concern growing plainer as the minutes ticked by. He stood out in stark contrast to the sub's crew, who were going about their duties calmly and with little outward sign of any kind of emotion. They mostly ignored the two interlopers from the recon mission. The sub's captain had extended them the courtesy of inviting them to wait out the mission in the control room, with the proviso that they keep out of the way.

Burrfish had surfaced shortly after midnight nearly a mile off the southern coast of Peleliu. Schroeder, Chief Ballard, and the rest of his team had gone on deck with an inflatable boat and the rest of the gear they'd needed for the op and had finished their preparations quickly and quietly. When all had been pronounced ready, the sub had slipped under the waves and left the boat and the five swimmers to do their job.

That had been nearly three hours ago. Commander Aiken had kept *Burrfish* moving slowly back and forth across the rendezvous area, making periodic periscope sweeps and taking photographs of the shoreline. And through the entire period Fitzgerald had been growing visibly more edgy, knowing full well that the entire mission rested with that handful of men outside the hull.

Forsythe had shared his concern but made every effort to suppress it. He still wished he had gone out with his team, and the forced inaction in the cramped control space was contributing to his feelings of helplessness. But Schroeder, White, and O'Leary were competent swimmers, and even the two Waipio men, Chief Ballard especially, seemed well suited for the task at hand. So he forced himself to wait without betraying any of the agitation he might normally have given vent to in some other setting.

"There they are!" Aiken said suddenly. "Mark this bearing!"

A crewman hastened to read the heading off his periscope. Forsythe let out a quiet sigh of relief and smiled to see that Fitzgerald was doing the same. "It's about damned time, too," the commander said. "What's the routine now, Skipper?"

Aiken flipped up the handles on the periscope. "Down scope," he ordered briskly. "Now, Commander, we maneuver over to them and surface. I doubt we'll come up right under them, but it won't take long to get them alongside and on board. If you and Mr. Forsythe would like to repair to the wardroom, I'll send your men down as soon as they're on board and we've got their gear secured." His words were phrased as a suggestion, but it was plain that he didn't intend to let them stay in the control room. Things would be confused and crowded when the sub started up, and they didn't need extra people underfoot. And a submarine on the surface was vulnerable, a situation that made even the most phlegmatic submariner as nervous as Fitzgerald had been all evening. They'd want to be sure no one got in the way if they had to make another sudden emergency dive.

Forsythe gathered up the charts they had been using, and he and Fitzgerald made their way to the wardroom without speaking. Again, they waited, but this time the atmosphere wasn't quite so tense. Fitzgerald was still fuming a little but looked more relaxed than before.

From the sounds that echoed through the hull the pickup seemed to go smoothly enough. After a time the diving alarm sounded and the noise of water rushing through sea cocks into the ballast tanks filled the compartment. Though he wasn't a submariner, Forsythe shared the feeling of relief he was sure swept through the boat at that moment, as they once again slid quietly beneath the concealing water, safely out of sight of any prying eyes that might be abroad in the night.

Schroeder arrived a few minutes later, still clad in trunks and with a towel draped around his neck. He had his slate in one hand with its cryptic lists of depths, conditions, and obstacles he'd noted during his swim. After he was seated, Forsythe and Fitzgerald made him go over his findings in detail, taking notes and letting the CPO point out places of interest on the chart as he ould ed the mission.

The rubber boat, with Chief Ballard acting as coxswain, had carried the party in to a distance of about two hundred yards. Then Schroeder and the others had gone into the water, leaving Ballard with the raft to await their return. They had spent the next two hours working their way across the zone, working in a standard grid pattern, locating and examining underwater obstacles and natural barriers that would be of interest to the high command.

As suspected, the Japanese had been busy. They had strung entangling wire underwater together with cribs full of coral linked by steel cables and coconut logs. But in Schroeder's opinion there wasn't anything there that couldn't be dealt with by standard UDT clearing operations when the time came for an invasion.

"As far as conditions on the beach are concerned, we weren't able to get a whole lot," the chief went on after finishing his account of the underwater obstacles. "The terrain —"

Fitzgerald held up a hand. "Hold it there, Chief. I thought I made it clear that your survey was to be confined to the water only."

"You did, sir, but I felt it wouldn't hurt to make a few observations —"

"So you spent extra time conducting operations I expressly told you not to carry out, and thus put your men and this whole mission in jeopardy. I'm very disappointed in you, Chief. I was told you were reliable."

"Sir," Forsythe broke in. "I think you're being a bit rough on Chief Schroeder here. He used initiative to gather additional material that will surely be an asset to your report —"

"My report, unlike Chief Schroeder's, is going to stick to the information Admiral Powell requested."

"But —"

"The matter is closed, Mr. Forsythe. I suggest we get on with the debriefings while we can." He glanced at his watch. "Our time is limited, after all."

Forsythe exchanged an unhappy look with Schroeder, but obeyed. "Anything else to report, Chief? On the underwater side of things?"

"No, sir. Nothing else."

"Good," Fitzgerald said, making a few final notes on his pad. "All right, Chief, you did a good job outside of your excess of zeal. I'll see to it you get full credit for your work. Now go grab a shower and some sack time, and send the next man in on your way."

"Yessir," Schroeder said, rising.

They debriefed each of the other men in turn, adding to their stack of notes and marking up the chart as they went along. It was close to dawn on the surface by the time they finished. Fitzgerald gathered up his clipboard when the last man was done. "All right, Lieutenant, that'll be it for tonight. I'm going to see Captain Aiken and have him take us up before it gets light out there, so I can fire off a preliminary evaluation to Pearl. Later on there'll be time to transmit a fuller report, but for now I know there's a lot of preparations being held up waiting for us to say yea or nay."

"You're recommending the invasion go ahead, sir?"

"You heard Schroeder and the others. The obstacles are extensive, but nothing the UDT can't handle."

"I'd still be happier, sir, if we had some more topographical information we could pass on about conditions ashore. I'm not sure if the air and sub recon can really do the same kind of job as a pair of eyes right up by the beach."

"Still harping on that, eh, Lieutenant. Thought I settled that before." Fitzgerald sighed heavily. "Look, I don't have time for a lot of arguments. If we get a chance over the next few nights we can supplement whatever Chief Schroeder already found out with additional observations. But all that's for the detailed reports we'll submit down the line. We've done what the admiral asked us to do, for this zone at least. The decision to invade or not is being made on the difficulty of the obstacles, not on our opinions of what the lay of the land is like. So back off, and keep your men on a tighter leash in the future. You got me, Lieutenant?"

"Aye, aye, sir," Forsythe said.

After Fitzgerald left, Forsythe stood up slowly and paced off the short length of the compartment. The commander was dead wrong, of that much he was convinced. But he was in charge, and he'd be the one to decide what information made it to Third 'Phib for evaluation. Forsythe doubted he'd include anything further in the follow-up reports. And of course that was his prerogative as CO.

But it was still wrong...

"Hey, Raider, what's the word?"

Rand rolled over in his cot as Stan Kowalski came through the tent flap. Thunder and the incessant pounding of a Florida rainstorm hammered away outside, and it was even damper and mustier in the tent than usual. But Kowalski seemed unaffected by weather as he was by just about everything else. Nothing could shake his cheerful grin or his interest in everything, and everyone, around him.

"Look what came in the mail," Kowalski went on without giving Rand time to answer his greeting. He pulled a folded newspaper out from under his dripping jacket. For some reason Kowalski's parents insisted on sending their son copies of one of the Chicago papers, and Kowalski relished the news from his home turf. He opened up the paper and stabbed a stubby finger at the headline. "See that? See it?"

RESISTANCE OVER ON SAIPAN, it proclaimed. Below, in smaller type, it added, JAPANESE NEAR THE END ON GUAM.

"So? Old news. We heard all that a couple days ago."

"Yeah, I know, Raider, but seeing it in print like this..." Kowalski sat on his own cot and laid the paper aside. "Seems like the whole war is winding down without us. Scuttlebutt says they're hitting somewhere in the Med again in the next coupla weeks, but it's all over in Europe. Even if we're not in Berlin by Christmas, you know it's gonna be an Army show from here on out. And it looks like the Japanese are going down, too. The way the Marines are knocking over one damned little island after another, there ain't gonna be anything left for us to do by the time they let us get into action."

"Hell, Ski, we're out of here in another couple of weeks. Probably be in the PTO in another month or two. There'll still be plenty to do. I don't think Tojo's just going to roll over because we grab a few islands here and there. We're going to have to go in and dig him and Hirohito out of their holes on the Home Islands in person, and if you thought Normandy was something wait'll you see that one. We'll be there, all right. In the thick of things. Count on it."

"Yeah. Maybe you're right." Suddenly his habitual grin was back. "Hey, I heard 'em call your name, too, back at mail call. What did you get? Something from home?"

"Just a letter," he said reluctantly. Then, "From my girl, if you must know."

"Not a 'Dear Frankie,' I hope."

"Naw, nothing like that." Rand looked down at the letter in his hand. "She's ... she's a little upset because a guy we went to school with bought it on Saipan. She worries about me, I guess. Thinks the next bullet'll have my name on it."

"Man, that's bad," Kowalski said. "That's the first sign, sometimes, you know? First they start worrying, then they start nagging, then they decide some Four-F four-flusher is a better bargain 'cause he's there and he ain't leaving. What are you gonna do, Raider?"

"I don't know, Ski," he said slowly. "I just don't know."

The conversation fell silent, but the hammer of rain went on against the tent. It was a depressing, dreary noise, entirely in keeping with Rand's mood.

He started reading again.

"Dearest Frank," it began.

I was so happy to get the letter you sent from Plymouth. Knowing you were over there, knowing the Scouts and Raiders had such a dangerous part to play, I was so afraid for you when we had the news of the landings in France. I don't think I slept a whole night through for three weeks, wondering if you were all right. It was such a relief when your letter came, to find out you were safe and on your way back to the States.

The letter you sent from Fort Pierce last month must have got lost in the mail, because it only got here yesterday. And since I wasn't sure where you were going to be, I couldn't write until I had your new FPO box. There's so much I want to say, so much to talk about, but I don't even know where to start. And what I really want to do is to see you, talk to you ... touch you. I know it's selfish, but sometimes I hate the Navy for keeping you away from me and I feel I just can't wait another day for you to come home again.

And it's been even worse the last few days, since Mrs. Ketteridge got the telegram about George. He was with the Marines who went in on Saipan, wherever that is, and he didn't make it. She was so proud because he'd just made sergeant, and then this had to happen. Last year it was Eddie Lustman, and now George. When will it be over?

Frank, Frank, I know we agreed to wait to be married until the war is over, but every night I lie awake and wonder if that day will ever really come. I love you, and I want to be a part of your life, but I'm so afraid of the future.

I'm sorry, Frank. I know the last thing you need to hear now are the fears of a silly schoolgirl. I want to be strong for you, because I love you so much. You know I'll wait for you for as long as it takes, until you get the job done. Then we'll be together forever. But sometimes I wish forever was now…

Was Kowalski right? It could be Nancy's first step toward dumping him. Or she could be falling back into the old coquettish habits of their school days, trying to manipulate him into an immediate marriage. But he didn't think so. As far as he could tell, her feelings, her fears, were genuine.

"Hey, look, Raider, I didn't mean to upset you, okay?" Kowalski spoke up hesitantly. "I didn't really mean anything by it. About your girl getting ready to dump you, I mean."

"Don't worry about it, Ski," he said quietly, still looking at the neat handwriting and wondering what he could do to relieve her frustration and pain.

"Hey, if you need a sympathetic ear or something … I mean, that's what your swim buddy's for, right?"

Rand started to shake his head, then sat up slowly. He was so used to being a loner, to handling things on his own, the reaction had become automatic. His mother was dead and he hadn't spoken or written to his father in nearly a year, and he'd never really been comfortable sharing his burdens with Nancy or with his sister, Sue. His only real confidants over the years had been Nancy's father, who had taken Rand under his wing and given him a job before he'd joined the Navy, and later Phil Bucklew, the founder of the Scouts and Raiders. He couldn't very well ask Mr. Brown for advice regarding the man's own daughter, and Bucklew was still in England overseeing the final missions of the Scouts and Raiders in Europe before closing down operations in a ould that no longer required their special expertise.

Maybe being a teammate really *did* cut both ways…

"Look, Stan, maybe you can help me out at that," he said finally.

"Anything you need, Raider. Anything."

"What I need is advice. Nancy … I think she wants me to set a date. I mean, we were going to wait till the war was over, but it sounds like she'd rather get hitched sooner."

"And you don't want to?"

"It's not that…" Rand trailed off, suddenly feeling awkward. It was like writing to Nancy and knowing the censors would be reading everything he felt and thought. "Okay, look. I just don't know if it's fair to her if I tie her down now. My dad came back from the last war messed up real bad, and things were never right at home. If I come back in pieces… Hell, if I buy the farm and leave her a widow … you see?"

Kowalski nodded slowly. "Yeah, I hear you, Raider. It's a real tough call, man. You can make her wait and break her heart, or you can marry her and maybe never come back, or leave a piece of yourself on a Japanese beachhead and leave her to look after a cripple for the rest of your lives." He looked away. "No good choices in there, huh?"

"You got that right."

"Well, then all I can say is since the down side's bad any way you go, you might as well not make your choice based on what could go wrong. You get what I mean, Raider? Try looking at what's *good* about each choice, and see where that leads you. Do you want to marry her? Are you in love with her?"

Rand thought about the doubts he'd been having, but they suddenly rolled away like a morning fog over the Indian River. Put straight and simple, there was only one answer to the question. "Of *course* I am…"

"Then if she feels the same way, I'd say you should marry her now, and be damned with what *might* happen. Look, if the war wasn't going on, you'd get hitched, wouldn't you?"

Rand nodded slowly. "Yeah … if she'd have me."

"Even though tomorrow you could fall down a flight of stairs or get in a train wreck or come down with influenza and die?"

"The odds are a lot shorter in wartime, Ski. They say the Demolitioneers took better'n forty percent casualties on Omaha. Two of the guys I went to school with have already died out there … my partner from S and R school, too."

Kowalski shrugged. "Odds … I guess it's all in the way you look at it. I come from a long line of Polish Catholics, Raider, and I was raised to believe that God has a reason for everything He does. If it's your time to go, then you're going, whether it's from a Japanese bullet or a car wreck. And if it isn't your time … well, it just isn't. You can't spend your whole life trying to second-guess God or fate or the future. Just get on with it. Live your life the best way you know how. Either that, or you might as well shoot yourself today and get the agony over with, because if you won't grab for whatever you're offered in life you might as well be six feet under." He looked sheepish. "That's the way I see it, anyway. It's free advice, and worth every penny, I guess."

Rand smiled, his bleak mood gone. "It's worth more than you might think, Stan. A hell of a lot more. Thanks."

He put down Nancy's letter and reached for the pen and paper in the footlocker beside his cot. Kowalski's words had convinced him. Now all he needed was Nancy's consent.

CHAPTER 17

Wednesday, 16 August 1944
U.S.S. *Burrfish*
South of Yap, Palau Island Group

The sleek gray hull of the *Burrfish* was barely perceptible against the inky black waters of the Pacific. Something clattered against the metal deck in the darkness and Alex Forsythe muttered a low-voiced curse. Noise carried all too well over the water, especially at night. The Japanese-held island was barely visible as a low humped shadow looming against the northern horizon, and Forsythe was constantly conscious of the menace it presented.

So far the *Burrfish* expedition had been fraught with difficulty and disappointment, and Forsythe was beginning to feel as if the entire operation was under the curse of some malevolent sea god.

A hoarse whisper broke the silence. "Ready, sir."

"All right," he replied softly. "Into the boat. Let's get this show on the road."

The other four men were hard to see in the darkness. Wearing swim trunks, masks, and silver-blue camouflage grease, they were like ghosts flitting eerily across the sub's forward deck as they boarded the inflatable rubber boat. Forsythe was the last man in. "All right, O'Leary, get ready," he ordered in a quiet voice. He picked up a shielded flashlight from the bottom of the raft, turned it toward the conning tower, and flicked it on and off twice, the agreed-upon signal that the recon party was ready.

Nothing happened right away, but Forsythe knew the signal had been seen by the deck officer and relayed below. The sub crew would be preparing to submerge, dogging down watertight hatches and double-checking dials and readouts on the bridge. After a few minutes there was a distant gurgling as water began to rush into the ballast tanks. The submarine began to settle beneath them, and the raft started to move. Then the sub was gone, leaving the raft afloat on the suddenly empty sea.

Crenshaw and Barker took up muffled oars and began to paddle carefully, virtually silent. Forsythe found himself smiling despite the tension. At least tonight he had nothing but OSS men swimming with him, men he'd trained with and could count on. Originally one of the Waipio men had been scheduled to be one of his swimmers, but he'd come up sick and O'Leary had volunteered to replace him. Maybe that was a good omen for tonight, he thought. After the debacle at Peleliu it was about time for their luck to change.

After Schroeder's first swim off Peleliu's southern beaches nothing had gone right again. When *Burrfish* had tried to move in to launch a second recon mission the next night, a radar contact had caused Captain Aiken to break off and retreat back to the bottom, and the following morning an attempted periscope sweep of the shoreline had been aborted by the appearance of another Japanese subchaser. For nearly two weeks the American sub had been engaged in a difficult and ultimately futile game of hide-and-seek with the well-coordinated naval and air patrols put up around the island. Finally Aiken had made the decision to leave Peleliu entirely and move on to Yap, the other major target they were supposed to survey.

Neither Schroeder nor Forsythe had been happy with the decision. They had both wanted to confirm the initial findings with more spot checks, and Forsythe had hoped to gather more information on the beaches so he'd have more ammunition in his fight to make Fitzgerald include that data in his reports to Pearl. But time was running out; Third 'Phib was already preparing to move out and had to know about Yap as soon as possible. And Aiken, responsible for the safety of the boat and crew, had the final say on what the submarine could and could not attempt.

So now they were off the southern end of Yap, hoping this survey mission would go smoothly after two weeks of disappointments.

The UDT men guided the boat toward the shadowy island. At about two hundred yards' distance Forsythe gave the soft-voiced order to stop, and Barker slid a weighted line into the water to serve as an anchor.

Forsythe studied the dark hump of the island, noting the bearings of a couple of distinguishable headlands in his mind so that he could navigate back. Then he strapped on his fins and checked his face mask one last time before turning to Phelps. "If we haven't returned in two hours, make your way back to the rendezvous point. Understood?"

"Aye, aye, sir," the man replied.

Forsythe nodded to the others. "Let's do it," he said. He rolled out over the side and into the warm water. His men followed quickly, making little noise. This was the kind of work they had practiced over and over in the Maritime Unit, and they knew their jobs perfectly. The only thing that would have made their work even easier, Forsythe thought as he dived under, would have been one of Doc Lambertson's LARUs strapped to each man's back so that they could have made the swim completely undetectable from the surface. With breathing gear, he thought idly, they might even have tried going out of one of the sub's escape hatches or torpedo tubes without ever surfacing. Something like that might have made the ould rence in conducting further work off Peleliu.

He forced himself to concentrate on the mission. Time enough for idle speculation at one of the bull sessions that had become a nightly UDT ritual back on the sub.

Forsythe and O'Leary made up one swimming team, while Crenshaw and Barker partnered each other. They split up early on, angling toward opposite sides of the beach. Everything was to be done by the numbers, just like one of the drills back on Maui. O'Leary was assigned to chart depths at twenty-five-yard intervals, while Forsythe followed behind him in a zigzag pattern, diving periodically to check for obstacles and obstructions. One of their principal tasks on this swim would be to check out several areas off the beach that had shown up in aerial recon photos as discolored patches in the water. If they were reefs, they could pose a major problem to getting landing craft inshore unless UDT swimmers were sent in early to blast gaps through them, but from the photos no one was even sure if they *were* reefs.

The swimmers soon discovered the truth when O'Leary ran into a patch of floating sea grass. They halted their careful grid pattern survey to investigate the area more thoroughly and soon confirmed that it was the drifting vegetation that had shown up in those photos. There was no sign of a blocking reef here … an important point to note in their reports, Forsythe thought.

The work was physically demanding, and the swimmers were kept on edge by the need to be alert to any sign of movement or activity on shore, but mostly it was just tedious and difficult.

Eventually the two parties came together near the center of the beach and compared notes in hushed voices. Both pairs of swimmers had encountered the floating grass, and Forsythe and Barker each had slates filled up with data on individual obstacles, the same types of underwater barriers reported by Schroeder's swimmers off Peleliu. So once again the news was good. They could let Third 'Phib know that the approaches to Yap were no more difficult than those at Peleliu.

Treading water, Forsythe scanned the shoreline longingly. He badly wanted to follow up on Schroeder's desire to scout the beaches themselves, but the hydrographic survey had taken longer than he'd hoped for and the allotted two hours would soon be over. They couldn't risk letting Phelps head back without them, nor did Forsythe fancy a run-in with Commander Fitzgerald over another recon swim that ran longer than intended. With a last reluctant sigh he signaled his men to head back for the rubber boat.

They rejoined Phelps without incident, clambering back aboard and stripping off their fins before taking up paddles and reeling in the anchor line. In a few minutes they were approaching the rendezvous point, and O'Leary's sharp eyes soon picked out the wand of a periscope a few hundred yards to port. Forsythe waited until he was sure the periscope was aimed in their direction and then gave another flashlight signal. Then they waited, alone in the ocean, for *Burrfish* to surface and retrieve them.

Chief Ballard supervised the party that helped recover the swimmers and their boat. While his work crew brought the raft aboard, Forsythe and the others headed below.

They barely had time to close and dog the hatch behind Ballard and his men before the Klaxon sounded and the ship's announcer started blaring a warning. "All hands, all hands, diving stations! Prepare to dive!"

The UDT men grabbed stanchions and other available handholds as the loudspeaker gave a final warning and water began to rush into the ballast tanks. Radar had picked up a surface contact, coming in fast. Aiken didn't make the ride down gentle, and the sub was soon maneuvering in a twisting course that made their footing uncertain.

Apparently they'd had a narrow escape. Did that mean their luck had changed? Or was it a sign of trouble to come?

Alexander Forsythe peered out into the darkness and cursed silently. According to his watch, Schroeder, O'Leary, and White should have returned over half an hour earlier. The night was wearing on, and he couldn't keep waiting here much longer.

It was the second night since the swim off the south beaches, and *Burrfish* had moved on to the eastern side of Yap to carry out further reconnaissance work, still dodging contact with the Japanese as the Americans tried to carry out their mission.

Tonight had been Schroeder's turn at swimming again, but at the last minute Fitzgerald had ordered Forsythe to accompany the team. Concerned that Schroeder would again exceed his orders and try to scout the shoreline, the commander had given strict orders to keep to the mission plan and to the scheduled rendezvous.

Rather than replace Schroeder or one of his men on the swim, though, Forsythe had chosen to take over for Chief Ballard and remain with the rubber boat. He resented Fitzgerald's interference and refused to do any more to disrupt Schroeder's team, which had already proven it could function effectively without any prodding from above.

So Forsythe had waited with the raft this time, wishing he could be out there making the swim and fuming at the whole situation. The team had paddled inshore until they reached the outer edge of a line of reefs about four hundred yards from the beaches. A few tiny islets dotted the reef line, identified on their charts as Tobaru, Lebinau, and Leng, bits of rock and coral that barely qualified as land when the tide was in. Once they'd dropped anchor by the reef, Schroeder and his men had gone into the water. Tonight it was much rougher than it had been when Forsythe's team had gone in. The choppy seas were an advantage in some respects, since It would be that much harder for any Japanese ashore to spot anything among the breakers, but it made the swim that much more difficult. Forsythe had been especially concerned for John O'Leary, who had filled in for one of his men last time out and was now making his third consecutive swim of the recon mission. He was a powerful swimmer and a capable scout, but Forsythe was afraid he might tire too quickly in the heavy seas.

As things worked out, though, O'Leary wasn't the problem. The swimmers had been gone for only fifteen minutes when Forsythe had seen two figures swimming across the reef toward him against the wind and the breakers. When they reached the raft, they proved to be Bob White, one of the ex-OSS men, and Mason, who was part of the Waipio group. In hushed tones they had explained that Mason had found the going too tough out there. Not accustomed to so much swimming under adverse conditions, he had decided he'd be more of a hindrance to the mission than a help, and White had been detailed to get him back to the raft safely.

Forsythe's immediate thought was to replace Mason and swim back out with White, but the Waipio man looked too exhausted to handle the boat if the need arose. Ideally the raft was supposed to stay put by the reef, but if there was real trouble inshore — an injury that precluded swimming out, for instance — the coxswain left behind was supposed to take the rubber boat in to assist the swimmers. If Schroeder and his men needed the raft, they'd need to know they could rely on the coxswain to get in and out quickly. Forsythe wasn't sure they could count on Mason for that, and according to White, Schroeder had said the same thing when he'd ordered them back.

So, reluctantly, he'd helped Mason aboard and watched White begin the return trip toward the island, staring after the man until long after he was lost from view.

Of all the bad omens on this jinxed mission, he had thought at the time, this one was the worst.

More than two hours had passed since then. Forsythe had told himself that it would take longer for the reduced team to finish up their work, that the sea conditions would complicate the matter even further, so he hadn't been all that concerned when they weren't back on time. But as the minutes ticked by his worries grew. The sub ouldd only remain at the rendezvous coordinates for so long. If they were too late getting back, dawn might catch them in the middle of a recovery op and *Burrfish* would be at the mercy of any Japanese ships or planes in the area.

He checked his watch again. Forty-five minutes overdue.

For a moment he considered going over the side and swimming across the reef to look for them but rejected the idea. He didn't even know exactly where they had started their survey, much less where they were now, and it was foolish to break up the unit even further now that part of it was already missing. It would be so easy for a lone swimmer to miss the others in the dark...

"Mason," he said, coming to a sudden decision. "Grab a paddle. They might have missed us and hit a different part of the reef on their way out. Let's do a sweep."

"Aye, aye, sir," Mason said. He sounded sheepish. They'd hardly spoken the whole time they had been waiting, but Forsythe had the feeling Mason blamed himself for fouling things up. And to be frank, Forsythe felt that way too. But it wasn't really Mason's fault. The real blame attached to whoever had decided they could put the Waipio men on an even footing with trained OSS and UDT swimmers.

He raised anchor and grabbed the other paddle, and the two men guided the boat along the reef line. Every so often Forsythe would signal a halt, then scan the water and the distant shoreline for some sign of the three missing men. But all they could see were a few lights moving along shore. There was no comfort in that. If Japanese patrols had discovered Schroeder's men, it might all be over…

But Forsythe wouldn't give up even with that grim idea gnawing at the back of his mind. They continued along the reef until Mason finally pointed out that they were pushing the end of the safety margin tacked on to the rendezvous schedule. They still had a long paddle out, and if they were late, there would be more than three men missing.

"Maybe they figured we'd head back on schedule, sir," Mason suggested hopefully. "If they knew they were running late, they might have tried to swim straight out to the sub."

Forsythe didn't answer immediately. It was a long swim even by UDT standards, and he doubted Schroeder would have risked it. The chief knew that Forsythe would understand if they were slow finishing their survey with three men trying to do the work of four and the sea conditions running against them, so he would at least have checked the reef first. Even if they'd lost their way swimming out, they would have paralleled the reef until they found familiar landmarks like Tobaru and Leng.

Still, it was possible…

"Okay," he said at length. "We'll head for the rendezvous. Just pray they're out there waiting for us."

As he and Mason steered the raft out to sea, Forsythe knew how hollow his words really sounded.

"They'll try for the reef again tonight, sir," Forsythe said urgently. "We *have* to be there to pick them up."

Commander Fitzgerald looked over at Aiken, the sub's skipper, who shook his head. "The decision is final, Lieutenant," Fitzgerald said. "I don't like it any better than you do, but I won't authorize another swim."

"Not a swim. Just let me take the boat out there and look for them."

"Lieutenant, we both admire your loyalty to your men," Aiken said. "But we have to face realities here." He started ticking points off on his fingers. "One, we know the Japanese are wary. Their radar was on all afternoon, and they might have already picked us up when we were trying to search for your men this afternoon. I doubt it, but it's possible. Two, we haven't any idea if your men are even alive out there. They might have gotten lost, or captured, or maybe they just couldn't handle the water conditions. Your man Mason certainly couldn't."

Forsythe turned a bitter look on Fitzgerald. "Mason wasn't a trained UDT swimmer," he said. "Schroeder and the others were. They wouldn't have had any trouble out there."

"Be that as it may, we don't *know* they're alive," Aiken said harshly. "Three, if they were captured the Japanese could very well know everything by now. They could be out there waiting for a rescue attempt. Or half the damned Japanese Navy could be closing in as we speak to try to pin us against the island. It's just too damned risky, Forsythe."

"I'm not risking any more of our men to save three who are probably beyond help anyway," Fitzgerald added.

"And I'm not going to risk my whole command," Aiken said. "I'm sorry. *Burrfish* has more work to do before the invasion flotilla gets here, and I'm going to order us to get started. The matter is closed."

Forsythe stood up slowly, crushed. "I see," he said quietly. "If I were in command here, we'd not abandon men to the enemy. Sir."

"You're not in command here," Fitzgerald said. "And your attitude is dangerously close to insubordination. I'm inclined to put it down to the strain, but don't say anything we'll both regret later. You hear me, mister?"

Forsythe was slow to answer. Schroeder, White, and O'Leary were out there somewhere, and it grated on him to even consider leaving these waters without at least trying to find out what had happened to them. But this was one situation where good breeding and high-placed contacts were worthless. Aiken and Fitzgerald were in charge, and that was all there was to it

Finally he gave a curt nod. "Aye, aye, sir," he said.

As he left the wardroom, he was seething inside. He felt helpless for the first time in his life, helpless and bitter and guilty that he hadn't found the men himself before the senior officers had been able to forbid further searches.

Someday, he told himself, someday he would have a command of his own, and when that day came he wouldn't let anyone keep him from doing what was right.

*

Red Schroeder heard the patrol long before anyone caught sight of it. He tapped O'Leary and White on their shoulders and signaled for them to remain quiet and still. Maybe the Japanese soldiers would pass by without noticing them.

Maybe…

The three Americans hugged the scant cover of the sand dune they'd taken refuge behind. On three sides there was nothing but open beach too wide to cross without attracting attention, while on the fourth side, behind them, was open sea. Schroeder's instinct was to seek refuge there, in the UDT's natural element, but in the mid-morning sun not even a UDT man would risk swimming right under the eyes of the enemy. Not when they had no place to go.

He wondered again, as he'd wondered a dozen times since they had taken refuge on the island, if they might have had a better chance with one of those underwater breathing rigs Forsythe had talked about back on Maui.

They had missed the rendezvous with the rubber boat Friday night, just plain overstayed their time limit trying to wrap up the beach survey. By the time they'd finally reached the reef, Forsythe, Mason, and the raft were all gone. Schroeder didn't blame the lieutenant for that. The scouting mission had just taken too long with Mason out of the picture and the water conditions so difficult, and there was no way Forsythe could have lingered out there long enough for the swimmers to make it back. With dawn already coming up on the eastern horizon

Schroeder had finally decided the three of them would have to take the chance of hiding ashore. They couldn't remain in the water all day, after all, and there was no hope of locating the submarine once it had left the original rendezvous point.

Somehow they had lasted all the way through the day on Saturday, hiding on shore within sight of the sea. White had suggested they'd be safer if they got under cover in the jungle beyond the beach, but Schroeder, tempted as he was, had finally decided against it. If they got into that tangle and lost their bearings, they'd be dead. They might blunder into the Japanese before they even knew the enemy was around, or they might get so thoroughly misdirected that they'd never find their way back to this same stretch of beach again. So they'd taken the risk of remaining on the beach, sheltered from view by a sand dune.

Saturday night, hungry and thirsty and feeling the effects of a long day in the sun, they had still found the will to swim back out to the reef in hopes of finding help. Schroeder had been fairly sure the *Burrfish* would have moved on, but he didn't share his fears with the others. No doubt Forsythe had argued in favor of going after them; he wouldn't willingly leave them without making some kind of rescue effort. But Fitzgerald and Aiken would have been right to overrule him, Schroeder told himself. They had no way of knowing if the swimmers had been captured or if the Japanese defenses were now alerted to the sub's presence.

So he hadn't been surprised when a night of paddling around the reef had yielded no sign of the sub or the raft or a follow-up survey party.

Dawn had again driven them ashore, knowing their situation was getting hopeless. Even if *Burrfish* was still in the immediate area she wouldn't stay indefinitely. In fact, it was probably already too late for the three Americans, and Schroeder had begun to wonder, inwardly, whether their best course was to surrender, or to try something desperate like attempting the jungles or taking the easy way out with their diving knives. That was a decision he wouldn't want to make for the others, but as for himself, death seemed preferable to the uncertainties of life in a Japanese POW camp.

The sounds were getting closer, sand crunching under boots and the jabber of voices speaking words he couldn't understand. O'Leary was nearest to the crest of the dune, and at Schroeder's signal raised his head just enough to peer over the top. He ducked down again right away. He made a quick hand signal. *Ten men. Approaching.*

The three men didn't speak or exchange any further signals, but almost as one their hands moved to draw their diving knives from their sheaths. Despite the danger, Schroeder almost chuckled aloud at the thought of the Americans challenging the Japanese garrison on Yap armed with nothing but knives and sheer grit. Everyone knew that the American swimmers were as crazy as they were tough, but those odds were insane even by UDT standards.

Knives held ready, the three Americans waited on their bellies, frozen in place. Hoping, praying…

A figure appeared at the top of the dune, rifle slung over one shoulder, fingers starting to undo the buttons of his uniform pants. The soldier caught sight of the UDT men and stopped in his tracks, gaping down at them for long seconds as if too startled to believe the evidence of his own eyes.

O'Leary's knife glittered in the sunlight as he surged to his feet to attack the man, but the soldier started backpedaling and stumbled back out of sight, giving voice to a harsh, guttural shout as he vanished from view behind the dune.

"Make for the water!" Schroeder shouted, and the three UDT men sprinted for the surf.

But the *snick-snick-snick* of rifle bolts brought them to a halt. A voice behind them cried out "*Tomare! Ugoku na!*" Schroeder didn't need to speak the language to know the meaning of the command. He stopped, then slowly turned to face the ring of Japanese soldiers who now stood along the top of the dune, their rifles held at the ready.

"*Buki o sutero!*" one of the soldiers said, gesturing sharply with his rifle. "*Te o agero!*"

Schroeder dropped his knife, then raised his hands over his head. His two companions followed suit.

As their captors advanced, Schroeder's thoughts were bitter. He had failed after all, failed in his mission, failed to protect his tiny command, failed even to kill himself rather than face capture...

But out of bitterness he felt a stirring of stubborn determination. The Japanese might take his body prisoner, but never his mind, his heart, or his spirit. He'd fight on with those as long as there was breath in his body, the way a UDT man should...

CHAPTER 18

Saturday, 26 August 1944
Marine City, Michigan

Frank Rand tugged at the sleeve of his dress blues, more nervous and uncertain today than he'd been facing the hostile beaches of Normandy or the calculated sadism of Hell Week. His stomach was one great knot, and it was all he could do to keep from pacing back and forth to try to work off his agitation.

"Calm down, Raider," Stan Kowalski said with a grin.

He, too, was in his dress blues, but unlike Rand he managed to look relaxed and even reasonably comfortable. "It'll all be over soon."

"That's what they tell death row inmates on the way to the chair," Rand said glumly.

"Hey, man, I'm not the one who told you to go out and get married."

Rand fixed him with a steely glare. "Actually, the way I remember it, you did."

"Oh, yeah." Kowalski's smile broadened. "See what you get when you ask for free advice?"

Rand laughed, but it sounded forced even to him. Everything had happened so fast. Had he really proposed to Nancy only three weeks ago? It seemed like an eternity since that rainy evening at Fort Pierce...

First he had written a letter which he promptly tore up. Then he'd phoned her instead and blurted out his proposal with hardly any preamble. Her "Yes" had left him speechless, and the rest of the call was nothing but "I love yous" and "I can't believe its." Later in the evening he'd written again, trying to be practical this time by spelling out everything they'd need to do or consider before they could actually make the marriage happen. Rand's class had been scheduled for a late August graduation and was sure to be posted overseas within weeks. Rand had felt overwhelmed by everything they'd need to get done if they were to have a wedding before he shipped out, and after he'd mailed the letter he started worrying that he'd been too pessimistic, too blunt. He'd spent days afraid Nancy would think he'd changed his mind — except for the times he was wondering if that wasn't exactly what he should have done.

And then, miraculously, things had started coming together. The orders for the graduating class of Demolitioneers were cut, and there was a two-week gap between the end of training and the date they were to report to the West Coast for transport to Hawaii. Rand's request for leave was approved. So Rand could make it to a late August wedding, if one could be thrown together with such a short lead time.

Luckily Christopher Brown, Nancy's father, was a rich and influential man by the standards of Saint Clair County, Michigan, and he had long stood as both a patron and a genuine friend to Rand. He took charge of the arrangements and shamelessly pulled strings to make everything fall in place, from the church and the minister to the honeymoon plans and all the rest of the myriad details. As letter followed letter recording the breakneck pace of the plans, Rand often found himself wondering how Nancy's mother was bearing up to these rapid-fire developments. The very epitome of propriety and good breeding, she probably found the hasty wedding of her daughter scandalous.

No doubt Louise Brown's opinion of Frank Rand as a son-in-law was no better now than it had been when he put aside his plans for attending Annapolis to join the Navy as an enlisted man and go off to the war...

So now the day was finally at hand. Rand had traveled north by train with Kowalski and Jennings in tow. The other Jaguars had all wanted to come, but there were other demands on their time in the brief period before they headed to the Pacific. Kowalski had to be there, since Rand had asked him to be best man. The rest of the team had cut cards, and Jennings had won the draw to represent them, giving rise to inevitable comments about what effect the Jinx might have on the happy couple.

The Navy men had spent the night at the Browns' rambling old house near the edge of town. Rand's poor relations with his father had made a stay at home too awkward to even consider, and Mr. Brown had refused to listen when Rand had suggested he do what he'd done the last time he visited, sleep on a cot in back of the workshop at Brown's Marine.

The whole situation with his father cast the one chilly shadow that marred the day for Rand. He had always pictured himself being married with his parents looking on, but Elizabeth Rand was dead and Howard Rand hadn't spoken a kind word to or about his son since the day she'd died in an auto accident, distracted and concerned over the news of the invasion of Sicily, where she knew Frank was serving in the dangerous Scouts and Raiders.

Rand glanced at his watch. Ten more minutes until the ceremony was supposed to start. Just time enough...

He looked across the room at Kowalski. "Look, Ski, there's something I have to do. Hold the fort for me here. I'll be back in a few minutes."

He slipped out a rear entrance to the church and made his way down the hill to the cemetery. Too late he wished he'd brought flowers; he'd have to come back later with the biggest bouquet he could find. She had loved flowers…

He found her tombstone and stood looking down at it, his mind a whirl of conflicting emotions. In just a few minutes there would be a new Mrs. Rand in Marine City, wife instead of mother. Would Nancy really take comfort from being married to him? Or would she end up as worried and fearful as Elizabeth Rand had been because Frank was somewhere overseas, in harm's way? Stan Kowalski's advice had sounded so right that day when Rand had screwed up his courage to propose, but now reality was staring him full in the face and all his doubts were back again…

"She would be proud of you," a gruff, rasping voice said behind him. "And happy to see you settle down with Nancy this way."

Rand turned, startled. His surprise gave way to a flash of anger as he took in the bent frame, the white hair, the cane gripped tight in the man's left hand. A single rose was in the other hand. Walking slowly, awkwardly, on the prosthetic leg that was a lasting reminder of the horrors of Belleau Wood, Howard Rand stepped forward and laid the rose upon the grave. His son stepped back, still angry at having his own time with his mother cut short, but feeling sad at the same time to see how much the elder Rand had aged in just a year.

"I … I just wanted a minute. To be with her before…" Rand's words trailed off awkwardly. He shifted from one foot to the other, feeling like a schoolboy caught in some misdeed. "I didn't know *you'd* be here. I'll go."

"No … wait a minute." The older man caught his arm as he started to brush past. "There's a lot of things that haven't been said between us…"

"I think everything was said."

"Let me finish!" his father said with a trace of the anger Rand remembered so well from their last encounter. "Let me finish. When your mother died, I felt the same way I did the day they told me the leg had to come off. Like I'd lost a part of myself and could never get it back. But then I did the stupidest thing I've ever done in too damn many stupid years on this Earth. I turned right around and cut off another piece of me the day I drove you away, Frank. I blamed you because you weren't there. And because it was easier to blame someone than it was to think about going on without her." He took a step back. "I'm sorry for that, son. Sorrier than I could ever say. Things can never be the way they were when she was alive, but I don't want them to be the way they've been this last year anymore either."

Rand didn't know what to do or say. They stood staring at each other for a long moment. Then the elder Rand stuck out his hand, and Frank took it, surprised at the firmness of the grip. They stepped closer together, and somehow the handshake became an embrace between father and son. "I said some pretty rotten things that night, too, Dad," Rand said. "I blamed you for everything that went wrong with my life because my own head wasn't screwed on straight…"

"Like father, like son, eh, Frank?" His father chuckled, a dry rasp that ended in a cough. "Is it too late to hope for an invitation to my only son's wedding?"

"It could never be too late for that, Dad," Rand said.

"Good. Because this is one day when I want everyone to know exactly how proud I am to have you as a son. I know I should have said that when you were younger. I always felt it, but I never knew how to tell you before. I'm proud of you, Frank. *Damn* proud of you. Never forget that."

Together, father and son walked slowly up the hill toward the church. And Rand realized that somewhere along the way all his doubts had vanished like they'd never been.

Jennings met them outside the church and offered to take care of finding a place for the elder Rand while Frank rejoined his best man. They had little time left before the ceremony, and Kowalski was just starting to get agitated over Rand's absence. They checked each other's uniforms one last time, and Rand made sure Kowalski still had the ring he'd invested most of his savings in at a jewelry shop in Fort Pierce. Then they took their places before the altar.

Rand studied the audience as they waited. Mr. Brown had done him proud, making sure the church was crowded with Rand's friends from school as well as the prominent families and business associates who were there to honor Brown and his daughter. He spotted Mrs. Ketteridge, still wearing black in mourning for her son, sitting next to Louise Brown in the front row. And Howard Rand was sitting across the aisle, looking proud and somehow younger than he'd seemed outside, as if ending the rift with his son had stripped away years in a matter of moments.

There was a stir by the door, and the organist struck the first chord of the wedding march. Rand swallowed. There was no backing out now.

One of Nancy's young cousins led the way as flower girl, followed by a pair of bridesmaids Rand recognized vaguely as friends of hers from high school. Then came his sister, Sue, the maid of honor, pretty enough to be a bride herself...

Then Nancy came in on her father's arm, and Rand couldn't take his eyes off her. She was wearing a gown that had belonged to her grandmother, all white lace and veil and long train. They advanced down the aisle with a measured, stately tread, until at last Christopher Brown handed Nancy off to Rand and stepped away.

Rand was hardly conscious of anything except for her. Even the words of the ceremony, the exchange of vows, were like some distant backdrop. He heard himself say "I do" almost as if a part of him was a spectator. But when Nancy's turn came, and she spoke those same two words, they filled his entire world. They were married…

"…I now pronounce you man and wife," he heard. "You may kiss the bride."

He lifted her veil, and her face was radiant under it. Their lips touched. The kiss lasted a long, long time.

The organist struck up the recessional and they started down the aisle together, only to be stopped in the vestibule by Jennings.

"Hold up, there, Raider," the young third class said with a grin. "Something's not quite right here."

"What are you talking about, kid?" he demanded. "What's going on?"

Kowalski came up beside him. "Well, Frank, the kid and me got to thinking. I mean, when the jarheads have a wedding, they send the bride and groom out under an arch of crossed swords, and we kinda thought you ought to have something like that for your wedding, too."

"Swords?" He stared at them. Neither was carrying a sword, but Jennings did have a small bag at his feet.

"Well," Kowalski said. "Not quite. Kid?"

Jennings picked up the bag and drew out a pair of diving knives with a flourish. Kowalski took one and stepped back, holding it in front of his face in a mock salute.

"Oh, no," Rand groaned. A few of the civilians behind them were laughing. So was Nancy.

"Here goes," Kowalski said. "PRE-sent ... *arms!*"

And the two UDT men extended their arms to cross the knives overhead. Rand and Nancy squeezed between them, and a few of the guests started applauding.

They emerged into the bright afternoon sunshine amid a shower of rice and stood for a moment at the top of the steps. Rand could hardly believe that any of it had been real.

As they started toward the Browns' big Oldsmobile at the curb — a loan by Nancy's father for the day, since Rand didn't have a car of his own — Nancy turned back to toss the bouquet. Sue caught it, blushing, and there were more laughs, especially from the people who knew her best. She'd always been popular, but everyone knew about her unconventional ideas of finding a job instead of a husband.

He held the car door for Nancy, then went around to the driver's side and got in. For a moment he just sat there, hands on the wheel. Then, finally, he turned to face her. "Mrs. Rand..." he said quietly, liking the way it sounded. "Mrs. Frank Rand ... have I told you today that I love you?"

Frank Rand had stood on this same railway platform three times before, and each time had marked the end of one chapter of his life and the beginning of something entirely new. His first visit to the Port Huron station had been the day he'd left home to start boot camp, abandoning all of his previous plans and saying goodbye to friends and family. The second time was after he had come home to recover from wounds received in

253

North Africa and he was on his way to become one of the Scouts and Raiders. Then, just over a year ago, he had stood here a third time, after his mother's death and the quarrel with his father and the night he'd promised to marry Nancy. That time the train had taken him to Fort Pierce and his stint as an instructor for the NCDU school, a stop on his way to England and the bloody sands of Omaha Beach.

Now he was leaving again, but this time he knew that the greatest change in his life lay behind him, not ahead. Marriage had already altered him in ways he could hardly understand or believe.

The honeymoon at the Browns' vacation cabin near Port Huron had gone by all too quickly. Kowalski and Jennings had made plenty of ribald jokes about how they'd never seemed to come out of the little cottage. In fact, though, passion had only been a part of what kept them in seclusion. By mutual but unspoken consent they had tried to cram as much time together into those few days as they possibly could, not just making love but sharing their thoughts, their feelings, their lives. Nothing in Rand's previous life had prepared him for the feeling of completeness that marriage had brought … or for the torture he was feeling now as he got ready to leave her.

She was standing with him now, fighting back tears, and at that moment Rand wanted nothing more than to take her in his arms and tell her he would never leave her side. But the train would be pulling away from the platform soon, and Rand would be aboard it, and nothing could change that now.

The platform was crowded, not just with friends and family but with well-wishers who had turned out to see him off. Stories of some of his Normandy exploits had spread around town, and his wedding to the daughter of one of the area's best-known citizens had only added to his local fame. It made it all the harder to give Nancy a proper farewell, especially when she wasn't the only one he needed to say good-bye to.

"Well, son," Christopher Brown said heartily, clapping him on the shoulder with a powerful hand. "I know you don't want to leave, and that makes me all the prouder, knowing you're off to do your duty. Plant a keg of powder under Hirohito and set it off with my regards, Frank!"

"I'll give it my best shot, sir," he answered, forcing a grin. Nancy would continue to live with her parents until he came home, and the Browns planned to build a house for them by the time he was back. Even Mrs. Brown, who had said her good-byes earlier and stayed at home, seemed ready to accept Rand as a son-in-law now. He owed them so much, and he wasn't sure he could even start to pay them back for all they had done. "And thank you again … for everything."

Brown pumped his hand and then withdrew, and Rand turned. His father and sister were waiting there, and Sue Rand stepped forward quickly to give him a hug and a sisterly peck on the cheek. "Come back, big brother. Come back as soon as you can, and safe." Then she was gone, before he could even respond.

"I've already told you how I feel about you, son," Howard Rand said over the noise of the crowd. "And you know I'm not very good with words anyway. But I did want to give you something before you left, something to show you how proud you've made me. Something that's meant a lot to me over the years … almost as much as you." He thrust a wooden box into Rand's hands.

Frank undid the clasp and opened the hinged lid. Inside, nestled in velvet, was his father's old M1911A1 pistol. A gift from the men he had saved at Belleau Wood, it had their names engraved on a presentation plaque. The elder Rand had always cherished it, and Frank had first learned to shoot, years ago, using this very weapon.

"Dad … Dad, not your Colt. How can I take that?"

"You say 'thank you' and you put it in your seabag with the rest of your things, that's how." The old man smiled. "It's time to pass it on, Frank. I don't know how many more years I've got, but whether I'm around for one year or for fifty, the Colt's yours now."

"'Thank you' doesn't seem like enough by a long shot, Dad."

"Then add a promise to me, son. Promise you'll keep going the way you've already started. That you'll always do your duty. That's good enough for me."

"I will, Dad. I will." They hugged, and the old man limped slowly away. Rand watched him, holding back tears. Sue had already told him that Doc Mitchell didn't expect him to last another year. No one had told his father, but it was obvious that Howard Rand already knew.

He hesitated, wanting to run after his father and say more. But there was so little time left, and someone else he had to spend those last moments with. Rand took Nancy in his arms. "It seems like we're always saying good-bye," he said softly. "And I'm sick of that word…"

"Then don't say it this time," she told him. "Just kiss me one more time. The only words I want from you are 'I love you.'"

Their lips came together in a long, lingering kiss, and when it was over Rand still held her close. His mouth brushed her ear. "I love you, Nancy Rand," he whispered. "And I'll come back to you. That's a promise…"

She released him reluctantly, tears sparkling in her eyes. Rand looked down at her, unwilling to turn away, to take that first step that would carry him away from her and back to the war.

A hand closed on his shoulder. "Come on, Raider," Kowalski said. "They ain't planning on holding up this train just for you."

"I love you, Nancy," he said again, then turned to climb aboard the railway car. Kowalski and Jennings were both there to give him a hand up the steps.

That was the other thing that was different today. All those other times he had left alone, but this time his teammates were with him.

And that almost made the leaving bearable.

CHAPTER 19

Saturday, 16 September 1944
Red Beach
Angaur Island

The UDT, Tangretti thought, had changed a hell of a lot since he and Richardson had been with UDT-1 at Kwajalein. He crouched in the bottom of the Higgins boat, packed in shoulder to shoulder with the other swimmers of UDT-8 as the LCP raced toward the distant beach, sending clouds of spray over the narrow bow ramp each time it slammed into a wave. An explosion sounded somewhere beyond the wooden bulwark pressed against his back. His bare feet rested on a large pile of canvas satchels piled on the bottom of the well deck, each containing several pounds of tetrytol and several yards of primacord. An inflated black rubber raft was lashed athwartships over the Higgins boat's stern.

Tangretti was wearing khaki-colored swim trunks and a belt for his knife. His mask was hanging by its strap around his neck. He'd left the beaded chain that held his dog tags and the souvenir Japanese bullet he'd caught in the waters off Kwajalein aboard the APD, and he felt a bit naked without it. Of course, "the naked warriors" was the new nickname given to the Teams by the press Stateside, along with "frogmen" and a number of sillier terms.

With his leg bare, the scar on his right leg a few inches above his knee was fiercely, angrily visible, a red welt that still showed the pucker and stretch marks of the sutures that had held it together.

That infection he'd picked up had guaranteed him a bed on a ward in the hospital in Falmouth for four weeks, followed by two weeks more in Portsmouth Naval Hospital in Virginia. After that, it had been touch-and-go as to whether he would even be allowed to stay in the Navy, much less in Navy demo.

Dismissed at last from the hospital at the end of July, he'd been given TAD orders to a naval headquarters detachment across the Elizabeth River in Norfolk. Tangretti had pulled a lot of strings to be assigned to the teams, including in the end a long letter to Lieutenant Commander Joseph Galloway, in Washington. Galloway was the officer on the Navy's special operations staff who'd wangled him his original assignment with the CDUs in England, and he'd known about an opening with UDT-8, then in training at Maui.

More than anything else, though, the strings Tangretti had had to pull had been his own, with a vicious, self-imposed regimen of push-ups and sit-ups and long, long runs along the sandy beaches east of Norfolk as soon as he was out of the hospital. By the time he'd joined Team Eight at Maui, he'd been pretty sure that he was at peak physical condition.

At Maui, though, the runs had been longer, and he found that Navy Demolition now emphasized long, long ocean swims. The one-mile qualifying swim in the choppy waters off Maui had nearly finished him.

Somehow, though, he'd made it.

"So, Gator!" the UDT man to his right said with a grin. "I guess this ain't much like Normandy, huh?"

"I was just thinking that, Slim," Tangretti replied. "We never did much swimming with the old CDU."

"Slim" was anything but slim. Standing over six feet tall, almost as tall as the lanky Tangretti, he weighed over 220 and was constructed head to foot of solidly packed muscle. His name was Edward Simmons, and he was a chief boatswain's mate born and raised in a small town on the Texas Gulf coast. As a BM1, Slim had been aboard the aircraft carrier *Hornet* during the now-famous Doolittle raid against Japan in April of 1942, and two months later he'd been at Midway. He'd had his ship shot out from under him, as he liked to say, at the Battle of Santa Cruz that October.

Rescued from the sea off Guadalcanal, he'd put in for a new ship. For the next year and a half, however, he'd been assigned to shore duty, working in the ordnance department at Pearl Harbor. That, he claimed, had been a mind-numbing exercise in boredom and gold-plated bureaucratic stupidity that had led to his repeatedly requesting combat duty, extra-hazardous duty, *any* kind of duty that would get him away from the lead-bottomed brass hats at Pearl. At last, in April of 1944, he'd been ordered to report to the Navy Demolition training command at Fort Pierce, Florida. After that, he'd been sent back to Hawaii, where he'd been assigned to the newly created UDT-8. At the UDT training center on Maui, Teams Eight, Nine, and Ten were sent through the UDT's advanced combat training course, given instruction in carrying out hydrographic surveys, and, of course, made to swim impossible distances, preparing them for the new and markedly different type of warfare that they would face in the Pacific.

"I wouldn't've put up with that CDU shit at Normandy for anything," Chief Simmons said, grinning. He reached up above his shoulder and gave the wooden hull of the LCP(R) a sharp couple of raps. "Give me a fast boat and a quick run into the beach anytime! The damned Japanese can't hit a thing if it's moving."

Tangretti reached down to the deck and picked up his swim fins, long rubber flippers that had only recently started reaching the teams. "We never had stuff like this at Normandy, either. Of course, if we'd tried running up the beach in these things, we'd've all fallen flat on our faces."

He didn't add that once, at Fort Pierce, he'd nearly drowned experimenting with the things. Those fins had been stiff and unbending, clumsy devices — and at that time none of the demo men had known how to use them. These were a newer model, more flexible ... and the teams at Maui had been training with them ever since Lieutenant Commander Chapman had introduced them.

"She-it," another UDT man drawled from the other side of the pile of explosives. He was a second class mineman named Frank Kelly, from Montgomery, Alabama. "I heard they made you guys wear rubber suits! What the hell was that like?"

"Hot and uncomfortable," Tangretti replied, shaking his head. "The brass thought we were going to face gas on the beach, so they issued us rubberized coveralls that we were supposed to wear with helmets, gas masks, gloves, and boots." He remembered his panic when, struggling ashore on Omaha Beach wearing all that gear, he'd stepped into a seemingly bottomless shell hole and nearly drowned. He still didn't care for deep water, especially deep *dark* water, but he'd made himself face it to stay with the teams. "I think most of us ditched the monkey suits as soon as we got ashore," he said. "You can't blow it up if you can't see or feel it."

"That's for damned sure," Kelly said. "If'n I learned anything in this here man's Navy, it's that when you need somethin', it ain't available, and if you *don't* need somethin', it's issued to you with three sets of spares, and you damned well better use 'em all or the CO'll damned well know why!"

"Ah, it's the fuckin' pencil pushers that'll lose the war for us," Simmons replied. "They get their little brown noses so far up some admiral's fat ass they can't see for looking. And the admirals are even worse. If something doesn't fit in with their tight-assed little picture of how the war ought to be, they don't look. They don't *want* to look."

"You sound like a man of experience, Chief," Tangretti said.

"Believe me, buddy, I am. I've had just about all I can take of officers and their shit-for-brains and their brown-nosing and their pretty gold stripes." He glanced across the boat and grinned at Lieutenant j.g. Clarence R. Dayton, Third Platoon's leader, who was listening to his tirade with evident interest. "*Except*, of course," Slim said, "for those rare and upstanding young officers who actually deign to rough it with their men!"

"She-it," Kelly said. "Only officers I ever met who was any good was the ones in demo. What you say t'that, Gator?"

"I've known some good officers," Tangretti said. The admission stung, deep down, as he remembered Richardson. The guy had had his faults, but he'd been a good man, and a damned good friend. "Especially the ones who went through the grind at Fort Pierce."

"Yeah, Fort Pierce officers are okay," Kelly agreed. "Leastwise when they ain't puttin' on airs, eh, Lieutenant?"

Dayton shrugged. He was a painfully young-looking man with sandy hair and fair skin that had a ragged, checkerboard appearance, part pink sunburn, part white patches of peeling skin. "You catch me putting on airs, Frank, and you have my permission to toss me over the side."

"Sounds fair, Lieutenant. We'll do jus' that, and that ain't no threat. That there's a promise!"

"Sounds like you'd better toe the mark, Lieutenant," Slim said. "Otherwise, you're gonna get wet!"

The others laughed, and Tangretti joined in, forcing down the lingering pain of his memory of Snake Richardson. Months ago, right after Normandy, Tangretti had blamed himself for Richardson's death. Since then, however, his feelings had been slowly changing, the blame shifting from his own shoulders to that vague and ill-identified group of shadowy figures in command whom enlisted personnel referred to as "the brass."

In fact, his growing bitterness was an indictment of the system more than of any individual people. Men like Richardson or Dayton went through the same training, the same discomfort and bad food and long swims and rugged PT as their men, and there was no difference Tangretti could see between them, except that the officers usually had more education behind them. But the *system* allowed men seated in comfortable offices as far from the front lines as Washington to make decisions that the men under fire were going to have to live with ... or die from.

The system had failed at Omaha. The Army-Navy engineering teams ashore had been operating under such precise and detailed orders that when the men found themselves under fire on the beach, separated from their units and from their equipment, they'd been forced to make do with whatever they could scrounge from the battlefield, inventing a new plan of operation from scratch. And, inevitably, the system had failed to recognize the possibility of the unforeseen ... such as the soldiers huddled in the illusory shelter of the beach obstacles that the CDUs were supposed to destroy. Again, the men on the beach had had to adapt and overcome, often against impossible odds.

Tangretti and Richardson had both been shot while trying to blow a hole in a roadblock that was supposed to be the responsibility of an Army engineering team. By the time the CDUs had made it up the beach to the sea wall at Omaha, however, there'd been damned little distinction left between

Army and Navy, between Navy demo man and Army engineer. They'd all worked together, those who'd made it that far, to get the job done, whatever it took.

But by rights, Snake should never have even been near that roadblock.

"Well, you can throw me in the drink later, guys," Dayton said, standing in the boat. "Looks to me like it's time for you to get wet now."

"Right," Lieutenant Culver, Team Eight's Exec and the senior officer in the boat, announced. "Stations, men! Get your feet on!"

The LCP(R) slowed, and the men farthest aft unshipped the rubber raft from the boat's transom and lowered it over the port side amidships, lashing it securely to the hull. Then the coxswain gunned the boat's engine, and they started in toward the beach once more, as the combat swimmers prepared to go over the side. Each man spit into his face mask and wiped the saliva over the glass, to keep it from fogging in the water. Then he donned the mask, positioning it up high on his forehead, and pulled the swim fins on, securing the straps behind his ankles in a snug fit.

Unit organization in the UDT had been reorganized somewhat since the Marianas operation. A team like UDT-8 was broken into four twenty-five-man operational platoons, each in turn divided into three squads of eight men each and led by an officer. Another thirteen officers and men formed a headquarters platoon and provided replacements for op platoon members hurt, sick, or killed. Each operational platoon had its own Higgins boat.

For this demo run, only Third Platoon would be deployed this afternoon, with Lieutenant Culver as boat officer, Ensign Milne as swimming officer, and Lieutenant j.g. Dayton in command of the demo platoon. The other three Higgins boats would patrol back and forth off the beach, attracting fire from the Japanese, if possible, to keep them off the swimmers, and using their .30-caliber machine guns to keep the enemy busy.

The deployment tactics had been refined too.

Splash-run deployment had been devised late in the Marianas campaign, in beach reconnaissance and demolition missions off Saipan and Guam, but the technique had been streamlined and honed by constant practice to a fine art. Racing at high speed to within a few hundred yards of the shore … or as close as intervening reefs or obstacles would allow them to get, the Higgins boat approached the drop-off line. Still travelling at full speed, the Higgins boat then swung sharply to the left, racing parallel to the shore, with the raft on the craft's seaward side, away from the beach.

Ensign Milne took his position on the LCP's port side just forward of the raft, facing aft with his hand raised, forefinger extended, while the UDT swimmers crouched in the well deck, awaiting his signal. Jamison and Colt, the first swimmer pair in line, scrambled over the LCP's side — *a* hazardous enough maneuver in its own right when the landing craft was bucking across waves or the splash ripples spreading out from shell bursts ahead — and took their positions lying side by side in the raft, facing forward.

Raising his head above the landing craft's gunwale, Tangretti stared toward the shore. It was hard to see much of anything, for the naval bombardment was thundering away, sending in a solid rain of shells that howled overhead, then slammed into the forest behind the beach in great, thundering eruptions of smoke and flame that had swiftly drawn a gray-white curtain across the island's face.

Angaur was a tiny island less than three miles across, consisting of gently rolling hills less than two hundred feet high. Six miles to the northeast lay rugged, mountainous, and heavily forested Peleliu, where the First Marine Division had landed yesterday and was encountering fierce resistance. Angaur's Red Beach was a stretch of sand and gently rising dunes four hundred yards wide along the island's northern coast, and the operations plan called for a landing there tomorrow by troops of the Army 81st Division. Team Eight had already made a reconnaissance swim to the beach that morning. They'd not found the expected mines or heavy defenses, but they had located a series of beach obstacles set into the coral and sand below the high water line on the left side of the beach, and now they were going back in to clear them out.

Lieutenant Culver gave the word, and Milne brought his hand down, pointing at Jamison and Colt. Together, the two men rolled over the side, and the next two in line, Parry and Mulhausen, slipped off the LCP and into their vacated places in the raft. At the same instant, two men to starboard tossed a pair of canvas satchels into the sea on the boat's landward side.

Kelly was Tangretti's swim buddy, and they were third in the chain. Fifty yards past the point where they'd dropped Jamison and Colt, Dayton signaled again and Parry and Mulhausen rolled into the water with a splash. Tangretti followed Kelly into the raft, careful where he stepped with the ungainly swim fins. Lying flat in the wildly bouncing raft, pressed shoulder-to-shoulder with the other man, he pulled his mask down over his eyes and nose, pressing it hard against his face until the air pressure outside held it tight, and watched Milne. Fifty yards more … and then Milne gave the signal. Tangretti rolled hard to the left, hitting the water with bruising force, then bobbing wildly in the LCP(R)'s wake as it continued speeding on along the drop-off line.

Together, Tangretti and Kelly swam across the chop of the LCP(R)'s wake to the satchels that had been tossed in over the side as they'd been rolling off the raft. Each pack contained a rubber floatation bladder that kept the satchel bobbing on the surface. Tangretti grabbed the strap on one of the packs, exchanged nods with Kelly, and started swimming toward the shore.

The drop-off line for Red Beach was about two-hundred yards out. The offshore bombardment was still going on, sending up great, crashing lines of explosions that continued to blot out most of the green hills behind the beach in drifting smoke and spray. There was no fire from the beach so far, at least none that Tangretti could see. The gunfire from offshore was steady and right on target, comforting in the shriek of shells passing over and the deep-throated roar of their detonation inland. Tangretti could hear the yammering chatter of machine gun fire too, but all of it seemed to be coming from behind him, from one or another of Eight's LCP(R)s weaving back and forth out beyond the drop-off line.

He couldn't help but compare the scene to his *last* demolition assignment, when he'd been wading ashore on Omaha, through water lashed white by machine gun fire and mortars.

Kicking steadily, their fins biting the water, Tangretti and Kelly made good time. With the fins, Tangretti didn't have to move his arms at all. He kept them out in front of his head, pushing the satchel before him like a kickboard, steering it toward the beach. He didn't think about what might happen if an enemy bullet hit the explosives inside.

Tetrytol was a solid, yellow-colored explosive blend, 70 percent tetryl, 30 percent TNT. While pure tetryl was shock-sensitive — meaning a bullet could set it off — it was given greater stability by the TNT, which was so stable by itself you could shoot it, hit it with a hammer, or even toss it into fire and it wouldn't explode. Tetrytol was considered only slightly more sensitive than TNT by itself.

Probably it wouldn't explode if it was hit…

CHAPTER 20

Saturday, 16 September 1944
Red Beach
Angaur Island

The obstacles the team had encountered on Red Beach that morning consisted of some fifty steel rails wedged solidly into the coral with their ends extended toward the sea, each ten feet from its neighbor. The rails were spaced in two lines below the high water mark and covered 250 feet on the left side of the beach. Compared to the wildly inventive and extravagant beach defenses that had protected Hitler's *Festung Europa* at Omaha, the Japanese obstacles were almost laughably primitive, but sometimes they had surprises attached, like mines and booby traps, and the beach areas were nearly always covered by intense mortar and gunfire.

Tangretti approached the seaward side of the obstacles slowly, alert to enemy troops on the shore, but seeing no sign of the enemy. The drifting smoke was so thick he could see very little of the beach save for the area directly behind the obstacles, and the steady crash and thunder of Navy gunfire continued to wrack the forest beyond the dune line.

The front row of obstacles was about three-quarters submerged, with only a foot or two of the steel rails projecting above the water. The second row, closer to the high water mark on the beach, was almost completely exposed, with surf curling around the base of each rail where it was wedged into rock and coral.

The demolition techniques employed by the UDT were essentially the same as those taught to the CDUs before Normandy and employed by them to clear the German beach obstacles. During the earlier reconnaissance swim, the men had noted the positions of the obstacles and made estimates as to how much explosive would be needed to take them out. Tangretti was making for a particular set of obstacles, toward the right center of the blocked area. Arriving at one of the submerged rails, he drew his knife and plunged it through the canvas of his satchel, rupturing the floatation bladder inside and causing the bag to sink.

Taking a deep breath, Tangretti jack-knifed at the surface and followed the satchel down, guiding it as he dove about six feet to the rail's base.

Working quickly, he pulled a charge from the bag and began wiring it to the bottom of the rail with primacord. Had the obstacle been larger, or set in concrete, he would have used the entire satchel, but as it was, a couple of pounds of tetrytol would be enough to blast the rail clear.

Following the pattern worked out aboard ship earlier, he carefully wrapped the charge several times with a length of primacord, then strung the cord across the ten-foot gap to the next rail. There, he surfaced for air and a quick look around. There was still no sign of a response from the Japanese, and the shore bombardment was continuing with unabated fury.

Underwater, the sound of the bombardment was muffled to a dull, throbbing thumping that filled the water around him. At the base of the second rail, he placed another charge of tetrytol, wrapped it in primacord, and used a square knot to tie that to the length of cord extending through the water from the first rail.

Primacord, also known as detcord, had proven to be one of the most useful pieces of demolition equipment yet devised for this war. Just over two-tenths of an inch thick, flexible, waterproof, weighing only eighteen pounds per one thousand feet of length, primacord consisted of a core of PETN — the letters stood for the jaw breaking formula pentaerythritol tetranitrate — wrapped in fabric, and it looked exactly like yellow clothesline. When detonated, either electrically or from a burning fuse, the stuff burned at a velocity of twenty-one thousand feet per second, and with sufficient force to set off any explosives it was attached to. Its greatest advantage lay in that speed of detonation, for it allowed one fuse to be used to simultaneously set off any number of charges across a very large area, without risking the possibility of one blast cutting the fuses set to other charges that hadn't yet exploded.

Tangretti finished placing his charges at the same time Kelly did. Together, they tied their adjacent charges together with more detcord, then ran a long length toward the shore.

Emerging from the water, Tangretti flopped clumsily in his fins through calf-deep surf over rock and coral, making his way to the second line of rails. Other UDT men were already there, attaching their own explosive packs and tying them all together with detcord. Tangretti and Kelly strung their long connector cord up to the space between two rails, where they tied it securely to the length of primacord already stretched from one obstacle to the next.

Tangretti heard a shout and turned in time to see Chief Simmons, fifty feet to the left, grabbing one rail in his arms and giving a hard, muscle-rippling pull. The rail snapped free from its coral base, as several UDT men laughed or shouted bantering taunts. Simmons heaved the rail into the sea, then whisked his palms up and down against each other, as though dusting off his hands.

It seemed foolhardy, this close to an enemy beach, and Tangretti took another hard look around, wondering if the Japanese had noticed them yet. The best reason for the enemy's silence seemed to be that the shore bombardment had driven them all into shelters off the beach, but there was no telling when someone might emerge to take a shot at them. These men, Tangretti reminded himself, had never been under fire before. Their first combat mission had been yesterday, when they'd swum toward another Angaur beach in a deliberate feint against the Japanese defenses, and that had been followed by their recon swim on Red Beach this morning. By this time, they were feeling pretty cocky — twice they'd been clear up to the beach and the Japanese hadn't so much as taken a pot shot at them.

With a loud grunt, Slim Simmons hauled another obstacle out of the coral and heaved it into the sea, to the cheers and applause of his teammates. Tangretti went back to work, making sure the knots in the primacord were securely and properly tied.

As the rest of the platoon set their charges and tied them together, two flank men had laid down a single, continuous master line of detcord offshore, parallel to the line of obstacles. As the men ashore finished laying their charges, Collins and Fitzhugh, the platoon's designated fuse pullers, began swimming from the seaward side of the obstacles out to the master line, unreeling a trunk line behind them, which they tied at right angles to the master line. They then surfaced and waited for the rest of the team to clear out of the area.

"Simmons!" Tangretti yelled. "Stop showing off and let's get the hell out of here!"

Lieutenant Dayton picked up the cue. "All right, people! Let's get a move on before the Japanese decide to die of old age, huh?"

Simmons grinned and waved. In small groups, the entire team was slipping back into the safety of the water. Swimming in line-abreast, the UDT men passed the waiting Fitzhugh and Collins and made for the pickup line, two hundred yards offshore.

Without the bulky canvas packs, their swim back out to sea was faster than the trip in. One of the boats had dropped floating markers in the water, marking the recovery line, and the men began positioning themselves along that line, waiting. Offshore, the low, gray shapes of the bombarding ships rested on the horizon several miles off, destroyers closer, the big cruisers farther out. Closer inshore were the four LCPs, still probing and darting and circling, as though daring the Japanese to open fire.

Swimmer recovery had come a long way since Saipan. Until then, Higgins boats had been forced to come to a complete halt — perfect, stationary targets for enemy shell fire — while men were plucked one at a time from the sea. This had always been the deadliest time of an operation, and the new techniques had been perfected to give both the boats and the swimmers a better chance. At Saipan, Lieutenant j.g. Robbins had tried tossing life rings to men in the water as the boat continued to move. This had soon evolved into the high-speed recovery system used now.

Spacing themselves out along the recovery line, the UDT men tread water, each man holding his left arm high out of the water to indicate that he was ready. The recovery boat made a final circle, then started its run...

The raft was still lashed to the boat's port side, and the LCP(R)'s coxswain angled in so that he was approaching the waiting line of swimmers between them and the shore. In the raft, a UDT man waited with a three-foot length of heavy rope knotted into a double ring. The man in the raft held one ring, reaching far over the side so that the other ring was extended just above the water.

Tangretti watched the approaching boat, keeping his place, his left arm high. He could see the man in the raft leaning out, see the ring rapidly growing larger. At the last instant, he thrust his left arm through the extended loop, grabbing the rope, feeling the sudden wrench in his shoulder as the speeding boat literally snatched him from the water and flung him back into the raft. Hitting the raft with a thump, he disentangled his arm, then let himself be helped up and over the LCP(R)'s side by a second UDT man.

The new recovery technique allowed the swimmers to be pulled out of the water while the recovery boat was still moving at full speed, a poor target for any Japanese gunners who might have been taking an interest in the LCP's activities. Tangretti had heard that when the technique had first been tried, a number of the men had suffered from dislocated shoulders. New methods were being tried all the time, however, and good results had been obtained using rubber rings, more flexible than one-inch rope. The important thing was not having the boat stop dead in the water.

The recovery boat completed the pickup, with the last swimmer flipped into the raft like a boated fish. Now only two men remained in the water — Collins and Fitzhugh, the fuse pullers.

A joke frequently heard in the teams held that the fuse pullers were the fastest swimmers in the air, that they could swim fifty yards without once touching water. Patiently, they held position offshore while the recovery boat finished picking up all of the other men in the platoon. Then, as the boat circled around for one final pass, they yanked the T-rings on the M-1 igniters neatly encased in waterproofing condoms. The igniters set alight the delay fuses, cut for a four-minute burn time, which were in turn carefully knotted to the primacord trunk line. With the fuses burning — two fuses ensured that one, at least, would set off the demo train — Fitzhugh and Collins swam as quickly as they could manage to the recovery line and took their places, spaced perhaps fifty yards apart.

Tangretti, slumped now against the side of the LCP(R), watched as the boat bore down on the first floating head; the recovery man extended the loop ... and suddenly Collins was flung full-length into the raft. Dripping and blowing, Collins was helped aboard the LCP(R), just as the Higgins boat bore down on Fitzhugh. Another flash of movement, and the last swimmer was recovered. The coxswain put the LCP's helm hard over to the left, and, still zigzagging against the possibility of fire from the shore, they raced again toward that line of gray ships waiting on the horizon.

In the Higgins boat, every man was either watching the receding beach or his waterproof watch. Minutes passed, with not a man saying a word ... and then a solid wall of smoke and white spray rose majestically a full one hundred feet into the sky, blotting out the left side of the beach, hanging suspended for a moment against the sky, and then cascading back to the shore with a rolling, thunderous crash.

On the Higgins boat, the men went wild, yelling and cheering and pounding one another on their bare, wet backs. From the size and the timing of the explosion, it was clear that, today, at least, it was "mission accomplished." Another boat run, or a pass by aerial reconnaissance aircraft later would be needed to confirm that the obstacles had been taken out, but Tangretti had already learned that only very rarely was a second demo swim ever needed.

Outside the bulkheads of the *Badger*, the wind howled and shrieked like a living thing, clawing at the APD as fifty-foot waves lashed and pounded, breaking across her decks in thundering explosions of water. The typhoon had broken yesterday, roaring down on the lead ships of Admiral Oldendorf's fleet, which included minesweepers detailed for the coming invasion of the Philippines as well as the transports for several of the UDTs.

Many of the men of Team Eight were gathered on *Badger's* mess deck. A few clutched mugs of coffee, trying to keep them upright as the ship heeled and pitched in the storm's swell. Nobody felt like eating. Men who'd been at sea for years and never been seasick had been stricken with mal de mer, the sleeping compartments and ship's heads stank of vomit. Only potential suicides ventured onto the upper decks in a storm like this, and the ship was pitching too violently for cleaning details to wield their mops and buckets.

"She-it," Kelly said, clutching the sides of the mess table. The ship's deck was heeled over at very nearly a thirty-degree angle. "I didn't join the teams to get drowned on my own ship's mess deck!"

"This storm's a whopper, all right," Slim said easily. He sipped at his coffee, ignoring the lurch as the *Badger* began to right herself. A crash sounded in the galley aft, as some piece of crockery broke its moorings and crashed to the deck. "Puts me in mind of one of our big Gulf storms. 'Course, if you wanted to see a really big storm…

Kelly clutched his head. "Slim, if you're about to tell us one of your Texas tall tales—"

"You are lookin' a mite green about the gills, there, Kelly. What do you think, Gator? Shall we spare this poor wretch?"

"I think you'd better have mercy on him," Tangretti said with a pallid smile. Truth to tell, he wasn't feeling too well himself. The deck lurched again ... and his stomach with it. Somehow, the compounded smells of hundreds of men crowded into cramped living spaces, the vomit, the stench from backed-up heads, the pervasive stink of diesel fuel had all combined to give him a throbbing headache that reached right down the back of his throat to twist and pull at his stomach.

They'd pulled out of the staging area at Manus in the Admiralty Islands on October 12, en route for the Philippines and what promised to be one of the biggest fights in the Pacific war so far. The typhoon had blown up that morning, just twenty-four hours before they were due to arrive off Leyte Island, the focus of an enormous invasion fleet.

"So," Tangretti said, changing the subject. "Did you guys hear the skinny on Peleliu?"

"Heard they was still fightin'," Kelly said. "Heard the First Marines lost over a thousand men already, and five thousand wounded."

"Yeah, but they say the Japanese are boxed up in one little area back in the hills," Slim said. "The Army's movin' in now to mop up."

"'Mop up,'" Kelly said. "Right. And that whole friggin' operation is just about useless."

"Useless?" Tangretti said. "What do you mean?"

Kelly shrugged. "Got it from a radioman on the skipper's staff. He overhead some traffic. Seems a lot of the brass is real steamed right now, cause the Peleliu invasion wasn't necessary in the first place."

"Aw, come off it," Tangretti said, disbelieving. "How could they plan an invasion like that if they didn't need it?"

Still, he'd heard plenty of scuttlebutt on the subject already, about a major tug-of-war in the high command over the best way to pursue the war against Japan. One faction, comprised mostly of the Navy and the Marines, had held all along that the fastest way to Japan was the celebrated "island hopping" up the central Pacific, capturing key islands along the way as air and naval bases, but avoiding strongholds like the Japanese naval base at Truk that could be bypassed, left isolated to whither on the vine.

The opposing strategy was held by the Army — and most specifically by General Douglas MacArthur, the former commander of America's Philippines garrison, who'd promised the Philippines shortly after the Japanese had captured those islands, "I shall return."

"Kelly's right," Simmons said. "I heard the same shit. They're saying we went into Peleliu because ol' Corncob wanted it taken, but we didn't really need the goddamned place at all. If you ask me, he's still trying to cure Nimitz of island hopping."

It was no secret that MacArthur opposed the central Pacific strategy, not after he'd taken his case to the American people with a controversial article in *The New York Times*. "Island hopping is not my idea of how to end the war as cheaply as possible" ran part of his page 1 quote.

Perhaps predictably, the Joint Chiefs of Staff had arrived at a compromise last March. America would pursue *both* strategies simultaneously, with Admiral Chester Nimitz leading the Navy and the Marines toward Japan by way of the Marianas, while

MacArthur fought his way back to the Philippines. Scuttlebutt had it that "Mac" planned on taking back his beloved Philippines island by island in the name of restoring American honor throughout Asia, while Nimitz covered MacArthur's flank during that advance ... which meant that some Japanese island fortresses that might have been avoided would have to be taken by the Marines.

Many Navy and Marine Corps personnel, including Tangretti, thought that American honor might be better satisfied by a quick end to the war with Japan ... and the quicker, the better. Splitting the war effort between the island campaign and the jungle-thick labyrinth of the Philippine Islands did not promise a quick anything.

"Way I heard it," Tangretti said, "Admiral Nimitz was the one who ordered the landings in the Palaus. He needed them as an anchorage, and as a staging area for the Philippines."

"Yeah," Simmons agreed. "That was one where Nimitz had to tag along with Mac-A. But old Bull Halsey decided we didn't need Peleliu at all. He tried to cancel the invasion."

That was news to Tangretti. "No shit?"

"No shit," Simmons said. "Only problem was, the invasion fleet had already lifted anchor. Nimitz didn't want to call the show off once things were already under way, so he overruled Halsey. The Marines went in ... and they've been fighting through pure hell on Peleliu for a month now. Losses worse than Bloody Tarawa, and the fighting's *still* going on, I hear."

"They shoulda had our UDT guys go into the beach," Kelly said. "If they'd had a *real* recon instead of just snapshots taken from the air..."

"Maybe," Simmons said. "Anyway, the Marines have what's left of the Japanese penned up in a few square miles of mountain, and they're rooting them out one fucking cave at a time with flamethrowers and tanks. Christ, what a way to fight a war. Bad as fuckin' World War One."

"And you want to hear the kicker?" Kelly put in. "Eight days after the landings on Peleliu, the Army landed on Ulithi Atoll, you know? Better anchorage for the fleet, better position to keep the Japanese neutralized on Yap Island ... and the fuckin' place wasn't even defended! The Army came ashore after the usual bombardment —"

"And after a thorough beach survey by Team Ten," Simmons put in.

"Right. And what do you think they found? The Japanese had snuck off and left the place empty!"

"She-it," Kelly said, shaking his head. "What a fucking way to run a fucking war!"

Tangretti had to agree. More and more, he had the feeling that the brass simply didn't care. Another thousand men dead? Too bad. Do we have enough pine boxes made up? Oh, well that's okay, then. Pack 'em up and ship 'em home. Our heroic boys will get a splendid military funeral ... and maybe even a shiny medal hanging from a strip of pretty-colored ribbon.

And a good many more good men were going to die taking the Philippines back from the enemy. Japanese tactics had been changing lately, especially on the larger islands like Saipan ... although they'd been doing it on small islands like Peleliu as well. Rather than throw everything they had into a savage defense of the beach, they tended to pull back into the island's interior and wait. Peleliu had been a nightmare of tunnels and caves — some of them with steel blast doors — buried deep in the island's soft coral basement. They tended to keep their artillery and tanks under cover until the landing forces were already ashore, then force the Americans to dig them out, one hole at a time. That had been why the UDT operations off

Angaur had turned out to be relatively easy, with no casualties among the teams. Nor had Japanese beach defenses proven to be as formidable as earlier military theorists had predicted. On most islands — with a few exceptions, like Tinian — there were so many possible landing beaches that the Japanese were simply unable to defend them all.

This strategy made the UDTs' tasks easier, but it made things worse for the Marines.

New strategy or not, though, it was still thought that the Leyte beaches would be strongly defended. Filipino guerrillas had reported that the approaches to Leyte Gulf were heavily mined, and there might be beach defenses as well. Leyte, after all, was not some remote, backwater atoll, all coral rock, sand, and palm trees. It was much more like Saipan, with a large native population, cities ... and a determined Japanese occupation force that could be counted on to pull every trick in the book ... and maybe even make up a few new ones of their own.

And the UDT, as usual, was going to be leading the way in. Seven teams had been gathered to assist "MacArthur's Navy," as the U.S. Seventh Fleet was known, and Halsey's Third Fleet in clearing the way for the landings on Leyte. An island half again larger than Long Island, Leyte would be the site of MacArthur's long-promised return to the Philippines.

The *Badger* gave another stomach-twisting roll, and Kelly groaned. "Oh, man," he said. "Somebody stop this damned thing and let me get off!"

"You figuring on walking to Leyte?" Tangretti asked.

"Aw, we're UDT, right? The sea's our natural element! Not this god-awful tub. Why do we have to go along with this Philippines crap anyway? You know what I heard? MacArthur hates special operations forces, hates the whole idea of them."

"I know the first UDTs that got assigned to him ended up working as Seabees, building airfields and shit like that," Simmons said. "He never allowed them to go in ahead of the landings."

"Well if that's the way he feels about it," Tangretti replied, "what the hell are we doing clearing his beaches for him at Leyte?"

"That's right," Slim said. "Let him clear his own beach approaches!"

"She-it," Kelly said, smirking. "Ol' Mac don't need to clear no damned approaches. When it comes time for the landings, he'll just walk ashore ... on *top* of the damned water!"

CHAPTER 21

Wednesday, 18 October 1944
Leyte Gulf

It was not the largest naval force mustered so far in the war — the fleet that had descended on Normandy four months earlier still held that distinction — but it was certainly the most powerful in terms of sheer striking power. The Seventh Fleet attack force consisted of 738 ships, including 157 combatant ships, 420 amphibious vessels, 84 minesweepers and hydrographic craft, and 77 other vessels of various types. Halsey's Third Fleet added Task Force 38 to the armada, with 17 of Mitscher's fleet carriers, 6 battleships, 17 cruisers, and 64 destroyers. Reconnaissance operations were set for the eighteenth and nineteenth of October; A day was set for the twentieth.

The first landings had actually already begun on the morning of October 17, when elements of the U.S. 6th Rangers began going ashore on the islands sheltering Leyte Gulf to the east and south in a driving rain. By noon of the next day, all four target islands had been secured, navigational beacons had been erected on Dinagat Island's Cape Desolation and fifteen miles across the strait on Homonhon. Shortly afterward, Admiral Oldendorf had maneuvered into the gulf with his fire support ships and begun the bombardment of Leyte's eastern coast.

The bombardment and the reconnaissance operations both started late — at 1400 hours instead of early in the morning, as originally planned. Mine-clearing operations were continuing, but the minesweepers had been badly handled by the typhoon a few days before. One had been sunk, and all arrived at Leyte Gulf well behind schedule.

Leyte Gulf is a sizable body of water, stretching over forty miles from Samar in the north to Dinagat's Cape Desolation in the south, and forty miles again from Leyte's eastern shoreline to Homonhon Island in the east. San Pedro Bay alone covers some one hundred square miles in the northwest corner of the gulf, tucked in between Samar Island and Leyte just south of the painfully narrow Juanico Strait. The invasion beaches were grouped in two primary areas, around the town of Dulag, squarely facing the center of the gulf proper, and thirty miles to the north, in San Pedro Bay. Leyte's provincial capital, the city of Tacloban, was located just beyond the northern beaches.

Operations began in the south. Five miles offshore, three cruisers and the battleship *Pennsylvania* sent salvo after salvo shrieking across the water and into the beaches, hammering the shoreline from Dulag north to San Jose. Closer inshore, beneath the shells howling overhead, four APDs, escorted by five destroyers, closed to within four thousand yards of the beach and began lowering their LCP(R)s into the water.

Only four of the seven UDTs present would be deployed on the first day of reconnaissance. Red and White beaches, in the far north on San Pedro Bay between the towns of Palo and San Ricardo, had also been scheduled for reconnaissance on the eighteenth by Teams Six, Nine, and Ten, but because of the delays in the minesweeping schedule, Admiral Oldendorf had decided to postpone UDT operations in that area until the following day.

To the south, however, UDT-3, off the U.S.S. *Talbot*, would go in on the invasion's far left flank, off Violet Beach directly below the town of Dulag, while the *Goldsborough's* Team Four surveyed Yellow Beach, between Dulag and a prominent hill north of town. The *Badger's* Team Eight drew beaches Blue 1 and Blue 2, north of that.

And on the right flank, beaches Orange 1 and Orange 2 would be investigated by UDT-5, now operating off the APD *Humphreys*.

Lieutenant Waverly was now the Exec of Team Five, while Lieutenant James R. Dulaney was the skipper. Waverly had received the promotion — in position, if not in rank — shortly after Tinian, just before the team had been transferred to the *Humphreys*. Coffer, it was rumored, was still aboard the old *Gilmer* back at Saipan, where the organization of the UDT's high command was supposed to be in for a shake-up of some kind.

Waverly didn't know how much truth there was in the scuttlebutt, and neither did Team Five's new commanding officer. Dulaney was a young, tough, athletic guy — he'd played first-string quarterback for Navy during his last year at Annapolis — who'd been thoroughly miffed during the Marianas operations by having to stay aboard a control boat while Coffer and others got to go swimming. He was set for a swim today, however … and this time Waverly, as XO, would be the stay-at-home. It was the skipper's privilege, after all, to name the swimmers, but if he named himself, then the second-in-command had to stay. Regulations forbade risking both men ashore.

Humphreys's four LCP(R)s had been lowered over the side by 1500 hours. When their swimmer deployment rafts were broken out and lashed alongside, they started in toward the beach. Waverly was riding in Boat One, along with Dulaney and the First Platoon. As they crested the first heavy swell, Waverly turned for a last look at Team Five's new APD. The eastern sky behind her was an ominous blue-black … the lingering remnants of the typhoon that had already played hell with the invasion schedule. *Humphreys* rode the swell off the beach with an easy, rocking motion. She looked a lot roomier from out here…

The *Humphreys* was one of the new breed of fast transports, converted from a destroyer escort instead of the old, four-piper DDs like the *Gilmer*. Though based on a smaller ship — she had an overall length of 306 feet as opposed to the *Gilmer's* 314 feet — she had a deeper draft and theoretically more space for troops. Most of Team Five's men agreed, however, and with considerable grumbling, that she wasn't much more comfortable than the *Gilmer* had been. Though she theoretically had space for 162 passengers in addition to her 212-man crew, quarters were still cramped, and space was at a premium, especially when the UDT aboard also had to find room for tons of explosives and gear.

One definite improvement over the old destroyer conversions was evident in *Humphreys's* armament. She carried a five-inch gun mounted in a turret forward, plus three 40-mm twin antiaircraft mounts and eight 20-mm guns. The older APDs carried four three-and-a-half-inch guns and five 20-mm mounts, mostly for antiaircraft defense. It was thought that the new APDs would be able to provide additional close-in fire support for the teams while they were on their missions.

Turning back again, Waverly studied the beach, four thousand yards away. Smoke was rising from several locations, and occasionally a puff of smoke would appear silently on the shore, followed seconds later by the rumble of the detonation. Still, the scene seemed deceptively peaceful, a low, rolling, green-clad island with perfect white beaches. Neatly spaced rows of coconut palms lined the dunes beside a coastal road. A patchwork of color almost directly ahead marked the little fishing village of San Jose.

Waverly had already gone over the charts and maps of the beach area and had taken compass sightings off several prominent features ashore to make certain he was off the right beach. In addition, *Humphreys's* radar was guiding him in, with the team's Ensign Gaines on the APD's bridge transmitting navigational bearings to all four LCPs and coordinating their requests for fire support.

With her boats clear, *Humphreys* was starting to make way slowly and beginning her turn in to the beach. The problem was that orders had been received that morning for all fire support ships, including the fast transports, to stay well clear of the shore. With mine-clearing operations throughout the gulf delayed by the storm, they'd been directed to remain at least two miles off the beach, while *Pennsylvania* and her cruiser groups would stay five miles out.

Worst of all, however, was the snafu over air cover.

Ever since Saipan, the teams had insisted on careful coordination of air attacks with UDT deployments off enemy beaches. Air strikes were more accurate by far than mass bombardment by battleships offshore. Guided by men with radios in landing craft right off the beach, planes could be called in on individual pillboxes or machine gun nests, and so long as the enemy was watching American aircraft circling overhead, they weren't likely to do much shooting at the swimmers. Too, a new weapon had entered the American arsenal during the Marianas campaign. Napalm — jellied gasoline — was a horrifying weapon, so horrifying that the brass had made the topic off-limits in press conferences, but it had proven itself time after time on jungle-infested islands from Saipan to Peleliu. A flight of Navy Avengers or Corsairs could streak in low over a hill, scattering napalm bombs across the jungle in a pattern that would instantly engulf the entire target footprint in flame and guarantee that those Japanese troops who survived would stay buttoned up tight in their caves and tunnels. Few of the American troops who'd watched napalm bombings worried about whether or not napalm was a *humane* weapon ... a word that had surfaced more than once in some press stories back home. After all, they would say ... dead was dead, right?

The UDTs had been counting on air strikes launched by the fleet of carriers offshore — and a healthy dose of napalm — to cover their approach to the Leyte beaches. Unfortunately, somewhere along the line during the planning for the invasion, there'd been a screw-up, one of those minor administrative or bureaucratic mistakes that seem trivial on paper but that could carry life-or-death consequences for the men on the front lines. The operational orders had stated that the UDTs specifically did *not* want air support, when in fact just the opposite was true. Waverly and Dulaney had just learned about the problem the day before, and by that time it had been too late to request a reshuffling of the invasion force's air assets.

The gulf was a bit rough, with a heavy swell running in the wake of the typhoon. The water looked muddy, an opaque, mottled brown-green, and the closer the LCP(R) got to shore, the muddier it became. Most of that gunk in the water, Waverly thought, must have been stirred up by the storm, but it would be even worse close inshore where the naval bombardment was tearing up the beach.

Some of the shoreline, though, didn't look like it was getting much attention from the bombardment groups at all. The *Pennsylvania* and her consorts appeared to be working Dulag over pretty well — Waverly could see a vast, black smudge rising from the horizon to the south — but here in the north, most of the fire was coming from the destroyers two miles offshore, and their fire was neither particularly accurate at that range nor concentrated enough to discourage Japanese gun positions.

Waverly could tell going in that this was going to be a rough operation … possibly the roughest he'd experienced so far.

As the LCP(R) closed to within nine hundred yards of the beach, a mortar burst rose majestically from the water two hundred yards ahead. "Coxswain!" Waverly yelled. "Let's not make it easy for the bastards!"

"Aye, aye, sir!" the coxswain, a third class boatswain's mate named Michaels, replied, and he threw the LCP(R)s wheel hard to the right, then reversed to the left. The zigzagging made the ride even rougher as the landing craft skipped and splashed and shuddered, smashing through one rolling storm swell after another. Another mortar burst erupted from the gulf, this time to the left, and some white splashes appeared, thrashing across the muddy water several hundred yards ahead.

Dulaney turned and grinned at Waverly. "Looks like they decided to notice us this time," he said. "I thought the briefing report said they were holding their fire on reconnaissance parties, saving up for the main force!"

Waverly shook his head. "You know, it's possible they think *we're* the invasion force. Sixteen Higgins boats, stretched from here to Dulag. That's a fair-sized little landing party."

Another mortar burst, to the right and still closer, while another thundered into the sky to the south, not far from Boat Two. Something howled overhead, something large … and traveling in the opposite direction to the shellfire coming from the fleet. Water and spray thundered into the air above the landing craft's wake, two hundred yards astern. "God, you could be right," Dulaney said. "This could get real interesting!"

The swimmers prepared for their swim, donning masks and flippers, checking slates and pencils and other personal gear and making sure it was all well secured. Waverly wished he were going with them. "Don't worry, Lieutenant!" Chief Davies called back when he saw Waverly watching the bronzed, hard muscled men forward. "This one's gonna be a piece of cake!"

"Just don't lose any important gear ashore, Chief," Waverly called back, and the men laughed. Tom Davies had received his crow — made chief — less than a month ago, and Waverly had suggested to Dulaney that he be made a leader of one of the platoon's squads. He couldn't look at the man, however, without remembering Davies's swim partner at Saipan, invalided out of the teams. The last Waverly had heard, Lamb was still in the hospital back in Pearl, recovering from the internal injuries he'd suffered from that mortar burst on the reef off Saipan. It was a reminder of the special dangers that these men faced each time they swam up to an enemy beach … especially in broad daylight.

A mortar shell burst to starboard, startlingly close. The fire, Waverly knew with grim realization, was heavier than it had been at Saipan, and a lot more accurate. If it was this heavy offshore, before they'd even dropped the swimmers…

He reached for the radio handset. "Bogart, Bogart!" he called, using the humorously derived call sign settled on for the *Humphreys*. "Bogart, this is Five-one! Do you read me? Over!"

"Five-one, this is Bogart," the voice of Ensign Gaines, the team's liaison officer aboard the *Humphreys*, came back a moment later. "Go ahead."

"Bogart, we need some covering fire in here. Pass the word to have the DDs concentrate their fire in sector Blue-one-Able. Over!"

There was a long delay, and Waverly could imagine the exchange on *Humphreys's* bridge as Gaines passed the word to the APD's communications officer.

"Five-one, this is Bogart. I'm sorry, sir, but the word is the DDs are busy with other targets and can't be spared. The Captain says he'll try to support with our five-inch. Over."

One five-inch gun against a whole beach?

They were five hundred yards off the shore when something slapped into the Higgins boat's side. Someone shouted. Still holding the radio handset to his head, Waverly turned and saw several wooden splinters sticking like daggers straight up from the starboard-side gunwale amidships, just above a pair of thumb-sized bullet holes. Several spouts of water snapped up to the right. There was another thump, and another bullet hole appeared in the boat's side, farther aft.

"Anybody hurt?" Waverly yelled. Several men shook their heads no, and Foglio gave him a thumbs-up. It was hard to imagine how a couple of rounds could have passed through the wooden hull of the LCP(R) without hitting *someone*.

Another mortar burst went off, even closer this time. God, those gunners ashore were good!

"Bogart, Five-one!" Waverly shouted into the radio. "You pass the word to those sons-a-bitches in Group Fire Control that they'd damned well better get off their asses and give us some fire support, or they're gonna have one boatload of very angry demo guys parked on their desks in about three minutes! You read that, Bogart? Over!"

"Uh … yessir. We're working on it, sir!"

Something whined overhead, but Waverly ignored it. There was a curiously detached feeling about being under fire and unable to fire back, as though his mind had disengaged some critical part of its fight-or-flight mechanism, allowing him to continue to work without thinking about the danger.

Four hundred yards from the beach, the LCP(R) swung to the left, turning parallel to the shore. If anything, the fire grew thicker as they raced south along the coast. Waverly signaled Lieutenant j.g. Dobson, the swimming officer, who was at his station amidships facing Waverly. The first pair of men, Foglio and Benning, were in the raft, with Horwitz and Perkins lying athwart the Higgins boat's port side.

Waverly took a last check on his navigational bearings, then pumped his arm up and down.

"Go!" Dobson yelled, bringing down his hand, and Foglio and Benning went over the side, vanishing in a splash, their heads reappearing a moment later in the Higgins boat's wake. With practiced coordination, Horwitz and Perkins fell into the raft, filling the space just vacated. When Dobson estimated the boat had traveled fifty yards, he signaled again. Two by two, the swim buddy pairs splashed into the muddy water to port, as men on the landing craft's other side tossed satchels over the gunwale to starboard. Since this was a reconnaissance swim, the satchels contained floatation markers, buoys, and reels of measuring line, and not high explosives. Each man carried everything else he would need on him, pencils and marker slates.

Mortar shells followed the boat, and Waverly felt a growing worry. Even if the Japanese mortars were trying to hit the LCP, when they missed astern they were dropping rounds squarely in among the long chain of swimmers trailing behind the fast-moving boat.

The moment Dulaney and McNally, the last two men in line, went over the side, Waverly barked a command and Michaels brought the boat hard about, sending it back up the coastline toward the north.

For the next hour, until it was time for rendezvous and pickup, they would zigzag back and forth off Orange 1, deliberately trying to draw off enemy fire and spotting targets for the *Humphreys's* five-inch gun. Mortar bursts continued to pace the craft, as Waverly began calling on the radio for more support.

Badger had dropped off her pups at just past 1500 hours, and the boats had proceeded in toward the shore, turning into the deployment run about three hundred yards out. Tangretti crouched in the well deck of Boat Three, waiting with the others, watching as Ensign Milne stood ready to send the first swimmers into the water. The first swim pair would be Slim and Jamison. Tangretti would go next, with his swim partner, Lieutenant j.g. Dayton.

"Hey, Slim!" Kelly called. Much to his disgust, he'd drawn duty aboard the LCP(R) that morning, where he would be serving as the ringman during pickup. "Don't you go gettin' in trouble without me there lookin' out for you."

"Hell, things'll probably go smoother than ever," Slim called back. "You just hold that ring steady during retrieval, hear me?"

"She-it," Kelly replied, laughing. "You won't be able to find the fuckin' beach without me!"

Laying along the Higgins boat's side, his face peeling from sunburn, as usual, Dayton looked scared until he noticed Tangretti staring at him. Then he flashed a quick grin.

"Nothing like a quick dip in the heat of the day to cool you off, eh, Gator?"

"No, sir," Tangretti replied. Thunder rolled as mortar shells detonated closer in toward the shore. "And maybe a round of tennis after?"

"If we can find space on *Badger's* fantail, that would be great." It was an old joke. The APD's fantail was largely taken up by two large depth charge racks. The men sunbathed there occasionally at sea, but only a few at a time.

Milne pointed at Slim, and the first two men rolled off the side of the raft. The moment the men were clear, Dayton slipped off the LCP's side and into their places in the raft and Tangretti followed, hitting the rubber deck with a thump cushioned by the water beneath. For a small eternity, he lay there, half on the raft, half on top of Dayton, as spray slashed aft from the LCP's bow wake and drenched his face and hair. Then Milne signaled again. Squeezing his mask tight against his face, he followed Dayton into the sea.

For a moment, Tangretti was wrenched about in murky near darkness while the boat's wake thrashed at his body. Then he surfaced, treading water until he could get his bearings. Their bundles of floatation buoys and markers bobbed on the surface a few yards away in the direction of the shore. Together, Tangretti and Dayton started swimming.

The mortar shells seemed to be falling faster now, and more thickly, a steady *whoom-whoom-whoom* that sent pillar after pillar of spray gushing into the sky. Tangretti thought they were still following the LCP(R), but the rounds were coming perilously near the swimmers in the water. "Getting kind of noisy out here!" Tangretti called to Dayton. Dayton just grinned, concentrating on his swimming. Sticking to the regs, the two men separated until they were about twenty-five yards apart.

Tangretti heard the whistle of the incoming round and almost instinctively ducked his head beneath the water, kicking harder even though he had no way of knowing just where the round was going to hit, and even knowing that when it *did* hit, the water would offer scant protection. Then the explosion slammed against his body, turning him over and over in a churning cloud of bubbles, ripping the mask from his face. The concussion blasted the air from his lungs, and he canted his body upward, fighting toward the surface.

The blast and the darkness brought back the nightmare with the abruptness of a flung-open door. He'd thought he had it licked, his irrational terror of deep, dark water. Once, during training at Fort Pierce over a year ago, he'd nearly drowned while he and Snake had been trying out the newfangled masks and flippers that — at that time, at any rate — had been rejected for use by the teams. He'd panicked, lost it completely, but Snake had pulled him out, dragging him ashore. It had been part of the bond between them, part of what had made the two men all but inseparable for the next nine months.

A Navy combat demolition swimmer afraid of the water? Tangretti had battled that black fear of his until he'd thought it was banished for good. He'd nearly panicked one other time since those early days … when he'd stumbled into a shell hole off Omaha while wearing helmet and gas suit and heavy boots. By the time he made it ashore, he *knew* he'd had it licked, because he'd faced it and survived. Even German gunfire hadn't seemed so bad after that.

In the muddy water off Leyte, though, the old nightmare surged up out of the smothering darkness, unexpected, unheralded. For a terrifying instant, he couldn't even be sure which way was up and which way was down, and he was afraid he might be swimming in the wrong direction.

His ears were ringing, his head pounding. His lungs, completely empty of air, were burning, burning, and he desperately needed to breathe…

CHAPTER 22

Wednesday, 18 October 1944
UDT-8
Off Blue 1

Tangretti emerged on the surface in a steady white drizzle of falling spray, gasping and blowing, shaking his head in an attempt to clear the savage ringing from his ears. Panic still clutched at his throat and stomach. He lashed out, thrashing in the water.

Then he heard the first scream. "My *eyes!*"

Twenty yards away, Dayton splashed and floundered on the surface, groping with clawed fingers at his face. Blood threaded the top of the muddy water. His own terror evaporated, and Tangretti started swimming toward the injured man. As he got closer, he saw that the glass front of his face mask had been smashed in, that a jagged flap of skin was hanging off his forehead, exposing white bone and welling blood beneath.

"Lieutenant! Lieutenant, are you okay?"

He realized how futile and stupid the words sounded the moment he shouted them, but he kept swimming until he reached the wounded man. Clutching at his bloody face with both hands, Dayton was beginning to sink beneath the water. Grabbing the man around his shoulders with one arm, Tangretti tried to pull his hands away with the other. He couldn't tell how bad the wound was; Dayton's face was a horrific mask of blood, the scalp wound bleeding profusely. "My eyes! Oh, Christ, my eyes!"

"Don't worry, sir. We'll get you back to the ship, okay? Just hang on!"

Kicking steadily with his fins, Tangretti found he could support both himself and Dayton high enough in the water to keep their heads clear, riding up and down with the shore-bound surge of the tide. Turning in place, he scanned the southern and eastern horizons, searching for the LCP(R).

There … that must be it. As per SOP, the Higgins boats were supposed to continue maneuvering along the drop-off line and in closer to the beach, watching for wounded men and using their twin .30-caliber machine guns to try to keep the Japanese snipers' heads down. He could see their boat perhaps half a mile out, circling back toward the north.

He wished he had a radio. Or a Very pistol. His one hope was that Milne and Casey, the boat officer, would be watching the progress of all of the swimmers, or trying to, through binoculars. If they noticed two heads bobbing near the drop-off line…

"God damn it!" Waverly screamed into the radio handset. "Get me some fucking air cover or I'm going to stay on this channel all afternoon. I don't care what your fucking orders are, we need air cover!"

Unable to get any surface fire support for his team beyond the five-inch popgun mounted aboard the *Badger*, Waverly had ordered the boat's radio operator to raise the bombardment group's fire control center and had spent the last several minutes blistering the airwaves with threats and invectives.

This, he thought, definitely was a step outside the proper bounds of protocol and military chain of command. Boat commanders and UDT executive officers were not supposed to communicate directly with the bombardment group … nor were they supposed to cuss out harried radio officers or threaten to tie up their communications frequencies.

"Ah, Five-one," the voice of the radioman aboard the *Pennsylvania* came back. "According to our op orders, you frogmen didn't want air support."

"Recite your op orders to me again and I will personally crawl up your anchor chain and ram them up your ass." He considered adding something about the "frogmen" crack and decided against it. "If you can't give us decent gunfire support, pass me to the air group commander. Or give me the frequency of somebody in the air. We need some fucking support out here!"

A moment later, a different, deeper voice came over the radio. "Five-one, this is Oboe. We have no ground support aircraft available for your area. You ought to know we can't change the order of battle at the last moment"

Waverly hesitated, wondering about the identity of the unseen speaker. "Oboe." Was that someone on Oboe's staff … or Rear Admiral Jesse Oldendorf himself?

"Sir, there has been a serious mix-up in the orders," Waverly said, trying to keep his voice from becoming shrill or breaking. "The new orders regarding the disposition of the ships in the bombardment group have placed them too far offshore to provide effective covering fire. We need air support over Orange beach. If we don't get it, we are going to be in a world of shit. Sir. Over."

There was a long silence, during which Waverly imagined official reprimands and court-martial proceedings.

"Five-one, this is Oboe. We don't have any dedicated ground support to give you, but we might be able to divert a flight of F6Fs. Stand by."

Minutes passed, as mortar fire thumped and boomed across the gulf.

Yes! Tangretti was sure now that they'd been seen. The boat had turned its squared-off bow until it was aimed almost directly at the two men, and the mustache of its bow wake had thickened as the coxswain rammed the throttle full forward. Japanese shells were searching for the Higgins boat now, splashing to left and right, but the coxswain wasn't bothering to zigzag, racing instead straight to where the two men floated in the water.

A lone spout of water splashed several feet high ten yards to the left. There was a pause, and another spout erupted, this one slightly closer. *Sniper*, Tangretti thought. *And he's got the range.* Three hundred yards or so was not very far at all for a rifle shot, especially if the guy on the trigger end of the gun had a sniper scope.

"Jesus, Gator," Dayton said. It was as though the man was just waking up. "What the hell happened? What's going on?"

"You got a little dinged up, sir. The boat's coming in to pick us up."

"Did we finish the mission?"

Shit, he's really out of it. "Yes, sir. Mission accomplished."

"Gator, I can't see."

"I know, sir. We'll get you back to the *Badger* and have the doc look you over. You're gonna be just fine."

With throbbing engine, the LCP(R) swung gently around the men, edging between them and the shore. Kelly, still wearing his greens and boots, jumped into the water as Michaels throttled back, walking the Higgins boat slowly closer. The raft bumped the back of Tangretti's head. Kelly helped him manhandle Dayton up into the raft, and then he and Kelly,

Ensign Milne, and Lieutenant Casey together pulled him from the raft and into the boat.

In the stern of the LCP(R), Kelly and Tangretti bent over the wounded man, pulling away the remnants of the mask and trying to pick shards of glass out of his face. Tangretti couldn't see any damage to the eyes themselves, but there was so much blood he couldn't tell for sure.

"He's gonna need stitches," Kelly said, looking up … and then blood exploded from Kelly's back and his eyes opened wide in an expression of utter astonishment and he lurched forward, colliding with Tangretti and then sprawling motionless across Dayton's legs.

"Frank!" Tangretti cried, reaching for him, trying to roll him over. The bullet had snapped into his back squarely between his shoulder blades. He was alive, but unconscious … worse than unconscious, for his eyes were still open with a dead man's stare.

There was a very great deal of blood, Kelly's and Dayton's mingling together on the deck of the LCP(R).

The two F6F Hellcats roared in low across the water, angling out of the southeast. Waverly's heart leaped at the sight, as the muzzle flashes of each aircraft's six Browning machine guns sparkled in the afternoon light, as neatly ordered white puffs of gun smoke appeared in the sky behind the Hellcats' wings. With a whining roar from their Pratt and Whitney engines, the aircraft flashed across the beach two hundred yards away, flying wingtip to wingtip at an altitude of less than one hundred feet. Dust exploded from the beach in front of them.

Then the Hellcats were lifting into the sky above the palm trees behind the beach, banking to the right as they broke from their strafing run. Waverly noted that the mortar fire from the shore had slackened considerably in the last few seconds.

"Get 'em!" Michaels yelled, shaking his fist toward the shore and bouncing up and down behind the LCP(R)'s helm. "Nail the sons-a-bitches!"

Two more Hellcats appeared in the south, flying low above the beach, firing in long, chattering bursts.

Though more than once Tangretti watched flights of American aircraft passing inland, none came close enough to strafe or bomb Blue Beach. Tangretti had heard rumors — nothing more substantial than that — of some sort of snafu with the air support for the teams. He'd heard stories about how promised air support had failed to materialize during the beach reconnaissance at Saipan. Now, it seemed, it was happening again.

Tangretti sat slumped in the Higgins boat's stern, sitting with the wounded Kelly and Dayton. If there'd been air attacks on the beach timed to coincide with Team Eight's reconnaissance, maybe...

The bitterness he'd been feeling toward the people managing this war had snapped into furious and crystal clear relief. Convinced that the high command didn't give a damn about the men who actually had to do the fighting and the dying on one miserable Pacific island after another, Tangretti was beginning to figure that he didn't care either. Fuck the politics that were running this war. Fuck the brass ... fuck the *Navy*. The only people he really cared about, he decided, were the other members of his team, Simmons and Fitzhugh and the rest.

And Kelly. And Dayton.

While the traditional separation between officers and men remained to a certain extent within the UDT, that separation was far less in the teams than elsewhere within the Navy. Most of the officers had been through the training at Fort Pierce, and as far as Tangretti was concerned, that made all the difference. He'd known Dayton since he'd joined Eight before Peleliu and Angaur, a young likable guy whose worst failing seemed to be his desire to be regarded as just one of the boys.

He hadn't known Kelly all that long either, but he liked the kid's brash cockiness, his self-assured good humor, his utter disdain for the *official* way of doing things … something dear to Tangretti's heart.

The LCP was under way at full speed again, hurtling around the northern curve in a huge, offshore racetrack. It was time for the pickup, and Lieutenant Casey had spotted the first of the swimmers' heads in the water as they approached the recovery line.

"Gator!" Casey snapped.

"Yes, sir."

"Kelly was going to be our hook man. Get portside and take over."

He took another look at the wounded men. Dayton's head was wrapped in gauze, the worst of the bleeding stopped; Kelly's back had been packed with gauze and tape. There was nothing more that could be done with them, not before they were returned to *Badger's* sickbay.

"Aye, aye, sir."

Moving forward, Tangretti picked up the double-looped length of rope and scrambled over the port side into the raft. Jim Parry, who was serving as the boat's radioman on this op, took his place inboard, ready to help the men aboard as Tangretti scooped them up.

Enemy mortar fire pursued them as they raced for the pickup line.

Waverly stood beside Michaels as the LCP(R) started its run toward the pickup line. The Hellcats had withdrawn — low on fuel or out of ammo — and the mortar fire from the beach was picking up again. The recovery was set uncomfortably close to that beach, 150 yards out, and the steady succession of mortar bursts was mingled with machine gun and rifle fire, much of it from the colorful houses of San Jose itself.

Both of the Higgins boat's gun wells were manned, not by UDT personnel but by sailors assigned to the duty from the *Humphreys*. Both of them, in dungarees, orange life jackets, and blue Navy helmets, were riding their weapons as the LCP(R) raced along the beach, laying down fire in short, steady bursts.

Perkins had the loop in the raft to port. Ahead, the first man in line floated slightly to seaward of the bow, facing the oncoming boat, his left arm raised. Perkins leaned out, the man's arm slipped through the loop, and he was catapulted clear of the water and into the raft with a thump that Waverly felt through the wooden landing craft's side.

One after another, the platoon started coming aboard, scrambling over the Higgins boat's gunwale and collapsing onto the deck, breathing hard.

Foglio was the first man aboard. Waverly walked forward to see him. "Blondie!" he called. "What's the word?"

Foglio, his chest heaving, his back against the starboard bulwark, looked up and managed a weak grin. "Good news, Lieutenant," he said. "No mines. No obstacles. Not a thing." He patted the slates hanging from his belt. "Got everything we'll need right here."

Waverly was just about to reply when his eye was caught by a flash of movement forward. One of the boat's machine gunners, leaning over his weapon, had suddenly straightened up on his toes. His helmet clattered across the Higgins boat's deck as his head appeared to explode in a bright red spray. He slumped backward over the rim of the gun well, his .30-caliber's muzzle pointed uselessly at the sky.

"Christ," Foglio said. He looked shaken. "When it's got your friggin name on it…"

Waverly checked the man, but there was clearly nothing to be done. The round had punched through his skull just above the bridge of his nose and blown out most of the back of head. The awful part of the death was its sheer randomness. Whoever had fired that round could not possibly have been aiming at that sailor in particular, not with the LCP(R) flying over the surface at full speed. The rifleman must have simply been firing in the direction of the boat, and by sheer, random chance the round had killed the man outright.

Lieutenant Dulaney was the third-to-last man aboard, followed by Davies and McNally.

"All accounted for, sir," Waverly told Dulaney. "Let's get the hell out of here."

"I'll buy the beer, Mike," Dulaney replied.

The boat raced away from the beach, angling toward the APD *Humphreys.*

Tangretti stood on the beach, watching the landing craft crowding the narrow approaches offshore. The crackle of rifle fire still sounded from the brush inland, interspersed occasionally with the heavier crump of artillery.

At 1000 hours that morning, the first landing craft had dropped their ramps, the first troops storming ashore onto

Leyte's beaches. The landings had been textbook perfect, on glassy seas that bore not a trace of the storms of several days before. The bombardment had been steady and effective, beginning with concentrated fire from six of Oldendorf's battleships, then giving way to close-range fire from cruisers and destroyers, and ending at last with a savage rocket attack from LCIs moving in close to the beaches.

The Army 1st Cavalry, sans boots and spurs, had gone ashore on White Beach, on the right flank of the San Pedro landing area just below Tacloban, while the 24th Infantry had grounded here on Red Beach. South, the 96th Infantry had landed on the Orange beaches beneath the green loom of Catmon Hill, and on the Blue beaches surveyed by UDT-8. To the south of that, the 7th Infantry had landed on Violet and Yellow beaches in the face of the stiffest opposition that morning. Despite the resistance, however, Dulag had been cleaned out and occupied by noon. Total casualties so far had been remarkably and unexpectedly light — less than fifty dead, certainly — and most of the resistance at this point appeared to be from isolated snipers. The Japanese defenders, no doubt, were organizing themselves inland. That, Tangretti thought, would be where the real fighting would take place.

He wondered if Leyte would turn out to be another Peleliu.

Tangretti, Simmons, and several other men from UDT-8 had been given the chance to go ashore on Red Beach this afternoon and, though Tangretti had been watching the proceedings so far with a jaundiced eye, he had to admit that it was good to get off the APD and stretch his legs on solid ground … something the UDT rarely enjoyed when their assignment called for long swims under fire.

The team had been given the opportunity as a kind of political gesture, a nod toward the UDT men who'd carried out their missions during the past two days despite problems with communications, with faulty planning, or in the face of enemy fire. This mission had been costly for the teams.

Team Three had managed to carry off its reconnaissance on the eighteenth without a hitch and with no casualties, but the others hadn't been so lucky. One of Team Four's LCP(R)s had been hit by four mortar rounds, with three men wounded. The boat had sunk, while the men inflated life jackets on the wounded men and, swimming through the waves, had towed them to safety. The APD *Goldsborough*, seeing what was happening, began maneuvering closer inshore to give the swimming men fire support ... something that had been notably lacking that afternoon. A Japanese shell had struck her number-one stack, killing two men and wounding sixteen. One of the dead and five of the wounded had been Team Four guys left on board.

Team Five had been the only team that had managed to wangle air support, and that, the story went, was only because the team's Exec had started yelling for support and refused to get off the frequency until it arrived. Even so, one boat had had its machine gunner killed, while another had suffered a near miss from a mortar round, with one man wounded.

Team Eight had suffered the heaviest casualties of all on the first day. Besides Dayton, four others in another boat had been wounded during the recovery when a mortar round exploded alongside. And Kelly had died of his wound the next morning.

On the second day of reconnaissance, Teams Six and Ten — the "Golden Horseshoe" — had come through completely unscathed, but Team Nine had been hurt badly. Their First Platoon boat had taken a direct hit from a mortar round before the men had even hit the water. One man had been killed, twelve others wounded. All in all, the operation had been the costliest the UDT had experienced yet in the Pacific.

Interestingly enough, only one of the casualties had been suffered by a swimmer in the water. All of the rest had been aboard their Higgins boats when they were hit, which tended to support the idea traveling through UDT circles that men in the water were not as vulnerable to enemy fire as some planners had originally predicted. The losses suffered by the teams during the past two days had been shocking because the teams had never faced this sort of thing before. Tangretti, though, remembered the fifty-two percent casualty rate suffered by the Navy CDU men at Omaha Beach and knew that this was nothing.

The thought was not in the least comforting. Kelly had been a friend and a fellow member of the teams, a swim buddy, not a statistic.

It had been drizzling off and on throughout the afternoon, and the overcast sky still held the promise of rain. It was muggy and hot. Tangretti was feeling soggy in his green marine fatigues and wished he could strip down to his more usual uniform — swim trunks. That wouldn't do today, however. The beach was already crawling with newsmen and other strange forms of life.

"There," Simmons said, pointing. "I think that's him."

A landing craft was making its way slowly toward the shore. It appeared to be lost. As it turned toward the beach about fifty yards offshore, it suddenly shuddered to a halt, hard aground.

The waters offshore were cluttered by four grounded landing craft, one of them still burning from a hit taken that morning. Nearby, the Red Beach beachmaster, a harried-looking Army major, was speaking urgently into a radio handset. "Look, most of the piers on this beach were wrecked in the bombardment," he was shouting. "And I don't have time to deliver guided tours." He listened to an inaudible reply, then gave an eloquent shrug. "I don't give a damn who you got on board, mister. Let 'em walk!"

Simmons grinned at Tangretti. "Beachmasters," he said. "They think they own the fuckin' beach."

"They do," Tangretti said. "Uh oh. Here it is."

The landing craft, obviously, was going nowhere. Slowly, the bow ramp swung down, landing with a splash in the surf. A moment later, a gaggle of men in khaki strode down the ramp, stepped into water two feet deep, and began making their way ashore.

In the lead was a man whose face Tangretti already knew very well, having seen it often enough on the pages of *Stars and Stripes* and other publications. Even if he'd never seen the man's hooked nose and jutting chin, though, the trademark high peaked hat and sunglasses would have been an immediate giveaway. General Douglas MacArthur had just made good his promise of two and a half years before; he had returned to the Philippines.

He looked furious, and Tangretti wondered if he was angry about the grounded landing craft or the beachmaster's intractability. A newsman at the edge of the surf snapped a picture. The people milling along in the general's wake included a number of other officers, the Filipino Sergio Osmena, handpicked by MacArthur to be the next president of the Philippines, and more newsmen and photographers. Ignoring the beachmaster, MacArthur strode up and onto dry sand. Gunfire crackled in the distance, a Japanese machine gun, but he appeared not to hear. After a brief discussion with his aides, he walked off into the trees behind the beach, presumably in search of the 24th Infantry's headquarters.

Later, Tangretti and Simmons stood in the crowd of reporters and soldiers standing nearby as a Signal Corps officer gave him a hand microphone.

"People of the Philippines," he said. "I have returned. By the grace of Almighty God, our forces stand again on Philippine soil — soil consecrated in the blood of our two peoples…"

Tangretti noticed the general's hands were trembling. Several drops of rain fell; several of the onlookers glanced up into an ominous sky. Thunder rolled … but it was the thunder of one of the battleships in Leyte Gulf, firing on targets inland.

"Rally to me!" MacArthur was saying, his voice rising. "Let the indomitable spirit of Bataan and Corregidor lead on. As the lines of battle roll forward to bring you within the zone of operations, rise and strike. Strike at every favorable opportunity. For your homes and hearths, strike! For future generations of your sons and daughters, strike! Let no heart be faint. Let every arm be steeled. The guidance of Divine God points the way. Follow in His name to the Holy Grail of righteous victory!"

Osmena took the microphone and began speaking, but Tangretti was having trouble hearing as trucks grumbled along the road behind the beach. A flight of Hellcats howled overhead. Eventually, the ceremony was over. MacArthur and Osmena walked to a fallen log at the top of the beach and sat down. Simmons and Tangretti walked away.

"The sanctimonious bastard," Tangretti said.

"What, MacArthur?"

Tangretti nodded. "He's the reason we came here, right? If it wasn't for him, we wouldn't have needed to send the Marines into Peleliu. And we wouldn't've lost Frank."

Simmons shrugged. He'd been very quiet since hearing about Kelly's death. "Hey, they don't pay us to make strategy."

Tangretti jerked his head toward the coconut palms behind the beach, and the crackling gunfire beyond. "Casualties were light in the landings. They were damned lucky, but the worst is yet to come. The *real* fighting's going to be inland. Lots of boys are going to die in there. You think that brass hat back there gives a damn? He's going to just keep on landing on island after island right here in the Philippines, and to hell with anything else or anyone else in the war. The way I heard it, MacArthur is running this whole campaign for his own satisfaction, just to get the Philippines back. Shit, Japan's the enemy. That's where we should be attacking. A *blind* man could see it." Then he thought about Dayton and angrily clamped his mouth shut.

"She-it," Simmons said quietly, as if in tribute to the dead Kelly.

There didn't seem to be anything more to say.

CHAPTER 23

Thursday, 26 October 1944
UDT School, Amphibious Training Base
Kamaole, Maui, Hawaii

"At ease, Lieutenant. And welcome back. I guess it was pretty rough out there…"

"Yes, sir." Alexander Forsythe barely relaxed from attention as he responded to Lieutenant Commander Chapman's greeting. Despite the man's friendly words and warm tone, Forsythe couldn't help but feel uneasy. *I screwed up bad at Yap…*

Burrfish had remained in the Western Carolines throughout the period leading up to the Peleliu landings, monitoring Japanese activity around the islands but making no further attempts to mount reconnaissance missions. Fitzgerald had been adamant about that. Since the American interest in Yap had been given away, he had argued, further recon missions would encourage the enemy to strengthen their defenses even further. Forsythe had urged him to let them try another mission, insisting that his tiny command needed to get back into action instead of remaining cooped up on the sub with nothing to do but brood. As usual Fitzgerald had ignored his pleas.

So they had remained aboard, crowded and distinctly underfoot as the sub crewmen went about their ordinary duties. When the invasion armada arrived, *Burrfish* found herself reassigned to picket duty near the fringe of the fleet, and there they had remained as the attack on Peleliu unfolded.

The Americans had decided, after receiving Fitzgerald's recommendations, to bypass Yap and focus on Peleliu and Angaur. Third 'Phib had moved in, confident of their advance preparations, but as Schroeder and Forsythe had originally predicted they ran into unexpected trouble because their information didn't include details of the terrain that awaited them above the surf line. The UDT operations had been fairly routine, and the hydrographic survey data faultless, but the periscope surveys and the aerial photos had not been able to penetrate the clinging jungle vegetation to spot the underlying rock. The Japanese had dug tunnels and built cave defenses that had turned the fighting on Peleliu into a yard-by-yard, foot-by-foot struggle, costing the Americans far too many lives when it came time to root them out. Listening to the periodic reports that the sub monitored on its lonely patrol, Forsythe had been gnawed by the feeling that he should have found some way to get around Fitzgerald's dogmatic foot-dragging and file a separate report of his own. Combined with his guilt at losing Schroeder and the others off Yap, the conviction that he'd failed had left him morose and depressed by the time the cruise was finally over.

Now *Burrfish* was back at Pearl Harbor. Upon arrival Fitzgerald and his men had returned to Waipio, while Forsythe, Crenshaw, and Barker, the survivors from the Maritime Unit — from UDT-10 — had returned to the training camp on Maui.

Being face-to-face with Chapman brought all of Forsythe's bleak feelings to the surface again. Couldn't he have done *something* more to help Schroeder and the rest of the team?

Chapman seemed to sense his discomfort. "Look, Forsythe, relax. You're not here for a reprimand. Far from it. Your boys did a damned good job scouting Peleliu. As for Yap … that was bad luck, pure and simple. House odds catch up with the best gamblers, Lieutenant, and we all knew that this mission was one high-stakes gamble."

"If you say so, sir," Forsythe responded, keeping his voice flat and level.

"Your report's been read by every level of brass from here to the Pentagon and back, and no one's suggested you could have done anything different. Chief Schroeder and the others missed their rendezvous and were captured —"

"I wish I could be sure of that, sir," Forsythe interrupted. "I mean, there's just something about *not knowing* what happened to Red that makes my gut churn every time I think about it."

"Oh, we know they were captured, Lieutenant. We intercepted Jap radio traffic that confirmed it. Three American swimmers were captured on the beach at Yap on August twentieth. So that much is sure."

"Do we know anything else, sir? About where they are now?"

Chapman shrugged. "Presumably they would have been sent to a POW camp somewhere. There's no way to be sure. And anything could happen in the meantime. POW life is no picnic. We do know they were questioned pretty thoroughly on Yap … and we know they didn't crack."

"Sir?"

Chapman actually smiled. "More intercepted Jap messages. We picked up a detailed summary of what the command on Yap had learned of American UDT operations. They call us the *Bakuhatai*, which is Japanese for Demolition Unit. According to their information, each of our teams is equipped with four submarines called LVPs which deploy swimmers ten miles away from an objective and let them swim the rest of the way in. The Japs are now busy taking extra precautions against future infiltrations by our dreaded swimmers, but I don't think they'll accomplish much if they're out there looking for LVPs, whatever the hell those are supposed to be. I tell you, Forsythe, when I gave you guys that send-off speech I never really figured anyone would actually be able to feed them false information. It was sure spooky when I saw the copy of that message, let me tell you."

"Sounds like Red Schroeder was in rare form that day, sir," Forsythe said with a grudging smile of his own. He was torn between pain and pride. Chapman was right about their chances for survival; POWs in Japanese hands died in droves in unsanitary camps with inadequate rations and cruel workloads. But Schroeder — those tall tales the Japs had believed must have come from him — Schroeder had handled his captors with the same combination of guts and humor he'd shown every day Forsythe had known the man.

"It hasn't been the same around here since he left," Chapman said quietly. "The three of them have been put in for Silver Stars. I hope they don't turn out to be posthumous. The rest of your team's up for the same awards. Yourself included, Lieutenant."

"Sir ... er, thank you, sir." Forsythe swallowed. He didn't want the medal. His instant reaction was an angry feeling that it wasn't fair to Schroeder, White, and O'Leary if the whole recon team got the same recognition. It cheapened the honor those three men deserved to be shown. The brass didn't seem to understand, sometimes, that handing out medals indiscriminately was a damned poor policy. It was individual achievement that they should have been recognizing...

"No thanks necessary, Lieutenant. You and your team went up against some pretty goods odds, and you did your jobs well.

The preliminary survey off Peleliu was some damned fine work."

"I suppose so, sir." His tone was neutral.

"Sounds like you don't agree, Lieutenant. What do you know about the op that I don't?"

Forsythe hesitated, then abandoned caution and plunged ahead. "Only this, sir. I think we could have kept a lot of the Marines we lost on Peleliu from dying unnecessarily if we had done a more thorough reconnaissance job."

"Most of the Marine casualties were due to gaps in our knowledge of the defenses ashore, Lieutenant. Intelligence outside your purview. Don't try to take the blame for something that was never your responsibility."

"The point is, sir, that Red and the others *did* gather information on the island terrain. They would have gotten more if *Burrfish* hadn't been chased off by sub hunters after the first night. The little material his people did get was left out of Commander Fitzgerald's report because of the very reason you just mentioned. He felt it wasn't our job. But I disagree. I think it should have been our job from the very beginning, that we should have gone out there ready not just to do the hydrographic work, but if necessary to climb right up on shore and check out the defenses at close quarters, spot their strong points and their troop concentrations and all the rest. The invasion plans could have taken account of all of it right off the bat."

"You lost three men as it was. How much more risk would you have run if you'd actually gone ashore as part of the mission?"

"If we trained the men for that kind of work, they'd know how to do escape and evasion. They'd be armed, if necessary. And the real point is, how many lives would we have *saved* if the Marines had gone in knowing just what to expect? I tell you, Commander, we're missing something crucial here. Over in Europe they tried to make the demolition men part of the actual invasion force, going in on the first landing craft and trying to blow obstacles while the rest of the army unloaded around them. I hear they were loaded down with heavy combat gear and canvas suits to protect them from gas attacks that never happened. Out here in PTO we've gone the other way. Here we have the Naked Warrior who strips down to swim trunks and mask and fins, and we didn't even use fins until my OSS boys showed how they were supposed to be used. We're supposed to do survey and demolition work long before the troops hit the beach, but the surf line's our rigid boundary even if it would make sense to go ashore. As far as I can see, the UDTs are going way too far overboard with this stay-in-the-water philosophy. We're wasting a valuable asset."

"You'd turn the UDTs into combat troops? Put them on the firing line? That won't make you very popular with men like Commander Coffer. He's been waging a one-man war against the Marines ever since Saipan because they keep trying to give us rifles and put us in the front lines."

"No, sir, I don't mean anything like that. We can't do everything. But I don't think we've found our true calling yet, and I don't think we will as long as we see our sole functions being obstacle clearing and wading around measuring water depth. Used the right way, combat swimmers could change everything we know about amphibious warfare. The UDTs, the old CDUs, the Scouts and Raiders, the OSS Maritime Unit ... I think each group has had a glimmering of what we're looking for, but I think the real thing's bigger and bolder than all of them put together. We want swimmers who can do an offshore survey, clear reefs and obstacles, do scout work ashore, maybe even attack key points or blow up defensive emplacements or create diversions while the Marines are coming in. Whatever the job required, we should be able to do it."

Chapman looked thoughtful. "You have some interesting ideas, Forsythe."

"I've had a lot of time to think them through, sir. On *Burrfish*, after what happened on Yap. And someday they'll be more than just ideas."

"Well, intriguing as they are I'm afraid they're too radical for the UDT right now. We've finally found our feet, Lieutenant. I really doubt that anyone is going to start tampering with an outfit that's already pretty damned successful."

Forsythe smiled at him. "Just wait and see, Commander. Someday I'll have my own team, and when I do maybe I'll have a chance to put some of my ideas into practice. And if the brass higher up see what we can do, maybe they'll make it official. Or maybe I'll get a shot at a policy job down the line. Who can say?"

The commander raised an eyebrow. "Is that so? You sound like a man who plans to stay in the teams for a while, Lieutenant. Not at all like a fellow who'd call down the wrath of God knows how many staff types in order to secure a transfer out of the UDT."

Forsythe kept himself from groaning aloud ... barely. The transfer! He had forgotten entirely about the transfer request he had filed the week he'd first been assigned to Maui, and the high-powered pressure he'd brought to bear on family friends in Navy staff jobs from Washington to Hawaii and beyond.

Back in July, disappointed over the way the Maritime Unit had been broken up and dubious about the whole UDT operation, Forsythe had seen a transfer as the only way to get his career back on track. That was before Peleliu and Yap, before he'd gotten to know Schroeder and to understand what the UDT was capable of. Before he'd realized that it could do so much more. As he'd told Chapman, he had spent plenty of time thinking about it during the past two months.

Forsythe no longer wanted out of the UDT. Now he wanted to see it reach its full potential. He wanted to be a part of it, to help shape its future the way men like David Coffer and Tom Chapman were doing.

He owed that much — and more besides — to the memories of Red Schroeder and the others.

Alexander Hamilton Forsythe III looked Chapman squarely in the eye. "Transfer request? Commander, right now a transfer out of the UDT is the furthest thing from my mind. And I'm sure anyone who has been trying to … help my career along … I'm sure they'll come to understand how important this is to me very soon."

Chapman smiled. "Very good, Lieutenant. Then you're available for a UDT assignment?"

"Yes, sir. Preferably a combat slot. The scuttlebutt says Team Ten's assigned to MacArthur's big show in the Philippines. Any chance I can hook back up with them?"

The commander shook his head. "I'll check on openings, but I'm pretty sure their TO and E is filled out already. What I really need is a training officer here on Maui —"

"But, sir —"

"To hold the job down on a *temporary* basis until the new guy I'm supposed to be getting in finally shows up," Chapman went on as if Forsythe hadn't interrupted. "We're in the middle of bringing a new batch of Fort Pierce men up to speed. They've been designated UDT-Fifteen, and they're short of senior officers. I've already promised the command slot to Tex

Kingsley. He was supposed to have Team Ten before your OSS crew was brought in and your buddy Coates had the seniority. He'll need an Exec, though, and I'd be willing to let you go when they graduate next month."

"Will this Kingsley be willing to take me, sir? Sounds like he might not be too big a fan of the OSS…"

"But you aren't from the OSS anymore, Lieutenant," Chapman said pointedly. "You're part of the teams … just like the rest of us."

Forsythe hesitated a moment longer. Deep down, he'd hoped to be offered a command of his own, but after all, he still hadn't done duty with a regular Team. He couldn't expect to step straight into a top job unless he started pulling strings, and for the first time in his life Forsythe didn't particularly want the preferential treatment. A few months as Exec would give him the seasoning he knew he needed. Another chance at a command would come along soon enough, he thought, and when the time came he'd be ready.

"I'll take it, Commander," he said at last. "Just so long as I get active duty. If I'd wanted to get buried on a staff somewhere I'd've wangled a slot at the Pentagon."

"Oh, you'll be active enough, all right, Lieutenant," Chapman told him with a grin. "Maybe more active than you ever figured on being."

"What can I get you, Lieutenant?"

Forsythe settled onto a stool and studied the Hawaiian bartender for a long moment. "Make it a beer," he said at last. Normally he didn't care for beer, but he was making an effort to start fitting in with his comrades in the UDT. Cultivating their tastes in drinks might help him break down some of the barriers that set him apart from the men he would be serving with.

He had the weekend to get himself squared away before taking up his new duties on Chapman's staff, so he'd decided to fit in a trip across to Oahu for an evening of relaxation. Unlike his bar-crawling the weekend before the *Burrfish* sailed, tonight he had no intention of carousing or finding some woman to conquer. He had no taste for that sort of thing anymore. Not after Yap. All he wanted was to toss off a few drinks in silent toast to Red Schroeder, Bob White, and John O'Leary.

"Alex? Alex, it *is* you, isn't it?"

The woman's voice behind him made Forsythe turn. For a long moment he couldn't place the tall, slender blonde in the WAVE uniform. Then he remembered.

Maggie ... the woman from the beach. The woman he'd romanced with the same calculating precision as an invasion plan.

A memory flashed unbidden through his mind. *I think I could handle it better if I knew for sure that Sam was dead, but* not knowing, *that's the worst.* She had been describing her feelings about the disappearance of her brother's sub, and he had been using her sadness to further his own campaign to get into her panties. He had said almost the same thing to Chapman when they were talking about Schroeder.

Alex Forsythe felt like a total heel.

"Maggie..." He trailed off, not knowing what to say to her.

"How long have you been back in port? Was your patrol okay?" Her eyes had brightened as soon as he spoke, and her words came out in an excited tumble. "I was really hoping for a letter or a call..."

He flushed. "Look, Maggie, I'm really sorry. I should have … I don't know. I guess … I guess I didn't really intend it to be any more than the one night."

She looked like he'd slapped her, and took a step back. "I … see." Her tone had gone cold and flat. "I'm sorry if I assumed too much."

He stood up and blocked her before she could leave. "Wait a minute, Maggie. Wait. That night … I was wrong, that night, taking advantage of you that way. I'm afraid that's the only way I ever treated a woman, but that doesn't excuse what I did to you."

"Get out of my way," she said coldly.

"I will … if you'll let me finish apologizing to you. Please?"

Her eyes studied him with a look he couldn't fathom. Then she nodded. "All right. Apologize. If it will make you feel better, you can grovel on the floor if you want."

He mustered an uncertain smile. "I'm a jerk, and I'm sorry, and I'm wrong, but I'm damned if I'm going to go that far! Maggie, if I'd been in my right mind that night I would have shown you a wonderful time, wined and dined you, danced the night away, and started a real relationship instead of maneuvering you out to that beach and … everything. But I really was a jerk, thinking of myself and nobody else. I wish there was some way I could undo it."

She didn't answer him for a long moment. Finally she spoke. "All right, you apologized. As far as I'm concerned, I don't know you. You're a stranger. And I don't talk to strangers."

He nodded slowly. "Okay. I deserve that. I'm sorry." He started to move off, but she touched his arm.

"I don't talk to strangers … not until they introduce themselves. Maybe buy a drink to break the ice." Her blue eyes held his, and he felt a thrill rush up his spine.

He thrust out his hand. "Good evening, ma'am," he said. "My name is Alex Forsythe, and I'm *not* in submarines, even though my last assignment did have me sailing in one. Right now I'm on a staff job, and as far as I know I'm not going on any classified missions or keeping any deep secrets. But if I'm not too terribly dull, I'd love to buy you a drink and strike up a conversation."

She smiled. "Maggie MacAllister. I'd love to have a drink and a talk … but I don't think I want to go swimming. Not when we've just met and all."

He laughed and signaled the bartender. Alex Forsythe had never been able to think of a woman as anything but an object of his lust, but he saw something more in Maggie MacAllister. He saw a chance to make a complete break with his past, to make a fresh start in every part of his life.

"Ten … HUT!"

Frank Rand drew himself to attention along with the rest of the hundred-man unit assembled on the lava-strewn field of the Maui camp. The senior officers of the UDT school, Commander Chapman and his staff, stood in a group facing the class, together with the instructors who had shepherded Rand and the others through then-advanced training for the past six weeks.

It was good to know they were graduating at last. The Fort Pierce men had come out to the Pacific believing they'd be funneled straight into combat, but they'd ended up spending as much time in UDT training as they had learning to be Demolitioneers in Florida. But all of that was finally behind them. As of this week, they were UDT-15, one of the teams that would be carrying the war to the beaches held by the Japanese empire.

Underwater Demolition Team Fifteen, Rand thought, would probably enter the folklore of the teams in short order. Seventeen six-man boat crews from a string of graduating classes had been gathered together for dispatch to the Pacific, Rand's class among them. Their journey to Hawaii had been an epic voyage of sorts. On the train trip from Florida to San Bruno in California, during a ten-minute stop in Nevada, Ensign Jones had won a hundred dollars at the crap tables. Team members were still talking about his run of luck, and the competition to get into his platoon, where that good fortune might rub off on his comrades, had been fierce.

Rand, Kowalski, and Jennings had missed that part of the team's travels, arriving at San Bruno a few days later. While waiting for available shipping, Jennings and Kowalski had adopted a stray dog they named Esther Williams for her swimming skills. The dog had rapidly become something of a mascot to the Fort Pierce graduates, and when the orders came to report to the Dutch merchant vessel M.S. *Tjisdane* at San Francisco's Pier Eighteen, they had naturally brought Esther Williams along. But the UDT men ran afoul of the ship's First Officer, who refused to allow the animal on board. The impasse had been solved by Stoky Stark, who'd bribed some dockworkers to hide the dog in a crate and smuggle it into the *Tjisdane's* hold. Team members had taken turns slipping food from the mess down to Esther through the whole trip to Hawaii. When they arrived at Pearl Harbor, Stark had managed to sway the dog's crate out over the fantail and into the LCI that was to take them to Maui along with the rest of the team's effects and gear. Esther Williams was still Team Fifteen's mascot, and Rand figured she'd be with them for a long time to come — at least as long as Chief Stark was able to work his magic.

At Maui they'd learned about the need for further training. Someone on the Kamaole staff had heard from a friend back at Fort Pierce that the new Team Fifteen had claimed to be particularly tough and well-trained. Supposedly they had boasted they could swim a mile with fifty pounds of tetrytol strapped to their backs, among other accomplishments, and the UDT instructors had decided to put them to the test right off the bat. Rand rather suspected that the source of the whole story had been Gunny Drake, a last practical joke directed at his one-time Scouts and Raiders comrade. Most of the team had flunked the swimming challenge, and Jennings had almost had to drop out of the unit entirely. Rand and the others eventually helped him get through the long-distance swimming qualifications, just as they had with the basic swim back at Fort Pierce, but it was a long and tough process getting through the whole UDT training program.

Now it was done. And at last UDT-15 would be a part of the war. Rand, usually so eager to see action, was torn for the first time as he contemplated that fact. He hadn't realized just how much marriage would change his outlook.

"Men of UDT Fifteen," Commander Chapman was saying. "The war in the Pacific is reaching a climax. The Navy, the Marines, and the Army are combining to push back the Japanese on all fronts. In the next few months we will be knocking at the gates of Tokyo, and the UDTs will be leading the way. Now that you have completed training, you'll be joining your comrades in the vanguard of America's advance.

"As you've gone through training, you've lacked officers senior enough to command your team. Today I am reassigning two of my staff. Some of you have seen them in action already. They are experienced veterans who will bring the benefit of their skills and knowledge to your unit. Lieutenant Austin F.

Kingsley will be the new CO of UDT-Fifteen. He is a Fort Pierce graduate who has been part of my staff here for several months. His Exec will be Lieutenant Alex Forsythe, from Team Ten, who recently earned the Silver Star for bravery in a classified UDT mission deep in enemy waters. I believe these two men are the ideal people to complete your team. Serve them well, and they'll lead you to victory."

Rand studied the two officers Chapman had indicated. Kingsley he knew more from scuttlebutt than from any direct contact, but Forsythe had been heavily involved in teaching the proper use of swim fins to the trainees. They were a study in contrasts. The new CO was a big, raw-boned man with a Texas drawl and a reputation as a little bit of a wild man, in keeping with his cowboy image. He was nicknamed Tex. As for Forsythe, he was smaller, trim and neat, always impeccably dressed in crisp, perfectly tailored uniforms. There were stories circulating that suggested Forsythe had come out of some secret spy operation rather than the more conventional Fort Pierce route, and no doubt there would be some in Team Fifteen who would resent an Exec who hadn't come through the NCDU training, but Rand had seen enough of the man to respect his competence.

Kingsley stepped forward and started talking, but Rand's mind wasn't on his words. He was thinking, instead, of Nancy. Team Fifteen was heading into the war at last, and Frank Rand would be there with them … but his heart would still be back in Michigan with the woman he loved.

CHAPTER 24

Wednesday, 15 November 1944
Noumea, New Caledonia

Their favorite establishment in the French territorial capital of Noumea was supposed to be off-limits, but the UDT had claimed the place as its own private watering hole, a bar just off the Grand Quai called Le Poisson. Tangretti had been told the name meant "The Poison," a joke played on every sailor arriving there for the first time. The shingle hanging outside had the name written on the scaly sides of a rather forlorn-looking fish. Inside, the deep-sea motif was continued, with fishing nets, dried sea fans, and enormous branches of coral hanging from the walls, mingled with hundreds of dried specimens of sea life — starfish, sea horses, sea urchin shells, and a number of odd-looking tropical fish that were, if anything, far more forlorn-looking in their desiccated state than their wooden namesake outside.

They'd arrived at the bar earlier than usual this afternoon, men from four different UDTs sent to New Caledonia for R&R, and with great ceremony had evicted four Army men already in the place. After all, the Navy men reasoned, how could they complain to the authorities about being tossed out of a bar when the place was off-limits? Even so, one man watched the door while the rest got down to the business of the meeting.

Roll call.

"Mineman Second Class Frank Kelly!" Tangretti shouted, holding his glass aloft. The other men in the room raised their glasses as well. Tangretti's hand trembled slightly. "KIA, Blue Beach, Leyte! Team Eight!"

"*Team Eight!*" the others chorused.

Tangretti tossed down the scotch in his glass, feeling it burn its way down his throat. The others drank too, punctuating the moment with the crash and tinkle of empty glasses and bottles smashing against a liquor-stained patch of bare cement wall that rose from a small mountain of broken glass. Just above the target area, the bony, tooth-lined circle of a shark's jaws gaped open. Someone had hung a sailor's white hat on the lower rows of teeth.

"*Messieurs!*" The bartender, a balding, worried-looking man with an immense handlebar mustache, hurried out from behind his counter. "*Messieurs! Arrêtez, je vous en prie! Les verres!...* "

Rising, with only a little unsteadiness, Tangretti blocked the furious bartender's advance. Since Tangretti, of all the UDT men present, had actually *been* in France, he'd been unanimously elected by the others to act as interpreter for the party, despite the fact that all he'd seen of the country was a stretch of hell-blasted sand and beach obstacles and fire-swept bluffs. Still, he knew more French than the rest of them. At one point during his stay in England, just before the invasion armada had embarked, Tangretti had started learning French from a book he'd picked up at an Army PX.

"*Ill nee pass de quoiy, monsuer,*" he said, reasonably enough.

The bartender stopped in mid rush and blinked at him. "Eh?"

"Uh, um, *quel est lay pricks,*" Tangretti continued, following up his verbal advantage. Gesturing broadly to include the watching UDT men, he plunged ahead. "Uh ... *noose payez view...* uh..."

"I speak English, monsieur," the man said stiffly. "*Considerably* better than you speak French."

"Huh?"

"But I tend to forget the English when I see my customers smashing my glasses! I assume what you were trying to say is that *you* will pay *me*, not the other way around!"

"Uh, right."

"Hey, Gator!" a young TM2 from Team Nine called from one of the tables. "What was that you were telling him about pricks?"

Ignoring the heckling, Tangretti fished into the back pocket of his white trousers and pulled out his wallet. "Look, this is kind of a memorial service, see? For some good buddies who didn't make it, understand?" He extracted a wad of U.S. currency. "We'll pay for the damage. Whatever you say."

With a practiced eye, the bartender examined the bills in Tangretti's hand, then reached over and deftly selected four twenties. "This will cover the damage done so far. You will pay me for anything broken, *oui*?"

"*Oui*. Uh, yes, sir."

"And take it easy, please!" He eyed the men in the room. "New glasses can be hard to get. There is, how do you say? There is the war on, and I have a business to run!"

"S'okay, Frenchie," Blondie Foglio called out. "When you run out of glasses, we'll just drink from the bottles!"

"Frenchie! Some more poison! And bring some fresh glasses!"

The bartender muttered something dark beneath his breath, then pocketed the money and returned to his counter, shaking his head. Tangretti slumped back into his chair. "Where … were we?"

"Engineman Second Class Peter Lamb," Chief Davies solemnly intoned. "Wounded at Saipan. Invalided out. Team Five."

"*Team Five!*"

They didn't hurl their glasses that time. That special tribute was reserved for the ones who'd died.

The roll call continued.

Most of the men in the bar had arrived in New Caledonia two weeks before, and their sixteen days of R&R was very nearly up. This assembly had been organized as a kind of farewell party for departed friends.

R&R, rest and relaxation. Most of the men in Eight had been eagerly anticipating what they preferred to call I&I, for intercourse and intoxication. There'd been little of the first available. There were prostitutes, of course, but for weeks before arriving at Noumea, the men had talked about little except the beautiful French girls they were going to meet in New Caledonia.

The island had been billed — by scuttlebutt as well as by official pronouncement — as a tropical paradise. The territory of New Caledonia had been part of the French empire since the 1890s, and Noumea, the largest town on the island of New Caledonia, had been a relatively sleepy and backward town until the coming of the Americans. The island's population was divided between Melanesian natives, Polynesian and Asian immigrant workers, and French colonists, administered, after the events of 1940, by a Free French government New Cal, as the Americans called it, had been occupied by Allied forces early in 1942. Its position, a thousand miles east of Australia and halfway between New Zealand and the southeastern tip of New Guinea, had made it an obvious strategic target for the Japanese in their effort to isolate the Australian continent, and the U.S. 164th Infantry had been stationed there against that possibility.

The 164th had moved on to Guadalcanal in August of 1942, but by that time the U.S. Navy had landed and had the situation well in hand. Noumea's harbor was one of the best in this corner of the Pacific, large, virtually landlocked, and quite deep, protected to seaward by a vast coral reef and further sheltered by the Ile Nou at the harbor's mouth. Even before Guadalcanal, New Caledonia had become an important staging area for naval operations a thousand miles to the north, in the Solomons.

With so much coming and going of military forces, of course, all of the unmarried French women on the island by now had either gotten married to someone in the first American wave or, more likely, had been moved by their parents to other, less accessible, islands. Plenty of men boasted of their exploits with the native Melanesian girls who lived in the New Caledonian capital, but most of that, Tangretti was sure, was just talk. "Nookie" — as naval personnel referred to all forms of sexual activity ashore — was simply not as freely available in Noumea as scuttlebutt had promised during the long months at sea.

There were prostitutes, of course; there were *always* prostitutes in places frequented by large numbers of servicemen. Getting to them was often something of a problem, though. The military authority, conscious of concerns back in the States about the troops' moral environment, had declared some parts of Noumea off-limits, a rule enforced by billy-club-wielding S.P.s.

Still, if a man was determined enough, stealthy enough, or had enough extra-hazardous-duty pay in his wallet, plenty of ways could be found around the rules and regs. Tangretti, like most of his mates, had availed himself of the girls at La Lumière Rouge, tucked in behind Le Poisson and one of the main reasons the military authorities had placed the area off-limits. After the sheer, enjoyable explosion of physical release during his first couple of visits, though, Tangretti had found the encounters to be monotonous and automatic to the point of boredom. The girls weren't all that attractive, and few spoke more than a smattering of English. Worst of all, though, they just *lay* there with their legs spread apart, not even looking at him as he pumped and slid and grunted on top of their sweat-slicked and unresponsive bodies.

He wanted something more than that … and there was simply nothing more to be had. So much for the first I of I&I.

If intercourse was not abundantly available in New Caledonia, however, the intoxication certainly was. There were strict rules about being drunk and disorderly, and there were the S.P.s to worry about while making your unsteady way back to the Navy barracks, but there were plenty of places to go where a man could get comfortably and happily drunk, and the UDT had reconned them all within a few days of their arrival.

Places like Le Poisson.

"Torpedoman's Mate First Class Charles Young," a big, red-mustached chief named O'Reilly announced loudly. "KIA, White Beach, Leyte. Team Nine!"

"*Team Nine!*"

This time the glasses flew, shattering on the bare wall beneath the shark jaws and its grotesque trophy.

At last the toasts were over. Someone took the white hat off the shark's teeth and passed it around, quickly filling it with a small pile of money from which Tangretti paid for the broken glasses, then paid for another round of bottles. The air, somber throughout the impromptu ceremony, grew noticeably lighter, then lighter still when the girls were invited back in. Some of them worked at Le Poisson, and the rest at the nearby Lumière Rouge. They, too, had been asked to leave during the roll call … a request put to them more gently than it had been put to the soldiers who'd been there earlier. Soon, the men were chatting almost happily with one another or with the young women who'd joined them. Cigarette smoke hung thick in the air, scarcely stirred by the slow-turning overhead fans, and the reek of liquor grew steadily stronger.

Tangretti ordered a new glass and ice, then tipped his quarter-full bottle of scotch to fill it up. Across the table, Simmons slid his glass within reach, and Tangretti poured him a shot as well. "The teams, mate," Simmons said, raising the glass.

"The teams."

When he set the empty glass down again, he saw Carpenter's Mate Chief O'Reilly standing by the table. O'Reilly was a powerfully built, six-foot-tall Irishman, complete with red hair and a bushy mustache that was not quite regulation.

"Pull up a chair for yourself, Chief. Have a hit?"

"Don't mind if I do. You're Gator?"

"That's me." They shook hands. O'Reilly had a tight, hard grip. "This here's Slim."

"I know. Met him here the other day. How ya doin', Slim?"

"Surviving. How's life in Nine?"

"It sucks." He slumped into the chair and accepted the drink from Tangretti.

"Haven't had a chance to talk to you guys about Leyte," Tangretti said. "How was it on your beach?"

"Wasn't good. I heard you were the guy who pulled one of your men out after he was wounded."

"Yeah." Tangretti managed a small grin. "Didn't even get in to the beach."

"I know how that is. We got hit before we even reached the drop-off."

"We heard it was bad up on White," Tangretti prompted. O'Reilly seemed to want to talk but was holding back. Sometimes it was damned hard reliving those memories.

Tangretti knew that from personal experience.

"Yeah, it was bad enough, I guess," O'Reilly said, shaking his head. He paused for another sip of scotch. "Some of our guys got within five yards of the shore. Got soundings, too, but they weren't too sure about mines. The water was damned muddy."

"I remember," Tangretti said.

"Our boat was four hundred yards off White Beach when we got straddled, one to each side, an' then a third came down smack on the boat's ass and a fourth blew a hole through the starboard side you could drive a truck through. The skipper was hit twice, in the chest and in the arm, but he was still on his feet, bellowin' out orders. We limped out another hundred, hundred-fifty yards, and then the engine quit. Then we were nailed but good in a crossfire from a little island offshore and from a house on the beach. Chuck Young, he bought it then. Shot right through the head. Another guy was hit in the arm. Damned thing was just hanging by a thread. The skipper, him and me, we used a sounding line as a tourniquet, and tied it off. Ten other guys were wounded in the boat."

Tangretti looked his new friend up and down. "They didn't get you. I see."

"Ah, laddy," he said, laying on a thick Irish brogue. "'Tis the luck o' the Irish, don't you know, an'll take aye more'n a houseful o' Japanese to put ol' Paddy O'Reilly down." He helped himself to another drink and chugged it down, slapping the glass hard onto the tabletop when it was empty and wiping his mouth with the back of his hand.

"How'd you get out, anyway?" Slim asked.

"Well, our boat was sinkin' out from beneath our webbed feet and we decided to swim for it. About then, two more of the team's boats came by, with fire from two directions layin' in like I never seen it before. They pulled us from the drink, they did, and we hotfooted it out to the fleet. Later that afternoon, two boat platoons were organized and sent back. Carried out the recon without the loss of a man."

Two more UDT men walked over, Chief Tom Davies and Blondie Foglio, both Team Five. "Hey, *paisan*," Foglio said, waving at Tangretti. "Telling lies again?"

"Damn it, Blondie," Tangretti said, "have some respect. We listen to your lies and don't ever question them, right?" He reached out with a leg and snagged an extra chair at a nearby table, dragging it over. "Park yourselves, men." He nodded at Davies. "Hey, Chief. This windbag giving you trouble?"

"Hey!" Foglio said, jerking his thumb toward his chest. "What do you mean, lies? When I speak, you can bank on it, okay?"

"Sure, Blondie, sure," Simmons said as the two sat down. He slipped a wink at Tangretti, but kept talking to the Team Five man. "Got any more trophies to show us?"

"What trophies?" O'Reilly wanted to know.

"You don't know this guy, do you?" Simmons said, indicating Foglio. "He likes to show off his trophies. Only nobody goes for it when we're in port."

"Right," Tangretti said. "See, Blondie, you've got to remember that guys only go for that shit after they've been at sea for about two months."

They'd met Foglio and Davies here in Le Poisson a week ago. Almost from the moment they'd shaken hands, Foglio had tried to charge him a dollar to see his collection of trophies taken from some willing WACs aboard the transport on the trip from San Diego to Pearl.

It reminded him so painfully of Snake — *he'd* boasted of a collection of panties too, liberated from willing girls — that at first Tangretti had hated the kid. That had changed over the past few days, though. Foglio was a likable enough sort ... and he had no idea of the effect his boasting and strutting had had on Tangretti.

Besides, Tangretti thought he knew a way to turn Foglio's boasting against him.

"That's okay, that's okay!" Foglio said, smiling. "While ol' Blondie is here in this luscious tropical paradise, be advised that I will be adding to my collection. And you all know where to find me if you need a little something to remember the joys left behind come next January or so."

"Might not need to come to you, Blondie," Tangretti said. "Lots of guys I know've been starting collections of their own, lately."

"Yeah? From who?" He laughed. "The whores over at the Lumière?"

"Nope," Tangretti said. "They wouldn't give their underwear away, you know that. And we've got better things to spend our money on now."

"Like what?"

"Like Lucy over there."

Lucy was one of the waitresses at Le Poisson, an attractive girl who was rumored to be married to an Australian soldier now serving in New Guinea. A blend of two worlds, her features were European, her skin the pale café au lait of mingled French and Melanesian blood. Tangretti found her attractive in an exotic way, though her bleached-blond hair was startling next to her darker skin.

"Aw, she don't put out," Foglio said. "Besides, she's married. Everybody knows that."

"All's fair in love and war, mate," Simmons said. "If the girl's willing…" He shrugged.

"Well, she's not," Foglio said.

"Yeah?" Tangretti said. "Did you ask her?"

"Huh? No!"

"Well, that's not what she told me last night."

"Aw, Gator, you're full of it."

In reply, Tangretti reached with delicate touch into the inside of his white jumper, just above the square knot in his black neckerchief. With tiny, jerky movements, like a magician producing some remarkable illusion, he tugged a wisp of sheer black silk out of his jumper.

"Seeing is believing," he said. He handed the garment across the table to Foglio. "And *I* won't even charge you for the privilege!"

In fact, Tangretti and Simmons had purchased the panties in a lingerie shop in Noumea two days before. They'd washed the newness out of them in a bucket of salt water, then added the distinctive aroma with a couple of drops from a bottle of musk.

Almost reluctantly, Foglio took the panties, then gave them a tentative sniff. "Whew!" he said.

Tangretti shook his hand. "Hot, Blondie. Incendiary."

"How do I know —"

"*Ask* her," Tangretti said. He nodded toward Lucy, who was busy serving drinks to some UDT Nine men at a table across the room. "She loves UDT guys, right, Slim?"

"Absolutely. She told me we're especially great in bed."

"That's because we're so good at holding our breath," O'Reilly said, struggling to keep a straight face. He wasn't in on this, but he'd smoothly stepped into the game, taking his lead from Simmons and Tangretti.

"And let me tell you, Blondie," Tangretti said. "She reciprocates. Oh, *man*, does she reciprocate!"

Blondie licked his lips, seemed about to say something, then changed his mind and handed the panties back to Tangretti. "That sounds … great," he said, less than enthusiastically.

"Listen, Blondie," Simmons said, "half the guys in Team Eight've already gotten to know the lady *very* well. She loves guys in demo, I tell you. Go on over and talk her up. I bet she'd give you her panties right now, if you asked her. Right here. All you've got to do is promise to see her tonight for a little late-night diving." He nudged Foglio with his elbow. "Know what I mean?"

"I don't think so, Slim," Tangretti said. "She wouldn't, not in here."

"Wouldn't what?"

"Give him her frillies. Not in front of everybody."

"Sure she would. She ain't shy." Simmons rolled his eyes. "*God*, she ain't shy!"

Tangretti reached for his wallet. "Ten says lover boy here can't get her panties off, not even in the back room. I think Lucy's more *discerning* than that."

"You're covered. If it swings between a pair of UDT legs, she'll go for it."

Foglio hesitated … and then a measure of his old, self-assured manner reasserted itself. "Shit, you guys can't railroad me! I'll bet you set something up with her."

"Hell no!" Tangretti said, feigning indignation.

"I never joke about nookie, man," Simmons said grimly. "There are some things a guy shouldn't joke about, and nookie's one of 'em."

"A reverential subject," Davies solemnly agreed.

"Go on," Tangretti urged. "*Ask* her. Ask her to give you her panties." He looked at Simmons. "Fifteen says he don't even ask her."

"Bet."

"Put your money away, damn it," Foglio said. "You guys know I only go for blondes. *Real* blondes, and she ain't no real blonde!"

"How do you know until you check?" Davies wanted to know.

"Anyway, what's the big deal?" O'Reilly said, waggling his eyebrows. "Blonde. Black. Polka-dot. They're all pink inside!"

"He's right, Blondie," Tangretti said. "Besides, you're defending your honor now. C'mon. Fifteen says you don't ask her."

"Aw ... *shit*!" Face reddening, Foglio got up from the table and stalked out, detouring well clear of Lucy on his way to the door. As the door closed behind him, Simmons, Davies, O'Reilly, and Tangretti all dissolved into helpless laughter.

"Son of a bitch!" O'Reilly said, leaning back in his chair and wiping his eye. "You guys are good!"

"Told ... told you he wouldn't go for it, Slim!" Tangretti said, laughing. "Where's my fifteen?"

"Hey! You said the bets wouldn't be for real!" Then Simmons started laughing again and reached for his wallet. "Oh, the hell with it. Here, you pirate! It's worth three sawbucks just to see the expression on his face!"

"Forget it, forget it," Tangretti said, shaking his head. "I was joking."

"You know," Davies said admiringly, "half the guys in Five've been wondering how to take Blondie down a notch ever since we were at Maui. My thanks, and my congratulations! That was a work of art!"

"Might've been better if he'd gone for it," Tangretti said, grinning.

"What, if he'd asked her?" O'Reilly asked. "Did you two set something up with her, like he said?"

"No. But did you hear about the last guy who made a pass at her?"

"Uh-uh."

"Seems Frenchie over there takes a kind of a protective, old-world-type attitude toward his girls, know what I mean? And he keeps a baseball bat behind the bar."

Simmons nodded. "It's true. I heard an Army guy reached up her dress and grabbed her ass about a month ago. She screamed and clobbered him with a tray, and then old Frenchie came out and broke his arm. Now, that *could* be a story…"

Davies eyed the bartender, who looked easily as muscular as any of the UDT men in the place. "That, gentlemen, is not a story I'd care to put to the test."

"So, Gator!" O'Reilly said. "I heard you and Slim, here, got to see MacArthur himself."

"Shit," Tangretti said. He drained his glass. "Wasn't that much to see."

"You don't sound all that impressed, Gator," Davies said.

"I hate officers," Tangretti said. "The damned, self-satisfied bastards. See, the way I figure it, what we need to do in this war is get all the officers on both sides to fight each other. Leave decent guys like us out of it."

"Hear, hear," Davies said, raising his glass. "Slim! Tell him about the exploders. Back at Pearl."

"What exploders?" Tangretti asked.

"I knew Slim back in Pearl, did you know? Used to hang out at the old Kilahuea. He used to be in the ordnance department at Pearl. You want to hear stories about officers. Go on, Slim. Tell 'em."

Simmons considered the question for a moment. "Aw, I spent eighteen months in ordnance, see? All through 'forty-two, our subs would come back from patrols and report that they'd get a nice, juicy Japanese target right in the crosshairs of their periscopes, only when they shot a torpedo at 'em, the warhead wouldn't go off. The torpedoes were hitting okay, but the exploders weren't firing, weren't setting off the warheads."

"I heard a little about that," Tangretti said. "The official report was that the sub skippers were missing their targets."

"Fuck that," Simmons said. "I talked to some of those guys, and they were mad as hell. They knew they were getting good solid hits. Hell, they could hear the things slamming into Japanese hulls through the water. Angled shots would usually explode okay, but slam a fish into a target square-on and it wouldn't go off.

"In fact, it turned out that the exploders were defective. We proved that at Pearl by dropping warheads onto steel plates from a crane. So what did we get from the brass? A new torpedo, only this one had a fuckin' magnetic exploder. The sub skippers were supposed to fire the thing deep, let it run beneath the Japanese ship's hull. The magnetic exploder was supposed to sense when the warhead was directly beneath the enemy ship and touch her off, breaking the ship's back."

"And how did that work?" O'Reilly asked.

"About the way you'd expect. Damned things didn't work. The fish would run right under the target and never give a quiver, and the sub skippers were getting more snide comments from the pencil-pushers about their poor marksmanship than ever. Then, along about mid–'forty-three or so, the warheads started working."

"Got the problems worked out, did they?" Tangretti asked.

Simmons laughed, then glanced left and right in a conspiratorial fashion. "Can you keep a secret, Gator?"

"Sure."

"O'Reilly?"

"Absolutely."

"The sub skippers started coming to us, the enlisted guys at Ordnance. We showed 'em how to disable the magnetic exploders after their subs had already put to sea."

"My God…"

"Not exactly regulation, huh?" O'Reilly said.

"Hardly," Davies said.

"If anybody back in Pearl ever figures out what those guys are doing…" Simmons shook his head, chuckling. "See, as soon as a sub clears the approaches to Pearl, her chief torpedoman starts disassembling all of the torp warheads on board, one after another, and disabling the magnetic exploders. It's dangerous. Those things aren't supposed to be tampered with outside of the ordnance depot ashore, but they break 'em down and fix every damned fish on the boat so they work on straight contact again. They work fine then, as an ordinary torpedo. If the skipper gets off a good shot and hits his target, believe me, it'll go boom. Then, on the way back into Pearl at the end of the patrol? The chief and his guys reset the exploders on all of the torpedoes left on the boat. That way, they never know the difference back in Pearl."

"And all this time, the stories we've been hearing about these great new magnetic torpedoes…"

"Are a load of shit. Right."

"I hate officers," Tangretti said again, shaking his head. The others were laughing at the story, but for him it merely confirmed the new attitude that had been hardening inside of him for months now.

He wasn't entirely sure where the attitude had come from, or what had caused it. Officers in the teams were okay, of course, men like Lieutenant Dayton and Lieutenant Casey ... and, of course, Snake. But they didn't count. They were UDT, not chickenshit martinets like the bastards that sent good men into hot beaches in broad daylight ... or who screwed up the orders so that the needed air cover wasn't there when the men who needed it went in.

He thought about Peleliu, and two thousand men dead so that MacArthur could make good his promise to return to the Philippines.

With great ceremony and a decidedly unsteady hand, Tangretti emptied the last of the bottle of scotch into his glass, thumped the bottle to the table, and hoisted another toast.

"God I *hate* fucking officers!"

The empty glass sailed across the room and smashed beneath the jaws of the shark.

CHAPTER 25

Thursday, 16 November 1944
Noumea, New Caledonia

Tangretti narrowed his eyes, trying to focus. "I'm not sure I understand, Blondie," he said slowly, enunciating each word carefully. "What is it you want to do?"

Blondie shoved a sheet of paper across the tabletop at him. Tangretti could see lines drawn in pencil on the paper, but they looked too fuzzy to read. He was having a little trouble putting the overall pattern together in his brain.

Tangretti had not sobered up much at all since the long round of toasting that had gone on in Le Poisson until closing time the night before. He dimly remembered wandering along the Grand Quai arm-in-arm with Davies, Simmons, and O'Reilly, singing "Anchors Away" at the top of his lungs. He supposed they'd made it back to the barracks — that part of the night was still a blur — but he remembered returning to Le Poisson with Slim at opening time this morning. He was painfully conscious of the fact that only two days remained of his sixteen-day stint of freedom, that after tomorrow it would be back to cramped quarters and no privacy, to bad food and a rolling, pitching deck in any weather heavier than a fresh breeze.

"*Trophies*, man, trophies! I know where to get 'em!" He slapped the shoulder of the kid sitting next to him. "Michaels here knows where to go!"

"I'm still not so sure this is a good idea, Blondie," Michaels said. He was a kid, Tangretti thought, a third class who was twenty, maybe twenty-one years old, but who barely looked old enough to shave. He'd been introduced to Tangretti and Simmons as Team Five's coxswain.

"I dunno," Simmons said, squinting at the map on the table. "Looks good t'me."

"Explain it again," Tangretti said.

"Aw, man," Foglio said, grinning. "I tell ya, you guys're gonna *love* this!"

The map, which had been provided by Michaels, had been meticulously copied from a chart provided to all coxswains and pilots navigating the channels in and out of the coral reefs surrounding Noumea. It showed one particular stretch of beach a few miles up the coast from the city, one that had become something of a legend among some of the UDT men during the past couple of weeks.

If French girls and native girls were largely unavailable for one reason or another, if prostitutes were boring and unattractive and bar girls uncooperative, there was yet one other source of sex on New Caledonia ... at least in theory: WACs.

A number of female Army personnel were stationed near Noumea, where they worked at an Army records office, in Personnel, or on one or the other of the senior officers' staffs. The difficulty was that WACs were carefully chaperoned everywhere, protected with the same dedication and alertness that might be given to the plans for some awesome secret weapon. The military high command, the censor's bureau, the press, and a number of well-meaning women's patriotic organizations back on the home front were concerned that servicemen overseas would take advantage of female military personnel — or vice versa — and were determined that moral standards would be maintained.

So far as the personnel actually involved, the question was not one of morals but of morale. Some sailors claimed to have made it into the barbed wire enclosures where the WACs were kept, but their claims were usually disregarded.

Of all of the claimants, though, the UDT was the only group that had even gotten close. For the teams, one of the principal attractions of Noumea — ahead even of off-limits bars and the Lumière Rouge — was a wide stretch of Army recreation beach northwest of the city, a beach that had one section set aside for the exclusive use of a number of WACs stationed there. Widely and variously known as either "Pink Beach" or, more bluntly, "Sex Beach," the area had been the target of numerous underwater reconnaissance missions by men in all of the teams. Using masks and swim fins, a man could get quite close to the action, close enough, at any rate, to catch a glimpse of girls sunbathing up on the beach or, if they came out any distance into the water, for a fish-eye's view of some long, bare legs. Some UDT men who'd made a recon swim even claimed that some women sunbathed nude now and then, a story usually discounted — but that, naturally enough, stimulated even more interest in Pink Beach.

What Foglio was discussing now, though, was more than a long-range reconnaissance, a sneak-and-peek from a distance. According to the chart Michaels had copied, there were some rocks offshore not more than thirty yards from the beach, rocks that would provide perfect cover for a small group who wanted to work their way in closer. The water there was seven to eight feet deep, depending on the tide, and the ground shoaled rapidly inland from that. A small team could swim all the way in to the beach unobserved. At least they could get in to where the water was only three or four feet deep.

What happened then would depend on the tactical situation of the moment.

That afternoon, Tangretti found himself floating with the gentle surge of the tide behind the rocks off Pink Beach, wondering just what the hell he was doing there. The swim from the spot up the coast where they'd parked their jeep had cleared a lot of the alcoholic haze from his brain, and he was finding it difficult to remember just what it was that had gotten him and Simmons so excited about this plan back at Le Poisson.

"There's the target for tonight," Foglio said, his voice low. "Man, oh, man, will you look at those knockers on that dame on the red towel!"

Tangretti had finally decided that Foglio was trying to make up for his humiliation in the bar the previous afternoon, and he wondered if the Team Five swimmer had some convoluted plan up his non-existent sleeve to get even with him and Simmons.

Now that they were here, though, he decided that Foglio probably just wanted to demonstrate his manhood in a way that wouldn't threaten him with a point-blank rejection — like the one he would have gotten had he approached Lucy yesterday.

Too, what they were about to attempt was not exactly the sort of thing they could brag about to others outside the group. Maybe, Tangretti thought, this was Foglio's way of shutting him and Simmons up about his failure to approach Lucy.

Well, it seemed like a good idea at the moment. UDT men might play elaborate gags on one another, but they stuck together where it counted, and rejecting Foglio's idea would have been a rejection of Foglio. They *owed* it to him, Foglio had insisted, and that had seemed quite reasonable, at least through the pleasant haze of scotch and bourbon. Foglio had also presented the plan as a way of "showing those Army sons-of-bitches a thing or two," and that, too, had seemed like a good idea … especially with the pun, hysterically funny at the time, on "showing."

Now that he was here, the pun wasn't as funny anymore, and Tangretti wished he could remember a little more about why those other things had all seemed like such good ideas.

But of course, there was no backing down, not now, not without looking as bad as Blondie had yesterday. Maybe *that* was Foglio's whole idea, to get him and Slim to chicken out?

Maybe. If so, it wouldn't work. The plan as they'd worked it out that afternoon at Le Poisson was just harmless fun, carrying enough danger to add spice. Tangretti shoved his doubts aside and concentrated on the objective.

Raising his mask, he studied the lay of the beach, his practiced tactical eye taking in the white sandy shelf, the dunes and jungle behind it, the distant fences that separated it from the rest of the recreation beach and theoretically assured the women of their privacy. A net walled off the seaward side of the cove, supposedly to keep out sharks, but they'd already dealt with that obstacle, as had other UDT men before them, through the simple expedient of diving deep and wiggling under the weighted bottom. There were no guards in sight, naturally enough, since males patrolling a female beach would have gone against the whole idea of the thing. Tangretti pictured armed guards walking sentry go up and down the strand blindfolded, and had to suppress a giggle.

It was a hot, summer's afternoon. The sun had been blazing from a deep, cloudless sky earlier, but now it was westering and losing some of its earlier strength. Better, from the swimmers' point of view, by 1700 hours most of the WACs got off duty, and that was when the largest number of them drove out to the beach for a post work swim or some after-the-heat-of-the-day sunbathing.

It was 1720 hours now, and from where he floated, Tangretti could see about ten or twelve women scattered about the beach, and several more in the water close to shore. None were nude, unfortunately, though there were plenty of bare legs and backs and shoulders in evidence, with not a single uniform in sight.

The men continued to watch and wait. They were looking for a most particular target of opportunity. This operation had been planned with all of the care and tactical precision of a reconnaissance against a heavily fortified beach. They'd gone over it time after time that afternoon in the bar, planning for unexpected contingencies. It would be, Slim had suggested, a hit-and-run raid, fast in, fast out, not a "sneak and peek," but a "sneak, peek, and tweak."

Foglio had laughed at that. "Naw, I got it. It'll be a snatch and snatch. Get it? Snatch!" He'd pantomimed yanking something off his hips. "And snatch!" He'd grabbed his crotch.

"There!" Slim whispered suddenly, rising a bit in the water as he peered past the algae-covered boulder that concealed him. "This could be it! We got four incoming."

"Action stations!" Foglio whispered, and then he giggled like a dirty-minded little boy.

Four women were running down the beach and splashing out into the water, one carrying a large, inflated beach ball under her arm. They waded out about fifty feet from the shore before starting to toss the ball back and forth between them, playing keep-away. One of the women was wearing a white bathing suit; the other three wore improvised suits — shorts or cut-off trousers, and shirts that had been tied off in front, leaving their midriffs delightfully bare. Three of them had their hair tucked away inside white rubber swimming caps; the fourth, however, the girl splashing back and forth among the other three at the moment, was a glorious, longhaired blonde.

"Perfect!" Slim said. "Four targets, and they're in range."

They'd not wanted more than four, to avoid interference during the raid, but they'd wanted more than two, just to keep things "sporting," as Blondie had put it. *And* the women had to come within reach of the rocks.

At least within a UDT swimmer's reach.

"Remember, guys," Foglio said. "The blonde's all mine!"

Michaels looked nervous. "Remember, guys. No rough stuff, okay? We just grab their pants and get the hell out."

"Don't worry, don't worry," Foglio said, smirking. "I don't have to stoop to rape to get what *I* want! It's just a damned shame we won't have more time at the objective! Otherwise, I'd show you rookies what a real master can do!"

"Aw, can that crap, Blondie," Tangretti said. His second thoughts were surfacing again, now that the desired tactical situation had presented itself. "Let's just do it, okay?"

"Right," Slim said. "Okay, if Blondie's got the blonde, Michaels, you get the one on the right and I'll take the one next to her. Gator, you go for the girl in the suit. Okay?"

"Sounds good."

"How you going to get her suit off, Gator?" Michaels wanted to know.

"Hey," Foglio said. "We're UDT. We overcome, and we adapt!"

"Everybody set?" Slim asked. "Okay, go!"

The men took several deep breaths, then slipped their masks down over their faces and ducked under the water. They all were equipped for beach reconnaissance, with masks, swim

350

suits, and flippers. Their swim fins, especially, gave them a tremendous tactical advantage, allowing them to move with tremendous speed for long distances under water. The tide was in ebb, but in this coral-sheltered cove there were no currents and only a slight swell moving in toward the beach. The water was moderately clear; any clearer and they would have had to call off the mission, because their targets would have seen them coming.

Tangretti propelled himself along the bottom until he couldn't hold his breath any longer, then carefully surfaced, rising just enough to draw in a breath and take a quick look around before submerging again. Another swim … and then, rising carefully, he took a last surfaced look at the objective, his head barely breaking the water. The women were less than fifteen yards away now, laughing and splashing as they tossed the ball back and forth. The relentless advance of the combat swimmers had gone completely unnoticed.

The others surfaced gently to either side, then descended again, without even raising a splash. Tangretti followed, slipping back beneath the water. To his left, Slim grinned beneath his mask and gave an OK signal with thumb and forefinger, while Michaels waved, then gave a thumbs-up. To Tangretti's right, Blondie gave a cruder signal, forming an OK with his left hand and vigorously pumping the middle finger of his clenched right fist in and out of the circle. Tangretti pointed up, then jerked his arm down, mimicking the over-the-side command of a UDT boat officer.

They sprinted the last few yards, staying close to the bottom, spreading out now as each swimmer zeroed in on his target. The water was about four feet deep here, reaching nearly to the women's breasts. Through their masks the men could see with crystal clarity in the sundance playing off the surface. Long, shapely legs stepped this way and that as they played their game, spaced out across a triangle perhaps ten feet across, with one set of legs scampering back and forth in the middle, sometimes walking on the bottom, sometimes lifting off and kicking with a great splashing and churning of bubbles. One of the women at one corner of the triangle, in a fetching gesture, reached down and tugged at the short hem of her shorts in back where it had been riding up on her buttocks, almost as if she were aware of the UDT men's covert scrutiny. With a thump, the beach ball landed on the surface almost above Tangretti's head, and the swim suited woman's body turned and started wading toward him.

Snake would've loved this, Tangretti told himself, and then he lunged forward on powerful, flippered kicks, his arms outstretched.

He swept in on his victim from straight ahead, wrapping his arms around her calves and knees, squeezing hard as he kept kicking, knocking her over backward with a tremendous splash. Bubbles and flailing arms filled his vision as he continued to drive forward, pushing her clear to the sandy bottom as she struggled and flailed at his shoulders and head with her fists. Shifting his grip to her waist, he reached up with his right hand and grabbed the strap on her right shoulder and yanked it down, pulling it over and off her arm, then repeated on the other side. He heard her burbled, underwater squeal of protest as he grabbed the suit's front and peeled it down. Large, naked breasts bobbed free in the water, almost as white as the suit and neatly centered by dark red-brown nipples that were fully erect, probably from stark terror at that point. They wobbled about as she moved, and then her arms crossed protectively over them as she twisted back and forth. Committed now, he kept tugging on the suit, turning it inside out as he bared first her navel, then her belly. The suit hung up for a moment on her hips and buttocks, but she was kicking wildly, trying to kick *him*, and he thought he was going to have to let go, but he hung on tight and kept pulling, and then a zipper somewhere in the back gave way and his prize slid easily down the woman's legs and off over her feet.

Desire flooded through Tangretti at the sight and feel of the struggling, naked woman. He had an erection that was squeezing up painfully inside his shorts. Dropping the suit, he reached up with one hand to pluck her rubber swim cap off her head, spilling a cascade of dark brown hair into the water. Pulling her closer, he squeezed her tight, flattening her breasts against his chest as she beat against him helplessly with tightly clenched fists. Her eyes, squeezed shut a moment ago, opened now to stare into his mask just before he could kiss her.

Unexpectedly, Tangretti was nearly overcome by a sudden surge of embarrassment … and a piercing shame. God … what was he *doing*? The violence of the encounter, and its suddenness, and the way the girl was struggling, all had somehow translated themselves into a raw and searing sexual excitement, and the realization horrified him. The beach raid was supposed to secure trophies and a quick, illicit grab and feel, nothing more. Never in his life had Tangretti imagined himself capable of *rape*, and yet…

Shit, shit, shit, he'd been *enjoying* this, enjoying the roughness and the wiggling … and the girl's squirming helplessness.

Worse, the way she'd clenched her fists as she struck at him had suddenly and unaccountably reminded Tangretti of Veronica, and of the way she'd clenched her tiny fists in her lap in that house in Weymouth.

With that memory, all of his urgent, pounding lust drained away, vanishing in a moment. Disgusted, sickened at himself, he released the woman and backed quickly away, colliding with the swimsuit that was still slowly floating to the bottom. The woman burst to the surface, and even under water Tangretti heard first her gasp for air, then her shrill, terrified shriek of fear and shock and outrage. Grabbing the suit, he started to stand up, to face her and apologize and give her suit back to her, but she was already vanishing toward the beach in a thrashing cloud of bubbles, bare legs scissoring frantically as she swam toward dry land and safety. He hesitated, unsure as to whether he should stand up and follow, or get the hell out.

He looked around and saw the other raiders were brandishing their own trophies. Michaels had the ankles of his woman pinned between his own legs as he doggedly unbuttoned her shorts and tugged them off her hips. She was wearing pink panties underneath, her pubic hair showing as a dark shadow through the sheer, wet material. Slim had managed to get both the shorts and the shirt off of his victim and was triumphantly waving them back and forth under the water as the girl swam desperately for the shore, wearing nothing but her swimming cap.

Blondie, though, had encountered a real surprise. Dragging the blonde to the bottom, he'd pulled her shorts off and yanked open the knot of her shirt, but instead of struggling the woman had aggressively moved into his arms and begun running one hand up and down his torso as she kissed him, her head turned far to the side so that she could reach his mouth beneath his mask. Foglio was obviously surprised, but he recovered quickly enough. His right hand started massaging a bared breast, rolling the nipple back and forth. Her right hand slid down to his stomach, exploring the top of his swim trunks, tugging insistently. Still holding their lingering, underwater kiss, he let go of her and reached down, unbuttoning them for her. She slipped her hand deep inside…

Blondie's eyes, closed behind his face mask, opened suddenly, bulging in a look of pure shock and pain. Bubbles exploded from his mouth. The woman, keeping one hand inside his swim trunks, reached up with the other and ripped the mask off his head.

Raising one flippered foot, Foglio planted it on her thigh and kicked off hard, just as the woman shifted her grip to his swim trunks. He thrashed in the water a moment, and the woman had his trunks in her hand and Foglio was surfacing explosively, clutching his testicles in both hands. Even beneath the water, Tangretti heard his bellow of raw pain.

Tangretti broke the surface for air. Pandemonium reigned on the beach, as women in shorts and bathing suits leaped to their feet, some running away up the dunes, others shading their eyes as they searched for the cause of all the commotion. Tangretti's victim splashed ashore screaming, clutching her arms tightly across her breasts as another woman met her at the waterline with a beach towel. Michaels's target followed more slowly, still more or less decent in shirt and panties. Slim's target was standing in knee-deep water with several other women, stark naked except for her cap as she pointed wildly toward the UDT swimmers' heads. Foglio's woman strolled out of the water fully dressed, her blond hair plastered down across her shoulders. She'd donned Foglio's swim trunks while still in the water — a tight fit over her generous hips — and finished buttoning them up before turning to hurl a taunt across the water. "You missed, you filthy perverts!" she yelled, waving Foglio's mask over her head. "Peeping Tom bastards!"

The other women on the beach took up the cry.

"Bastards!"

"Get them, girls! There's only four of them!"

"Let's strip them! See how *they* like it!"

"Get 'em where it hurts the most!"

"Come on! Get them!"

"We'll give em to the M.P.s! Somebody call the M.P.s!" A number of the angry women started to advance toward the water. The UDT men were badly outnumbered.

"Time for a strategic withdrawal," Slim said, laughing. "Where the hell's the pickup boat when you need it?"

"Grab Blondie," Tangretti added. "I don't think the poor guy can make it on his own!"

"Yeah, and I don't think we want to leave him for *them*" Slim said.

Some of the women pursued the UDT force for a short distance, but the chase was half-hearted at best, and with swim fins, the men easily outdistanced the women, even with Blondie and a bundle of stolen clothing in tow.

By the time they made it back to the beach around the point on the coast where they'd begun their swim a few hours earlier, Tangretti was miserable. War, he decided, could bring out the best in people ... but also, too often, it brought out the very worst. What had made him think he had the right to attack another person that way? She must have been terrified out of her mind, certain that he'd meant to rape her, or drown her, or both. How was she feeling now, after being knocked down and grabbed by a stranger, half drowned, stripped naked, groped, humiliated...?

They'd wrapped Foglio in one of the towels they'd left on the beach, piled into the jeep they'd requisitioned from the motor pool, and driven back to the barracks. Foglio was still in considerable pain, and twice they'd had to stop while he vomited on the side of the road. By the time they got him inside, his scrotum had swollen up as large as a baseball and taken on an ugly purplish hue. "Oh, God, I wish I was dead," he moaned, leaning forward on the edge of his rack.

"Me too," Tangretti said quietly. "Fucking me too."

"Come on," Slim said quietly. "We'd better get him to sick bay."

CHAPTER 26

Tuesday, 12 December, to Wednesday, 13 December 1944
Hollandia, New Guinea

They never did find out who was responsible for the raid at Pink Beach, though the fact that the culprits were four individuals of the UDT was self-evident. Only men of the teams could have navigated the shark net or managed the long underwater swim from the rocks halfway to the beach and, as if further proof were necessary, a WAC sergeant produced the final evidence: a swim mask of the type issued to the UDTs.

Lieutenant Russel K. Taylor, the CO of UDT-8, gave a stern lecture to the assembled team after they'd reported back aboard the *Badger*, but it was fairly obvious that the matter was not going to be pursued further. There were no demands that the culprits come forward, no threats of group punishment. The worst that happened was the lecture itself, which emphasized the need to respect fellow military personnel regardless of their sex. Taylor had told them that it was known that the culprits were in the teams, and that if there was any *more* "conduct prejudicial to good order and discipline," as the notorious catch-all Article 134 of the Uniform Code of Military Justice put it, and if he found out that his men were involved, he would be coming down on them hard.

Tangretti couldn't help thinking that the guy who'd needed to hear the lecture most wasn't there to benefit from it. When Team Five's *Humphreys* set sail from New Caledonia in formation with the *Badger*, heading northwest into the Coral

Sea, Foglio was still in a hospital shoreside, recovering from what his medical record called a "softball-related accident."

Well, claiming that he'd been injured when a soft-ball had hit his groin during a pickup game behind the enlisted mess had been the easiest way past some uncomfortable official questions. Still, the wording of his injury's description had already started circulating through the teams. *Softball* indeed. If not *soft*, exactly, Blondie Foglio was going to be extremely tender in a delicate area for a long time to come. At the moment, there was some question about whether he would even be able to rejoin the teams.

As for Tangretti, he'd seriously considered going to Taylor's office aboard the *Badger* and confessing to his part in the Pink Beach raid. Ultimately, though, he'd decided that it would be better all the way around if he simply kept his mouth shut. A confession would put the whole affair on an official level, no doubt with an attendant investigation, and Tangretti had gotten the distinct impression during Taylor's lecture that the brass would probably rather forget the whole affair. Any publicity at all leaking into the home front press would quite probably hurt the Navy ... and the teams. Besides, in an investigation he would be ordered to name his accomplices, and Tangretti knew he couldn't do that. Simmons was a member of his team, of his platoon, and swim buddies didn't spill the goods on each other. As for Michaels, Tangretti was pretty sure he'd been maneuvered into the affair by Foglio, and a black mark on his service record now would follow him throughout his career ... a damned high price to pay for some bad judgment.

Tangretti didn't even want Foglio to get into trouble ... or, at least, to get into any more trouble than he was already in. Certainly he couldn't turn in a fellow member of the teams.

Besides, Tangretti was pretty sure that Foglio had learned his lesson.

Before he'd shipped out from Noumea, however, Tangretti had made one final solo swim to the Army recreation beach, this one at 0100 hours. In the dark of a moonless night, he'd crept ashore to a point on the sand well above the high-tide line and left there the stolen white swimsuit, the swimming cap, and a note written on an underwater slate. The note said, simply: *I'm sorry. It was a drunken prank. Not all UDT guys are jerks.*

He figured that whoever found the note and the clothing would know who it was for. The whole WAC community on Noumea must have been buzzing with rumor, speculation, and outrage over what had happened.

After the incident, Tangretti found himself thinking a lot about Veronica, wondering where she was and what she was doing. He'd had a letter from her at the hospital in August. She'd told him then that she was three months pregnant with Snake's child, that she would be getting out of the service on a medical convenience-of-the-Army discharge and going back home to Milwaukee. When would the child be due? He counted months and decided that the date must be sometime in January.

Somehow, at Le Poisson and at the rec beach afterward, Tangretti had forgotten that a WAC was a person. Most guys in the service had the same general idea about WACs, that they'd joined the Army just to meet guys, that they wouldn't have joined at all if they didn't want the sexual attention of men. *She was just asking for it* was a phrase Tangretti had heard more than once from sailors or Marines describing in lurid detail some encounter, real or imagined, with a woman in uniform.

Knowing Veronica let him put a face and a personality and an intelligence behind what otherwise would have been a faceless nonentity, a *thing*, something to make jokes about or to inspire wild and erotic stories.

He wished he could have gotten to know her better.

After their sixteen days in Noumea, Teams Five, Eight, and Nine were sent to Hollandia, on the shores of Humbolt Bay in northern New Guinea. Though they would be on active duty, the assignment was virtually a continuation of their R&R routine. Once again they picked up their calisthenics routine, largely neglected in New Caledonia, and began conditioning themselves with long runs along the beach, with mile-long swims in the bay, and with an hour of calisthenics before breakfast each morning.

Hollandia, while not as idyllic as New Caledonia, still had the look of a tropical paradise, a rawer, more remote paradise where the jungle behind the bay, lying like a thick green blanket over the mountains rising above the coast, gave the region the look of a primeval and isolated wilderness. Just two miles inland a five-hundred-foot waterfall sprang from cloud-shrouded Mount Cyclops. Where Noumea had been a fair-sized town with coconut palms and flame trees lining streets between decidedly European-style stone buildings, the base area at Hollandia was still raw and new, prefab huts squatting in bare-earth slashes in the jungle.

There were plenty of reminders of civilization, however. MacArthur had wanted to shift his HQ there from Brisbane, so the place had been converted into a major base shortly after its capture the previous April. Three shingle-and-beaverboard prefabs had been joined together on the slope of a six-thousand-foot mountain overlooking Lake Sentani. Painted white, the palatial structure was easily visible from the beach, where the troops had nicknamed it "Dugout Doug's White House," even though the general had spent only four nights there.

Every effort had been made to assure the comfort of the lower-ranking officers as well. There was a widely circulating rumor that MacArthur's chief of staff had arranged for his mistress — the wife of an Australian officer stationed in the Middle East — to accompany him from Brisbane, that he'd finagled a WAC captain's commission for her and assigned her as a secretary in his office even though she couldn't type, take dictation, or even file reports.

So far as the UDT men were concerned, the local WAC detachment was the most important aspect of Hollandia's rugged, natural beauty. Best of all, there was another recreational beach here, fenced off and set aside for the women. The day Eight had arrived, scuttlebutt had already spread a description of the base layout to every man in the team, and as their APD cruised slowly past that particular stretch of beach on its way to the dock, a number of men had availed themselves of going on liberty a little ahead of the rest of the ship's crew, leaping into the sea in masks, swim trunks, and flippers to pull a fast advanced reconnaissance despite Lieutenant Taylor's lecture.

Tangretti wondered how much of the recon activity was due to the widely circulating story of what had happened in Noumea. He half expected to hear of a similar incident after *Badger* docked in Hollandia, but the UDT men's exploits, if there were any worth mentioning, were kept well under wraps. Maybe, he reasoned, the women's beach at Hollandia had a better shark net, one that could keep out two-legged sharks as well as the gilled variety. Or possibly the demo men were more subtle in their reconnaissance methods this time around.

Tangretti didn't know, and he wasn't going to try to find out. He'd had enough of voyeurism, of sexual innuendos, of outright attacks on women no matter how good-natured or humorous the intent.

Attacks on the bureaucratic naval hierarchy that seemed so determined to lose the war and increase its casualty figures — specifically, attacks on the non-UDT officers who kept trying to manage the UDT as though the unit was a part of the *real* Navy — were another matter entirely. What had been born in the pain of Snake Richardson's death and nurtured by his experiences so far in the Pacific had grown in recent weeks into a wholehearted detestation of the system.

One week after the teams' arrival at Hollandia, Tangretti and O'Reilly were sitting in wicker chairs at a field expedient table — a square piece of plywood nailed to the side of a large empty spool for wire rope — in the lounge reserved for enlisted men at Hollandia. They each had a beer, the only alcohol available on the base, and the chief was telling Tangretti about Team Nine's latest work order.

"So the son-of-a-bitchin' officers are on our case to blow a channel through the sandbar," O'Reilly told him. "See, their O Club is on a point right above the water, and they want to build a marina and pier right there, overlooking the bay. That way they can sit on the veranda, don't you know, and sip gin and tonics fetched by the club's steward's mates, and get their damned little sailboats and powerboats and yachts in and out of the harbor in time for luncheon."

Tangretti groaned and shook his head in sympathy. The story was typical, from what he'd heard. The teams were supposed to be in Hollandia for training and to get back into a decent physical regimen ... so of course the damned officers were going to twist things around to see to their comfort. The base needed a better approach channel for cargo ships unloading at the main dock, and the enlisted personnel at Hollandia needed everything from better mess facilities to less crowded barracks space … and here the officers were ordering the teams to dig them a channel for their O Club's new marina.

"So," Tangretti said with a wry grin. "What's the story? You guys gonna do it?"

"Hell, if they give the order, we gotta do it, right?"

"Seems like a hell of a way to run a war. The Navy spends … what? … thirty thousand bucks apiece to train each and every UDT man? Is that the figure?"

"Something like that."

"Okay, and then they ship him halfway around the world to dig channels for an officers' marina! Shit!"

"Yeah, well, that's the way it is, right?"

"There's three ways of doing anything," Tangretti said. "The right way, the wrong way —"

"And the Navy way," O'Reilly said, completing the aphorism that had probably been ancient in John Paul Jones's day. "Sure, but what you gonna do? The officers gotta be entertained and keep up their social class standards, right? And we gotta be kept busy."

"Tell me something," Tangretti said suddenly. "You got any explosives? Demo gear? Or are they supposed to provide your blasting stuff for this project?"

"Huh? Sure. We have plenty on hand. Remember Yap? Team Nine got to go recon the place," O'Reilly told him. "We were set to go in and blow the reefs, too, but then the brass got cold feet and called the show off."

"Good thing," Tangretti said. "I heard Yap was a bitch."

"Maybe. Even considering how bad Peleliu was, Yap probably would've been a lot worse. Thing is, we got five, maybe six tons of tetrytol packed into lengths of fire hose and safely stacked away aboard ship. We were supposed to use it to blow a gap through the Yap reef for the Marine tracks, but since we never had to go in we've just been hauling it around on our APD ever since. Why?"

"Six tons, eh?" Tangretti chuckled. Then the chuckle turned into a laugh.

"What the hell's biting you, Gator?"

"Chief," Tangretti said, wiping tears from his eyes, "I think we ought to go out and dig that channel for our superiors."

"I know you, Gator. You've got something up your sleeve besides that muscle-bound arm of yours. What gives?"

"I'll tell you, Chief," Tangretti said. "I'm sick of the goddamn officers jerking us around. You hear about what they're gonna do to the Skipper?"

"The Skipper," when said in that tone of voice, could mean only one man — Lieutenant Commander Coffer.

"Yeah. That's a bitch, ain't it?"

Tangretti chugged a swallow from his beer. "The bastards just can't leave well enough alone," he said, slamming the bottle back to the plywood tabletop. "Always gotta be screwin' with things that're just fine the way they are."

The news had been percolating through the teams for the past several weeks, though no one had yet been able to confirm it. After Leyte, the U.S. Naval command structure in the Pacific had ordered a full-scale reorganization of the UDTs.

By now, there was no denying the importance of the teams in Pacific theater operations. They'd proven their unique abilities and usefulness time after time — at Kwajalein; at Saipan, Tinian, and Guam; at Peleliu and Angaur and Leyte. While some commanders — MacArthur among them —

continued to resist the idea of specialized naval forces carrying out missions once reserved for Marine Recon or the Army's Rangers, more and more Marine and naval commanders were requesting UDT contingents to support their own operations. Even MacArthur was reported to have requested UDT support for the planned landings at Lingayen, on the northwest coast of the major Philippine island of Luzon. There was simply no other way to learn what kind of emplacements and defenses the enemy had put in place at a target beach, no other unit that could ascertain beach conditions and reef depths and channel access for landing craft like the UDTs. More and more Teams were in service — twelve at Tangretti's last count — with at least six more planned or already in the organizational pipeline.

Unfortunately, so many men scattered across so much ocean was a command far larger than that assigned to a mere two-and-a-half-striper. The scuttlebutt had it that a new man was being brought in as CO of the UDTs, some captain named Raymond R. Hanrahan.

Hanrahan was not a graduate of Fort Pierce and he'd never been involved in UDT operations, and that left a sour taste in the mouths of most men in the teams. "The Skipper" had built the teams out of nothing, had created the Fort Pierce program, had made the UDT what it was today, and it damn well wasn't right that Washington should bring in some outsider to boss the Skipper's unit.

In Tangretti's Team Eight, morale had plummeted among the men since word of the impending changeover had started to spread.

"Well, whatcha gonna do?" O'Reilly said with a philosophical shrug. "They say the Skipper can't fill a captain's billet, and you know how particular the chair-warmers are about proper chains of command. What do you want to do, stage a mutiny?"

He smiled as he said it, but the word was spoken softly, and with an uncomfortable shifting of O'Reilly's eyes to left and right. There'd never been a mutiny aboard an American naval vessel or within any Navy unit ... but the word was not one to be casually or lightly tossed about.

"Shit," Tangretti said, using that all-purpose vulgarity to lightly shove the suggestion aside. "Who said anything about mutiny? I just wondered if we could stage a little ... um, demonstration, is all."

"A demonstration, huh? What did you have in mind?"

"Well, I used to be a Seabee, before I was in demo," Tangretti explained. "Damn, that seems like about a million years ago. Anyway, I know a little thing or three about blasting. And this is what I think we ought to do..."

Late the next afternoon, a special ad hoc UDT platoon, consisting of seven men from Team Nine and one from Team Eight — Tangretti — made its way slowly toward the sandbars just offshore from the O Club, its Higgins boat sliding through the still water until it gently grounded on the bottom. O'Reilly dropped the boat's ramp, and the men began hauling out the explosives and dragging them onto the sandbar. It was low tide, and the bar was more mud than sand, dark gray, calf-deep muck covered by a layer of water only a few inches deep. Despite the mud, offloading the explosives took the men only a few hours. By the time they were done, however, the incoming tide had increased the depth of the water until the men were wading about in a viscous soup that reached above their knees.

TM2 Griffith jerked his thumb toward the officers gathered on the point in front of the O Club to watch. "Don't you think we should warn them off?"

"Screw 'em," Tangretti said. He was sweating heavily with the effort of lugging lengths of fire hose filled with high explosives, and struggling back and forth in the muck. "If they want to get wet, that's their lookout, right?"

"They look awfully damned pretty in their whites, don't they?" O'Reilly said with a sadistic grin. "God, this shit is going to make a *splendid* bang!"

Clambering back into the LCP(R), MM1 Edwards shouted the order, and the boat began backing down off the bar, the engine rumbling and belching smoke from the aft exhausts. Tangretti and O'Reilly remained standing in the thigh-deep water, wearing shorts, masks, and swim fins. They would be the fuse pullers for the op.

When the boat was circling in deeper water a hundred yards off the bar, Tangretti and O'Reilly looked at each other for a moment. Then O'Reilly drew a deep breath. "Well, might as well do her. It's been so damned boring here, maybe this'll liven things up, right?"

"Can't have a boring war," Tangretti agreed. Together, they stooped in the water and fastened their condom-wrapped pull ring M-1 igniters to the trunk fuse. "Set?" Tangretti asked him.

"Set!"

"Fire in the hole!" Together, they yanked their igniters, then waded as quickly as they could manage toward the edge of the bar and dove headfirst into deeper water. Swimming hard, they splashed across the water toward the Higgins boat, which was holding station with engines idling. When Edwards saw them swimming, he gunned the engine to life and put the craft into a tight turn. Weiss was already in the raft with the pickup ring extended.

Tangretti reached the buoyed recovery line first and held up his arm. Engine howling, wake churning, the LCP(R) came out of its turn and bore down on him hard and fast. Weiss leaned out, Tangretti reached out, and suddenly he'd been plucked from the water and hurled into the raft. He scrambled clear and into the boat just as O'Reilly joined him the same way. Edwards was at the helm, guiding the boat farther into the bay. Jackson, meanwhile, held up a Very pistol and fired, sending a bright green flare arcing through the sky on a lazily curling trail of smoke.

On the shore, the officers in front of the O Club suddenly seemed to catch on to what was happening, and began to scatter.

Tangretti, sitting in the aft end of the LCP(R) with a towel over his shoulders, was staring at his watch. "Okay, guys! Any mo —"

Astern, a wall of mud and water erupted high into the sky as six tons of tetrytol detonated in a thunderous explosion. Like the solid, dark loom of a cliff, the water hovered there for a moment, then began the long fall back into the bay, cascading across water and land alike in a torrential black downpour of mud.

"Told you," O'Reilly said in the almost reverential silence that followed. "A splendid bang!"

It took the base maintenance personnel a while to find the officers' club again. Most of that part of the shore was buried in several feet of black ooze and mud blasted out of the harbor by the explosion. When working parties plying streams of water from a dozen hoses finally managed to sluice the thick coating of mud from the building's walls and roof, they found every screen window smashed in, the front door missing entirely, and every glass and bottle and chandelier in the O Club's bar smashed to bits. There was mud in the main dining hall, in the food preparation area, and flowing down the steps to the hollowed-out basement that served as a wine cellar. It was a foot deep in the bar, and three feet thick on the veranda, where wicker furniture and formerly glass-topped tables were all but submerged in the stuff.

Adding insult to injury, the channel up to the proposed marina site wasn't even very good. The blast had been so powerful that most of the sand and mud had simply been thrown straight up into the air ... and what hadn't fallen on the O Club had ended up right back in the water again. The silt was so thick that that end of Hollandia's harbor was all but useless for small craft for months afterward.

And for months afterward, no one dared mention the UDT to the naval officers stationed at Hollandia.

CHAPTER 27

Saturday, 6 January 1945
U.S.S. *California*, Lingayen Gulf
Luzon, the Philippines

It was mid-afternoon of another hazy, tropical-humid day. The battleship *California*, a seagoing fortress bristling with guns and turrets and towers, steamed majestically at the head of a long column that consisted of five other battleships, six cruisers, nineteen destroyers, twelve escort carriers screened by another twenty destroyers and destroyer escorts, ten APDs carrying the underwater demolition teams slated to check the Lingayen beaches and participate in mine-clearing operations, eleven LCI gunboats, and an enormous fleet of minesweepers and various service vessels. Rounding the headland of Cape Bolinao, the attack force moved slowly southeast into the sheltered waters of Lingayen Gulf.

Aboard the *California* and the other ships of the American fleet, all hands were at General Quarters and had been for the better part of three days. That meant that every man aboard was at his battle station, with life jacket and helmet, eating and even sleeping at his post save for brief rotations with other hands. Day and night, officers and men alike scanned the skies, searching for an enemy who suddenly had assumed a new and terrifying aspect in this struggle that already had assumed the character of a total and all-out war of extermination.

Two days earlier, the Japanese had introduced a new and awesome weapon. According to Tokyo Rose, the sultry-voiced

Japanese propagandist on the radio, the weapon was called *kamikaze*, "the Divine Wind."

The first known kamikaze attack had occurred the previous October, in the furious and desperate fighting off Samar, when three American escort carriers had been attacked by enemy planes crashing into their flight decks. *Santee* and *Suwanee* had been damaged in that fight, and the *St. Lo* had been sunk. Since then, kamikaze attacks had been launched at American convoys moving between Leyte Gulf and Mindoro in the Philippines, but not until the invasion fleet had approached Lingayen had the terrible new weapon been unleashed with all of its hellish fury.

As Admiral Oldendorf's battleship group had passed through the Philippines south of Luzon on the morning of January 4, four Japanese aircraft had broken through the group's fighter umbrella and vectored for the American column. As every ship in the fleet threw up a seemingly impenetrable wall of antiaircraft fire, each enemy plane had selected a different target and plunged out of a sky filled with cotton-candy puffs of ack-ack and lazily drifting tracers, deliberately trying to crash themselves into an American ship. One had struck a destroyer. Another, burning furiously and trailing a contrail of smoke that stretched clear across the sky, had slammed into the flight deck of the escort carrier *Ommaney Bay*.

The Japanese, every man in the American fleet agreed, had to be getting damned desperate to try such tactics. The Lingayen invasion was another in a long chain of amphibious operations carried out by MacArthur's forces in the Philippines since the previous October, but these landings were particularly important. Lingayen Gulf is the body of water on Luzon's west coast that gives it the appearance of a mitten with its outstretched thumb, a deep slash into the mountainous body of Luzon that points directly at the Philippines's capital. The beaches selected for the landings at the head of the gulf near the sleepy villages of Lingayen and San Fabian were only 130 miles northwest of Manila, and the enemy appeared determined to throw everything they had against the Americans to keep them from taking the city.

There was a grim, almost fatalistic feeling among many of the Americans watching the self-immolation of the Japanese pilots. *Ommaney Bay* had been sunk, with the loss of one hundred men, by a single man in a single plane, determined to trade his life for that of an American ship. Sixteen kamikazes attacked the fleet in the gulf the next day, damaging the escort carrier *Manila Bay* and the cruisers *Louisville* and *Australia*.

How could you possibly fight against men already determined to die?

Lieutenant Commander Coffer stood on the *California's* bridge, together with members of his staff and with Captain Hanrahan, the new UDT skipper. Hanrahan was a big, red-haired man with pale, freckled skin and a sharp mind, both ambitious and methodical. *An organizer*, Coffer thought of his replacement. *Someone who can step in, take charge, and get things done.*

Coffer did not resent Hanrahan's takeover of his beloved teams. The principal reason for the change, in fact, besides the obvious one that Coffer didn't carry clout enough in his two and a half gold stripes to command a unit this big, was that Coffer was finding it increasingly difficult to manage both the UDT *and* Team Five. The changeover had been effected so that Coffer could concentrate more on his team ... only it wasn't long before he'd been offered another position entirely.

As expected, there'd been some immediate resistance within the teams to Hanrahan's takeover by men who felt that Coffer, and *only* Coffer, had the right to lead them. Partly to smooth those ruffled feathers — and there were a lot of them among the lower ranks — and partly because Coffer still knew more about the running of the UDT than anyone else in the Navy, Coffer had been offered the post of Hanrahan's chief of staff.

After considerable thought he'd accepted the assignment. A naval officer didn't get far with his career turning down such offers, and the new post would still allow him to work closely with the men of the various teams.

Besides, he felt as though the resistance of the men was somehow his fault, and serving as the UDT's chief of staff might let him head off any possible trouble before it had a chance to begin.

Hanrahan's official title now was Commander, Underwater Demolition Teams, Amphibious Forces, Pacific, which in true Navy fashion was abbreviated to Com-UDTsPhibsPac … a jawbreaker that was quickly and inevitably shortened again by the men of the UDT to "Mudpac." Team Five's old APD, the *Gilmer*, re-equipped and refurbished, was to be the unit's headquarters ship, with new accommodations for staff, communications, and planning. Facsimile machines had even been installed to allow the rapid printing and distribution of depth charts and maps, something that Hanrahan was particularly eager to improve. Too often in the past, good, hard, firsthand intelligence returned from a beach by members of a UDT had arrived too late to be of any use in the increasingly complex and cumbersome amphibious operations. With better copying and distribution of the swimmers' reports, their hard-won information could be used by the whole fleet … and save far more lives in an invasion than would otherwise be the case.

Shortly, Coffer would be transferring to the *Gilmer* permanently. For now, though, during the Lingayen operation, his temporary headquarters was with Hanrahan on board the battleship *California*, along with a number of Mudpac's staff. He stood on the port wing of the bridge, binoculars pressed to his eyes, as the battlewagon thundered away with her fourteen-and-a-half-inch guns at the forest-green hills of Luzon. All of the big ship's guns were in action. The dozens of 40-mm and 20-mm antiaircraft guns scattered along her six-hundred-foot length were slamming away constantly at the Japanese planes that appeared to fill the haze-paled sky.

And the damned Divine Wind kept coming. One had crashed into the *New Mexico* at noon, though the old, World War I vintage battlewagon had shrugged off the damage and kept on shooting. The destroyer *Walke* had downed two kamikazes seconds before they could ram the ship, but a third had crashed into her bridge. Her skipper, horribly burned, had directed firefighting efforts and continued conning the ship until he'd been sure she was out of danger before allowing himself to be taken below. Word had just come through to *California's* bridge, however, that *Walke's* skipper had just died of his wounds.

Shortly after the *Walke*, the minesweeper *Long* had been rammed, blown up, and sunk. Next, the minesweeper *Southard* and two destroyers, *Allen B. Summer* and *Barton*, had taken hits, though all three vessels were still afloat and in no immediate danger.

And *still* the kamikazes kept coming.

At Coffer's side, Hanrahan lowered his binoculars and shook his head, which looked tiny within the embrace of his blue-painted Navy battle helmet. *California's* antiaircraft guns delivered a steady, hammering *thud-thud-thud* that pounded on the ears and the brain, hurling long streams of tracers into a sky pocked by bursts from heavier shells. Clustered at their stations, gun crews served their guns with a mechanical and relentless endurance, as though the men themselves had been transformed into machines. Their shouts were lost in the incessant thunder of the guns; many stood almost knee-deep in the expended shell casings spilling from the breeches of their weapons. Far in the distance, a plane twisted wildly on the end of an uncoiling streamer of black smoke, impacting in the sea in a billowing surge of white spray. It was too far to tell whether the aircraft had been friendly or enemy. Almost certainly it had been Japanese; American aviators were concentrating on the outer ring of the fleet's defensive umbrella and staying clear of the deadly free-fire zone above the invasion armada.

"The men," Hanrahan said, shouting so that Coffer could hear him over the incessant roar and boom of the guns. "The men in the UDTs must find this damned frustrating, being sitting-duck targets and not being able to shoot back!"

"They're used to it, sir," Coffer shouted back. "Swimming around in a lagoon, armed with nothing but a knife and a pair of swim fins while the Japanese use you for target practice, that's harder to face than this any day!"

"You may have a point there, Commander."

Another aircraft, burning furiously, swept in from the hills to the southeast, as a dozen of the battleship's antiaircraft mounts swung about to receive this new assault. Yellow-white tracers crisscrossed above the waves, then found their target, hammering bits and pieces of metal from its hull as it kept bearing down on the *California's* port side amidships. The flames streaming back from the engine cowling were brilliantly reflected in the water underneath. At the last possible moment, the plane's left wing crumpled like cardboard in a strong man's fist. The aircraft seemed to hesitate a moment, then flipped onto its back and plunged nose first into the sea. Spray geysered as high as *California's* mainmast, and Coffer felt the shudder of the concussion as the plane's bombs detonated in the water less than a hundred yards abeam of the *California*.

"Close one," Hanrahan said. "Those bastards are damned good."

Coffer was watching his new superior closely, more interested in his performance than in the performance of the suicidal Japanese pilots. The man was calm, firm, and absolutely unflappable in a battle situation that would have rattled lesser men, however brave or determined. Better still, Coffer thought, was Hanrahan's concern for the men. The APD *Blessman*, with the brand new Team Fifteen aboard, was running parallel to the *California's* course a mile to port, and Hanrahan had spent much of the afternoon watching her through his binoculars, almost as though he wanted somehow to help the helplessly watching UDT men aboard her, and couldn't.

Though there was still resistance from a lot of the men to the new UDT skipper, Hanrahan was wearing down that resistance fast. He had a reputation for listening to the men, and that went a long way with the UDT ... farther than rank or any recitation of medals or service schools. Coffer had heard one story making the rounds, how Admiral Turner himself had told Hanrahan: "Have patience with screwball ideas and people. Many of them have value."

That sounded like old Turner, sure enough, and Hanrahan seemed to have taken the words to heart. Coffer hoped the men would give the new CO a chance to show what he could do.

"What the hell is *kamikaze* supposed to mean, anyway?" Lieutenant Commander Carl Jones, one of Mudpac's new junior officers, wondered, breaking Coffer's chain of thought.

"Divine Wind," Coffer replied. "It's named after a big storm that saved the Japanese tail a few centuries ago."

"That's right," Hanrahan added. "The Mongols were threatening Japan with invasion in, I think it was 1570. Their fleet was already at sea when a terrific storm blew up, a typhoon that scattered the Mongol fleet and sank a number of its ships. The Japanese figured the gods had sent the storm and called it *kamikaze*, the Divine Wind."

Coffer was impressed. Hanrahan had certainly done his research.

"Here comes another one," Jones said, pointing. "Looks like he's after us."

The aircraft was a Nakajima of the type known to the Allies as an Oscar, skimming across the surface of the gulf from the southeast scant feet above water that was being lashed to an angry froth by the concentrated antiaircraft fire from the *California* and several nearby ships, including the *Blessman*. Closer and closer it came, bearing down on the *California's* port bow with a fascinating slowness, a fixedness and a deadliness of purpose that raised the hackles on the back of Coffer's neck. *That guy is trying to kill me*, Coffer thought, and he desperately wanted an antiaircraft gun, a machine gun, a pistol, *anything* to allow him to join with the battleship's gun crews in trying to knock that suicide-prone aviator down.

The Oscar was burning, scattering the glow of the flames along the water's surface. Tracers converged on the aircraft, shredding parts of the wing and fuselage, smashing into the canopy, hammering at the cockpit. Surely the pilot was dead by now!

Abruptly, a thousand yards out, the aircraft pulled up sharply, obviously under perfect control as it rolled onto its back and nosed down toward the battleship, plunging from an altitude of about eight hundred feet. Coffer could see the huge, red meatballs painted on the wings as the kamikaze fell toward the bridge. In the last instant, he thought he could see the pilot's face behind the bullet-shattered windscreen, hanging upside down less than a hundred feet away.

"*He's going to hit!*" Jones yelled, echoing perfectly Coffer's unvoiced thought. Reflexively, the men ducked behind *California's* bridge splinter screen as the suicide plane slammed into the battleship's aft fire control tower, above and behind the bridge, close by the base of the ship's foremast. There was a shattering explosion, and the deck bucked beneath the soles of Coffer's black shoes. Something whined off the splinter shield, and suddenly the air was filled with boiling clouds of black, greasy smoke.

"Now fire, fire, fire on the aft gun control tower," a voice announced over the bridge speaker. "Damage control and fire parties, lay to the aft fire control tower on the double!"

Flaming gasoline had engulfed much of the battleship's towering, central island. On the deck below the bridge wing, sailors were picking themselves up and returning to their guns. A number of men in dungarees and cumbersome breathing gear pounded aft along crowded decks, lugging fire hoses and foam gear with them. The main guns, meanwhile, let loose another thunderous salvo, which rocked the ship nearly as hard as the crashing Japanese plane had. *California* had been hurt, but she kept on fighting.

"It sure would be nice if we could fight back," Coffer said absently. "You'd think the government would issue us something more than a diving knife for situations like this."

Hanrahan laughed. "You know, a few weeks ago, a friend of mine, line officer, came up to me and said, 'You know, the Navy spent thirty thousand dollars educating you at Annapolis and another thirty thousand giving you postgraduate instruction in ordnance and modern weapons and ballistics.'"

"Yeah?"

"Then he says, And now you're going to go spend your time swimming onto beaches and throwing rocks at the Japanese.'"

Coffer chuckled. The tension among the Mudpac staffers, raised to a fever pitch by the crash of the Kamikaze, was broken. "Maybe so," he said. "But you know, right now I'd even appreciate having a few rocks to throw."

In the next fourteen minutes, five more American ships were hit.

"Shit, I've never seen anything like this. Never!"

Rand stood on the fantail of the *Blessman*, fists on hips, staring up into a sky that seemed to be filled with aircraft and contrails and suddenly appearing puffs of smoke. Lieutenant Forsythe stood next to him, watching the spectacular aerial display.

"Those people must be crazy," Forsythe said, shaking his head as though he still couldn't quite comprehend the enormity of the thing. There'd been a lot of speculation at first among the men in Team Fifteen that the kamikaze pilots were aiming their planes at American ships only after the pilots themselves were badly wounded and knew they could not land, but that clearly wasn't the case. So many planes, plunging through fire-laced skies to reach the U.S. ships. These men *wanted* to die … if they could take a shipload of Americans to some fiery Japanese Valhalla with them.

It was unlike anything any of them had ever had to face before.

"One of the boys over there claimed to have counted thirty-five Japanese planes splashing into the water in thirty minutes," Forsythe continued, his voice just loud enough to carry above the yammer of a 20-mm mount nearby. "I told him he must have counted some twice."

"I wouldn't be too sure of that, Lieutenant," Rand said. Movement caught his eye, and the flash of sunlight on an aircraft's canopy. "Hey! Look there!"

Astern and to port, another Japanese plane was bearing down on the *Blessman*, angling in from the hills behind San Fernando, to the east. Smoke streamed from the plane's cowling, but the wings dipped back and forth in delicate, carefully manipulated movements, clearly under the pilot's control. It looked like it was heading directly for the spot on the deck where Rand and Forsythe were standing.

Other men in Team Fifteen standing nearby saw the approaching plane, and some nudged one another uncertainly. "Should we go?" Rand heard one ask nervously. "Should we go?"

"What the fuck, you gonna pull a Ten?" his buddy said. Several men laughed, though the humor was strained. The day before, a Japanese suicide plane had plunged straight toward the deck of the *Rathburn*, Team Ten's APD. The kamikaze had missed — barely — skimming over the ship from stern to bow, avoiding the superstructure seemingly by scant inches before crashing into the sea ahead. Just as a crash into the APD's stern had seemed certain, half a dozen of Team Ten's men had leaped off the *Rathbum's* fantail and into the water; when they were picked up later and scolded by the ship's captain for deserting their posts, one had replied that the

UDTs didn't *have* posts during attacks against the ship. And besides ... the UDTs' job was in the water, right?

That story had been making the rounds of the other teams with that magical speed inherent in shipboard rumor and legend. Rand wondered what Forsythe thought of it.

The Japanese plane was closer ... closer...

It's going to hit, Rand thought. Incongruously, he suddenly saw the situation as a titanic game of chicken. Could he stand here, rooted to the APD's fantail as the kamikaze dove straight for him ... or would he break and run and dive for the imagined safety of the water? His fists clenched at his side. Glancing to the left, he noticed that Gunner's Mate First Class David Skinner had taken a place in the 20-mm mount. Evidently, the UDT man had tired of just standing and watching, and had elected to temporarily go back to his original rating. He'd discarded helmet and life jacket and shirt; stripped to the waist, he was leaning into the mount's curved shoulder rests as the twin barrels pom-pommed in and out, hurling yellow tracers toward the oncoming plane.

Rand turned back and felt a small stab of fear as he realized the Japanese plane was almost on them, a hundred yards off the port stern quarter. His thoughts leaped in that instant to Nancy — to their honeymoon...

He got ready to jump...

At the last possible moment, the aircraft's right wing dipped precipitously toward the sea, the wingtip snagging a wave and throwing up a dazzling rainbow-highlighted rooster tail of water. The sudden drag yanked the aircraft hard to the right, its pale gray belly exposed to the *Blessman's* stern. Then its engine cowling hit the water, and the plane began cartwheeling tail over nose over tail over nose, before slamming to a halt in the *Blessman's* wake eighty yards astern. An explosion hurled tons of water into the sky. On the *Blessman*, men were cheering and shouting and waving and jumping up and down … most of them. Rand noticed one sailor on his knees, crossing himself reverently. Others were pounding Skinner on the back. It was by no means certain that his mount had brought down the suicide plane, but no one seemed to care. One of their own had struck back. The jubilant cheers from the UDT men were louder than the thunder of the massed guns of the fleet.

I didn't break, Rand told himself, but he knew that that was a lie. Another instant, and he would have been over the side … and to hell with anybody slower than he. *Has being married changed me that much?*

He felt ashamed. He glanced sidelong at Forsythe. How did the Boston-born, Oh-So-Social guy stay so cool? The man hadn't even twitched as he'd stared into approaching death. Ice, Rand thought. The man must be made of ice.

Somehow, the American fleet came through the devastating firestorm of Japanese suicide attacks. Twenty ships had been hit or sunk on January 6 alone, but Admiral Halsey had been hammering every airfield on Luzon with carrier aircraft ever since, trying to kill the kamikazes in their lairs. The suicide attacks were definitely dwindling now, and the men were beginning to hope that the worst was over. One intelligence report suggested that there were no more than a handful of operational Japanese planes left on the entire island of Luzon.

The landing operation, meanwhile, was under way at last. On January 7, UDTs Five, Nine, and Fifteen had gone in to survey the beaches near Lingayen, while teams Eight, Ten, and Fourteen checked the landing area at San Fabian. The swimmers, their bodies weirdly coated in silver grease as camouflage against sand and water, had swum ashore with their slates and markers under the closest, most savage shore bombardment yet hurled against the enemy's beach defenses. Visibility in the surf-and shell-churned water had been poor, but the teams had carried off their missions with only a few reported instances of fire from the shore, and no casualties at all. Newly instituted operational orders, which placed UDT liaison officers aboard the bombarding LCIs and destroyers, allowed the supporting craft to rake the beaches with devastating fire from only a mile offshore. On January 9, the landings had begun, the Army troops splashing ashore virtually unopposed.

It had been three days now since the landings, and Chief O'Reilly was beginning to think that they'd actually managed to live through another one.

It was 0800, and the *Belknap*, Team Nine's APD, was on screening duty on the perimeter of the American fleet. An alert had sounded a few minutes ago when a couple of Japanese planes had been sighted, but things were quiet at the moment. O'Reilly had gone up to the enlisted mess and grabbed a cup of coffee, then brought it outside. He was standing on the ship's boat deck now, leaning against the railing and watching the touchdown of a Navy PBY Catalina off to starboard. Only a few other ships were in sight — a destroyer and a couple of troop transports already empty of passengers. It promised to be a quiet day.

Something caught the edge of his vision. Staring toward the east, shading his eyes against the morning sun, he could just make out four tiny, circling dots beneath a line of scattered orange clouds.

An alarm was shrilling. Seconds later, the *Belknap's* antiaircraft guns were pounding and banging away, and the peaceful sky erupted into the now all-too-familiar puffs of ack-

ack explosions. One by one, canopies and wingtips catching the sun, the four distant aircraft peeled off and dove for the American ships.

As they came closer, O'Reilly stared at the planes, fascinated. He'd been studying Japanese aircraft silhouettes from a recognition manual for days now and recognized them almost at once, Kawasaki Ki-61s, the type known to the Americans as a Tony. Every gun on the APD was firing now, throwing up a curtain of tracer fire. One Tony, separated from the others, bore down on the *Belknap*, circling past the bow, dropping lower, coming closer…

"What do you think, Chief?" Machinist's Mate First Edwards asked, coming up beside him. "Suiciders? Or a regular bomb run?"

"Hard to tell," O'Reilly replied. He could see two bombs, one slung under each wing. The Tony was firing now, coming in on a strafing run. Tracer fire from the *Belknap* converged on the aircraft, slamming into it, smashing off pieces. The engine was smoking … then belching black smoke. One of the bombs was knocked loose and sent tumbling into the sea five hundred yards away. The aircraft was a solid mass of flame now as its fuel exploded … but its speed and mass kept the wreckage coming, hurtling down at two hundred miles per hour and crashing into the base of *Belknap's* number-two stack.

The explosion knocked O'Reilly and Edwards off their feet as two of the APD's landing craft splintered with the blast, then were whirled away in the firestorm. An instant later, ammo stored in the ready locker atop the APD's galley deckhouse was touched off, and the explosion seared across the ship's upper structure, catching O'Reilly and hurling him across the deck. He felt his spine snap when he hit a stanchion.

Edwards … where was Edwards? Couldn't see him. Too much smoke, too much fire. The ship's alarm was shrieking in the distance somewhere, but all O'Reilly could really hear was the roar of the flames. God … he'd been burned. What he could see of his arm was all black char and raw red cracks. He couldn't move. Surprisingly, there was no pain at all, but he couldn't move and he couldn't breathe and the flames were getting closer…

O'Reilly's last thought, irrationally, and with a mad touch of twisted humor, was of the channel clearing at Hollandia … and of what a *splendid* bang that op had been…

CHAPTER 28

Thursday, 25 January 1945
U.S.S. *Badger*
Ulithi

"Gator," Tangretti told himself as he was shaving in the tiny head reserved for his platoon, "you are a fucking fugitive from the fucking law of averages."

The pain in his soul just seemed to go on and on and on. He wondered what it would be like to die.

It was early in the morning two weeks after Lingayen, and the *Badger* was riding at anchor at the Ulithi anchorage now, marking time between one campaign and the next. Everyone on the ship knew another big operation was in the works, but so far nobody knew what it would be, or where.

Another island.

And more deaths.

Tangretti had only found out about O'Reilly and Edwards and several of his other Team Nine friends a few days ago, when the casualty lists from the *Belknap* were finally published. Eleven men, wiped away, just like that. Snake. Then Kelly. Lieutenant Dayton, invalided out of the teams, maybe even blinded for life. Now O'Reilly. *Shit*, he thought. *I'm starting to feel like a damned Jonah. Everybody I get close to ends up dead.*

He knew he was feeling sorry for himself, but he no longer cared. Deliberately, now, he felt close to no one, not even to the other men in Team Eight. If he liked somebody, sooner or later that person was going to die.

He scraped off the last bit of lather and rinsed off the razor. It wasn't that he was superstitious, exactly…

Or was he? As he stared into the mirror, his eyes strayed down the center of his bare chest to the bullet dangling by its chain around his neck.

He'd once heard that sailors and soldiers were two sets of people who always harbored a little superstition in their souls. The sea and combat were both so vast, so implacable, so utterly beyond any man's control or even understanding that those who faced them were always looking for some deeper meaning to it all … not to mention some charm or talisman or sequence of thought or prayer or omen that might, somehow, give them an edge, however slight, against the odds.

"Hey, Gator," a deep voice said behind him. Slim walked into the head, wearing boxer shorts and carrying his shaving kit. He propped his stuff up at the sink and mirror next to Tangretti and started to lather up. "Damned shame about the guys in Nine, huh? I just saw the list last night."

"Fuck it," Tangretti said. "Dead's dead."

Slim glanced at him from above a mask of shaving cream. "Cheerful goddamned son of a bitch this morning, ain't you?"

"Not a lot to be cheerful about, is there?"

"Hey, I'm sorry, Gator," Slim said, backing away from the hardness in Tangretti's eyes. "I know you were buddies with that one chief in Nine. I didn't know those guys that well."

"Maybe you were lucky." Hastily, he rinsed his face, gathered up his gear, and shouldered his way past Slim before the Texan could ask him any more questions. Damn it, he *liked* Slim … and he didn't want to see the big-boned Texan get hurt, or worse…

When he stopped to analyze it, he knew the superstitious feelings were irrational, maybe even a little crazy. Maybe, he thought, it was just the old defensive mechanisms kicking in, a way to keep from going any crazier than he already was. Then again, he'd read somewhere that a man's senses were tuned to an ultrahigh pitch by danger, by combat especially. He'd heard lots of stories about guys in the military who'd suddenly gotten the feeling that they were going to die, had paid off their debts and given away their possessions ... and in the very next battle they'd been killed. In the past, he'd always figured that those were self-fulfilling prophecies. If a guy was certain he was going to die, he'd end up being less careful than usual, maybe not ducking for cover the way he would otherwise. Hell, maybe the fact that he thought he was going to die meant he really wanted to die, that he would seek death in combat and find it.

Screw it. All Tangretti knew was that his friends kept getting killed, a different kind of prophecy entirely. He'd been thinking about death a lot lately ... not to the point where he thought he was going to die, or even to where he wanted to die, though the depression, the bleakness of spirit that had gripped him ever since Kelly's death at Leyte was growing worse. He could *imagine* wanting to die.

Standing by the three-high tier of bunks that he shared with Jamison and Colt, Tangretti reached up and touched the good-luck bullet. Maybe this was what was keeping him alive. But if it was, did that mean the bad luck was deflected somehow? To his friends?

How do you outguess the fucking universe? he asked himself. He knew superstition was nonsense. Hell, he'd been a Seabee once, a builder. Someone who could calculate the stress on a load-bearing wall, or the thickness of concrete needed to shore up an abutment. That was all science and math. There was no room there for magic.

Was there?

All he really knew for certain was that, sooner or later, there would be another island … and another … and another after that. One damned island after another, all the way to fucking Japan, and on one of those beaches this side of Tokyo, he was pretty sure that there was a bullet or a mortar shell or a kamikaze aircraft waiting for him to cross its path. This, this *luck*, if that's what it was, that kept him alive while so many others close to him died or were wounded just couldn't go on for ever. Hell, everyone knew that the odds balanced out sooner or later, that the string of lucky sevens would end up snake eyes.

Tangretti wondered what the name of that next island in the chain would be.

"Good morning, Commander," Waverly said, stepping onto the quarterdeck and saluting Coffer. "It's damned good to see you again!"

"Good to have you with me again, Mike," Coffer said, grinning as he returned the salute. "Welcome aboard!"

"Thank you, sir." Waverly patted the fat, string-tied envelope he'd been holding under his left arm. "I understand I have you to thank for my orders."

"You don't mind, do you?"

He gave a lopsided grin. "It'll be good to be working with you again, Commander. I was starting to miss you."

"You may miss the peace and quiet of a regular team pretty quick, let me tell you," Coffer said. "Come on down to the wardroom and we'll talk over some java."

The *Gilmer* had changed a lot since Waverly had last seen her. She was cleaner, for one thing, as befitted a command ship … albeit a tiny one. She was less crowded too, though some of the compartments he glanced into as he followed Coffer down the passageway leading to the officer's wardroom were clearly jam-packed with new gear. Waverly recognized no one and felt a little bit lost.

"So," Coffer said as they got their coffee and walked over to the table neatly covered in white damask. "You didn't care to go Stateside with Team Five, I hear."

"No, sir," Waverly said. "There's still work to do out here."

Team Five was being broken up, at least partly to make room for the flood of new men and equipment pouring into the Pacific from the States. Most of these were being organized into new teams, rather than being used to reinforce and re-equip the old. Team Five was going home.

Many of Team Five's men, however, had requested assignments with other UDTs.

Waverly's request, however, had been turned down. Instead he'd been surprised to receive a new set of orders directing him to report to the U.S.S. *Gilmer* at Ulithi, where he was to join the Mudpac staff as Coffer's executive officer.

"You'll find plenty to do in Mudpac," Coffer assured him. "You see, they made me Captain Hanrahan's chief of staff, which means I get to do all of his dirty work. Now I'm making you my Exec, which means I get to pass it all on to you. Neat, huh?"

Waverly laughed. "Shit always flows downhill," he said, repeating the ancient Navy aphorism.

To tell the truth, Waverly was a bit disappointed by the assignment, though he was being careful to mask those feelings from Coffer. He'd been hoping for a combat billet, possibly as Exec in one of the new teams.

His real dream, of course, was to command a team of his own, though that was damned unlikely at this point in his career. There were a lot of young and eager officers out here, many with more seniority than he had, and everyone wanted to run one of the teams. By now, the mythos of the "frogmen" — the "naked warriors," as the press back home was calling them — had taken on a glamour all its own. Command of a UDT might well lead to promotion, commendations in the officer's personnel records, official recognition in the after-action reports, and better commands down the line.

"I know you were looking for a combat slot," Coffer continued, and Waverly wondered if the man was a mind reader. It always seemed as though he could tell what his people were thinking. "Maybe we can arrange something later. Right now, though, I need you with me. We've got a lot of organizational work to do if we're going to pull these new teams together. And some of the old teams, as well…"

"Team Nine," Waverly said, and Coffer nodded.

The kamikaze attack on the *Belknap* had been a disastrous blow, one that had sent ripples through the morale of every Team in the Pacific. Thirty-eight men had died aboard the *Belknap*, and another forty-nine were badly wounded. Of those, eleven of the dead and thirteen of the wounded had been members of UDT-9.

Since the beginning of UDT operations in the Pacific, with ten landing operations and dozens of reconnaissance swims, demo ops, and channel-clearing missions, a total of eight UDT men had been killed. Now, eleven had died in one savage flash of aviation gasoline and exploding munitions, the worst single loss to date since Omaha.

Worse, it seemed that Team Nine was bearing more than its fair share of casualties. Between the losses they'd suffered when one of their boats had been shelled at Leyte and the disaster at Lingayen, they'd lost a total of thirty-nine men, dead and wounded. The team's strength was down to just twelve officers and forty-seven men. Some things just didn't figure. There was Team Ten, the Golden Horseshoe, never scratched. And then there was Nine.

"Are you breaking up Team Nine too?" Waverly wanted to know.

"Probably, eventually," Coffer replied. "In the meantime, I've been arranging for the men to take Stateside leave in shifts. God knows, they deserve it."

"You know," Waverly said, "I'm not sure this idea of taking old units apart in favor of new ones is such a good idea. There's something to be said for the British idea of having units with a long history and plenty of traditions, something to be proud of."

Coffer took a sip of coffee from his mug before answering. "You're right, of course," he said. "I worked with the Brits for a time, as you know. Some of them take an absolutely passionate pride in belonging to, oh, some regiment that stood in the squares and held off Napoleon's best at Waterloo, or whatever. Sometimes, when I was over there, I'd be in a pub and hear some kids sitting at another table arguing over their respective regiments' battle histories … nineteen-year-old boys boasting about something that had happened a hundred years before they were born. It was eerie sometimes, let me tell you. As though the ghosts of all those men long dead and buried were still marching with the living."

"Esprit de corps," Waverly suggested. "Pride in your unit. Wouldn't that sense of belonging be a good thing to have in the teams?"

"That 'sense of belonging' is what Fort Pierce is all about, Mike. Every man in the teams knows that every other man in the unit has been through Hell Week too, same as him."

"Well, almost every other man," Waverly said, rolling his eyes in the traditional expression indicating some higher authority — the Man in Charge.

"Is that a problem for you?" Coffer asked sharply.

"No, sir. It is for some of the men."

Coffer relaxed slightly. "I know. It's something you and I are going to have to deal with. And let me tell you right now, if you have any problem at all with the idea of working for the Captain —"

"No problem, sir."

"Good. So far as the unit tradition goes, I think the men will get that out of knowing that they're members of the teams, whatever the numbers happen to be. I've seen that happening already."

"I know there've been a hell of a lot of fights between UDT personnel and other sailors ashore, fighting for the honor of the teams."

"That sort of thing's happened shipboard some, too. A lot of the regular sailors think the UDTs are getting some kind of special treatment. They don't share the day-to-day routines, don't have the same working parties or details. There's some jealousy."

"Sure. And an APD's sailors don't have to swim to an enemy beach. Or handle tetrytol. Or make a run through mortar fire in a wood-hulled LCP. Or —"

"Or stand around helpless while enemy suicide pilots try to land on them. I know. But that jealousy is going to be another problem you and I will have to work on. The teams need the guys shipboard to get them where they're going and support them once they're there."

"Affirmative to that." Waverly was silent for a moment. "Commander?"

"Yeah?"

"How come the brass is breaking up the old units like Five? I'd think having new hands join a team with old hands to teach 'em the ropes would be pretty damned valuable."

"Maybe. I've often thought that would be the way to do it. The fact is, though, there's a perception among the senior officers that those old hands, as you put it, get to feeling like they're cheating the law of averages after a while. They go on mission after mission, and one day they look around and realize that all of their old buddies are dead and that sooner or later Fate is going to catch up with them. It makes them cautious, and it slows them down. Maybe it even makes them wonder whether or not they should obey a tough order."

"That's garbage, Commander, and you know it," Waverly said. Still, he recognized a certain amount of truth in what Coffer was saying. A man *did* get to feeling like he was shooting craps with the devil after a while.

"Maybe it is, Mike. But that's one we're stuck with. The Navy believes that the men will work better if most, if not all of their buddies were with them at Fort Pierce, the whole team raised together, trained together, serving together. Oh, some of the men will cycle through other teams, of course." He smiled. "My office has been flooded by requests from guys in Team Five, putting in for transfers to fighting teams."

"Like me. Are you going to approve any of those requests?"

"Some. I happen to believe that experienced hands in a new unit is a damned good idea. Others, especially the stubborn old troublemakers, get assigned to cushy staff jobs."

"I hear you, sir." He drank a sip of coffee, thoughtful. "Commander?"

"Hmm?"

"I'll agree with everything you've said. Still, it's a shame Team Five's gone. I mean, a hundred years from now, a guy could say, 'Yeah, I'm in Five,' and people would know that his unit had been at Saipan and Tinian and Leyte, even if the people in it were different. Wouldn't that be something?"

Coffer waited a long moment before answering. He sat at the wardroom table, his half-empty mug held between both hands, staring into the brown liquid as though he were trying to read the future there. "Do you think there's going to *be* a UDT a century from now?" he asked.

"Hell, I don't know. Things are changing so fast. Look how different this war is from the last one. Blitzkrieg. Amphibious landings. In 1918 the latest wartime fashions were machine guns, airplanes, and barbed wire. In the Civil War it was massed artillery, trenches, and ironclads. What kind of weapons are we going to have issued for the next war?"

"I know we're opening a lot of doors to the future with what we're doing out here," Coffer said. "Clandestine UDT missions off of submarines, for instance. Maybe that rebreather lung of Lambertson's would let our people stay under water while they're working."

"Hell, the way the chrome domes talk about things, the next war is going to be fought by scientists. What do they call it? Push-button warfare."

"They could be right. Look at what the Nazis have been doing lately with their V-one and V-two weapons. Giving London a pasting from clear across the Channel. Buck Rogers stuff."

"Bullshit," Waverly said. "As long as governments fight wars they're going to need *men* to go in and grab beaches and fight inland and hold the high ground, things that buttons and machines and V-two rockets simply can't do, not in a million years. And *that* means they'll need the teams to show 'em the way."

"'Welcome Marines,'" Coffer said with a grin.

"Damn straight."

"Tell me, what do you think of the possibility of UDTs moving off the beach? Carrying out reconnaissance inland?"

"The Marines do that already with their recon teams and raiders," Waverly said. "And there's always aerial reconnaissance. I can't see that something like that would be necessary."

"Well, aerial reconnaissance can give you some pretty twisted data. Remember Tinian?"

"The things that looked like mines from the air and turned out to be postholes. Yeah. But the Marines handle that recon shit, Commander."

"Maybe. You know, I've been giving it a lot of thought. A lot of the Marines' problems on Peleliu are being blamed now on the fact that no one knew what to expect on that island. Our boys were there, swimming around right off the beaches. They could have reported on conditions ashore almost as easily as they did on coral reefs and beach obstacles. It might have saved some lives."

"Maybe. But hell, the men would have to be armed if they were going to go ashore, right?"

"I guess so."

"Hell, yes. Unless you want them to be sitting targets on the land as well as in the water. So you give them carbines. Or grease guns. More shit to carry with them on their swim. And that would mean more training, too. Half of the guys in the teams now don't know one end of a rifle from the other, you know. They'd have to go through something like a Marine weapons familiarization course before they could be trusted with a gun."

"Maybe. Still, we've been giving them some hand-to-hand and small arms training at Maui. That could be expanded."

"Well, sir, I still prefer that sharp divide in organizational responsibility in the planning. Like at Tinian. The teams take care of everything up to the high-tide mark. The Marines handle everything beyond that. They don't end up shooting each other in the dark, and everybody knows exactly what's expected of them."

Coffer laughed. "Which is why I wanted you for this job, Mike. You're organized. You have an organized and methodical way of looking at things. You know what needs to be done to pull something off."

"Maybe. Some folks say I'm a stick-in-the-mud, too. I tend to lose it when things get out of whack." He was thinking about that night off Tinian's White Beach 1, when everything possible had gone wrong. "I *am* learning about the need to stay loose and be ready to adapt."

"Excellent," Coffer said. "You know, all the experience in the world doesn't help one of those old hands if he doesn't learn from it."

Coffer drained his cup, then rose to take it back to the small coffee mess that occupied one end of the wardroom. Several other officers came in, greeted Coffer, looked Waverly over curiously, then got coffee for themselves and set up at the far end of the table.

"So what's next on the board for the teams, Commander?" Waverly asked as Coffer returned. "I don't mean next century. I mean in the next few weeks."

"Another island."

"I didn't think it would be the Chinese mainland."

"This one's going to be a doozy, though. The objective isn't all that big, but we think the Japanese are going to fight hard to hold it. Like Saipan. Or Peleliu. We've already started the preparation work, of course, getting ready for it. The teams are going to be involved in this one in a big way. We're looking at deploying Twelve, Thirteen, Fourteen, and Fifteen. You'll find out about the new training program later. The Captain's been running them ragged."

Waverly nodded. He'd heard that Mudpac had set up a new advanced base for UDT training on Ulithi, where they could practice working with the LCIs and destroyers, and try out newly developed tactics. "Any special problems with this one?" he asked.

"Every island has its own special problems, Mike. You know that. But, yeah, you're right. We'll be operating a lot farther north than the men are used to. The water'll be cold. That will present all kinds of new problems."

"Maybe we could have them rub down in fat or grease or something, like we do for camouflage now. Bear fat's supposed to work for Indians in Alaska, I hear."

"Interesting idea. We'll have to look into that, though I wonder what the supply officers back in Pearl will say when they get a requisition for two tons of bear grease."

"Maybe they'll substitute Vaseline. To go with all those condoms, right?"

Coffer laughed. "Could be. Kidding aside, though, this cold water is going to require a lot of thought. Clothing won't work, of course, since anything the men wear will just become waterlogged and drag them down."

"That wouldn't help with the cold anyway. Best way to die of exposure is to keep your wet clothes on. So what the hell's the target, anyway? Someplace in Siberia? Or have they found some Japanese still holding out up in the Aleutians?"

"Not quite that bad. It's a little tiny speck of volcanic rock just four and a half miles long, plopped down way out in the middle of nowhere, seven hundred miles from Saipan and seven hundred miles from Japan. Smack-dab between the two, which is what makes the place so all-fired important."

"What's it called?"

Coffer told him.

"Never heard of it," Waverly said, shaking his head.

"Neither had I," Coffer said. "But from what I've heard, I have the feeling that a month from now everyone in the world will have heard of Iwo Jima."

CHAPTER 29

Saturday, 17 February 1945
UDT-15, 1st Platoon Boat
Off Blue Beach 1, Iwo Jima

Three thousand yards out, the destroyers pounded away at each enemy gun that dared reveal its position. Closer in, the LCIs moved steadily toward the beaches.

And in the pitching LCP(R)s, the weirdly painted swimmers of four UDTs listened to the grumble of shellfire and wondered what this one would be like.

Pear-shaped, with the stem pointing southwest, Iwo Jima was an unprepossessing bit of real estate that had never possessed any importance whatsoever save to the handful of native people who'd once made their homes there, and they'd all been evacuated long since. Only the Japanese garrison remained on the island, and by now they knew the Americans were coming. The only question was where.

Iwo's northern coast was inaccessible, bounded by hundred-foot cliffs rising straight out of the sea to a rocky plateau. Four and a half miles to the southwest, at the stem of the pear, the rocks at Tobiishi Point give way swiftly to the dome-shaped glower of Mount Suribachi, an extinct volcano with a crest 550 feet above sea level. At its widest, in the north, the island was only two and a half miles wide, and at the narrow neck above Suribachi it was barely nine hundred yards wide. Little more than a large volcanic rock in the ocean, a part of the widely scattered Bonin Islands group, Iwo Jima appeared to be worthless to anyone reading the map, and it would have been except for one thing.

It was needed for the B-29s.

Late in November of 1944, the first B-29 raids against the Japanese home islands had been launched from Tinian in the Marianas, a round-trip of nearly three thousand miles. The B-29 Superfortress could make that long a flight — barely — if it carried a minimum weight of bombs, but any fighter escort across such a vast distance was completely out of the question. Worse, if a plane was damaged in the skies over Tokyo, its pilot and crew faced a fourteen-hundred-mile marathon of nursing the crippled giant along, of prayer, of cursing, of wondering if they could be found so far from home by an American sub or PBY, of desperate choices between bailing out ... or trying to make another critical few hundred miles before ditching in a vast and empty ocean.

But there was Iwo, squarely at the halfway point between Tinian and Tokyo. There were two airfields on the island now, and room for a third. If the Americans could take Iwo Jima, crippled B-29s could land there. Fighters could be based there and sent aloft to accompany the raiders all the way to their targets. Eventually, B-29s might be based there as well, halving the length of the trip and increasing the number of bombs each could carry.

Of course, the Japanese could read a map as well as their opponents. And if they'd not guessed that Iwo was a likely target for invasion at first, they knew now. Ever since early December there'd been daily naval air strikes against the island supplemented by heavy bombardments from the sea, as well as two heavy poundings by B-29s flying out of the Marianas.

By the time the UDTs had arrived off Iwo, on the rain-gloomy morning of February 16, the once-green island had been reduced to black sand and the splintered, burned-over stumps of a vanished forest. The entire island looked sere and desolate, as blasted and as lifeless as the face of the moon. Aboard the APD *Blessman*, the men of UDT-15 had leaned out over the rails, trying to catch a glimpse of their objective between the darkly scudding rain shadows of fast-moving squalls. Offshore, eight battleships — four of them veterans of the armada that had bombarded Normandy eight months before — five heavy cruisers, and a swarm of destroyers and lesser craft pounded away at the island until it seemed that nothing could possibly have survived that hellish, infalling rain of steel and high explosives. From *Blessman's* upper works, the men of Fifteen could see the flash and sparkle of shells slamming into Suribachi, the looming pall of gray-black smoke hovering above Iwo like its own private storm cloud. Some of the men made bets with one another: *Twenty bucks that this one's a walkover. You're on! My money says that the Japanese stay and fight, and this one's going to be as bad as Peleliu.*

The seventeenth had dawned clear and bright, without a trace of the squalls of yesterday. Now, Frank Rand was standing in an LCP(R), bracing himself on the gunwale against the small craft's unpredictable pitches and yaws.

The boat crews wore dungarees, helmets, and life jackets. The swimmers, ten in each boat, wore thick layers of cocoa butter and silver grease, which made the hard-muscled men look like heroic Greek statues of white marble come to life. The grease, as usual, was intended as camouflage in the water. The butter was for protection against the cold. The water temperature that morning was sixty-five degrees — warm enough when measuring air temperature, perhaps, but deadly for an unprotected swimmer. Below seventy degrees, the water sucked a man's heat from his body like a sponge; hypothermia could set in within an hour. At sixty-five degrees, the men might have as little as thirty minutes before being overcome by cramps, chills, and exhaustion. The cocoa butter should extend that time, though nobody knew for sure how much … if at all.

With the cold water, the buddy system was going to be more important than ever this morning.

"Ready to get wet, Raider?"

Rand turned to see Jennings coming up behind him.

"You going to be able to keep up with me today?" Rand growled.

Jenning's face fell. "Uh, sure, Raider." He flexed his arms. "I've been working real hard on the swimming."

Rand still had misgivings about Jennings's inclusion in the swim party. He remembered the trouble the kid had had both at Fort Pierce and with the one-mile open sea test at Maui. Jennings was his teammate, his friend, had been at his wedding, but Rand couldn't let personal feelings stand in the way of the mission. He wouldn't be able to carry him out there the way he had in training.

Usually, Rand would have been teamed with Kowalski … but Ski had a bad cold, and the *Blessman's* doc had down-checked him for the recon swim, much to the tough little Pole's dismay.

"You'd damned well better not slow me down, kid," Rand told him, "or I'll kick your ass clean out of the water."

Jennings slapped the mess of grease and cocoa butter on his chest with a wet plop. "Aw, with all this grease on, Raider, I'll just *slide* through the water as fast as a dolphin. You just watch me!"

Rand could hear the edge behind Jennings's words. Was it fear? Or was he just grating against Rand's own hard edges? The kid's eagerness was almost contagious. At Lingayen,

Jennings had been assigned to a boat crew, very much to his loud-voiced chagrin. This would be his first op as a swimmer, and Rand was afraid he'd get himself in trouble again.

Almost reluctantly, Rand nodded. "You'll do okay, kid. Just stick close, okay? And don't get in the way!"

"Right, Raider. You can count on me!"

Rand turned his back on Jennings and began studying the beach approaches ahead. Iwo possessed two possible landing areas, one on the east coast, one on the west, both of them running north from the rounded nub of Suribachi. Those beaches were black as coal, a crumbly, black volcanic sand like some of those the men of the UDTs remembered from Oahu, near Diamond Head. Both coastlines appeared suitable for landings when examined from the air. PHIBPAC had a moderate preference for the eastern beaches, since those were slightly more sheltered from wind and waves than those to the west, just across the island's narrow, connecting strand.

The men of the UDTs would check out both coastlines, of course, in an ambitious schedule that called for a recon of the eastern beaches this morning, and the western beaches at 1630 hours this afternoon. For the morning reconnaissance, Team Thirteen would take Green 1, on the left flank, directly under the towering slope of Suribachi. Teams Twelve and Fourteen covered the closely spaced beaches in the center, identified as Red 1 and 2 and Yellow 1 and 2. Team Fifteen had been assigned Blue 1 and 2 on the right, farthest from Suribachi, but hard up against the towering, rocky plateau that stretched north toward the island's widest point. There were no reefs to survey or blast this time — the water was too cold for coral growth — but the UDT swimmers would look for obstacles and mines as always. In addition, they would try to gather samples of the volcanic sand from both below and above the waterline and bring them back in tobacco pouches, an attempt to discover whether or not the beaches would support tracked and wheeled vehicles. From the air, the sand on those beaches looked well churned up and quite deep, as though it were not packed down at all. If vehicles became mired in loose sand during the landing, it could turn the landings into real nightmares.

Seen close-up, the view from the sea off Iwo's southeast coast was daunting — Suribachi far to the right, the hundred-foot cliffs to the left, and between them, the black-sand beach and the churning surf, killing grounds waiting for anyone foolish enough to enter those dragon's jaws of interlocking fields of fire.

It was already well known that Suribachi was honeycombed with caves and fortified gun positions. Likely, the Japanese were planning on making this fight another Peleliu, contesting every square foot of volcanic soil in a bitter, to-the-death stand. Rand looked up at Suribachi's rounded, smoke-patched top and tried to imagine what Japanese artillery spotters must be seeing from up there.

Hell, Rand thought, they must be scratching their heads and wondering about those LCIs in the van.

Rand didn't know yet what to think of Hanrahan, the new UDT CO, but he did know the man had been reworking the teams' command structure to bring greater efficiency to the UDTs' efforts. He'd been training the men hard, and he'd been going all out to get the men what they needed, and that was a damned good sign in Rand's book.

Hanrahan had also introduced two innovations, and most of the men in Fifteen liked the sound of both of them: smoke and gunboats.

Laying smoke along the beach, either from aircraft fondly known as "smokers" or through a barrage of white phosphorous shells, was expected to considerably reduce the risk to the swimmers by drawing an impenetrable white curtain across the enemy's line of sight, forcing them to fire blindly. Gunboats, or LCI(G)s, were something entirely new, odd-looking hybrids converted from standard LCIs but with troop space converted now to stores lockers and magazines. Designed to fit a perceived niche between the two .50-caliber mounts on an LCP(R) and the heavier but necessarily more distant armament of a destroyer, they were supposed to move in close to the beach and deliver almost point-blank cover for the swimmers. There were various types, but all carried a mix of 40-mm guns, 20-mm guns, and as many as ten .50-caliber machine guns. Most carried several rocket launchers as well, and one model had been equipped with three 4.2-inch chemical mortars for laying down smoke screens. With a full load, the sturdy little craft displaced 385 tons; they had a length overall of just 160 feet and, depending on the type, carried crews of anywhere from fifty to seventy officers and men.

So far the promised smoke was nowhere in evidence, but the LCI(G)s certainly were. Each of them wore a zigzag pattern of green and orange paint, a dazzle-scheme camouflage intended to break up the gunboats' outlines, but Rand could imagine each of them bearing a huge sign in Japanese reading "shoot me." There were seven of the craft in all, and they presented a strange and bizarrely surreal sight as they moved in toward the beach ahead of the LCPs.

A thundering gout of water erupted skyward five hundred yards ahead and to the right, close alongside an LCI gunboat. A second splash struck in the same boat's wake. The volume of fire from the island appeared to be increasing, answered by the crash and crack of the five-inch guns of the destroyers to the LCP lines' rear. Shells howled overhead, to flash and flare against the black, shell-blasted wasteland that was Iwo Jima. The battle was joined in earnest.

"Son of a bitch!" Jennings said, at Rand's back. "How's anyone supposed to live through all of that?"

Rand couldn't tell from Jennings's voice whether he was thinking of the swimmers who would soon be moving up close to that beach, or of the Japanese defenders in their caves and bunkers, hunkering down now beneath the thundering salvos from the American fleet.

It didn't much matter.

"Don't sweat it, kid," Rand said. "Just do your job and you'll come through okay."

He just hoped that his words would turn out to be true.

Waverly looked at his watch with growing frustration. It was past 1030 hours, the boats were on their way in to the beach, and still the promised smoke screen hadn't materialized. Another shell, probably from a three-inch gun, whistled into the sea and exploded with a crash fifty yards away. He looked up at Commander Coffer, who was standing with the command staff's radioman on the LCI(G)'s bridge wing a few feet away.

"Where the hell's the smoke, Commander?" he called. "We're goddamn sitting ducks out here!"

"Supposed to be on the way," Coffer yelled back. Another explosion went off in the water, closer this time. The Japanese spotters, up on Suribachi to the right and among those cliffs to the left, must have a perfectly triangulated fix on each of the gaudily painted LCIs cruising slowly into their overlapping fields of fire.

"Don't expect miracles though, Mike," Coffer added as the thunder died away. "You can stretch a smoke screen only so far. I doubt that they'll be able to cover the whole beach."

Three more shell hits threw up towering splashes to port … probably from guns somewhere up on Suribachi. "God, I hope the spotters in the fleet are watching this close!" Waverly yelled. "I'd hate to think I was suckering the Japanese into giving away their damned gun positions for nothing!"

To left and right, the other six gunboats could be seen, proceeding in line-abreast toward Iwo Jima's southeastern shore. Astern, the LCP(R)s with the platoons from four UDTs were slowly catching up, exactly according to the meticulously planned schedule Hanrahan had worked out.

Today's op would be a critical test of the new command structure; Coffer, in command of all four UDTs, was maintaining his advance headquarters here aboard one of the gunboats, where he could stay in direct communication with the individual LCP(R)s. Captain Hanrahan would remain aboard the *Gilmer* farther out, coordinating Coffer's operation with the tactical command of the armada of gunboats, destroyers, transports, and support aircraft involved in the beach reconnaissance.

The battleships had been pounding Iwo all morning, their thunder rolling across the sea and bouncing back in death-dealing echoes from the slopes of Suribachi. Japanese return fire had been steady, if not spectacular. Waverly glanced down at a chart he was holding, one that showed Iwo with a thick scattering of red dots, a deadly acne with each spot marking a known gun position. Most of the Mudpac officers, and those in the fleet as well, agreed that only a fraction of the enemy's guns had been revealed so far. The Japanese appeared to be continuing with the strategy, formulated at Peleliu, of turning the island they were defending into a fortress literally honeycombed with shelters, tunnels, bunkers, and steel-doored caves, of waiting until the Marines were ashore before hitting them with everything they had.

Suribachi — aptly code-named "Hot Rocks" on the chart — was going to be a real bitch. Over a hundred gun positions had already been identified, but none larger than three-inch. The Japanese *must* be holding back their five-and eight-inch coastal batteries. Where were they?

Gunfire barked and chattered, steadily increasing in volume, an ear-torturing cacophony of raw noise. Somehow, despite the racket, Waverly heard a new sound above the gunfire, a high-pitched droning, and looked up. In the crystal-blue sky overhead, wave after wave of Navy carrier aircraft, Hellcats and Avengers, were peeling out of formation and plummeting toward the island, loosing rockets in shrill, yellow salvos of flame, targeting the beaches and the high ground beyond, adding to the wholesale devastation ashore.

Then it was time for the LCI(G)s to add to the bombardment. From two thousand yards off shore, they put down a yammering, thundering hail of 20-mm and 40-mm rounds, sweeping back and forth across the beach. Rockets followed, hissing into the sky like flights of fiery arrows balanced on trails of orange-yellow flame. Explosions rose on every visible part of Iwo, erupting in twos, in fives, in tens, until the entire island appeared to be blanketed under churning columns of smoke and black cinders. White phosphorous exploded in great white globes rimmed with white-glowing embers that arced across that panorama of destruction, trailing smoke. The first tenuous haze of a smoke screen appeared, like the drawing of a filmy curtain across a window.

The LCIs were moving parallel to the beach now, as the LCP(R)s passed between them, continuing at high speed toward the beach.

Despite the bombardment from sea and sky, however, and despite the thickening curtain of smoke, the fire from shore was growing heavier.

Waverly leaned against the splinter screen on the bridge, staring through the pall of smoke above the island. He could still see the flash of enemy guns lighting the smoke, tiny, crisp sparkles that were sharper than the broader flashes of exploding American shells. Larger geysers of water were appearing now among the approaching forces, great, white, towering plumes of spray that reached high above the highest masts in the inshore fleet. One after another, the plumes burst from sea to sky.

Waverly moved across the wing to Coffer's side.

"Getting pretty hot, eh, Mike?" Coffer asked with a grin.

"A bit. You know, sir," he said, "I wonder if the Japanese might think we're the main invasion? Up until now they've been holding back ... but those look like eight-inch splashes over there."

Coffer raised his binoculars to his glasses and peered through them for a moment. A big shell exploded close astern of the command gunboat, sending a shudder through the deck.

"You know, Mike," Coffer said, lowering the binoculars, "I think they're concentrating on the gunboats."

"Not surprising, the way these paint jobs stand out. We must look like a circus parade to those jokers up there."

"Maybe. And maybe if they're shooting at us, they'll ignore the boats with our people."

"Oh, *wonderful!*" But he grinned as he said it.

Coffer laughed. "You could be right, though. The brass thinks that that's what happened at Leyte. The Japanese commanders mistook the UDT landing craft for the main invasion, and that's why they opened up so hard. Look at it this way, though. Each new battery that joins in against us gives the boys in the fleet a chance to spot it and mark it."

"What's that make us?" Waverly asked. "Decoys?"

Another shell landed to starboard, close enough to send a drenching rain of falling water across the LCI(G)'s decks.

"You know, Commander," Waverly said, straightening up again behind the dripping splinter shield. "All things considered, I think it was safer in the regular teams."

"You want to go back?" Coffer asked with a grin. "Put in your request!"

Another shell to port. Bracketed! "Show me to a typewriter!"

"Commander Coffer?"

Coffer turned to face the LCI(G)s young radio operator, who'd just emerged from the enclosed bridge. "What is it, son?"

"Sir, message from the *Gilmer*, They want —"

In the next instant, the air was shattered by a thunderclap so loud that Waverly wasn't entirely sure he'd even *heard* it at all. He was engulfed by the sound, by the sheer, raw blast of force that picked him up and slammed him against the wing's aft splinter screen. Something snicked past his left ear and buried itself in the sheet metal with a loud *ping*.

Waverly was lying on his back, blinking up at the sky stained by smoke. For a moment, he couldn't remember where he was … or why. His ears were ringing, his face burning. What in God's name had happened?

Flame and black smoke boiled across the sky overhead, and Waverly felt a stab of panic. Groggily, he managed to sit up.

The smoke was thick and choking, burning his eyes. He took a breath and the stuff bit his throat, sending him into a racking chain of coughs. He could hear screaming somewhere, and the barks of men shouting orders.

"Commander!" he yelled, his voice harsh and raw.

God, a shell, a damned big one, probably an eight-incher, had slammed into the LCI directly below the bridge and exploded. Damn, where was the Skipper? Had he been hit?

Waverly struggled to his hands and knees and blinked hard, trying to clear his burning, tear-streaming eyes. "*Commander Coffer!*"

CHAPTER 30

Saturday, 17 February 1945
Command LCI(G)
Off Red Beach 2, Iwo Jima

"*Commander Coffer!*"

"Mike!" Coffer's voice yelled back out of the boiling smoke. "Mike! Where are you?"

"Here, sir!" Waverly started crawling across the deck toward the voice. His back hurt like hell where he'd slammed into the splinter shield, but he decided that if he could feel it and move, he was probably okay. "Are you all right?"

"I'm okay," Coffer's voice came back, and Waverly felt a surge of relief. Struggling to his feet, he lurched forward, feeling his way along the bridge wing's railing.

Coffer was kneeling above the horribly mangled body of the radio operator. When he looked up, Waverly could see the pain in his eyes.

"He … he was just standing there talking to me, Mike," Coffer said.

A hurtling piece of shrapnel had taken off most of the top of the boy's head. Blood and brains were splashed liberally across the deck.

"We can't help him now, sir," Waverly said. Bending over, he helped Coffer rise to his feet.

"I think we're starting to find some of those eight-inch batteries, Mike," Coffer said, standing upright. The LCI(G) had taken a pronounced list to starboard … about ten degrees, Waverly estimated, and it was wallowing heavily in the sea.

That first shell had landed in the deck directly in front of the bridge, but Waverly doubted that it had pierced the hull. The list must have been brought on by another hit at about the same time.

"Are we going to have to abandon her?" Waverly asked.

Coffer surveyed the damage before answering. "We may have to," he said. "But I'd like to stay in the line as long as we—"

Another incoming shell smashed into the LCI, this one taking out one of the 40-mm gun mount tubs forward, hurling gun and crew into the air and sending fragments of metal shrieking past the smoke-blackened bridge.

"We can't take much more of this, sir!"

Another shell slammed home. God … it was as if the Japanese had scented the LCI's blood, as if they were concentrating now on the cripple, trying to tear her apart before she could escape their sights. The list was becoming more pronounced. It was getting harder to stand upright on the deck now without grabbing hold of a railing or lifeline for support.

The lieutenant in command of the LCI(G) staggered out of the bridge and onto the wing. "Commander Coffer!" he said, choking against the smoke. "We've been holed pretty badly, sir. I'm putting a D/C party to work dropping a mattress over the hole."

"Very good."

"What are your orders, sir?"

Technically, the lieutenant was in command of the gunboat and had the final say in how to save his vessel, but Coffer was in overall command of the entire flotilla. "You still have power?" he asked.

"Yes, sir. We can make maybe four knots. We won't be going anywhere until that hole is patched, though."

Coffer nodded as another shell burst nearby. "Okay. As soon as you can make speed, take us out of the line. It's nuts to just sit here and be knocked to pieces."

"Aye, aye, sir!" It was clear that that was exactly what the boat's commander had hoped to hear. He turned back toward the bridge, barking orders.

"Let's see if we can still raise anyone on the radio, Mike," Coffer said, glancing once briefly at the lifeless, bloody body at his feet.

"I can run a radio, Commander. Who do you want to talk to?"

"The *Gilmer*, for one. And we'll need one of the reserve gunboats."

"Sir, you're not planning on coming back out here *again*?"

"Until the job's done, Mike, this is where I belong." He jerked his head toward the LCP(R)s, now churning like big, dark gray beetles through the surf between the gunboats and the beach. "With *them*."

"Go!" the swimming officer yelled, and Rand rolled over the edge of the raft, squeezing his mask tight against his grease-covered face. *Christ*, the water was cold! Even with the layers of cocoa butter over his body, the chill bit through skin and muscle and clear to the bone in an instant.

The pack tossed in off the opposite side of the Higgins boat contained reel and fishing line, plumb bob and marker slates. As Rand placed the baseline float, Jennings took the reel and plumb line and without a word began swimming toward shore. When the float was secure, Rand turned and followed, kicking hard with his flippers, hoping the exertion would warm him up.

Soon he drew up on his partner's left, about twenty yards away. Jennings was pushing along with a pretty strong breaststroke, a look of sheer and utter determination on his face as he reeled out the knotted fishing line. Hell, maybe the kid was going to be okay after all. Jennings saw him looking at him and waved. Rand replied with a quick thumbs-up.

His initial shock upon hitting the cold water had dissolved in moments, leaving Rand feeling clearheaded and alert, almost refreshed. He estimated that they were about two hundred yards from the beach, and about twice that from the smoke-shrouded heights of the cliffs to the right. Swimming steadily, they moved toward the beach.

As searcher, Rand spent more time under water, jack-knifing below the surface and zigzagging back and forth along their line of advance, while Jennings plugged along on the surface, stopping every twenty-five yards to take and record another sounding.

It was quiet under water, though Rand could still hear the far-off thud and rumble of the bombardment. He almost hated to surface for air, because the noise was so much louder, so much more *demanding* up there. Beneath the surface, the water was clear and deep, but shoaling rapidly as they drew closer to the beach. The bottom, like the beaches, appeared to be made of black, volcanic sand. Visibility was at least seventy feet, though distances were always notoriously difficult to estimate under water through the magnifying glass of a face mask. He saw no sign of beach obstacles and no mines, nothing at all, in fact, to block the Marines' amtracks when they went ashore.

Floating in the depths midway between the black bottom and the silvery surface, he paused to record an observation on his slate.

Strange. He was having trouble grasping the pencil in his fingers. He found that he had to clench it in his fist, then drag the point with great deliberation to scrawl crude, childlike lettering across the slate.

The pain hit without warning, a sharp, gouging agony in his left calf muscle that almost crumpled him up double. Letting slate and pencil drift on the ends of their safety lines, Rand reached down and grasped the muscle in both hands, forcing his heel down, his toes up toward his face, stretching out the cramp.

It was the cold. It had to be. Gradually, the pain eased, and he was able to straighten up and float to the surface.

He broke into the open air, panting for breath. The key to surviving a sudden cramp like that, he knew, was to keep your head and not panic. *Panic* drowned more people than water by itself did.

But that thought brought a new worry. Where the hell was Jennings?

Something thrashed white in the water a few yards off. At first Rand thought it was another bursting shell, but then he saw one white-greased arm groping in the air before sinking out of sight.

Shit!

Jack-knifing with a splash, Rand arrowed beneath the surface, swimming hard. Jennings was descending in a cloud of bubbles a few yards away, his head jerking wildly back and forth as he clutched his belly. Rand reached him in a moment, grabbed his arm, and started kicking for the surface. Jennings struggled a moment, then relaxed. In another second, they'd broken through to the air once more.

"Jennings! You okay?"

"Y-yes!" Jennings gasped, his eyes wide behind the glass of his face plate. "Stomach…"

"Just float here for a minute until it passes. Roll your head to the side when you need to breathe."

Jennings did as he was told, his silver back bobbing on the surface as Rand held him.

The smoke blanketing the shore was growing thicker now, and it didn't seem as though any of the mortars or cannon shells were landing anywhere nearby. No machine gun fire, either, which was a blessing. American aircraft roared low overhead, strafing the beach beyond the haze of concealing smoke.

"I-I'm okay, Raider," Jennings said, gasping a bit. "Thanks."

"You sure?"

"Yeah. I can go on now. I'm fine."

"Negative." The floatation sack that had stowed their gear was bobbing on the waves a few feet away. Rand swam over and retrieved it. "Here," he said, shoving it toward Jennings. "Use it as a life preserver. Paddle back out to the recovery line and wait for pickup."

"But Raider —"

"Stow it, Jennings! I'm not your goddamn baby-sitter, okay? I can't afford to watch you every second all the way in to that beach and back! Got it?"

"Got it." His lower lip, blue with the cold, was trembling.

"C'mon, then. I'll give you a hand."

He helped Jennings swim back toward the buoy, staying with him to make sure he didn't have another attack of cramps. The kid was clearly exhausted and in no condition to swim much farther.

Leaving Jennings afloat on the pack next to the buoy, Rand followed the fishing line hand-over-hand until he found the reel, lying on the bottom where the kid had dropped it. Checking the depth at that point, he made a clumsy, almost illegible mark on his slate, then kept swimming toward the beach.

The commander of Coffer's gunboat had kept the little vessel's guns firing while a mattress was rigged across a gaping hole in its starboard side, but after a few more minutes, the LCI(G) had taken several more hits. Limping back out beyond the destroyer line at three thousand yards from the beach, Coffer, Waverly, and the other Mudpac staff officers had transferred to a reserve gunboat, then closed once more with the beach. Within five minutes, that LCI too had been hit amidships and set afire.

Smoke spilling from its deck, the LCI(G) had followed the first gunboat to relative safety, her damage control parties had extinguished the fire, and she'd started to return to the beach. Plumes of white water thundered and burst around her. A direct hit detonated in the center of a 40-mm gun tub forward, hurling bodies and twisted bits of wreckage into the sea.

"They're definitely aiming for the gunboats," Waverly yelled at Coffer, holding a radio telephone to his ear. The LCI(G) shuddered as another round struck her waterline. "According to *Gilmer*, every damned LCI has been hit. One is reported sinking. There are no more reserves."

Coffer scowled. "That's going to make it hard for the beach run this afternoon," he said. Turning on the bridge wing, he stared out at the destroyer line. "There! Commander Harding!"

The new LCI's skipper joined them, his face streaked by smoke. "Sir?"

"Put us alongside the *Twiggs*."

"Aye, aye, sir."

"I know her skipper," Coffer told Waverly. "We'll transfer to his ship and continue the operation from there."

Moments later, the crippled LCI bumped alongside the destroyer. Overhead, the ship's forward five-inch gun crashed and recoiled, slamming a round into the shore less than two miles away.

Coffer looked up and saw an old Navy friend, Commander Greg Phelps, leaning out over the side of one of the wings on his bridge, along with several of his officers. "Permission to come aboard!" Coffer yelled, cupping his hands around his mouth.

"You Jonah!" Phelps yelled back, but his grin robbed the name-calling of any sting. "Why the hell did you have to pick *my* ship?"

"Tell him his ship is safe, Commander," Waverly told Coffer as the *Twiggs's* deck crew began lowering a ladder to take the Mudpac officers aboard. "It's against Navy regs for anyone to have more than two ships shot out from underneath him in less than fifteen minutes!"

Rand was shaking with the cold by the time the black, grainy bottom rose beneath his knees and hands, and the surf broke and tumbled in white rollers across his back. He crawled forward a little farther, then lay flat on the sand as the water continued washing over him and up onto the beach.

He'd already taken several samples of sand from the bottom. He wanted to get some from the land as well, but the small arms and machine gun fire had been picking up steadily as he moved closer in.

The smoke screen laid down by American aircraft and the mortar LCIs was still in place, but capricious winds off the island kept tattering and thinning it, especially here, close to the cliffs on the right flank. Shells continued to howl in from the sea, slamming inland with thunderous detonations that Rand could feel through his belly as the ground thumped and lurched beneath him.

He was tired. The cold water had sapped him almost completely, and he wondered if he was going to be able to make it all the way back out for pickup. Checking his watch, he saw that he had just twenty minutes left to retrieval. He'd better move, and move fast.

Crawling a little farther, keeping flat on the black sand, Rand inched his way forward up the sloping beach. A stubborn, hard chattering sounded from inland; it took him a moment, and the sight of gouts of water splashing up from the wet sand and inch-deep water behind him, to realize that someone up there was shooting at him. Searching for the source of the sound, he thought he saw a flicker …

There! A rapidly winking white flash showed itself against tumbled black rock at the top of the beach, accompanied by something snapping sharply through the air inches above him. Narrowing his eyes, squinting against the pitch-black shadows, Rand tried to trace the shapes he could see in the rock pile. Like one of those optical illusions with a picture hidden within a picture, he saw nothing at first … and then the shape came together almost magically.

It was a bunker, with sloping concrete walls painted black to match the sand, rising no more than a foot above the dunes at the top of the beach and almost entirely covered over with chunks of volcanic rock and loose piles of sand. Watching carefully, he could see the slender, rectangular shape of the gun slit — and the winking white light, he knew now, was the muzzle flash of a machine gun.

Rand was lying in a slight hollow on the shingle of the beach, and that had saved his life, because it looked like the machine gunner was having trouble depressing the muzzle of his weapon enough to fire at Rand directly. The bullets were whip cracking six inches above his head and striking the water behind him. Glancing down at his arm in front of him, he was suddenly, painfully aware of just how well his white-greased body showed up on black sand. "Nothing like a little camouflage to throw the Japanese aim off," he told himself. He decided he'd better do what he'd come here to do.

Calmly — he was too tired and cold to do *anything* with haste at the moment — Rand pulled his slate up to where he could write on it and began sketching in details of the top of the beach, marking the machine gun's position. As he lay there sketching, he gradually became aware of another bunker, behind the first and twenty yards to the left. And another … to the right. God, the Japanese must have bunkers and fortified positions almost shoulder to shoulder up there, and from the way they were firing, it didn't look like that hellish bombardment had even scratched them.

His sketch complete, Rand pulled out his last empty tobacco pouch and scooped up some of the black sand in front of his face. It was hard-packed here, with plenty of "fines," or soft powder, mixed in with the larger chunks. He eyed the dry sand farther up the beach with something almost like longing. To do this job right, he really needed samples from all the way up the shingle … but with those machine guns positioned up there, he wouldn't make it halfway to the high-tide line. What he had in the pouch would have to do.

Off to his left, perhaps fifty yards away, Rand saw two more swimmers on the beach, as distinctly visible in their white-on-black camo scheme as he was. They were huddled together, flat on their bellies at the edge of the surf, and they appeared to be working diligently on something in front of them. He wondered if one or both of them was wounded. Maybe they needed help.

Well, first he had to look out for number one, because he couldn't check on the neighbors if that machine gun managed to pick him off right here. Carefully, he started inching backward off the beach slope. When he felt cold water sluicing past his ankles, he started moving faster, backing away, keeping his eyes on those guns. At some point, he would be backing into their clear line of fire.

Spouts of water shot up from the surface a few feet to his left. Rolling quickly away from the marching line of splashes, he plunged sideways into the surf just as the breaker rolled over him, turning around so that his head was going downhill, digging in with his flippered feet, fighting the rough-and-tumble tug of the current to get clear of that deadly beach as fast as he could go. Then the wave was past and he was into the undertow, letting the current drag him swiftly along the bottom and out toward the sea. Bullets slapped and splashed in the water around him.

As the bottom dropped away, he angled down until his bare stomach scraped the volcanic sand at the bottom. When he glanced up, he saw dozens of metallic objects scattered through the water above him, sinking slowly like so many glittering, copper-colored snowflakes. Reaching out, he caught one as it drifted down, and he almost laughed. *Damn, a guy could get killed around here!*

Tucking the spent bullet into one of his pouches, he looked around to get his bearings, then started swimming quickly along the surf line toward the southwest, the direction in which he'd seen the other two swimmers on the beach. If they were stuck up there, pinned down by another enemy gun, maybe he could distract the Japanese long enough for them to wiggle clear and get into the water.

Surfacing for air, he saw that he'd covered half the distance to the other swimmers ... and that both of them had backed off the beach and were in the surf again. That was good. But there was something more ... something starkly white against the black sand just above the water line. Was it a third swimmer, left for dead?

He started moving toward the two men, submerging as much as he could to avoid being shot at from the beach. A moment later, he recognized Lauber and Bailey, the next two swimmers in the string dropped off from the 1st Platoon boat after him and Jennings.

"Lauber!" he called. "Hey, Rog!"

"Ho, Raider Rand!" Torpedoman's Mate First Class Roger Lauber yelled back. "Ain't we got fun?"

"Who the hell did you leave back on the beach?"

"Huh?" Lauber glanced back over his shoulder, looking puzzled. "What do you mean?"

Rand looked back at the white body, blinked, then pulled his mask up onto his forehead to get a better, less water-blurred view.

He'd not been able to see it clearly before because of the angle of view. He'd swum far enough along the beach, however, to see the thing full-on.

It was a sign, painted on what looked like a strip of white cloth, possibly a cut-down bedsheet. It had been unrolled on the beach, stretched taut between a pair of uprights driven into the sand. On the cloth were the now-immortal words:

WELCOME MARINES!
UDT-15

"Damn it, you guys!" he shouted. "You scared me half to death! I thought somebody got killed up there!"

"Shit no, Raider," Mineman Second Class Ralph R. Bailey called back. "We did everything we came to do and thought we'd leave a little surprise for the Gyrines."

"Hey, you're not gonna tell on us, are you?" Lauber asked. "I mean, everybody's been doing it."

Rand scowled. He was furious, in part because he really *had* been afraid that one of the men in his platoon had been shot on the beach.

"You mean everybody's been *trying* it," Rand growled in response, treading water as the two swimmers drew closer. Ever since Guam, UDT skippers had been finding Welcome Marines signs in their men's gear and confiscating them.

Machine gun bullets slapped into the water a few yards away. Lauber nodded toward the open sea. "Raider, if you're gonna chew our asses, could you do it someplace a little less exposed?"

"Swim, damn it," Rand said. "At this point I'm about ready to shoot you myself and save the Japanese the trouble!"

"Aw, we didn't mean anything by it," Bailey said.

"Some guys in Twelve bet us we couldn't do it," Lauber added. "C'mon, Raider! The honor of Fifteen was at stake!"

"Shit, I'll give you the honor of Fifteen. I ought to put the both of you on report. You risked losing every bit of information you were sent in here to collect!"

"No we didn't, Raider. We gave our slates and samples to Cunningham. He's already got 'em out at the pickup area by now."

The brass had been working hard to discourage the practice of planting signs for the Marines to find, claiming that they were a serious breach of security. In fact, the practice probably wasn't so much a security breach as it was a breach of common sense. Oh, the Japanese might learn from the sign that UDT-15 was operating in the area, but no one in the teams thought that a problem. Hell, the Japanese themselves might decide the unit number was a deception. Who in his right mind, after all, would go to all that trouble to give the enemy an important piece of military intelligence? Rand could imagine a group of Japanese military intelligence officers somewhere looking at one of those signs and scratching their heads, trying to figure out what those crazy Americans were *really* up to.

Sooner or later, though, one of these kids was going to go too far trying to pull off one of those stunts, and then there really would be a body on the beach.

"So, are we on report?" Bailey asked.

"No," Rand said. "You damned well ought to be, and if you ever pull a gag like that again I'll personally drag you back onto that beach to pick that shit up. C'mon. Get your dumb asses back to the retrieval area. On the double!"

Together, the three men began swimming back out to the sea. Behind them, the sign fluttered a bit in the breeze coming off the island, as patches of white smoke drifted down across the beach.

CHAPTER 31

Sunday, 18 February 1945
Off Iwo Jima

Commander Coffer had no more ships shot out from under him that morning. The final count was eleven gunboats damaged, one sunk — every LCI(G) on the line and in reserve hit. Forty-eight men had been killed in the brief, furious action, and another 155 wounded. One of the dead and two of the wounded had been UDT liaison officers. After that hell of shellfire from the cliffs of Iwo, it seemed a miracle that casualties in the heroic little flotilla had been as light as they were.

For all that, the reconnaissance of Iwo had proven to be a success. Evidently, the Japanese had been tricked into revealing most of their guns, and the destroyers had begun methodically taking out the recorded positions, one after another. The swimmer teams, meanwhile, had completely swept the beach approaches. No obstacles had been reported, and only a single mine. Returning to the retrieval line, the cold, exhausted swimmers had been startled to find the covering gunboats missing, but Hanrahan, meanwhile, had ordered the destroyers to close to within two thousand yards of the shore in order to lay down a heavier and more accurate covering barrage. The LCP(R)s had gone in, zigzagging sharply to avoid enemy gunfire, plucking the swimmers one by one from the chilly water.

Despite the fierce gunfire from shore, only two UDT men had been lost in the reconnaissance teams — one swimmer from Team Twelve, who'd last been seen swimming beneath Suribachi's cliffs with mortar shells landing all around — and one member of a boat crew with Fifteen, shot through the head during recovery operations.

Casualties could have been a lot worse.

Hanrahan's new system for dispersing UDT intelligence throughout the fleet seemed to have worked well. The samples of bottom and beach sand returned in the tobacco pouches had been analyzed, and the pronouncement was made that the beaches could support all types of vehicular traffic. Despite concerns that the Japanese, now fully alerted, would turn the beach reconnaissance on Iwo's western coast into a slaughter, the day's second swim had gone smoothly, with no casualties. Again, Hanrahan had ordered the covering destroyers in close, laying down a thick screen of smoke with white phosphorous shells to shield the swimmers, and the tactic appeared to have worked. The men of the UDTs were especially pleased to hear Radio Tokyo's assessment of the day's activities: *Today a major landing force was repulsed from the shores of Iwo Jima with heavy losses. An American battleship was hit and sunk instantaneously.*

It seemed a fair tribute to the gallant, sunken gunboat, and to the men who'd died that bloody, thunder-torn morning, to prepare the way for the Marines.

"Hey, Frank. Bum a light?"

"Hello, Jennings." Rand extended a pack of Camels to the younger UDT man, who selected a cigarette. Rand struck a light, the match flare momentarily illuminating the kid's face.

"Thanks." He puffed the cigarette's tip to glowing orange brilliance, then exploded in a ragged chain of coughs.

Rand smiled. "Still getting the hang of it?"

"Nah, smooth." Jennings coughed again, then almost defiantly took another drag. A strip of bandage was set across his face, bracing two tight rolls of gauze to either side of his nose and holding them in place.

The evening was dark and overcast and there'd been some isolated rain squalls earlier, but the night sea gleamed with an eerie phosphorescence, especially astern where the APD's wake churned up the water. They were racing through the darkness at twenty-two knots — flank speed for the converted DE — and the ship's roiling wake shone like a silver-white line drawn across the sea.

The seventeenth had been a grueling day off the black, sandy beaches of Iwo, but the men of UDT-15 had been told they were standing down, and on the evening of the eighteenth they were enjoying the prospect of some time off. The survey work was done, the Marines' landings were set for the next morning, and their APD had been assigned to picket duty as one of the light screen of ships surrounding the anchored American fleet off Iwo. Besides the 100 officers and men of UDT-15 aboard, *Blessman's* complement numbered 212.

"Where the hell are we going in such a hurry, Frank?" Jennings wanted to know.

"Way I heard it," Rand replied, "we're standing in for another ship on picket duty that had engine trouble."

"Well, we're sure busting a gut to get there." He leaned against the railing, staring aft a moment at the eerie phosphorescence of the sea. "Listen, Raider, I never got a chance —"

"Skip it," Rand said curtly.

"You saved my life off Blue Beach yesterday."

"And you nearly got every man in that boat killed."

Jennings's face fell. "I didn't mean to. It wasn't my fault!"

As Rand had heard the story later, by the time a pickup boat had reached Jennings, the swimmer had been too tired and too cold to reach for the recovery ring. After several passes, with enemy mortar fire growing more and more accurate, the LCP(R) had stopped dead in the water while members of the boat crew had hauled Jennings aboard bodily. Jennings's nose had been broken when some anxious member of the UDT boat crew had slammed him facedown into the bottom of the Higgins boat just as the coxswain had given it the gas. Weaving erratically, they'd cleared the area, mortar shells slamming home in the spot they'd been idling at an instant before.

Rand softened. "No, it wasn't your fault," he said. "But I think you ought to give some thought to dropping from the teams. You've got to carry your own damn load in this outfit. People get killed if they have to carry it for you."

"I'm not dropping," Jennings said. His voice was so low Rand almost couldn't hear the words, but he could hear the determination behind them.

"Suit yourself," Rand said. He turned away, staring at the APD's wake.

After a moment, Jennings spoke again. "I'm going up to the mess deck, Raider. I heard the guys were getting up a game of poker. You want to come?"

"Later maybe."

"Okay. See you later."

Rand closed his eyes as the kid's footsteps receded. *Why are they sending children out here to fight a man's war?*

Maybe, he answered himself, it was just that wars were always fought by children, for the most part. Right now, though, he felt about a thousand years old.

*

431

Many of Team Fifteen's members were on *Blessman's* starboard mess deck amidships, playing cards or writing letters home. A few were topside, enjoying the breeze as *Blessman* carved her way through the sea toward her rendezvous.

But there were hunters in the night. One of them, a Mitsubishi G3M2 twin-engine medium bomber of the type known to the Allies as a Betty, had spotted *Blessman's* wake miles astern. Following the straight, gleaming arrow across the sea for miles, the Betty soon spotted the blacked-out ship against the silvery sea, swung right, came about 180 degrees, and descended toward *Blessman's* starboard side.

As lookouts shouted warning and the ship went to General Quarters, most of the men on board thought that this was yet another suicide attack. In fact, this time death came by more traditional weapons of war. At 2120 hours, two five-hundred-pound bombs shrilled out of the black sky, one crashing into the sea close aboard with a thunderous crash and an avalanche of white water spilling across the deck, the second punching through the overhead and landing squarely in the starboard-side mess hall before exploding in a searing blast of flame and noise.

Forsythe was in the officers' shower head when the general quarters alarm went off. Following shipboard water conservation routine, he'd only wet his skin, then turned the water off while he lathered up. The alarm caught him covered with soap from head to foot.

With a sigh, he reached up and pulled the handle to sluice off the soap. How were the Japanese able to time things like this? Was their secret service so good that they knew exactly when an attack would be the most inconvenient to Forsythe personally?

Suddenly the lights went out and the ship lurched violently to port. The impact flung Forsythe backward out of the shower stall, and he slammed hard into the bench set into the opposite wall. Other men in the compartment yelled.

Stunned, he rose, trying to find his feet. The ship gave a hard shudder, and her list slowly started to right itself. "Damn it, where's my life jacket?" someone yelled.

"Out! Everybody out on deck!" another voice called. Blindly, Forsythe followed that voice, his bare wet feet slapping on the deck as he made his way out of the head and into the passageway beyond.

"What the hell happened?" someone wanted to know.

"Torpedo!" someone answered. "We've been goddamn torpedoed!"

"Nah. Must've been a suicide plane..."

"Now hear this! Now hear this!" blared over the ship's speakers. "Damage control and fire parties lay amidships!"

Forsythe tasted smoke in the air of the passageway, a raw and evil stink that burned his throat with each breath he took. Following the press of other men navigating the darkened corridor to a ship's ladder, he let himself be swept up out of the ship's belly and into the cleaner, colder air of the night.

It wasn't until he was almost on deck that he realized that he was naked except for some clinging patches of suds. The suddenness of the attack, the panic of the other men in the darkness, the muddled shock of being dropped on the deck, had all conspired to make him forget to get dressed, and suddenly his embarrassment at being found on deck nude seemed more pressing than the danger that the ship was in. This sort of thing never happened in Boston. He tried to turn around, tried to make his way back below deck to his quarters and the clean uniform waiting for him there, but the surge of scared-looking sailors pouring up out of the ship's smoky passageways blocked him.

Outside, orange light glared off sky and sea. The davit-mounted LCPs aft of the impact were smashed to splinters, and the entire center of the APD was a raging inferno, with gasoline-fed flames mounting to the night in a roaring blaze that must have been visible twenty miles away.

Forsythe could sense the nearness of panic in the sailors around him. The intercom was still blaring the General Quarters alarm, and a few men in that milling mob wore life jackets and appeared to be moving with purpose.

"Okay, men!" he yelled, and he hoped his voice didn't sound too shrill, too uncertain against the babble of noise around him. "Stand to your D/C stations! On the double!"

Almost instantly, the magic of having someone in authority tell them what to do worked its magic on the men. "Fire party!" a first class yelled. "Form with me!"

"Life jackets!" another called, cracking open a locker on the deck. "Here! Pass 'em around!" Order formed out of near chaos, and the men began working together with a purpose.

It had to be that way if they were to save their ship.

Throughout the ship, men stumbled through smoky darkness, helping one another grope toward doors or hatches leading topside, breaking out damage control gear and firefighting equipment, belatedly donning life jackets and helmets as the ship wallowed powerless in moderate seas. Wounded men were hoisted into fireman's carries, or dragged along the deck to get them clear of the rapidly spreading flames, as the fire gongs clanged incessantly.

There was little the fire parties could do. Pressure in the firefighting hoses was already dropping to nothing. Water mains had been ripped open by the blast, pumps destroyed, holding tanks ruptured. With the ship's head of steam falling, there was no pressure to work the fire mains, and soon the only water available for fighting the flames was from hand-operated pumps or from bucket brigades hastily organized among the ship's company.

Explosions began going off as the fire reached the APD's magazine stores. Hundreds of rounds of 20-mm and 40-mm ammo for the ship's guns began cooking off with a furious pop-pop-popping that sounded like a full-scale attack.

The exploding ammo had another and more deadly significance, however. Stored below decks were some forty tons of tetrytol, the high explosive used by the UDT for clearing obstacles and blowing passages through obstructing reefs. As survivors of Team Fifteen began gathering on the *Blessman's* fantail, the word spread. The decks were getting hot, and the tetrytol was heat-sensitive. Before too long the APD was going to vanish in a savage explosion that would kill every man on board.

The ship's radio officer got off an SOS, but there was little hope that the ship could be saved. With the explosives aboard, with the fire spreading and no means of fighting it, the ship was literally a helplessly drifting bomb.

And the fuse had already been lit.

"Jesus, look at her burn!" Waverly said, pressing his face against the bridge windscreen to cut down some of the glare. The fire engulfing the APD's upper deck and superstructure abaft of her bridge appeared to be totally out of control. *Gilmer*, which happened to be the closest ship able to leave its position in the screen, had picked up *Blessman's* SOS nearly an hour earlier and come racing through the night at twenty-five knots to render aid.

The question now, though, was whether any aid was even possible.

"You want me to put us alongside?" *Gilmer's* skipper, Commander Benjamin Wilson, sounded dubious. He stood beside the ship's helmsman, a foul pipe clenched between his teeth as he stared at the inferno ahead.

"I don't think so," Coffer replied. "How about lowering a couple of boats? I can take a damage-assessment party over there without risking your ship."

"Suits me," Wilson said with a sharp nod of his head. "What are your estimates concerning the explosives aboard?"

Coffer whistled tunelessly through his teeth. "I'll tell you the truth, I don't know. The stuff's only a little more sensitive to heat than TNT. Detonating temperature of three hundred forty-five degrees. When it goes, though, it'll all go at once."

Captain Hanrahan walked onto the bridge. "Commander Coffer? What do you intend to do?"

"Put a damage-assessment party aboard and find out how bad it is. Maybe take some of her wounded off in small boats. Then if it looks like we can bring the *Gilmer* close aboard, we could use her hoses to fight the fire and maybe cool off her decks. And we could stand by to take her whole crew off if that seems the best thing to do."

Waverly could see the wheels turning in Commander Wilson's mind. He had a responsibility to render all assistance possible to a ship in distress ... but he also had a responsibility to his own ship and crew. If the *Blessman* exploded with the *Gilmer* alongside, both ships would go down in seconds. For his part, Hanrahan remained silent. He was the ranking officer, but he'd come onto the bridge after Coffer had already taken charge of the situation, and he seemed willing to let his chief of staff handle things, at least for the moment.

Wilson turned to Hanrahan. "With your permission, sir, I think we can get the *Gilmer* in there pretty close."

Hanrahan nodded. "Do it."

Gilmer's skipper clapped the helmsman on the shoulder. "Take us in, half speed," he snapped. "Lay us one hundred yards off the *Blessman's* port side."

The man's hand went to the engine telegraph, and he dragged the handle back from ahead full to half speed. There was no hesitation, no wavering. "Ahead one-half, aye, aye, sir. Coming around to *Blessman's* port side."

"Mr. Gilchrist!"

"Yes, sir."

"Pass the word. Break out two of the LCPs for the boarding party."

"Aye, aye, sir."

On the other ship, ammunition for one of the 20-mm mounts went off with a clattering rush of fireworks.

"Captain Hanrahan," Coffer said, turning to his CO. "I would like permission to lead the boarding party."

Hanrahan thought about it for only a second. "Permission granted, Commander."

"I'd like to go with you, Commander," Waverly said.

"It's going to be hot work, Mike."

"Just like UXB, right?"

Hanrahan caught Coffer with a hard look. "That's right. You used to work in demo with the Limeys, didn't you?"

"Guilty, sir."

"Never had a UXB go off while you were working on it?"

"Actually, Captain, yes I did. Once."

Hanrahan gave him a funny look. "Well, I'll take that to mean you've got a charmed life, and this one won't kill you either. Good luck!"

"Thank you, sir."

"Don't forget, sir," Waverly added as Coffer hurried off the bridge. "Yesterday he had two ships shot out from under him and came away without a scratch."

"That," *Gilmer's* captain said, "is hardly reassuring. His luck doesn't seem to rub off on the people around him."

"I think it does, sir," Waverly said, and he turned to follow Coffer into the flame-shot night.

Rand was on the *Blessman's* fantail, singing at the top of his lungs. After the explosion, he'd grabbed every UDT man he could find in the tangled, yelling confusion and organized a bucket brigade. There'd been an initial flash of panic, fueled by the flames leaping into the night, but the men were working together smoothly now, singing to keep the rhythm of their movements together as they passed bucket after bucket of cold seawater forward and down a hatch to dump it over the tetrytol below.

Anchors aweigh, my boys!
Anchors aweigh!
Farewell to all these joys,
We sail at break of day Hey! Hey! Hey!

They'd been singing for an hour now, and their voices were dry, parched, and cracking. When some of the voices faltered, Rand moved up to take them out of the line and replace them from a small pool of reserves he'd formed on the fantail.

"Sing!" he yelled. "Damn it, sing!"

To our last night ashore,
Drink to the foam.
Until we meet again
Here's wishing you a happy voyage home…

A happy voyage home? Not damned likely, not with the deck growing so hot now that men still in bare feet could scarcely stand in one spot for long. The way things were going at the moment, the only thing that would make it home out of this whole ship's company would be a very large number of telegrams.

We regret to inform you…

More men with the ship's rescue parties stumbled out of the boiling black smoke forward, dragging wounded with them. Every spare foot of space on the fantail was already taken up by wounded men, some with the ship's company, others from Team Fifteen. A ship's pharmacist's mate was with them, bandaging wounds and injecting the worst cases with Syrettes of morphine.

Quickly, Rand hurried forward to lend a hand with the wounded. He met GM1 Skinner, who was half dragging a horribly burned sailor along the deck. The man's face and arms were badly charred, and blackened swatches of his burned dungaree shirt had merged in a horrible patchwork with the skin of his chest and back. One of his feet was missing, and the stump left a dark smear trailing on the deck as Skinner dragged him along.

The face was unrecognizable, but as Rand moved close to share the body's weight with Skinner, tortured eyes opened in the char-crackled face and Rand knew who it was.

The kid, Jennings.

"Oh, God, no…"

Jennings tried to say something, but his mouth was full of blood and a pinkish froth. Together, Rand and Skinner found a clear spot on the port side aft gangway and laid him down on a blue Navy blanket.

"Corpsman!" Rand yelled.

The pharmacist's mate hurried over, bringing his medical bag, but after one quick look at Jennings he simply shook his head. He gave Jennings two shots of morphine, but it was clear there wasn't anything else to be done. There were other wounded men who needed him … and who first aid might help.

"Any more down there?" Rand asked Skinner as the corpsman moved on.

"Hell, I don't know, Raider. Probably. There were a bunch of guys on the mess deck, and the bomb just came through the overhead right smack in the middle of them. It's … it's awful down there…"

"But did you get all of the wounded?"

"I think so."

"'I think so' isn't good enough. Come on."

"Where are we going?"

"Back to the mess deck!"

"Raider, it's no good! That whole area forward from section thirty is burning. Everybody's out who's going to get out."

Rand sagged inside. Jennings was dead.

He headed back toward the fantail to make certain the bucket brigade was holding together.

Coffer, Waverly, and the rest of the Mudpac officers coming aboard the *Blessman* were met at the top of the boarding ladder by a tall, smoke-blackened young man wearing nothing but a towel. "Commander Coffer!" the man exclaimed. "I … what are you doing here?"

"Holding inspection," Coffer snapped back. "You're out of uniform, son."

"Uh, yessir."

"Never mind. Your bridge still operational? Where's the captain?"

"This way, sir."

"What's your name?"

"Lieutenant Forsythe, Commander. UDT Fifteen."

"A bad business here tonight, Lieutenant."

"Yes, sir. They really —" He broke off suddenly.

"What, Lieutenant?" Waverly asked as they followed the officer toward the bridge.

Forsythe gave a humorless, tight-lipped grin. "I was going to say that the bastards caught us with our pants down, then I thought better of it."

Coffer chuckled. "And a good thing, too."

The damage to the ship was starkly self-evident. A gaping hole showed in the *Blessman's* starboard side, and the interior of the ship where the mess deck had been was a seething mass of flame. Firefighting and damage control parties worked desperately both fore and aft, trying to contain the fire.

On the bridge, they found Commander Harold Stinton, *Blessman's* skipper, and several of his staff. "Welcome aboard, Commander," Stinton said, extending his hand. "I wish to hell this were a courtesy call on your part."

"Me too, Harry. What's the score?"

Stinton unrolled a large diagram on the bridge chart table. It showed the *Blessman* deck by deck, in plan and profile views. The chart had already been liberally marked in red and black ink.

"We're holding our own, but just barely," Stinton told them. "Some of your people have organized a bucket brigade aft, but we're having trouble getting aft to join up with them. Fire here … here … here. The bomb landed right here, on the mess deck, and blew through to the number-two engine room directly below. We lost steam, and we lost pressure for the pumps. No water. If we don't get some pressure damned soon, the fire's going to push us right off the bow and the stern and into the sea."

"And the tetrytol?"

Stinton gave an expressive shrug. "So far, so good. But it won't hold for long."

"Your radio still up?"

"This way."

Moments later, Coffer was on the ship's radio and raising the *Gilmer*. "Okay," he said, after reaching the other ship, "I recommend that you bring her alongside and start hosing down the *Blessman's* decks. The fire hasn't reached the explosives yet."

"I gathered that," Captain Hanrahan's voice came back. "Stand by."

While *Blessman's* wounded were being evacuated to the two landing craft dispatched from the other ship, the *Gilmer* circled around and moved to within fifty yards of the stricken vessel, as fire control parties on her deck played streams of water across the fire. The sea was growing rougher, and a rising wind was fanning the flames. The landing craft rose and fell with the passing swell, and men had to steady themselves against safety lines as they worked their hoses.

The *Gilmer*, meanwhile, circled once more, came up on *Blessman's* stern at full speed, went into reverse, and gentled into a perfect starboard-to-port docking despite the roughening seas. Additional damage control teams and fire parties leaped across the railings, spreading through the stricken ship to shore up her exhausted crew.

Ammunition continued to go off at unpredictable moments. Aft, the fire had reached *Blessman's* 40-mm clipping room, and rounds were cooking off, snapping and exploding in the heat like popcorn. But for everyone aboard both ships, the real danger lay in the fact that a large quantity of tetrytol was stored close by the clipping room. *Gilmer* edged closer despite the danger, sending cascades of cooling water across the other ship's decks. Hose parties descended into the smoky bowels of the *Blessman*, plying streams of water directly over the explosives, which had already started to melt. Volunteer parties hurled flammable material — including packs of explosives — off the ship and into the sea.

Finally, by 0100 hours, over three hours after the bombs had struck, the fires were out. The *Blessman* wallowed along in the swell next to the *Gilmer*, a thick, stinking haze of smoke still pouring from her interior, catching the *Gilmer's* spotlight beams and spilling out across the sea. More ships had arrived, and the *Gilmer* supervised the evacuation of the wounded.

The dead were gathered in silent rows of blanket-swaddled forms, awaiting the dawn and burial at sea.

Once again, the UDTs had been lucky during what was supposed to be the dangerous part of their mission, carrying out a daylight reconnaissance of an enemy beach … only to suffer savage losses aboard their transport. As Waverly returned to the *Gilmer* early that morning, he wondered if there was anything that could be done about what was obviously a major problem in deploying the teams.

Probably not. To get one hundred men from point A to point B, you had to send them by ship or by plane, and either way they were vulnerable to attack.

Still, he didn't like the idea of the teams' being so dependent on another unit … even if that unit was part of the Navy. Damn, the UDTs had always been more or less odd men out, not quite belonging, not fully accepted. It was hard for a maverick group like the teams to control fleet assets, and the UDT had never comfortably fit in with normal fleet operations, no matter how smoothly the recon and beach survey missions had gone.

He wondered if there was a better way.

CHAPTER 32

Monday, 19 February 1945
Red Beach 1, Iwo Jima

Team Fifteen was very much on Coffer's mind early the next morning as he waded through the surf and up onto the beach. Thirty-eight men had died aboard the *Blessman*, with another thirty wounded — fifteen of them seriously. As Coffer and Waverly had tallied up the casualty reports early that next morning, they learned that eighteen of the men killed had been from Team Fifteen, and another had been the team's Marine observer. Twenty-three of the wounded had been UDT as well, bringing Fifteen's total losses in that single attack to over forty percent — a percentage second only to the casualty rate suffered by the Navy's CDUs at Omaha.

And speaking of Omaha...

The beaches at Iwo were a shambles, their slopes littered with wrecked vehicles and crowded with Marines who lacked even Omaha's sea wall for cover. The first Marines had waded ashore at 0859 hours. Two hours later, they'd pushed inland several hundred yards at most places, but artillery fire was shrieking in both from the high ground to the north and from Suribachi to the south. The water's edge was a nightmare of stranded or burning landing craft, of stalled vehicles, of struggling knots of men racing against the crack and thump of mortar shells to offload ammunition and gear.

Coffer could tell immediately that one part of the beach reconnaissance report, at least, had been seriously in error. The black volcanic sand was hard-packed at the water's edge, but above the high-water mark it was as soft and as yielding as flour. Wind and waves had piled the stuff up in a steep terrace fifteen feet high, blocking the Marines' fields of fire inland and acting like an enormous fly trap, slowing their advance to a painful crawl as the Japanese mortars pounded them from the heights to either side. Men struggled uphill, each step a battle, each step sinking into the sand ankle-deep. Tracked vehicles managed to flounder ahead in great, billowing clouds of ash, but wheeled vehicles like jeeps and amphibious DUKWs sank in to their hubcaps, transforming the beach into a tangle of trapped and helpless machinery. Incoming mortar fire had left wrecks scattered everywhere and set several landing craft afire. Though the Marines had pushed inland off this section of the beach, there were still large numbers of wounded here awaiting evacuation, and Coffer could hear the shrill, hoarse cries of "Corpsman! Corpsman front!" as he walked along the water line. There were bodies everywhere, half buried in the sand at the edge of the surf, or sprawled about in the sand and among the stalled vehicles in sad, twisted heaps.

Stopping to get directions from a party of Marine officers, Coffer was told that the beachmaster was down this way. He heard the familiar voice before he saw the man himself: "You there! Get that goddamn contraption off my beach!"

Mouse Halverson, the Force beachmaster, looked just as he had at Saipan, short, massive, and wearing torn-off shorts and a tattered, sleeveless jacket.

"Hello, Captain," Coffer said. "It's been a while."

"Goddamn," Halverson said. He extended a beefy hand. "It's the tourists again. Welcome to Sulfur Island."

"Is that what you call it?"

"That's what 'Iwo Jima' means. Can't you smell it?" Now that Mouse had mentioned it, Coffer could … a faint, unpleasant stink of rotten eggs. He'd dismissed it with the mingled odors of cordite, diesel oil, and recent death that already clung to the beach like a shroud.

"Fire and Brimstone Island, more like it. My people have been assigned to you for beach clearance."

"Glad to have you. Your work's gonna be cut out for... *You* there!" he yapped suddenly. "Yes, goddamn it, you! Don't you park that thing there! Get it off my beach!"

"It's stuck, sir!" a young Marine climbing out of a sand-mired jeep said.

"Then goddamn get out and goddamn *carry* the bastard!"

Coffer waited while the beachmaster organized a team to move the bulky vehicle. "Goddamned sand," he said, returning a few minutes later. "This stuff's worse than mud."

Coffer stooped, picking up a handful of lumpy, fluffy black grains and letting them trickle from his fingers. "You know, I checked out some of the sand samples my men brought back myself. It looked like it would be packed enough to handle any kind of traffic you wanted. Looks like we were wrong."

"Easy mistake," Halverson said. "Your guys must've just taken samples from the wet part, or at the low-tide mark. See, storms and tides can wash all the fines out'f the top of the shingle, and pack in the stuff lower down. Leaves the shit up here with no cohesion at all, like loose gravel."

Coffer took an experimental step in a soft pile of black cinders, and almost lost his footing. The stuff was as treacherous as walking through a pit filled with marbles. "I see what you mean."

"Not to worry. The 'Bees are going to lay an artificial surface. We'll have traffic moving again in a bit." A mortar blast fifty yards off punctuated his sentence. Gravel rained from the sky.

A second burst hit in the water among some stranded LCVPs. A machine gun chattered in the distance.

Coffer felt responsible somehow. He knew that, even if the invasion's planners had known, there wouldn't have been much they could have done to change things with forty-eight hours' notice. Still, the teams had been tasked with getting information about this beach and how well it would support vehicular traffic. Some of the men had reported getting up onto the sand itself, but none had been able to advance to the high-water line.

Might they have, if the covering bombardment or smoke screens had been heavier? What if they'd reverted to Coffer's original idea, and come ashore at night?

Would anything have made a difference?

Halverson strode through the shifting sand toward an amtrack parked nearby, and Coffer followed. Explosions thundered nearby, sending standing and crouching Marines to cover. Coffer ducked as well, but Halverson kept walking.

"Captain, don't you believe in duck and cover?"

"Hell, they can't hit me. They've already had too many chances and blew 'em all."

Water geysered into the sky offshore. A flight of Hellcats screamed overhead, machine guns blazing as they strafed Japanese positions just yards ahead of the Marine lines. On the horizon, the line of covering cruisers and battleships continued sending tons of metal and high explosives slamming into Suribachi and the northern plateau.

"At least the incoming's not as bad as it was when you guys took those gunboats in the other day," Halverson told him.

"Seems bad enough."

"Nah. Light stuff. So far, at least. The bombardment group was real happy 'bout your gunboats getting shot up, let me tell you."

"The Japanese thought we were the invasion." Perhaps, he thought, the gallant sacrifice of the gunboats hadn't been in vain.

"That's the way it looks. Anyway, they revealed a lot of their heavy stuff, and the battleships and the flyboys have been having a field day." Another explosion sounded, closer this time. Halverson ignored the patter of cinders, scanning the barren, shell-blasted terrain inland. "She looks all right," he said. "You want to go in?"

"No," Coffer replied.

Halverson shrugged, then clambered up the amtrack's side. "Suit yourself."

Coffer followed him.

"I thought you weren't coming."

Coffer grinned. "You asked if I *wanted* to go. The answer is no! Let's get this bucket moving."

They toured much of the beach in the next few hours. Inland, things were even more crowded than on the beach, where eight full assault battalions had swarmed ashore within the space of ninety minutes. Enemy artillery fire was gradually stiffening, raining down on the chaotic beachhead between the high ground to the north and the vast bulk of Suribachi to the south.

Halverson summed it up at the end of their inspection. "Iwo," he said grimly, "is gonna be ten square miles of Hell."

By the end of that first, long day, Halverson had already been proven right. Thirty thousand Marines were ashore, but nowhere had the first day's objectives — which rather optimistically had included Suribachi itself — been met. One battalion — the 3rd Battalion, 25th Marines — had finally captured the heights to the north after an eight-hour battle, but at the end of it they had only 150 men fit for duty. The unit was pulled out of the line and replaced by 1st Battalion, 24th Marines.

In combat, a unit — whether it be a platoon, a regiment, or an entire army — is subject to the same stresses and strains of the men who compose it ... more, perhaps, since an individual can hide his own doubts and shaken morale more effectively than can a team of men trying to work together. By the end of the day, Coffer knew that Team Fifteen would have to be sent home. They'd taken too hard a beating, and no one could tell what effect the casualties they'd suffered, the comrades they'd lost, might have on the men who remained. What was left of Fifteen would be given a month's leave in Saipan, rotated back to Hawaii, then disbanded.

Some of the older units would be going home soon, too. Five was already disbanded, of course. Six and Eight would soon follow, to be either disbanded or reorganized back at Fort Pierce. That would be good news to most of the men, Coffer was sure. They'd done their bit in this hell of a war, on beaches from Saipan to Lingayen. A few of the old hands would want to stay, of course, men like Mike Waverly, but their combat experience would be more valuable at Maui or at Fort Pierce than it would be here.

Or would it? The Navy frowned on mixed units containing old hands and raw recruits. Still, there might be a way around that.

He would have to see about what could be done.

*

"Enter."

Forsythe, his billed cap under his arm, opened the compartment door and walked in. "Lieutenant Forsythe, reporting as ordered, sir."

Captain Hanrahan glanced up from the paperwork covering his desk. "At ease, Lieutenant. Be with you in a sec."

Forsythe remained standing, listening to the scratch of Hanrahan's pen. The Captain looked tired, Forsythe thought, tired and drawn, as though his stint with the UDT was wearing him down.

Well, it was doing that to everybody. Commander Coffer had been looking like a ghost lately, down to 130 pounds from his usual 175. Forsythe had been losing weight too, a combination of backbreaking work, irregular meals, and the relentless and unremitting schedule of planning, operation, and planning once more.

Scuttlebutt had it that Captain Hanrahan wanted out of his position as head of the UDT, that he was an ambitious officer looking for a major ship command. True or not, Forsythe was pretty sure he wouldn't get much farther if he stayed with the teams. Specialized units like the UDT, like the Seabees, tended to become backwaters that trapped otherwise fine officers, blocking promotions, side-tracking their career paths.

Forsythe, of course, already had his future planned down to the last detail. His first step would be to secure command of one of the new teams. And after that, after he'd had a chance to make a name for himself…

The scratching of the pen ceased, and Hanrahan sat back. "Sorry to keep you waiting, Lieutenant. The paperwork around here gets deeper by the minute."

"No problem, sir."

"Won't keep you long." He reached out and picked up one of the papers piled on his desk. "This arrived with the regular traffic this morning. Thought you might like to see it."

Frowning, Forsythe took the paper and scanned it quickly.

OP-25-BC4
L34-[5]-4
SERIAL 0012

DATE: 28FEB45

FROM: COMMANDER IN CHIEF, PACIFIC FLEET
TO: COMMANDER, UNDERWATER DEMOLITIONS TEAMS, AMPHIBIOUS FORCES, PACIFIC

REF: FORSYTHE, ALEXANDER H., LIEUTENANT
1. EFFECTIVE THIS DATE, LIEUTENANT FORSYTHE IS HEREBY PROMOTED TO THE RANK OF LIEUTENANT COMMANDER.
2. LIEUTENANT COMMANDER FORSYTHE IS HEREBY DIRECTED TO REPORT BY FASTEST AVAILABLE MILITARY TRANSPORT TO UDT TRAINING COMMAND, MAUI, HAWAII, THERE TO ASSUME COMMAND UDT-21…

There was more, a lot more, but Forsythe scarcely saw the words. His eyes skipped to the bottom of the sheet.

BY DIRECTION:
RADM CHESTER W. NIMITZ
CINCPAC

"Jesus H. Christ…" Forsythe said softly.

"Not quite, but Admiral Nimitz is close enough for my taste," Hanrahan said. "Congratulations, Commander."

"Thank you, sir."

"I've heard you have friends in high places. Looks to me like they've been pulling for you."

Forsythe stiffened. "I wouldn't know about that, sir." Still, he couldn't help wondering if this was his uncle Donald's doing.

"Right." He didn't look as though he believed Forsythe, any more than Forsythe did.

It didn't matter. *Nothing* mattered. He had his command … and the two and a half gold stripes. He was on his way now. A team of his own! He still had some ideas he wanted to try…

"Twenty-one's finishing up their UDT training at Maui," Hanrahan told him. "We can have you there by PBY within twenty-four hours."

"Thank you, sir. How long will I have to get settled in with the men?"

"Not very long, I'm afraid. Iceberg is in full swing. We'll be bringing in ten teams on this one, Mr. Forsythe, and we'll need them all in position and ready to get wet no later than March twentieth."

"Do you have the team objectives worked out yet?"

"Not yet. That will be sent along to you once you're aboard the *Bunch*. That's Twenty-one's APD."

"Yes, sir."

"I can tell you that Twenty-one will be right in the thick of it. This one is going to be hot."

"If Iwo Jima was anything to go by, sir, I'd say that was an understatement."

"Better get your gear together, Commander. Your PBY will be ready to leave within the hour."

"Yes, sir. Thank you, sir."

"Don't mention it. Dismissed." Hanrahan went back to his papers, hesitated, then looked up. "And ... good luck with your new team," he said. "See you on Okinawa."

Saipan might have been the first territory the Japanese considered their own ground to be assaulted by American forces, but Iwo Jima had officially been a part of the Japanese prefecture since 1891, when Japan had claimed the island for its own. The attack on Iwo had been considered to be an attack on Japan itself.

Okinawa would be even worse. Lying just 350 miles south of Kyushu, Okinawa had been assimilated into the Japanese empire in 1879. If the Okinawans themselves had never become fully reconciled to being Japanese, however, the Japanese considered Okinawa to be as much a part of the home islands as Honshu itself. With a population of half a million, with a landscape dominated by a patchwork of farmers' fields and paddies and low, rolling, limestone hills, Okinawa presented a more civilized aspect than any island yet assaulted in the Pacific campaign. Sixty miles long, but rarely more than five miles across along its snaking and irregular width, Okinawa would be the principal advance base for the invasion of Japan itself.

Planning for Operation Iceberg, as the Okinawa assault was called, had begun with a CINCPAC study ordered late the previous October, and Admiral Turner had submitted a detailed operational plan to CINCPAC on February 9, 1945. Here, at last, the two separate campaigns of the Pacific — Nimitz's island-hopping advance across the central Pacific and MacArthur's drive up from Australia by way of New Guinea and the Philippines — would be joined together; the invasion force would be the Tenth Army under the overall command of Lieutenant General Simon Bolivar Buckner, consisting of three Marine divisions of Three 'Phib Corps, plus the four infantry divisions of the 24th Army Corps, with a fifth division in reserve, a total of 172,000 combatant troops and another 115,000 service personnel.

Against this force, the Japanese were thought to have between 77,000 and 100,000 troops dug into the island — its soft limestone cliffs would allow the same sort of tunnel and bunker complexes that had proved so deadly on Iwo Jima. They would be employing their new and highly successful weapon as well, the kamikaze. There were hundreds of enemy-held airfields within reach of the island, among the Amami and Sakishima islands, on Formosa and on Kyushu, not to mention at least five airfields on Okinawa itself.

The invasion, second in size and complexity only to the D day landings at Normandy, were scheduled to begin on Easter Sunday, April 1. As always, the UDT would lead the way, with ten teams operating in two groups, Able and Baker. In the week before L day, Able Group, with Teams Twelve, Thirteen, Fourteen, and Nineteen, would first lead the attack on the Kerama Retto Islands, clustered fifteen miles west of Okinawa's southern tip, which would provide the massive invasion armada with a safe anchorage. Group Baker, operating against Okinawa itself beginning on L-minus-two, included Teams Four, Seven, Eleven, Sixteen, Seventeen, and Twenty-one, plus two of the teams from Kerama Retto.

As tough as Okinawa would be, however, everyone in the invasion force, from Admiral Turner down, knew that the bitter fight the Japanese put up for this island would only be the merest foretaste of what was to come.

For as the planning for Operation Iceberg had begun while troops were still going ashore at Leyte, Turner's planning staff had already turned their attention to the next two operations in line, Olympic and Coronet.

The invasion of Japan itself.

CHAPTER 33

Monday, 12 March 1945
The Grass Skirt, Honolulu

The nightclub, like most such establishments in the islands, catered to servicemen. Opposite the bar, a trio of comely *wahines* in long grass skirts, green-and-white bras, and flaming pink leis undulated with enticing bumps and rolls of their hips to Hawaiian music atop a low stage. Fishing nets and strangely fashioned war clubs, swords, and scowling Polynesian masks decorated the walls, while several Māori canoes were suspended from the coconut palm logs that formed the building's rafters.

Tangretti and Slim Simmons, resplendent in their dress uniforms complete with the colorful rows of ribbons on their left breasts, sat at one of the tables with glasses, bottles, and a flickering candle in a green glass bowl. Their companions were the two young women they'd picked up much earlier that evening.

On a forty-eight-hour liberty from the Maui UDT training base, the two Team Eight men had started the evening at a USO club in Honolulu. They'd had a buffet dinner of southern-style chicken and rice and a few beers, and done some swing-time dancing with the bevy of girls there, but the atmosphere had been entirely too serene, too *controlled* for Tangretti. He'd wanted some action, even if he hadn't been entirely sure what he meant by the word, so he and Slim had talked two of the girls into slipping away from the sharp-eyed matrons and chaperones who'd been perched about the dance floor's perimeter like roosting vultures and joining them for a foray into Pearl's bar district.

That had been several hours and several bars ago. The current place was called the Grass Skirt. Tangretti remembered that much, thanks to the gyrating hula dancers on the stage, though he was having trouble remembering much else, including the names of the two young women they were with. Slim's date was a petite brunette in a flower-print dress and with an orchid in her hair. Tangretti's girl was a blonde — he couldn't help but think of Blondie when he'd first taken her out on the dance floor. She wore a low-cut green dress that did nice things for her green eyes and still nicer things for an interesting cleavage.

"Steve? Steve? Are you okay?"

Tangretti tried to focus on the voice … a woman's voice, coming to him from a long, long way off, somewhere on the far side of the table. It didn't belong to the cleavage, and he forced himself to look up. The voice, he decided, must belong to the brunette. But Steve?

Who was Steve? It took him a moment to recognize his own name. He'd been "Gator" for so long that "Steve" sounded foreign, the name of someone else entirely.

"Aw, Gator's okay, Ann," Slim's voice said. "But it sure does look like he's feeling no pain, that's for sure!"

Ann. That was the brunette's name. Now, what was the name of the blonde?

Whatever her name was, she was leaning forward over the table, exposing even more skin and giving Tangretti a long, long, lovely view down the front of her dress. If she would just lean forward a little bit more, he might get a glimpse of her…

"Stevie!" the blonde said.

458

Stevie? He blinked. That wasn't his name. That wasn't even close.

"Eddie," the blonde said, turning to Slim with a swirl of golden hair across her bare shoulders. "If Stevie gets any drunker he's going to just *ruin* the evening!" Then she giggled.

Tangretti frowned. The girl — what the hell *was* her name anyway? — the girl tended to punctuate her sentences with a high-pitched giggle that he distinctly remembered finding amusing earlier in the evening, but which was beginning to grate on his nerves like fingernails dragging across a blackboard. Reaching out, he grabbed the half-full bottle of bourbon in front of him and, ignoring his glass, took a long, hard swallow. The liquid mingled cold and hot, exploding in his throat and gut, then sending white fire sizzling up his spine to detonate like forty pounds of tetrytol somewhere behind his eyes. The room whirled around him for a moment, then steadied. Carefully, he placed the bottle back on the table.

Slim gave him a long, hard look. "You take it easy, buddy, okay? I don't want to have to carry you home."

"I'm fine," Tangretti announced with considerable pride. "In fact, I'm great. *We're* great! We're demo ... demo ..."

"We're in demolitions," Slim suggested.

"That too."

"Ooh!" the blonde said, and her green eyes opened very wide. "You're *frogmen*."

"Never, ever call a frogman a frogman," Tangretti said carefully, correcting her. "Frogs ... eat flies. And live on lily pads. We're demo..." He stopped, then tried again. "We're *Demolitioneers*."

"Aw, nobody ever calls us that anymore," Slim said sadly.

459

"Is it true what they say about UDT guys?" the blonde wanted to know. She giggled. "I mean, about how long they can hold their breath?"

"Bonnie!" Ann said sharply.

"What did I say?"

"Nice girls don't talk about things like that!"

"Well, maybe I'm not a nice girl!"

"You're Bonnie," Tangretti said, looking at the blonde.

"That's right." She giggled again. "You're Stevie Tangretti."

"Tell me something."

"If I can."

"You ever know a guy named Blondie?"

"Blondie?" Giggle. "That's a funny name for a guy."

"His full name, for your information, was Torpedoman Second Class Charles Foglio. Ever meet him?"

Bonnie shook her head.

"Pity. He'd've liked you. Long as you kept your hands to yourself. What color are your panties?"

"*Stevie*! What a question!"

"I thought you said you weren't a nice girl?"

"Um, I just love all those ribbons on your uniform," Ann said brightly, turning to Slim and quickly changing the subject. She reached over to single out one in particular, worn to the left of his top row of three. It was mostly red, with thin white borders at either end and a blue stripe edged by white in the center. Three tiny gold stars were centered in a row across the ribbon. "Isn't that the Silver Star?"

Tangretti burst out with a half-stifled guffaw. "Silver Star! That's rich! When did you become a fuckin' officer, Slim?"

There was a moment's shocked silence at the table. "Gator," Slim warned quietly. "Ladies present."

"I fucking know there're ladies present." He took another long swallow from the bottle, then set it down again, centering it carefully between two empties. Exact control of hand and eye and balance was important in such matters, and he took pride in the meticulous care and military precision with which he lined them up.

"Gator! Damn it, watch your mouth!"

"What'd I say?"

"It's okay, Eddie," Ann said, laying her hand on his arm. "We girls know how it is, being out in the war zone for so long. You were telling us about your medals. Isn't that one with all the stars a Silver Star?"

Slim grinned indulgently at his companion. "No, no," he told her. His words slurred a bit, and he was working hard to keep each syllable clear and distinct. "The Silver Star's something else. Different medal. Actually, this red 'un here is the Bronze Star."

"But there are three little bronze stars," Bonnie said. She peered at Tangretti's chest. "See? Stevie has them too!"

"*Gold* stars," Tangretti corrected her. "And Silver Stars for ossifers. And Bronze Stars for —"

"The three little stars just mean we got the award four times," Slim explained, interrupting.

Bonnie shook her head, a puzzled crease appearing above the bridge of her nose. "I don't understand."

"Gator here's a little mixed up," Slim explained. "The Silver Star and the Bronze Star are medals, see? The Gold Star isn't a medal. You get one of those instead of a second decoration."

"In *lieu* of a second decoration," Tangretti corrected him.

"Right. And three gold stars on the ribbon means four awards all together."

"But that means you both have four Bronze Stars," Ann said, surprised. "Is that just a coincidence? Or did everybody in your unit get the same awards?"

"Well —"

"See, ladies," Tangretti said, interrupting, "the admirals and the generals and all the fucking brass got t'gether, and they decided that every time an, an ossifer … uh … an officer swims in to the beach, he gets the Silver Star. Now if an *enlisted* man swims in to recon that same enemy beach, he's gonna get a Bronze Star. An' he gets a *fuckin'* little gold star every time he does the same stupid *fuckin'* thing again…"

"Gator!"

"What'd I say?"

"You girls'll have to forgive old Gator here," Slim said. "I think he's been hitting the juice a little hard."

"Not hard enough, Chief Slim, ol' buddy. Not nearly hard enough."

"So, uh, the three little stars mean you got the medal four times?" Ann asked cheerfully. "Wow!"

"Where did you guys get them?" Bonnie asked. "What did you do to get them?"

"One for Angaur," Slim said. "The original award was for that. Like Gator says, we swam in to the beach. Then we got one for Leyte. One for Lingayen."

"And one for fuckin' Iwo Jima!" Tangretti proudly announced. "Just got that one last week!"

"Iwo Jima," Bonnie chirped. "The papers have been just full of the wonderful things you were doing over there."

"I liked that picture in the paper," Ann said. "The one with the Marines raising the flag. What was the name of that mountain?"

"Suribachi," Slim said.

"Were you boys there when they took that picture?"

"Well, not when the picture was taken," Slim said. "But we were at Iwo —"

"Fuck!" Tangretti spat. "Yeah, we were fuckin' there, fuckin' two weeks after the landings and —"

"Gator, don't you know any other words?" Slim asked him sharply. "Watch your language, okay?"

"I am, I am. I'm jus' tellin' 'em, okay?" He reached for the bottle again. Grasping it firmly by the neck — he wasn't going to let it escape him — Tangretti guided it to his mouth, then tipped the bottom toward the rafters.

"Gator, don't you think you've had enough?"

"What ... whatcha mean, 'enough'?" he said, setting the bottle down with a loud thump. "Ain't had enough. Evenin's still ... still real young. Real young." He reached for the bottle again and nearly missed, but he was able to sneak up behind it, secure it in a strong, two-handed grip, then raise it once more to his mouth. Oh, *God*, it burned going down, but the explosion that followed was sheer bliss, bringing with it the first black tatters of a sweet oblivion.

"You know, Gator," Slim said, reaching for the bottle, "I really do think you've had enough to drink."

"*Never* gonna get enough to drink." He waved Slim off. "G'way!" Slim started to say something and Tangretti waved him down. "No! Let me say m'piece! Uh ... what was I sayin'?"

"You were at Iwo Jima," Ann suggested.

"Right! I was. We were. See, Team Eight — that's our unit, see? Team Eight came in t' Iwo on March third, an' we were there jus' long enough for one fuckin' air raid an' for the fuckin' ossifers to decide we could all get another pretty gold star 'cause we'd participated in fuckin' combat, but we didn't, see? 'Cause the other Teams was already done an', an' see, we —" He fell partway out of his chair, catching himself heavily on the table and with one knee on the floor. "Oops," he said.

The girls looked at Tangretti uncertainly as he righted himself, dragging himself back into his chair. "What do you mean, Stevie?" the blonde asked. "You mean you weren't at Iwo when the fighting was going on?"

"He means our unit wasn't at Iwo for the initial beach reconnaissance," Slim explained. "The fighting was still pretty bad ashore, up toward the north end of the island."

"I hear the fighting's still pretty bad," Ann said. "I read in the paper this morning that there was a banzai attack on the island just a couple nights ago. It said the Marines wiped the enemy charge out, though."

"I think the Marines are *wonderful*," Bonnie said.

"Marines?" Tangretti said, rolling the word around his mouth as though it had an unpleasant taste. "Marines? What's so great about the fuckin' Marines? Always claimin' they're the first. *We're* the first! Always are!" Unsteadily, he lurched to his feet, spread his arms wide, and shouted, "Welcome, Marines!"

"Listen, swabbie, you wanna keep your voice down?"

Unsteadily, Tangretti turned and found himself eye-to-eye with an unpleasant-looking face set directly above a very large expanse of khaki without, so far as he could see, the benefit of a neck. "Who're you?"

"I'm the guy that's tellin' you to pipe down so's the rest of us can enjoy the show, see?" He reached out with a meaty hand and gave Tangretti a shove on one shoulder that plopped him hard into the seat of his chair. "An' if I hear you bad-mouthin' Marines any more, I'm gonna have to pound your face so far down your scrawny little neck that you're gonna be breathing through your asshole!"

Tangretti started to rise, but Slim reached across the table and held him down with a hand on his shoulder. "Sorry, Sergeant," he said. "My buddy's had a little too much to drink, okay?"

"Just have your swabbie friend hold it down, Chief," the Marine growled.

The khaki-clad giant lumbered off, and Tangretti shook his head. "Damn, why'd y'stop me, Slim?"

"Hey, I didn't want you to kill the poor guy," Slim said. "You're here to relax, remember? Unwind. Take a load off. We don't need to fight with the jarheads."

But Tangretti was already focusing on the entrancing movements of one of the hula dancers on the stage, the Marine forgotten. "I wonder," he said thoughtfully. "Do hula girls wear panties under all those weeds?"

"Stevie," Bonnie said seriously. "Why are you so interested in girls' underwear?"

"Sorry. Jus' thinkin'… thinkin' 'bout a buddy of mine."

"Someone … someone who died out there?"

Tangretti broke up, trying to contain the laughter. The two women watched him with mildly concerned expressions. "Nope. Wounded in action." He grabbed the bottle and tilted it vertically, chugging the last few fingers of liquor remaining.

"Whoa, easy there, Gator," Slim said. "You're three sheets to the wind already. Better slow down if you want to see the rest of the party."

"Fuck the party," Tangretti said suddenly, slamming the empty bottle down. The laughter was gone as suddenly as it had come. He wiped his mouth with the back of his hand. "*Fuck* the party. And fuck all of us for laughing and living and having such a gay old time when good guys like Snake an' O'Reilly an' Kelly're all dead, and the damned fuckin' Japanese

465

are all … they're all just beggin' for us to kill 'em only they don't mind it, 'cause … cause they want us to kill 'em and they jus' keep comin'…"

Ann pushed back her chair and stood up suddenly. "Ed, I think it's time Bonnie and I went home now."

"But I don't want to go yet," Bonnie protested.

"I think we've been more than patient," Ann said. "I don't know which your friend here is drowning in worse, booze or self-pity. I don't mind a little rough language, especially where you two have been, but he's been deliberately offensive all evening and he's been getting worse. Now he's blubbering like some shell-shocked jerk. I've had it."

"Wait a minute, Ann," Slim said, rising. "Please don't go. I can explain…"

She picked up her pocketbook. "Don't bother. Bonnie? Are you coming?"

"Well, fuck you, too," Tangretti told her.

She gave Tangretti a look that made glaciers seem balmy in comparison. "*Sailors!*"

"Wait a minute," Bonnie told Tangretti. "You can't talk to my friend like that!"

"Is this gob botherin' you ladies?" It was the khaki giant again, looming over the table like an ugly Suribachi, and Tangretti had to blink a couple of times hard to make sure he wasn't seeing double. No, there really were two of them now, a big one and a not-quite-as-big one, both Marines and both wearing combat ribbons. The smaller one's fruit salad led off with the red, white, and blue of a Silver Star.

"Ah ha!" he said, rising from his chair and pointing. "There! Now that's a Silver Star! This guy mus'… mus' be an ossifer!"

"It's okay, Sergeant," Ann said. "We were just leaving."

"Can we take you ladies anywhere?" the smaller Marine asked.

"No you don't!" Tangretti bellowed, lurching forward a step. "We saw 'em first, an we're in demo … demolition. Welcome, Marines! We was fuckin' on the beach first!"

"Stow it, frogface," the big Marine growled.

A hand grabbed Tangretti's shoulder from behind. "C'mon, sailor. You're causing a disturbance. Time to call it a night."

Rising, Tangretti spun a little too quickly and had to grab the corner of the table for support. Blearily, he focused hard on the figures closing in on him from three sides. All appeared to be in civilian dress. The nightclub management, perhaps … or the establishment's bouncers.

"A … a dis*tur*bance, is it?" he said. Why were the words coming so slowly? He raised his voice to a full-bodied shout. "I'm making a … a dis*tur*bance? I'll fuckin' show you a fuckin' dis*tur*bance…"

An older woman at a nearby table gasped, then hastily looked away. One of the men next to Tangretti grabbed his arm. "All right, Mac. That's it. Let's —"

Tangretti whirled, bringing up his elbow and catching the man hard beneath the ear, staggering him. The big Marine moved in, and Tangretti threw everything he had into a hard-driven uppercut squarely into the base of the man's jaw.

Several women screamed and a man squawked with surprise as the Marine landed flat on his back across a neighboring table. Several sets of hands grabbed at Tangretti but he shook them off. "Slim!" he yelled.

"I'm here!" Slim shouted, tripping a charging bouncer and sending him careening into a table.

"Get th' girls out!" he yelled. "I'll hold 'em here!" He swung wildly and missed. Somebody hit him in the side but he shook off the blow and swung again, connecting this time with a meaty crack.

Aw, shit! He realized with a sudden flash of clarity that the adrenaline charge from the fight had just made him … if not *sober*, exactly, then certainly a lot less drunk than he'd been a moment ago. His reflexes were as fast as lightning, his timing as quick as —

A fist came hurtling in from the left and Tangretti started to duck … but somehow his reflexes weren't quite as fast as he'd imagined them to be. The fist connected with the side of his head, and for a moment the whole world went red and black in a dizzying whirl of stars. Shaking his head, Tangretti wondered for a moment how he'd gotten on the floor. No matter. The fight was in full glory now, with Marines and sailors across the room mixing it up. Someone was shrilling on a whistle, and that meant the Shore Patrol would be here any minute.

Well, better to go down fighting. Staggering to his feet, he scrambled up on top of a table, reaching for one of the Māori war clubs on the wall. Yanking it down, he turned, braced his feet, and prepared to make his stand, swinging the club from side to side. "*When our Marines reach Toky-o*" he bellowed, singing wildly off-key and keeping time with the club, "*And the Rising Sun is done…*"

The song, usually recognizable as sung to the tune of "I'm a Rambling Wreck from Georgia Tech," was the unofficial anthem of the men trained for the UDTs and CDUs at Fort Pierce.

…They'll head right for some Geisha house
To have a little fun.
But they'll find the gates are guarded
And the girls are in the care

468

Of the shootin', fightin', dynamitin'
Demolitioneers!

He'd held all comers at bay throughout the verse with the swings of his club, but as he was winding up to deliver another, the table suddenly tipped to starboard, spilling him, war club and all, to the floor. Things grew quite fuzzy for a time, and when he blinked his eyes open, he realized he was seeing the world from a very peculiar angle.

"What the hell?"

"Easy, Mac," a voice said close to his ear. "We're getting the hell out of here."

Tangretti shook his head, then wished he hadn't. He was suspended in space, hanging partway across the shoulder of another sailor clad in whites. Tangretti was not a small man, but he'd been hoisted into a fireman's carry and was being hauled head down past the chairs and tables of the nightclub like he was a sack of meal.

A *light* sack of meal.

"I can walk! I can walk!" he protested.

"You sure?" The sailor set him down. Tangretti blinked back at him. The guy, a first class boatswain's mate, looked vaguely familiar...

"Do I know —"

"No time to talk. This way!"

Glancing back over his shoulder, Tangretti saw chairs flying and people running and the big mirror above the bar disintegrating under the impact of a hurled bottle. At the front door, the mob parted like the Red Sea separating for Moses, and a platoon of white-helmeted S.P.s hove into view, billy clubs at the ready.

"Come on," his rescuer said, grabbing his elbow, and Tangretti was yanked through a doorway and into a short corridor. Running now, they turned left, then burst through another door and into a room on the right.

A dressing room, occupied by a number of attractive women in various stages of undress, all shrieking loudly as the two men barged in. Tangretti noticed with considerable interest that hula dancers *did* wear panties beneath their grass skirts ... or some of them did. There was one just coming out of a shower in the back...

"'Scuse us, *wahines*," the boatswain's mate said, and with Tangretti in tow, he pushed through to the far door, banged through it and out onto the street.

"Damn it, who *are* you?"

"A fellow alumnus of Fort Pierce. Come on!"

"Wait! Wait! How'd you know I was Fort Pierce?"

"With that song you were singing? How could I miss it?"

"Oh."

Down the alley, then across a street to a park fronting the ocean. It was late at night with a moonless but gloriously clear sky. Even the lights of Pearl at their backs couldn't mask that glittering depth and profusion of stars.

They stopped, breathing hard. "I think we're okay," the sailor said, looking back toward the Grass Skirt. A neon sign, a two-part animation of a hula girl shifting her hips, jittered above a small mob of shore patrolmen still forcing their way inside. The civilian police were arriving as well. "Just the same, let's put some distance between us and them, okay?"

Tangretti stared hard at the man's face. He was so damned familiar...

"I know you from somewhere."

The other sailor looked him up and down. "You should. We knew each other at Fort Pierce."

"Huh? Were you in my class?"

The man grinned. "No. I taught your class." He extended a hand. "Frank Rand."

Tangretti shook hands, his eyes opening wide. "You were one of the Marine instructors!"

"Not Marine. Navy. August 'forty-three? I *was* with the Navy and Marine Scouts and Raiders. They had me over at Fort Pierce teaching your bunch."

"Drake, Harrison, and Rand!" Tangretti exclaimed, reciting the long-hated names of the S&R instructors of his NCDU class. "You're Raider Rand! I'll be a son of a bitch!"

"Small Navy, huh?"

"I'll say! You guys put me and Snake —" He faltered. "So ... you're still S and R?"

"Nope. Not since Omaha. I put in for Fort Pierce myself." He grinned. "Thought I'd see what it was like from your perspective."

"No shit? You're UDT?"

"Webbed feet and all."

"Christ, this is like a reunion." Something Rand had just said gnawed at Tangretti's awareness. "Wait a minute, what'd you just say? You were at Omaha?"

"Sure was. You know, I think I saw you there. With Richardson. With Snake, I mean. I helped him drag you out of that draw after you'd been wounded."

And then Tangretti was crying.

CHAPTER 34

Monday, 12 March 1945
The Kamana, Honolulu

"I don't ... don't really remember seeing you at Omaha," Tangretti told Rand.

They were sitting at another bar in Honolulu, an hour after leaving the Grass Skirt. Tangretti, eager to regain the pleasantly detached lack of sobriety he'd lost during the fight and in the long walk in the pleasantly cool night afterward, had ordered scotch. Rand, however, had rather sternly suggested black coffee instead.

Tangretti had been too tired, too emotionally drained, to protest. This was at least his third cup.

"To tell the truth, I wasn't sure it was you, either," Rand said. "Not at the time. But I remember you from Fort Pierce."

Tangretti hoisted his coffee cup. "To Fort Pierce."

Rand echoed the toast. "To Hell Week!"

"So why'd ... why'd you go and join the UDT?"

Rand shrugged. "I'm not sure I know, even now. It had something to do with the ... I don't know. The whole concept of the *team*. I guess I saw something there I thought I was missing."

"You find it?"

"Yeah. For a while." He frowned. "Or I thought I had. Now, I'm not so sure."

Tangretti took a sip of coffee. It was bitter, and he grimaced. He preferred his coffee with cream and sugar, not raw and black like this. But his head *did* feel a bit clearer. Funny, though. He was having trouble remembering what had happened at that nightclub a while ago.

He also felt a churning nausea in the pit of his stomach, and his head hurt. He wondered if he was going to be sick.

"You married, Frank?"

"Yup."

"Too bad…"

"How come?" He grinned. "I kind of like married life … what I've seen of it, anyway."

Tangretti stared into his half-empty cup. "Well … sometimes I think it would be nice having someone waiting for you back home…"

"I take it you don't have anybody."

"Nah." Tangretti stared into his coffee for a time. "You know, Snake was married. A WAC he met and married in England."

"Yeah. I remember hearing about that."

"I saw her, after D day. Went to tell her … tell her what happened. She still writes me, every once in a while."

"How is she?"

"Oh, she's doing okay. Her last letter, she told me she'd just had a kid. Snake's kid."

"No kidding?"

"No kidding. She named him Henry Steven Richardson. Snake was Henry. I'm Steven. So he's named … for both of us."

"Bet he grows up with webbing between his toes."

"Hope … I get to see him … someday."

"Must be tough, being a young war widow with a newborn kid."

"Yeah. She's still waiting to get back to Milwaukee."

"She's still in England, then?"

"As of last month, yeah."

They sat and drank their coffee in silence for several moments.

"Listen, Steve…"

"God, don't call me that. It's Gator."

"Yeah, I remember now. Snake and Gator. Castor and Pollux. The inseparable twins."

"War has a way … of separating people."

"That it does. So how about you, Gator? What's happening with you?"

"Shit."

"That doesn't sound encouraging."

"I'm with Team Eight."

"Eight?" Rand's eyebrows raised. "Leyte and Lingayen."

"Yeah. And you were…"

"Team Fifteen."

"Right down the coast, both places."

"Yeah, we swam around some of the same pieces of beachfront property, didn't we?"

"And you were on the *Blessman*," Tangretti said. "God, that was a bad deal."

"I lost some buddies."

"I know what that's like."

"Yeah, I guess you do. What's Eight doing in Maui?"

"Fucking running the training center up there. Only that's just make-work, cause next we're headed back Stateside."

"That's good."

"Is it?"

"I gather you don't like the idea."

Tangretti's earlier belligerence flared again. "What, just because some asshole of a bureaucrat has the idea that we're all worn out? Combat fatigue or some crap like that?" He brought his fist down hard on the table. The coffee cup clattered on its saucer. "Damn it, they want to put me out to pasture, Raider."

"Hmm." Rand looked at him for a long moment. "You don't like the idea of selling war bonds, is that it? Or a soft training billet turning out more UDT men at Fort Pierce?"

"Aw, shit, Frank! I'm *demo*! I've been a lineman and a searcher and a goddamn fuse puller! You think I can go back and have them drop me behind a fucking desk someplace?"

"Yeah. You'd rather be out blowing things up."

"Damn straight!"

"Tell me the truth, Gator."

"Huh?"

"Tell me the *real* reason you want to stay in the war."

"I hate the Japanese."

"Hate only takes you so far. After a while, you get tired of killing." Rand's eyes narrowed. "Besides, how many Japanese have you killed anyway?"

"None, I guess." Tangretti smiled. "Usually *they're* trying to kill me."

"A knife isn't exactly a decent offensive weapon when the other guy has a machine gun," Rand conceded.

Tangretti was silent for a moment. Finally, he reached inside his white jersey and brought out the bullet on its chain around his neck. "You know, for a while there, I think I was getting pretty superstitious."

Rand grinned, then reached down into the pocket of his white trousers. Drawing out his hand, he set something on the table in front of Tangretti.

It was a bullet, copper-jacketed, thicker and longer than Tangretti's souvenir.

"Machine gun?"

"Yup. Iwo. The bullets and the shrapnel were floating down underwater like snowflakes. You could just reach out and snag them."

"Did you get ... get superstitious about it?"

"No. I don't think so. I just did it for kicks. Why, did you?"

"Well, for a while there I had the idea — kind of crazy, I know — I had the idea that maybe I was being so lucky because all my buddies were unlucky."

"You were alive. They kept dying."

"Something like that."

"What changed your mind?"

"The realization that there's no magic to war. Just a lot of pain and suffering. And heroism. And fear. And goddamned fucking stupidity."

"That's a rather profound thought for an enlisted man."

"You know, more than the Japanese, I think what I hated most of all was the way the officers were mismanaging things."

"Hell, every enlisted man goes through that, Gator. Starting his first day at boot camp."

"Maybe. Except ... look, what do you know about Iwo Jima? Why are we trying so hard to take that damned, barren speck of rock?"

Rand spread his hands. "I just know what I read in the papers. They want to use it to land B-29s."

"Yeah? How many Marines have died on that miserable rock already?"

"I don't know. Two, three thousand, maybe?"

"I heard closer to four. What I'm wondering, Raider, is whether our having Iwo Jima is going to save the lives of at least four thousand American aviators."

"Shit, Gator, you can't juggle lives like that. You're saying that the life of this guy over here isn't worth sacrificing for the life of that guy over there. How the hell can you know a thing like that?"

"Maybe you can't. But don't you wonder if it was worth it, worth the lives of those guys who died on the *Blessman*?"

"I don't think I've ever thought about it. C'mon, Gator. They were there because they had to be, okay? Maybe they were in the wrong place at the wrong time, but they died doing something they believed in. And that's just about the best epitaph you can carve for yourself."

Tangretti was silent for a long time. "You know what cranks me off?" he said after a while.

"What's that?"

"It's knowing that, if the high command had gotten its ass in gear and invaded Iwo Jima, oh, say, last September. Right after the Marianas? The way I heard it, the Japanese didn't have anything at all on Iwo until after then."

"I heard the same skinny."

"Look, there we were, leapfrogging across the Pacific, hitting the Japanese where they were weak, leaving them to wither on the vine at places like Truk, where they were dug in and fortified."

"They weren't exactly weak on Saipan or Guam."

"No. But the point is, we were heading straight for Japan, right? Tarawa and Kwajalein and Eniwetok. Then the Marianas. Iwo was next, right? Seven hundred miles from the Marianas and halfway to Tokyo. Right?"

"Right."

"Then what happens? Doug MacArthur gets a hair up his ass and decides we just *gotta* go invade the Philippines. He talks Roosevelt into a whole new Pacific strategy. Next thing you know, the whole of 'PhibPac makes a hard left and we head due west and start piddling around with places like Peleliu. You know Halsey called off Peleliu 'cause it wasn't necessary, but the invasion fleet had already left port?"

"I heard."

"So we lost three thousand guys on Peleliu and Angaur. And then came Leyte. And Lingayen. And the *Belknap*. And the damned, damned kamikazes, falling out of the sky like damned leaves. We were stuck in a fucking sideshow, getting good guys killed, and all the while the Japanese are getting the idea that just maybe they ought to hollow out some caverns up on Mount Suribachi. Just in case we ever got off our tails and come calling at Iwo Jima. When we finally get there five months late, *pow*! They're waiting for us."

"You know, Gator, I've been in the Navy for a bunch of years. And I've been in my share of battles. Sicily. And Normandy. And the Philippines. I've learned one thing."

"What's that?"

"That strategy and tactics always look a hell of a lot different from the foxhole — or from the deck of an LCP — than they do in some chart room back aboard the flagship. Or in Washington."

"You got that straight, brother."

"Question is, what are you going to do about it? You can fight the system, or you can work inside the system."

"What do you mean?"

"C'mon, Gator. Remember back at Fort Pierce? Remember when the government didn't send enough paddles for the rubber boats? What'd you do?"

"We adapted."

"You and Snake and the rest of your boat crew were the only ones with enough paddles to go around. Hell, I heard you were the cumshaw king of Fort Pierce."

Tangretti smiled at the memory. Cumshaw — getting what was needed through whatever means were necessary, legal or semilegal, was an ancient and venerable tradition in the Navy … especially in the Seabees. "What can I say?" Tangretti said. "I was with the Seabees before I ended up at Fort Pierce."

"Enough said."

"What's your point?"

"That you can always find a way to make the system work for you. If you don't, you're going to find yourself slamming your head against a concrete wall. You're going to get a bloody nose."

"But it's such a damned *waste*."

"I know it is, buddy. But you overcome and you adapt. Or you go under." Rand reached out and clapped Tangretti hard on the shoulder. "Are you going to let the bullshit get you, or are you going to dish some out yourself?"

Tangretti grinned at that, but then the smile slipped. "I see what you mean. Sometimes though…"

"What?"

"Well, I've been pulling strings ever since I got to Maui. Calling in markers. Looking up old friends and offering to trade favors. Trying to wangle myself a billet on an APD going west, y'know?"

Rand nodded.

"And I've come up empty. Maybe that was what was hurting the most. For the first time in I don't know how long, I came up empty. And somehow, the thought of 'overcoming' and 'adapting' and even just plain doing my duty doesn't sound all that appealing in some grimy little office back Stateside."

Rand's face split in a merry grin. "Gator, old man, things just might not be as bleak as you think they are…"

*

"I … I don't quite know what to say, Commander."

Waverly looked at the orders in his hands again, half afraid they would say something different the second time he read them.

Coffer grinned at him from behind the desk. "Don't say anything, Mike. Especially since it's not the command that ought to be yours."

"Hell, I don't have that much seniority yet."

"The fact of the matter is that the new CO of Team Twenty-one is a heavyweight. A bit cold, but a real professional. Used to be with a special team with the OSS."

"Ten?"

"That's the one."

"Well, with someone out of the lucky horseshoe team, how can we go wrong?"

"I gather this guy was at Peleliu, with the preliminary recon off a sub. Very sneaky, very hush-hush stuff. Then he was XO for Team Fifteen."

"God. The *Blessman*?"

"He came through it okay. Forsythe is his name. Alex Forsythe. Princeton grad. Good family connections, including some pretty high up in the Navy, I hear. Solid Navy career type."

"I'm sure we'll hit it off fine."

"I'm sure you will." Coffer tugged at his ear, as though uncertain whether to say more. "Mike, I put your name in the hat for the skipper's billet with Twenty-one. They turned me down cold. I just thought you should know. I'm sorry things didn't work out better."

"Hey, don't apologize, sir. It's way more than I deserve. XO of another team? Listen, that's great! I figured I was going to be desk-bound for the rest of the war!"

"Well, just you don't go and get yourself killed, okay? I'd never forgive you if you did. Or myself."

"Don't you worry about that, Skipper." He shrugged. "The way things have been going, I'll be safer in the water than I would be aboard the *Gilmer*."

Coffer laughed. "You may be right." He handed several typewritten pages across the desk to Waverly.

"What's this?"

"Thought you might like to see it. It's Twenty-one's muster list, as of last week."

"And the check marked names?"

"Are the ones who've had experience with other teams."

"My God!"

"Who do you see?"

"Chief Tom Davies? He was with Five! A damned good man!"

"Thought you'd like to get him."

"And Blondie Foglio! Son of a gun, this is going to be like old home week."

"You remember Foglio?"

"Yes, I do. He had a reputation as a tomcatter and ... I don't know. A bit of a braggart. But he was a dependable man. He ended up in the hospital, as I recall. Noumea?"

"That's right."

"Thought he got invalided out."

"No. After he got out of the hospital, he was assigned to a Seabee unit in New Cal. I gather he's been bombarding Pearl with requests for a transfer back to the teams ever since. Somebody finally gave it to him, probably just to shut him up."

"That's Blondie."

"Is he going to be a problem?"

"I don't think so. And his stories were always pretty entertaining. If you didn't blush easily."

"There are a couple of other names on that list you should look at. Frank Rand, for one."

"Yes, sir?"

"Rand is going to be your right-hand man, you hear me? You get into trouble out there, you listen to what he has to say. He's former Scouts and Raiders. Seen more combat than any six men I know, including D day. Used to be one of my instructors, back when I was running Fort Pierce."

"No kidding?"

"No kidding. He was with Forsythe in Fifteen, so he probably knows the man's habits, his likes, his dislikes. On the *Blessman*, he organized a bunch of UDT men into a bucket brigade. Had them singing 'Anchors Away' to keep time. He's worth his weight in gold, Rand is. Rely on him."

"I'll remember that, Commander."

"The other name to remember is Machinist's Mate First Class Steve Tangretti. The men call him 'Gator.' He's another good man. He and another demo guy were with Team One at Kwajalein and then were transferred to the CDUs in England. He was at D day. Wounded. Afterward, he put in for the UDTs and ended up with Team Eight."

"He didn't want to muster out?"

"I gather he didn't. That seems to be a special problem with the teams, doesn't it? Once you're in, you're in. In Tangretti's case, he'd been trying to get transferred to another outfit with no luck. Happened that Rand ran into him in Honolulu, and they got to talking old times. Rand finagled a spot for him with Twenty-one." Coffer smiled. "And that's a first. Tangretti is the finagler. If you ever need anything, can't get Supply to get you what you need, just put in a word with Gator Tangretti.

Chances are, you'll have whatever it was you needed within the hour. Probably in the original packing."

"I'll keep that in mind, Commander. But … what's the idea? I thought the Navy didn't recycle the old hands."

"Normally they don't, Mike. And just between you and me and the binnacle, Mike, I think that's a mistake. The way I see it, experienced senior petty officers are the backbone of the Navy."

"So Twenty-one's going to be different?"

"Yup. The teams are expanding so fast, these last couple are being thrown together with anybody who'll volunteer. Guys from the fleet, even. I was able to work it that some experienced hands who didn't want to get rotated back to the States got billets with Twenty-one."

"Sounds good. I'll be glad to have them."

Coffer nodded. "Especially remember Davies, Rand, and Tangretti. They're three of the best UDT men I know. They'd be valuable back at Fort Pierce training new men, I know, but the kids need that kind of steadiness with them out here, especially the ones that haven't had Fort Pierce training. It helps a lot, swimming in to a hot beach, to know that some of your buddies have done this sort of thing before. Right?"

"That's for damned sure. If nobody else on my team had done something like that before, I'd be tempted to say it couldn't be done." He laughed. "For that reason, I'll even appreciate Blondie. When he isn't talking about his romantic conquests, he might tell the guys about what it was like at Saipan and Tinian."

"Exactly." Coffer glanced at his watch. "You'd better hustle, Mike. Your new team is scheduled to arrive here at Ulithi sometime this evening. You might want to find a clean uniform."

"Aye, aye, sir. And … thanks. For everything."

"You just take care of yourself. And your new team. I'll be seeing you at Okinawa."

"Good." Waverly turned to go.

"Mike?"

"Sir?"

"I'll miss you. You were a damned good Exec for me. Be a good XO for Forsythe. And maybe the *next* time…"

Waverly grinned. "I'll sure do my best!"

In the passageway outside, Waverly's smile faded … but only a little. He *had* wanted a CO's slot, he couldn't deny that, and he'd almost dared to believe that that was what had been in the orders when Coffer handed them to him to read.

Still, number two in a combat-duty team was a damned sight better than shuffling papers.

Or working up death certificates and casualty lists for all of the teams in an operation. He preferred working with one team, with men he could get to know.

It suddenly occurred to him that the Skipper was certainly stacking the deck. Twenty-one might be a brand-new team, but it had at least three experienced team veterans among the enlisted personnel, and it had Forsythe as Skipper.

And Waverly, with quite a bit of experience of his own, as second-in-command. He wondered if Coffer knew something about Twenty-one's mission orders … or if this was just some kind of experiment, some way to find out whether a team would work better with a core of experienced officers and senior POs.

He found himself wondering what this Forsythe character was going to be like.

CHAPTER 35

Thursday, 29 March 1945
Waverly
Boat 3, UDT-21
Off Orange 2 Beach, Okinawa

"So what's with you always bein' the XO, Lieutenant?" Chief Davies asked with a wide grin. I thought you'd've gone on to bigger and better things by now.

"Always a bridesmaid, never the bride," Foglio called from the other side of the boat. Waverly cast a quick glance to port, where Lieutenant Commander Forsythe was talking on the radio, but the man didn't appear to have heard. That, or he didn't care.

"Well, I knew you old Team Five guys just couldn't get along without me here to keep you out of trouble," he told them, raising some laughs from them and their shipmates.

Good, he thought. *Their morale's up, and they're eager to go. Everything's working, despite the problems with the new skipper. God, I wish I were going with them.*

Third Platoon, UDT-21, was on its way in to the beach on a demolition run. Forsythe would be leading the team in, with Waverly staying in the LCP(R) as boat officer. So far, at least, there was little fire from the shore, little response of any kind to the thunderous barrage being hurled inland by the massed battleships, cruisers, and destroyers gathered off the west coast of the island.

The invasion beaches stretched for nearly ten miles along a stretch of coastline called Hagushi, on the west coast fifteen miles from the southern tip of the island. Two important airfields, Yontan and Kadena, were located just beyond the dunes above the beaches, and the Marines hoped to capture these swiftly. South was Naha, Okinawa's capital. Almost the entire length of the Hagushi beaches was guarded by a coral reef; the exception was at the center, between the landing beaches designated Yellow and Purple, where the Bisha River flowed down from the inland hills and met the sea.

To port and to starboard, the other boats of Twenty-one were on their way in, slipping through the line of destroyers, gaining steadily on the line of LCI(G)s that, as at Iwo, were leading the UDT boats in. The offshore bombardment was continuing throughout, a thunderous, unrelenting roar of artillery, from the volcanic rumble of the big-bored monsters aboard the battleships three miles out, to the high-pitched bark of the 20-mm and 40-mm guns on the LCIs, to the shrill whiplash crack of six-inch rockets.

Quietly, Waverly studied the men of the Third Platoon surrounding him in the boat. He was not entirely happy with the way the team had come together. Commander Coffer, he was sure, had intended for the old hands, the men with combat experience, to be distributed throughout the team, but somehow, when it had come down to pairing off into swim partner teams, it hadn't worked out that way. Most of the old hands had ended up pairing with other old hands, while the kids fresh from Fort Pierce or drawn from the fleet paired off with each other, forming tight and separate little cliques that Waverly knew were no part of Coffer's original idea. Hell, Forsythe had led things off for this operation by selecting Tangretti as his partner, and the others had followed — Foglio pairing with Davies, Kowalski with Rand.

The tendency for the experienced hands to link with one another, Waverly realized, was only natural. Kowalski and Rand, he'd heard, had been swim partners at Fort Pierce and again, later, in Team Fifteen, while Foglio and Davies had known one another in Five. Even if the men hadn't known one another previously, no one who'd been under fire before, no one whose life depended on the guy swimming twenty yards behind him, wanted to be paired with a rookie who might break and run or lose his gear or just plain screw up.

But doing it this way robbed the system of what Coffer had been trying to create in Twenty-one, a mixing of old hands with new, of experience with inexperience.

Waverly had quietly spoken with all of the experienced men aboard the *Bunch*, suggesting that they mingle more with the new men. That hadn't happened … and Waverly was beginning to wonder whether the reason it hadn't happened was Lieutenant Commander Forsythe.

Forsythe was a hard guy to figure. Competent, obviously, and quite self-assured … sometimes to the point of arrogance. He knew what he wanted and he always found the most direct way to get it, and since Forsythe had been the one to approach Tangretti with the idea of being partners, Waverly thought the pairing of experienced men with experienced men was either his idea … or something he was willing to go along with.

Throughout the voyage from Ulithi, Waverly had had the feeling that he was engaged in some kind of a subtle tug-of-war with Forsythe, with orders countermanded, with suggestions ignored. It was enough to almost convince Waverly that Forsythe had it in for him … until he realized that what he was witnessing was simply a marked difference in leadership styles. Waverly had worked so closely with Coffer, first in Team Five, then in Mudpac, because their leadership styles complemented each other.

Coffer definitely tended to lead from the front, but he was excellent when it came to delegating authority, and Waverly, with his methodical and careful attention to details and preliminary planning, fit smoothly into Coffer's management style with few, if any, rough edges. Forsythe also led from the front, but he tended to be more aggressive, more flamboyant, a cowboy with swim fins and mask instead of boots and ten-gallon hat. Waverly noticed he rarely sought the advice of others.

Was that why Coffer had been so insistent back in Ulithi about Waverly's listening to Rand and Davies and the other old UDT hands? Maybe it was. Forsythe seemed always to know exactly how something ought to be accomplished and didn't waste time discussing it.

Which, of course, left Waverly feeling very much out of things. In any Navy ship or unit organization, it was the Exec's job to manage the men and handle the interior details, leaving the CO free to concentrate on exterior matters such as mission planning, the unit's goals, and its interaction with other units.

Unwilling to challenge Forsythe directly — indeed, unable to do so, since it *was* Forsythe's team — Waverly had thought it best to leave well enough alone, but he was still uneasy. Forsythe was trying to do everything, to *run* everything himself.

And Waverly knew from experience that that approach to military management simply never worked.

Tangretti had settled in well with Team Twenty-one almost from the first day. Hitting it off so well with Rand helped. Rand was quiet, the kind of guy who was hard to get to know initially, but Tangretti sensed the kinship there that came from having walked through the same stretches of Hell. Rand had been at Omaha … had been under fire plenty of other places as well. He'd lost friends; he'd told Tangretti about Jennings on the *Blessman*. He *knew*…

And the reunion with Foglio and Davies at the Maui UDT base had been nothing short of riotous.

On the whole, Tangretti liked the guys in Twenty-one, even though he wasn't sure he liked the idea of so many of the kids coming in straight from the fleet, with little or no training or preparation of any kind. They'd been through some training and hydrographic recon schooling in Maui, and they'd all had to qualify on the long-distance swim, but the ones who hadn't been through Fort Pierce had a kind of callowness about them … and some rough edges that Hell Week might have worn smooth.

Well, those rough edges would get knocked off soon enough. Tangretti wasn't too worried about it … though he'd been a bit hesitant about being teamed with one of the kids as a swim partner.

Of the whole group, the only guy Tangretti really felt unsure about was the CO. There was a lot of scuttlebutt going through the team about Forsythe's rather mysterious past, about secret missions off submarines and training with the ultra-secret OSS maritime commandos. The problem was, Forsythe hadn't been to Fort Pierce either, and that, for Tangretti, was the dividing line between an officer he respected and one he merely tolerated.

It seemed ironic, then, when Forsythe had approached Tangretti aboard the *Bunch* en route to Okinawa, asking him to be his swim partner. Tangretti had agreed and taken a first step toward losing some of the bitterness that had been gnawing at him for so long. He still didn't trust the guy, but the fact that

Forsythe had been in other UDTs, Ten and Fifteen, and the fact that even as skipper of Twenty-one he was planning on making the swim with his men the way Coffer had used to do, together made a hell of a big difference so far as Tangretti was concerned.

"Hey, Blondie!" Davies called from the opposite side of the boat. They were passing the LCI(G) line now, and the men were starting to trade nervous stories, especially the greenhorns. It wouldn't be much longer. "Let's hear about your collection."

Foglio scowled. "I told you, Chief, don't call me that no more. I gave it up for Lent."

"It's Easter," a first class gunner's mate named Petrovic said. "Whatever it was you gave up, you can have it back now."

"Not this kid," Foglio said. "I'm reformed."

"What was it he gave up, Chief?" Petrovic asked Davies.

"Man, you'd never believe it. I sure didn't."

"Gator?"

"Hell, Petrovic," Tangretti replied. He locked eyes with Foglio and gave the man a broad wink. "I used to have the same collection, so I'm not going to tell!"

"Hey, Gator?" said another greenhorn, a kid from North Dakota everybody called Cowboy. "You think this is going to be a rough mission?"

"Hard to say, Cowboy. The recon boys had it pretty easy this morning. We could be in for a smooth ride."

"Yeah," Foglio said darkly. "Or else the Japanese are all woke up from their siesta now, and are waiting for us!"

"April fool!" Davies called.

"The Japanese don't take siestas," Cowboy said.

Tangretti laughed. "They did this morning."

It *had* been quiet during the first run. Three other teams had made the run in to the beach that morning, at high tide. They'd taken depth readings of the entire stretch of landing beaches up to within fifty yards of the shore, measured the reef, and confirmed the presence of beach obstacles first spotted by aerial reconnaissance several weeks ago.

The obstacles appeared to be stakes, eight to twelve feet long and about a foot thick, driven into the bottom mud or the coral much like those at Angaur. It was possible that some were mined, though the morning reconnaissance had not found any explosive devices in the stakes that they'd checked.

Now it was 1530 hours, mid-afternoon, and the tide had gone out. The obstacles were exposed now, stretched in multiple lines across long stretches of flat mud or shallow water. Teams Seven, Eleven, Sixteen, and Seventeen were hitting the obstacles north of the Bisha River. Four and Twenty-one were operating to the south. Each team was responsible for a separate section of obstacles. They would swim in, attach explosives, and get the hell out ... all completely routine.

It was eerie not having any response from the Japanese at all, though. The offshore bombardment was continuing unabated, sending salvo after salvo screaming into the once-quiet island. The morning swimmers had reported some sniper and mortar fire, but said that the cold would be more of a problem than the Japanese. The water temperature was lower than it had been at Iwo ... around sixty-three degrees. Once again, the men were coated in a thick layer of grease, partly as camouflage, partly as protection from the cold. Over their heads they wore gray hoods to keep their hair color, dark or light, from making them easily distinguished targets. Since the tide was out and they would be working in shallow water on coral, they'd abandoned their swim fins this time in favor of deck shoes.

"Here's the line!" Petrovic shouted, and the LCP(R) swerved to port, running parallel to the beach. Tangretti rose far enough off the deck to get a good look at the shoreline. The reef was about one hundred or one hundred fifty yards farther in, some fifty yards off the beach. There was no surf, save a little off the mouth of the Bisha River. Behind the beach were lines of low, grass-covered dunes, and beyond that the land bulked high in a series of low, white bluffs. He'd heard that those bluffs were limestone ... ideal for tunneling. In fact, many of the cliffs he was looking at now had been used for generations by the islanders as cemeteries, with tombs carved into the soft rock.

He wondered if the Japanese had done as much tunneling here as they had on Iwo.

"Hey, Gator!" the big, muscular Swede from Wisconsin named Johanssen called out. "What you see, more suicide boats?"

"Not this time."

Everybody in the team had been talking about the suicide boats that day. Early that morning, as the *Bunch* had been moving into position to release her boats for the morning swim, two small motorboats had been sighted, charging in fast from starboard. The *Bunch* had opened up with 20-mm and 40-mm guns, and one machine gun had been manned by demo men from Twenty-one. Both motorboats had been sunk — the second with help from a destroyer that had charged in at the last, its five-inch gun blazing.

The suicide boats were just the latest twist in the Japanese cult of the kamikaze. The landings in the Kerama Retto islands a week before had captured hundreds of small boats hidden there among the bays and lagoons, designed to be piloted by one or two men and carrying explosive charges — manned torpedoes to be hurled against the sides of American ships. Ever since, all American ships had mounted so-called "fly-catcher patrols" each night, with small boats or landing craft circling the anchored ships and manned by sailors or Marines armed with carbines, pistols, and grenades. Tangretti had pulled duty on several fly-catcher patrols during the past week.

He'd not seen a suicide boat until that morning, however. One piece of scuttlebutt making the rounds in the enlisted mess was that the Japanese still had hundreds of small boats hidden in inlets and rivers in Okinawa, and that the Japanese were saving them for the main landings, when they'd be sent to crash into American landing craft filled with troops.

Remembering the fierce and fanatic determination of the kamikaze pilots to hurl their aircraft into U.S. ships, Tangretti could well believe it.

"So, what do you think, Gator?" Davies called above the engine's roar. "How come they didn't bring Doug MacArthur in to run this show?"

"Yeah," Foglio said. "Who's this Buckner guy anyway?"

"Sounds like MacArthur's still playing tag with the Japanese in the Philippines," Tangretti replied.

"Shit," Foglio said. "If'n we do it *his* way, we're never gonna get to Japan!"

"Take your positions!" Ensign Avery, the swimming officer, warned.

"Maybe the brass has wised up," Tangretti said. "They gave MacArthur the Philippines to play with, and now they're getting on with the rest of the war!"

There might have been some truth to that. There were rumors that MacArthur had protested the redeployment of part of Nimitz's fleet from the Philippines to support the Okinawa landings. Maybe the brass *had* wised up … though Tangretti still distrusted the motives of any officer who hadn't been to Fort Pierce.

Including Forsythe.

Johanssen was first into the rubber boat, with his partner, a little guy from Texas that everyone in the team called "Wetback" taking his place on the gunwale. Ensign Avery, a freckle-faced kid from North Carolina, took his position.

Tangretti looked aft, watching Waverly studying landmarks ashore and checking the boat's compass. He'd heard that Waverly had been XO of Team Five, then on the Mudpac staff, and wondered what he was doing back in the boats again. He had the muscled, weathered look of most UDT people, and Tangretti wondered if the man might not simply prefer boat duty to conning a desk.

Waverly's hand came up. "Get ready!" There was a pause. "Now!"

"*Go*!" Avery piped, and Johanssen rolled into the water as Wetback dropped immediately into his place, then followed him into the sea. On the opposite side of the boat, two enlisted ratings from the *Bunch* started tossing over the packs.

The canvas satchels carrying the explosives had been redesigned. Called Schantz packs, now each was a kind of apron with a floatation bladder and pockets holding four two-and-a-half-pound blocks of tetrytol. Those blocks had been carefully prepared the night before by the individual swimmers, wrapped up in primacord, and bundled with a length of wire which would be used to attach the charge to an obstacle. Each swimmer would carry five Schantz packs, for a total of fifty pounds of explosives.

Foglio and Davies were next in line. Tangretti was glad to have them in his platoon. They, too, had jumped into the water off a lot of beaches, from Saipan to Lingayen.

Next it was Rand and Kowalski, the Polish guy from Chicago.

And then it was his turn, and Forsythe's. Scrambling down into the raft just after Kowalski vacated it, Tangretti set his mask in place, taking deep breaths and watching Avery at the gunwale. Avery's hand came down...

Forsythe watched Tangretti vanish into the spray and leaped into the rubber boat in his place, feeling the chill of the water breaking across the raft's bow. Avery brought his hand down again. "*Go!*"

Holding his mask on tight, he rolled off the raft and hit the water with an icy shock. Surfacing, he treaded water for a moment to get his bearings, then breast-stroked toward his Schantz packs floating on the other side of the boat's wake. Tangretti had already reached his gear and signaled with a thumbs-up that Forsythe returned. Together, then, they started swimming toward the beach.

Forsythe was aware that the new XO, Waverly, had been trying to get the experienced men split up through the team and had taken steps to quietly block the idea. It was a question of politics. He needed a hard core of men in the unit, experienced men who would be loyal to him, and he knew the old hands wouldn't appreciate being forced to pair with rookies. He understood Waverly's motives ... and understood, too, that Coffer and his anti-elitist views were probably behind them.

Coffer was a believer in democracy in its pure form — no one was any better than anybody else. That was why the man had never comfortably fit in with Navy life and protocol. God, Coffer was still only a *Reservist* and didn't understand the way the real Navy worked at all, while Forsythe with his background and his connections knew exactly how things operated and could manipulate them to his benefit.

Forsythe knew he'd changed in one important way during these past months. He appreciated the quality of the Fort Pierce men, which was one reason he'd chosen Tangretti as his swim partner. He'd rather have one of them covering his back any day than one of those raw kids out of the fleet, or even someone like Davies, who had experience but who'd not been to Fort Pierce. He still remembered how that Waipio man, Mason, had come up short in the swim off Yap. Teaming untrained men with trained ones, in Forsythe's opinion, was a recipe for disaster.

He glanced at Tangretti, swimming twenty yards to his right. The main reason he'd selected Tangretti as a swim partner was a hope to win the guy over. He wasn't sure what the problem was, but Tangretti appeared to have … not an open disrespect, but a certain aloofness when it came to officers other than Coffer or Waverly. Probably, it was that magical aura of Fort Pierce again. If Forsythe could get Tangretti on his side, he would have a solid base to build up his popular support in Team Twenty-one.

And from there, God alone knew how far he'd be able to take it.

Tangretti was pulling ahead. Forsythe started kicking harder, pushing his floating bundles of explosives ahead of him like a bulky, olive-drab kickboard.

Rand and Kowalski did not have explosives in their packs. Instead, they carried the slates and float markers and reels of knotted fishing line usually carried by preliminary reconnaissance swimmers.

The reason was that, due to a confusion in orders, the morning swim had gone no closer to the shore than the coral reef, a ten-yard-wide barrier set some fifty yards off the beach. The coral walled off a shallow lagoon; the invasion planners wanted to know *how* shallow … and they wanted to know if the bottom was firm enough to support tanks.

According to the charts, this was actually an outer lagoon; beyond those sand dunes was a kind of inlet or marsh, an inner lagoon only intermittently open to the sea. That was none of the team's concern, however. The outer lagoon most certainly was. Since there were more than enough swimmers available to deal with the wooden obstacles, Rand had volunteered to check the outer lagoon's depth.

He had volunteered … but Kowalski, damn him, had won the coin toss in the boat. Rand would wait on the reef with the slates, while Kowalski swam in to the beach.

At low tide, the coral reef was only just beneath the water. In many places, fantastic coral rock shapes thrust above the surface, many of them looking like oddly carved mushrooms. Rand squatted on his coral shoes next to one, holding the measuring line as Kowalski paid it out.

He was watching Kowalski swimming toward the shore, but he found himself thinking instead of Nancy. She was so beautiful, so loving, so…

Angrily, he jerked his mind back to the mission. That had been happening a lot lately, and it worried him. Somehow, having a wife at home had wormed its way in to the utter devotion he'd felt toward the team.

It was as though he were caught between two lovers, Nancy and the UDT.

Nancy...

He slammed the heel of his hand hard against the rough coral at his side, using the pain to focus his thoughts.

Stop it, you silly bastard, and pay attention to the job!...

Kowalski surfaced for another breath and looked around. He was a lot closer to the beach now — less than twenty yards, he estimated — and still there'd been no response from the shore. Except for the drifting smoke and the continuing crash and rumble of exploding ordnance, there was no movement at all. So far as Kowalski could tell, the island could have been completely deserted.

He decided to swim a bit closer.

The lagoon here was quite shallow, less than three feet above a muddy but reasonably firm bottom. Swimming to the next knot in his line, he surfaced again, then checked the depth. Two feet ... and he was less than ten yards from the shore.

From here, he could see a three-foot sea wall behind the beach, much like the one he'd heard guarded Omaha Beach in Normandy. Directly behind the wall was a row of sand dunes, most of them capped by tufts of beach grass. To the left was a gap in the dunes, and a muddy channel or gully that was supposed to be full of water at high tide, muddy and impassable at low. According to the maps he'd seen of the beach area, there was a large marsh or inland lagoon behind those dunes, intermittently connected to the sea by the rise or fall of the tide.

It was damned tempting to go farther, to see what was on the other side of those dunes.

But from here he could also see the limestone escarpment that rose behind the lagoon about 150 yards beyond the muddy channel. There were cave openings or hollowed-out shelters in the face of that white rock. He could see them from here, and the sense that he was being watched from that terrace was almost overwhelming.

He decided it was time to turn back.

Dropping his reel, he started swimming back toward the reef. He could just make out Rand's head in the shallow water on the reef's seaward side.

Throughout his reconnaissance, Kowalski had been aware of the shore bombardment, of course. It was hard to ignore it, the insistent screech of shells and the hiss of rockets, the cacophonous detonation of high explosives across the hills and fields behind the beach. Still, the thunder had been going on for so long that he'd managed to let the noise become a part of the background, heard but largely ignored.

It was impossible to ignore the infalling howl of the mortar round, however, as it whined down out of the sky and hit the water less than ten yards in front of him. Another few seconds and Kowalski would have been directly over the shell's impact point.

The concussion hammered at Kowalski's chest and head, the explosion engulfing him in sound and white water. For a dizzying moment, he hung in the water, unable to move, unable to hear anything at all, unable even to think ... and then a second shell slammed into the water just a few yards away, this second explosion flinging Kowalski skyward like a limp rag doll.

He didn't feel the impact when he landed.

CHAPTER 36

Thursday, 29 March 1945
Rand
Orange Beach 2

Rand had been watching Kowalski's head alternately appearing and vanishing in the water as his partner moved across the lagoon. The lack of Japanese interest in the proceedings off their beach didn't surprise him. Since Peleliu, the Japanese had been refining their island defense tactics, preferring to allow the invaders to establish themselves ashore before attempting to destroy them together with their logistical support. At Iwo, those tactics had been sharpened further by turning the entire island into a fortress riddled by caves and tunnels and hidden gun positions and forcing the Americans to clean them out, one by bloody one.

Likely, the Japanese were trying the same thing at Okinawa, only more so, since this island was a hell of a lot bigger than the last one. If the scuttlebutt was true, if the defenders of Iwo Jima had mistakenly fired on the gunboats covering the UDT recon swims and accidentally given away their positions, the enemy commanders at Okinawa might be under especially severe constraints, ordered to ignore all reconnaissance activities and save their strength and their ammunition for the main landings to follow.

Hell, so far Rand hadn't seen a thing to stop any of the demo men from going clear up on the shore if they wanted to.

The first mortar burst caught him by surprise. At first he thought it must have been a shell from the bombardment group that had landed short, but that second round, and the third and fourth and fifth that followed it, were definitely mortar rounds coming from somewhere inland.

He was swimming across the reef almost before he realized what he was doing. Proper tactical doctrine required him to deliver his slates to the ships offshore, but that was Kowalski in there, his swim buddy, and he needed help.

Rand stayed on the surface as he swam, pulling along rapidly with a strong, overhand crawl. The reef was too shallow for comfortable underwater swimming, and in any case, Rand wanted to keep an eye on Kowalski. Was he dead?

No. Despite the near miss, Kowalski was on his feet, standing in knee-deep water only a few yards from the beach.

"Kowalski!" Rand shouted as loudly as he could, never breaking his stroke for an instant. "Kowalski, damn it! Get down!"

He could see his friend moving now ... stumbling a little, weaving as he moved ... not away from the shore but *toward* it. At the water's edge, Kowalski collapsed onto hands and knees, crawled a few feet farther, then collapsed face down on the white sand.

Rand swam faster, as fast as a fuse puller sprinting for retrieval, splashing across the shallow lagoon. The mortar fire had ceased — thank God — but it seemed fairly clear that someone up on those limestone bluffs must have the lagoon under observation, and they might be calling in more mortar fire, or a volley from hidden snipers, at any moment now.

The ground shoaled beneath his kicking feet. Crawling now, only his head exposed, Rand moved toward the beach and the limp, grease-coated sprawl of his friend.

A machine gun yammered from the heights behind the beach, and Rand sprawled face down in the wet sand.

*

Forsythe had also seen the salvo of mortar shells kicking up their characteristic poplar-shaped geysers of white water in the lagoon just off the beach. From some eighty yards to the north and fifty yards from the beach, he could see the splash as one of the two swimmers — he couldn't see whether it was Rand or Kowalski — started swimming to his buddy's rescue.

"Damn!"

Tangretti surfaced nearby, clinging to one of the partly exposed wooden poles. They'd almost completed planting all of their charges, and Tangretti was in the process of stringing them together with a long length of primacord. "What's the matter, Commander?"

Forsythe stood up in the shallow water, supporting himself on the nearest pole. It looked … yes! It looked like there was a man down ashore, and a second man swimming in to try to get him.

"Trouble," Forsythe told Tangretti.

Tangretti stood, shading his eyes against the light coming off the water.

"I'm going over there," Forsythe said.

"Sir?"

"Are the demo charges set?"

"All set, Commander. Tied to the trunk line and ready for the shot."

"Then get back to the boat. Fast. Tell them we have a man down on the beach. I'm going to try to go pick him up."

Tangretti's eyes widened. "Oh, shit!"

"What is it?"

"Machine gun!"

"Where?"

502

"I can't see, but it must be up in those bluffs somewhere. Can you hear it?"

"Not with the shelling … no." He listened again, and he could just pick out the chatter above the rumble of the offshore bombardment. "I do hear it."

Forsythe balanced himself higher, trying to see. At this distance, he could just make out two figures on the beach. Had they been hit?

"Get back to the boat and report," Forsythe told Tangretti. He picked up the last Schantz pack, which still had four prepared blocks of unused tetrytol. "Tell them I've gone in to pick those men up."

"But sir —"

"Go back, damn it! That's an order!" And he began bounding with long, splashing steps through the shallow water across the reef toward the lagoon. When he ran out of reef, he dove, arms outstretched, and hit the water swimming.

Forsythe would have been hard-pressed to explain his reasoning at the moment, or the emotions behind it. He didn't realize until he was halfway across the lagoon that he'd not been thinking about what this would look like on his service record.

All he knew was that he'd lost people on the beach before, Schroeder and White and O'Leary.

He was damned if he was going to lose anybody else.

From the LCP(R) cruising back and forth at the two-hundred-yard line, Waverly had been following the events ashore closely through his binoculars. He was pretty sure that it was either Rand or Kowalski who'd gotten in close to the beach and been knocked down by a mortar barrage — dead or simply stunned, Waverly couldn't tell. He could also see other swimmers moving toward that part of the beach from both the north and the south.

"Miller!" he shouted, alerting the boat's coxswain. "Take us in toward the reef."

"Toward the reef, sir? What about recovering the swimmers?"

"I'll worry about the swimmers. You get us as close to that reef as you can manage!"

"Aye, aye, sir."

"Smith!"

The boat's radio operator looked up from his set in the stern sheets. "Yes, sir!"

"Raise the *Bunch*. Get me Commander Coffer."

"I have him now, sir."

"Give it here." Taking the radio handset, Waverly brought it to his ear. "Whiskey, this is Echo One."

"Whiskey here," Coffer's voice said, crackling from the earpiece. "Go ahead."

"Whiskey, we have a problem on Orange Two. Brunette, repeat, brunette. Over." They were using the blonde-brunette code, first introduced at Tinian, for swimmers lost and swimmers recovered.

"Ah, Echo One, it's not time for recovery yet, over."

"Roger that, Whiskey. We've got a brunette on the beach. I'm going in to get her. Recommend you send in another Echo to pick up the blondes."

There was a short pause. "Whiskey copies that, Echo One. Approved. Good luck."

"Thank you, Whiskey. Echo One out."

By this time the LCP(R) was flying toward the reef, the little boat's bow ramp well clear of the water, a rooster's tail of spray cascading over the wake. Miller was putting the helm from port to starboard to port again, throwing the boat roughly back and forth in a zigzag that took it ever closer to the shore. So far, the Japanese hadn't responded to the provocation, however. Any mortars or other artillery ashore remained silent.

"Mr. Waverly!" one of the helmeted, life-jacketed ratings manning a forward .50-caliber machine gun shouted back, hands cupped to his mouth to be heard above the roar of the Higgins boat's engine. "Swimmer in the water, five points off the port bow!"

Waverly laid a hand on the coxswain's shoulder. "Miller! You heard?"

"I got him, Lieutenant." The coxswain pointed. "Eighty yards."

"I see him." It was a lone swimmer, his head bobbing in the swell. As the Higgins boat throttled back and bore down on him, the swimmer raised both arms out of the water, the signal that he needed help.

"Ensign Avery! Standby to go in after him! He may be wounded!"

"Aye, aye, sir!"

"He's swimming again, sir," Miller said. "I don't think he's hurt."

Moments later, the LCP(R) hove to alongside the swimmer. It was Tangretti, panting after a hard, fast swim out from the reef. Together, Miller and Waverly reached over the boat's gunwale and hauled him dripping out of the sea.

"Lieu-Lieutenant!" Tangretti gasped out between panting breaths. "Kowalski and Rand are ashore! One of 'em's hurt, I think. Mr. Forsythe swam in to see if he could help."

Waverly stood up, holding the binoculars to his eyes. It was hard to make out what was happening ashore. It looked … yes. That was Rand, lying on the beach next to Kowalski, who was sprawled out in the manner of someone either dead or unconscious. As he watched, a line of waterspouts walked across the water, seemingly right next to the two men, though the foreshortening of the binoculars could easily deceive the eye. An instant later he could hear the sound as well, the distinctive, far-off chatter of automatic weapons fire.

"*Shit!*"

"What's the matter, Mr. Waverly?" Tangretti asked.

"Looks like our people are pinned down," Waverly replied. "Machine gun."

An instant later, the machine gun ashore had changed targets. The line of waterspouts was walking across the reef, splashing and spurting as the hidden gun sought to hit the Higgins boat.

Rand lay face down in the wet sand as bullets snapped inches above his head. He could tell without looking where the fire was coming from: that cave-notched limestone bluff on the far side of the muddy channel and beyond the inner lagoon. The Japanese bastards up there had a clear line of fire at him and Kowalski, aiming down between the gap in the sand dunes where the inner lagoon met the main outer lagoon and the sea.

They sure as hell couldn't stay here. Grabbing the back of Kowalski's shorts, staying as flat as he could, Rand started crawling toward the sea wall, which was some twenty yards above the water line. Twice he stopped and ducked as bullets struck the sand nearby, but most of the time the unseen gunners appeared to be firing at something else — what, Rand could not tell. Each time the gunners seemed distracted, though, he resumed his awkward crawl through loosely packed sand, dragging Kowalski with him.

When he reached the relative safety of the sea wall, he stopped, his back pressed against the sun-warmed, three-foot-high concrete barrier, breathing hard. Three quick breaths … and then he checked Kowalski more closely.

As far as Rand could tell, Kowalski hadn't been scratched. There were no obvious wounds on his body. The layer of grease would have covered up any bad bruising, but there was no major bleeding, no open wounds, no sign of broken or dislocated limbs. He was definitely out cold, however, and there were trickles of blood from his right nostril and his right ear that might or might not mean a broken skull. When Rand peeled back the man's eyelids, he honestly couldn't tell if one pupil was larger than the other, but they appeared fixed, and that could mean a skull fracture. Ski had been moving around on his feet before he'd collapsed on the beach, so his spine and neck were probably okay, but there was a possibility of skull fracture, and a near certainty of a concussion.

All of which meant there wasn't a damned thing Rand could do for him at the moment. Here behind the sea wall and the dunes they were safe enough from the machine gun, at least for the moment, but there was no way to reach the sea without having again to cross that fire-swept corridor exposed by the gap in the sand dunes.

"Gun it, Coxswain!" Waverly yelled.

The engine roared; the boat lurched forward. Bullets slapped wood as they roared away from the beach, but no one was hurt.

For Tangretti, the moment held a terrible, floating sense of waiting, knowing that someone on the shore was trying to kill him while he was unable to do anything in reply. In that instant, Tangretti knew once and for all that he didn't have a death wish. Quite to the contrary, he wanted to *live*!

But he also knew that Rand and Kowalski needed help, and they needed it fast.

And Rand was married...

The sense of déjà vu was sharp, demanding. "Lieutenant Waverly?"

"Yeah?"

"We've got to get them out of there!"

Waverly didn't reply right away. He was still studying the beach, and the limestone bluffs behind the dunes, with his binoculars as the LCP(R) zigzagged out clear of the reef.

"Miller!" Waverly snapped suddenly.

The coxswain continued conning the boat, but he glanced back over his shoulder. "Sir?"

"What kind of weapons do you have aboard this bucket?"

"You mean beside the two fifties? We got a couple of carbines, and, I think, a couple of pistols. Fly-catcher stuff."

"Break 'em out. And all the magazines you have. I'll take the con."

"Aye, aye, sir!"

Under Waverly's hand, the LCP(R) swung about in a broad one-eighty and started back toward the beach. The coxswain dug around for a moment in a locker on the deck, then produced a pair of Army M1 carbines, two bolstered .45-caliber pistols attached to Sam Brown belts, and several canvas pouches stuffed with loaded magazines for both weapons.

"Is that all we have?"

"That's the lot, sir."

"It'll have to do. Ensign Avery!"

"Yes, sir!"

"You and Tangretti, break out the other raft. And get me the waterproof walkie-talkie!"

"Aye, aye, sir!"

Tangretti felt a sharp inner thrill. "Mr. Waverly! Are we going in to get them, then?"

"I'm going in, Tangretti," Waverly said. He was already peeling off his shirt, shucking off his trousers. He wore white cotton shorts underneath — his swimsuit, ready in case he needed to get wet. He kept his shoes on — heavy, black boondockers — and grabbed a spare mask from a stowage locker aft.

"Request permission to accompany you to the beach, sir!" Tangretti said. It sounded more like a demand than a request, but he added nothing, staring at Waverly as though defying him to say no.

"Very well, Tangretti," Waverly said after giving him a long look. "We'll go in together."

Returning the helm to Miller, Waverly pointed toward the shore. "I want you to take us in as close to the reef as you can manage. After you drop us off, I want you to patrol back and forth. Maybe you can give us some cover with your fifties."

"Will do, sir!" A mortar burst surged skyward to port. "Whee! Ain't we got fun!"

The second raft was the same size as the one used to take swimmers aboard, a four-man rubber boat carried along in case a bullet or a shell fragment nicked the first one. Avery and one of the Higgins boat's sailors had it inflated in moments. As the LCP(R) coasted to a near stop just off the reef, Tangretti and Waverly heaved the rubber boat over the stern, then tossed in weapons, ammo, and two paddles. Tangretti leaped into the water with a splash and paddled up to the raft, clinging to the side.

As Waverly was about to follow, Avery called, "Sir? You want greased up?"

"No time," Waverly replied. Then he jumped.

The water felt ice-cold, and he gasped and sputtered as he surfaced. Tangretti reached out and gave him a hand, pulling him into the raft. "Paddle or swim, Lieutenant?"

"Swim, Tangretti," Waverly decided. "It's faster, and we're poorer targets in the water."

"Swim it is." Clinging to the stern of the raft, they started kicking, propelling the craft toward the reef. "And Lieutenant?"

"Yeah?"

"Call me 'Gator.' Everybody else does."

"Gator it is! Now *kick*!"

"Aye, aye, Mr. Waverly!"

It was slow going wearing shoes instead of fins, but they soon were over the reef, pushing the rubber boat along at a splashing run as they pushed their way over the coral.

Davies had just completed attaching the trunk line to the last of the primacord leads coming off the line of beach obstacles when Foglio yelled to him from the inner edge of the reef.

"Hey, Chief! We got a swimmer on the beach!"

Davies looked up sharply, angry. If this was another of those goddamn welcome Marine stunts...

Foglio was pointing up the beach to the north. "See? Up there by the sea wall. It must be Rand and Kowalski. I think they're in trouble, Chief."

"Damn. Looks that way." He looked down at the condom-wrapped fuse igniter he'd been about to attach to the main fuse. There was a terrible choice here ... to continue with the mission or to delay blowing the obstacles until those men could be brought off the beach.

He didn't consider the problem long. Reaching into a Schantz pack, he pulled out a condom, held the open end to his mouth, and inflated it, tying off the bottom. He then tied the improvised float to the end of the fuse and left it bobbing on the waves, easy to find later.

"Let's go, Blondie."

"Where? To the beach?"

"A stroll on the beach, Blondie. A piece of cake."

"I told you, Chief. Don't call me Blondie."

They started swimming northeast across the lagoon.

Sand spurted into the air several feet away, and Rand jerked involuntarily. A sniper, he decided, must have worked his way along the bluff to a point where he could see Kowalski and Rand, though the sea wall still gave them adequate cover. Still, it wouldn't be long before somebody up in those bluffs decided that the pair of trespassers on their beach were both alone ... and unarmed. Gently, Rand slipped his hunting knife from the sheath strapped to his leg.

He eyed the sea wall, and the dune behind it. Sheltered as they were at the moment, that sand dune made him damned uneasy. Anybody could come up behind it unobserved, and from the top they'd have a clear shot at the two men on the beach, like shooting fish in a *very* small barrel. He decided he wanted a better view ... and a look at whatever was behind that dune.

Kowalski would be okay where he was. There was nothing Rand could do for him in any case. Knife in hand, he rolled over the top of the sea wall, then scrambled up the seaward face of the dune.

The top of the dune crested about ten feet above the beach in a tangled clump of tired green grass. He had a good view of the bluffs from here and saw enough cave or tomb openings to give the place the look of a Pueblo cliff dwelling in the American Southwest.

Closer, and to the right, the dune dropped into a small swale, then rose in another, lower dune. And behind that dune was the inland lagoon, a stagnant four or five acres of water connected with the sea at high tide, isolated, as now, when the tide was out.

And what in the hell were *those*…?

He wished he had a pair of binoculars. From here, though, it looked like a portion of the near shore of the inner lagoon was covered over by camouflage netting strung from vertical posts, into which numerous clumps of beach grass had been woven. Whatever the Japanese were hiding in that marsh, it wouldn't be visible from the air.

It looked like *boats*…

Realization hit him then. They *were* boats, eight or ten of them pulled up onto the shore of the marshy lagoon, with more probably hidden behind the smaller sand dune.

Suicide boats.

A tiny, carefully hidden flotilla of motorboats like those that had attacked the *Bunch* this morning, probably with explosives already stowed, waiting for the first wave of American landing craft and amtracks.

Suddenly sand splattered into the air just in front of him, the grains stinging his face. From the far side of the inner lagoon, the machine gun chattered angrily, and Rand ducked down behind the shelter of the dune.

Trapped … unable to go forward, unable to go back off the beach — at least not while dragging Kowalski along — and no way of signaling the fleet about the suicide boats.

Rand searched desperately for options, for alternatives … and realized he had none.

CHAPTER 37

Thursday, 29 March 1945
Forsythe
Orange Beach 2

With the Schantz pack draped over his shoulder, Forsythe splashed through ankle-deep water and up onto the sand. He'd brought the unused explosives along because they represented the only weapons the UDT men had aside from their knives. If the Japanese were closing in on the men trapped on the beach, those four blocks of tetrytol, rigged with detonators and short-cropped fuses, might serve as crude but powerful hand grenades. At least they might create diversion enough to let Forsythe get the men off the beach and into the relative security of the water.

When he reached the beach, he saw Kowalski lying on the sand next to the sea wall, and Rand on top of the dune just beyond. The machine gun was firing with harsh, clattering sound. It stopped, then resumed ... and this time sand and water geysered just behind Forsythe, sending him diving face first onto the beach. Crawling now, he worked his way swiftly forward, scrabbling across the dry sand above the tide line and into the comforting shelter of the sea wall.

Kowalski was unconscious.

Moments later, Rand rolled across the top of the wall and dropped to the sand at Forsythe's side. "Hello, Commander," Rand said. "Lovely day for a picnic on the beach, eh?"

"What the hell happened?"

Rand nodded at the unconscious man. "Ski there was checking the lagoon's depth, according to orders. A mortar barrage caught him. I think he must have been stunned, or maybe he just got confused and went the wrong way. But he ended up on the beach, and I came in to get him. What are you doing here?"

Forsythe gave the man a wry grin. "Same thing you are, I guess. Think we can make it past that gun?"

"By myself, maybe. Not dragging Ski, though. And I'm not leaving him behind."

Forsythe hefted the explosives pack. "Maybe I can create a diversion."

Rand stared at the pack, then locked eyes with Forsythe. "There's something else, sir. Behind those dunes."

"What?"

"Looks like maybe ten small boats, covered over by a heavy roof of netting and grass. I think they might be kamikaze boats."

"Waiting for the landings."

"That's what I was thinking."

The Japanese would know that the invasion planners would be aiming to bring the first wave ashore at high tide — which on L day would be at 0900 hours. At high tide, the inner lagoon would be connected to the outer by a channel deep enough for a small boat to navigate. A flotilla of suicide boats breaking from the sheltered cove just as the landing craft were coming ashore wouldn't be enough to stop the landings … but they sure as hell would cause a lot of confusion — LCVPs and amtracks swerving from their precisely aligned courses to evade the charge, possibly colliding with one another or stranding themselves on the reef … and all the time, mortar and artillery fire dropping into that chaos to keep the pot boiling.

A nasty surprise for the troops scheduled to hit this part of the beach.

"Listen," Forsythe told Rand. "That sounds like the sort of diversion we need. How far are the boats from that dune?"

Rand's eyes narrowed. "Sixty … maybe eighty yards." Reaching down, he used the point of his knife to sketch in the sand. "Here's us, here's the dune. There's another dune here, right beside the inner lagoon. It should provide cover."

"Will I be able to work my way to that second dune?"

"Listen, sir. Why don't I —"

"I asked you a question, damn it!"

"You'll have to crawl from this dune to the next. And you'll be exposed to fire once you go over the top of this one. I don't think it's a real good idea, Commander."

"And I don't really care what you think, Rand. Now here's what we'll do."

He already had the tetrytol blocks out of the pack and was busily using his knife to cut off the fuses, leaving just enough for a few seconds' burning time. Estimating how long a given length of fuse would burn was always tricky, but he'd tested this batch last night and knew that it burned at the rate of about forty seconds per foot. Three inches between the fuse igniter and the primacord bundling the four blocks of tetrytol together ought to be just about right…

"You wait here with Kowalski," Forsythe told Rand as he worked, "ready to make a dash for the water. When you hear the explosion, go! Ten pounds of this stuff ought to create quite a commotion, and if we're lucky, it might touch off more explosives squirreled away inside those boats."

"What about you, sir?"

"Don't you worry about me. I'm the fuse puller on this one, remember? I'll probably be in the water before you are!"

"Commander, may I remind you that you are the team leader? This isn't your responsibility."

"Don't tell me my business, Rand. Set?"

Rand hesitated, then nodded. "Set. Sir."

"Then I'll see you back at the boat."

"Mr. Forsythe?" Rand extended a hand. "Good luck, sir. Keep your ass down."

"I'll do that. You just be ready to make your move with Kowalski."

Replacing the explosive charges carefully in the Schantz pack, leaving only a condom-wrapped fuse igniter dangling from the pocket, Forsythe clambered over the sea wall and started up the dune. The hill of sand bulked a little higher to the north. If he could go over the crest a little to the south, he ought to be able to stay under cover until the last possible moment ... crossing the open area down the east face of the dune before the machine gunner could react.

At the top of the hill, he lay motionless a moment, getting his bearings and checking the view with Rand's crude map. Yes ... there was the second dune ... and just beyond was the camouflage netting. He could see several of the motorboats, resting half in shallow water and half in the mud.

Forsythe felt his heart hammering. He'd always wanted to be a hero ... if for no better reason than that the recognition would advance his career. There was something more this time, though, the sense that he couldn't leave his men to be caught or killed on the beach, that he had to do something to get them off.

Doing *something*, even the wrong thing, was sometimes better than doing nothing at all.

With a last glance toward those looming, ominous, silent limestone cliffs, he sprang forward, literally diving headfirst down the steep eastern slope of the dune. He heard the machine gun chattering, heard the whipcrack of bullets snapping past close by.

He landed at the bottom in a tumble, his impact with the ground at the base of the dune softened by deep, loose sand. He sprang to his feet, running…

The unseen machine gunner followed his movements, sending a stream of bullets slashing across his leg, the impact driving him down again before he could even recover his balance.

Forsythe blinked back surprise. He couldn't move his left leg. Rolling to his side, he looked down and saw the blood … and the jagged white thrust of a bone jutting through the mangled flesh between his ankle and the knee.

Strange. It didn't hurt at all. It was like looking at something horrible, something gut-wrenching that had just happened to someone else.

"Commander! Commander Forsythe!"

He could hear Rand's voice calling from the far side of the dune, but when he opened his mouth the breath to reply wasn't there. Instead, he started choking on blood.

That was when he realized that he'd been shot through the throat as well.

The rubber boat grounded in shallow water. Tangretti reached over the side, grabbed one of the carbines, and worked the charging lever, chambering a round.

The M1 carbine was the little brother of the military's bigger, bulkier M1 Garand rifle, designed for use by MPs, officers, truck drivers, or other behind-the-front types who might conceivably need something more than a pistol but who weren't expected to find themselves in combat. Tangretti found himself wishing he had an M2 instead … a carbine identical to the one in his hands except that it could fire on full-auto, instead of the one squeeze/one shot of the semiautomatic M1.

Hell with it, he thought as he sighted down the barrel. *Why not wish for a battleship while you're at it?*

"Watch that machine gun!" a voice called down from the line of dunes behind the sea wall. Glancing up, Tangretti could see Rand crouched high up on the dune just below the crest. He pointed, indicating the limestone bluff. "They've got an enfilading field of fire across that part of the beach!" he yelled.

Tangretti wasn't sure what an "enfilading field of fire" was, but he got the idea. From here, he could see the limestone bluff and its ominous-looking cave openings, looking down at him from a range of perhaps 180 yards.

Why weren't they shooting?

"Gator?" Waverly called from the other side of the raft. "Can you handle that carbine?"

"I was a Seabee before I was a swimmer, Lieutenant," Tangretti replied. The Navy construction battalions offered at least some weapons training. More than once so far in this war, Seabees had been forced to defend their half-built airfields from a sudden Japanese attack before returning to their bulldozers. Tangretti had logged a fair number of hours on the rifle range.

Of course, he'd never had to shoot at a *man* before.

"Good enough," Waverly said. "Cover me and I'll drag the raft up to the wall."

Lying in the shallow water, Tangretti drew a bead on the cliff. He couldn't tell which of several cave openings might conceal a machine gun, but firing in that general direction might make them keep their heads down. "Okay, Lieutenant. Go!"

He squeezed the trigger and the carbine bucked against his shoulder, startling him with its ear-splitting crack. Ignoring the ringing in his ears, he squeezed off four more shots, firing as fast as he could work the trigger.

Waverly was on his feet and running up the beach, dragging the raft behind him by the lifeline that ran around its inflated rim.

Then the machine gun opened up again, and Tangretti understood why it hadn't been firing earlier. Only a small part of the bluff was visible, peeking between the eight-to-ten-foot-high dunes that rose to either side of the muddy channel leading from the inner lagoon. The far dune had blocked the enemy gunner's line of sight ... but as soon as Waverly dashed up the beach, the Japanese gunner had seen him and opened fire.

Waverly dropped flat as bullets geysered in the sand in a line running past him and the raft, but he signaled that he was all right. Tangretti lunged forward, running five feet up the beach until he could see the flickering muzzle flash of the enemy gun and flopped onto the sand again, bringing the carbine's butt to his shoulder and slamming off five more fast rounds. Then he was up and running once more, tumbling to safety behind the sea wall just as Waverly reached cover with the raft.

"Raider!" Tangretti yelled at Rand. "Have you seen the CO? He was coming in to find you!"

"He's down," Rand called back from the slope of the dune. "He's on the other side of this hill, about twenty feet away. He's still moving, but it looks like he's hit pretty bad."

"Damn it," Waverly said. "Can we get to him?"

Rand dropped to the sand next to them. "Maybe," he said. "If we can put down enough covering fire from those M1s."

"We have a radio, too," Tangretti said. "Maybe we could call for some extra fire support."

"Not until we get off this beach," Waverly said, shaking his head. "We call in battleship fire support, or even a DD, and we're going to be sitting smack on top of the bull's-eye."

"Friendly fire," Rand said with a grim smile. "Kills you just as dead as the other kind. Hand me that rifle, Lieutenant."

"Where are you going?"

Rand nodded south along the beach. "The long way around. I want to see if there's another way to get at the Commander without going down that naked slope. And Lieutenant —"

"Yeah?"

"There's something else." Quickly, Rand told Tangretti and Waverly about the motorboats hidden in the lagoon. "The Commander was right. We should try to take them out."

Waverly shook his head. "Now that we know they're there, Rand, we can call in fire from the fleet. Or an air strike."

"Just the same, sir, if we can take some of them out with the Schantz pack, it might make a good diversion."

Tangretti was rummaging in the bottom of the raft.

"What are you after, Gator?" Rand asked.

Tangretti produced one of the .45 pistols, slipping a fully loaded magazine into the pistol grip and slapping it home, then yanking the slide back to chamber the first round. "I'm coming with you."

"I can move better on my own."

"Scouts and Raiders stuff, huh?" He tossed his carbine to Waverly.

Rand didn't answer.

"He's right, Rand," Waverly said, taking the carbine, then reaching into the raft for the walkie-talkie. "I can lay down covering fire from the dune. I can raise Commander Coffer on the horn and have the fire support ready. You're going to need two sets of hands over there … especially if you want to try for those boats."

Rand didn't look happy. "I guess, sir, but —"

"Looks like the tourists are really out in force," Tangretti said, nodding toward the beach. Forty yards down the beach, two more dripping figures — Foglio and Davies — were crawling out of the water and onto the beach.

"I'll give them cover," Waverly said, picking up two of the canvas pouches holding extra .30-caliber rounds for the carbine. "You two, *move!*"

They moved.

Slinging the radio over his shoulder, grasping the carbine in his right hand, Waverly scrambled up the packed sand face of the dune until he reached the crest. Looking down into the swale on the other side, he saw Forsythe … a shocking, wrenching sight with blood all over his face and head and leg.

But Waverly had no time to spare for the wounded man. The machine gun was firing again, probably at the two UDT swimmers coming ashore behind him. Sighting carefully at the twinkle of the muzzle flash, just visible inside one of the largest of the cave openings, he held his breath and squeezed gently, just as he'd been taught in a weapons familiarization course he'd taken at Maui. The sharp bang startled him and he fumbled about for a moment, trying to reacquire the target, and then he was firing again and again and again.

He couldn't tell whether he was even coming close to that damned cave opening. He kept on firing, though, until the carbine abruptly wouldn't fire anymore. Looking down, he saw that the bolt was locked open, his fifteen-round magazine empty.

He plucked another magazine from the pouch, dropped the old, slapped in the new, then released the slide to chamber the round. The machine gun was still firing ... but this time he felt the snapping of bullets cleaving the air a foot above his head, and realized with a lurch to the pit of his stomach that it now was shooting at *him*.

He kept shooting, however, engaged now in a deadly firefight where the advantage of firepower definitely lay with the enemy.

Tangretti reached Forsythe's side an instant ahead of Rand, dropping into the sand. Forsythe was still alive, weakly moving his arms and the unbroken leg, and making unpleasant gurgling sounds. It looked to Tangretti as though a bullet had passed clean through his neck, in one side and out the other, tearing open his throat.

Glancing up, Tangretti was relieved to see that he couldn't see the Japanese machine gun ... which meant that it couldn't see him. Forsythe had been hit coming down the dune, but he'd landed behind the shelter of a low, sandy hummock a few yards away.

Rand was probing the wound. "Damned lucky," he said.

"Lucky?" The wound looked horrible, and it sounded as though the man was drowning in his own blood.

"Yup. Another inch one way and that round would've gotten the jugular or nicked the carotid artery." Rand was working over the wounded man now, bending his head back and feeling the throat beneath the Adam's apple. "Hell, if the carotid had gone," he said, drawing his knife, "we'd have seen a red geyser six feet high … for as long as his heart kept going. An inch the other way and it would have gone through his spine."

Rand neatly slashed the knife's blade across Forsythe's throat.

"Christ! What are you doing!"

"Tracheotomy," Rand said. "Keep him from choking on his blood. Now, to keep it open…

Reaching into the Schantz pack, he found a length of soft, stiff wire, and worked it back and forth until it broke off in his hand. Next, he doubled the wire up several times into a piece as long as his thumb, then folded it into a U shape.

Tangretti watched him working the wire U into the inch-wide slit in Forsythe's throat with a faintly queasy feeling. Forsythe, fortunately, appeared to have passed out. "You know a lot about field first aid?"

"Enough," Rand said. "Scouts and Raiders. We had to be pretty self-sufficient without a corpsman, so they taught us a lot of rough-and-ready first aid. That ought to do it. Now, for that leg."

Rand unfastened the canvas sling from his carbine, and used that to tie Forsythe's legs together. "Not very elegant," he said, "but the one leg will serve as a splint for the other, at least until we get him back to the ship. Help me with him now."

Gently, they hoisted Forsythe's shoulders up and, keeping low to stay out of the enemy gun's line of sight, they dragged him through the sand back the way they'd come. They'd only gone a few feet when Rand sagged suddenly, dropping to his knees.

"Frank! What happened?"

"Nothing … much," he said, his teeth showing white through the grease on his face. He was cradling his right arm in his left. "Hit my wrist."

Tangretti looked around wildly. There must be a sniper out there somewhere, but he couldn't tell where the shot had come from.

"Come on, Frank! Double-time!"

Obviously in pain, Rand staggered to his feet and started to run, still cradling his wrist. Tangretti followed, dragging the limp weight of Forsythe.

Halfway back they were met by Foglio and Davies, who were dragging the raft between them. With their help, Tangretti lowered Forsythe into the raft.

"You three go on and get him back to the sea wall," Tangretti said.

"Why?" Rand said. "Where do you think you're going?"

Tangretti jerked a thumb over his shoulder. "He was trying to get those charges to the suicide boats, Frank. I think I ought to make a try for 'em."

Rand frowned. "You heard the lieutenant. We can call in an air strike."

"Maybe. And maybe they can't find the damn thing. Go on, get him back to the beach. I'll wait a couple minutes to give you time. When you hear the explosion, make your break."

Reluctantly, Rand nodded. "Good luck, kid. See you at the retrieval. Here. Take this."

He handed Tangretti the carbine. Tangretti gave him a cocky salute, then turned back toward the spot where they'd found Forsythe.

The Schantz pack was lying where Forsythe had dropped it. Tangretti took a moment to check the pack. It looked like Forsythe had set the fuse for about ten seconds or so, which ought to be fine.

Then, snaking along on his belly to stay beneath the shelter of the hummock of sand, he started inland, toward the inner lagoon.

"That's right, Whiskey. We'll need fire on my command, map reference one-five-five by three-seven-two. Over."

"Ah, Echo One, we read that as one-five-five by three-seven-two. Over."

"Affirmative, Whiskey. Set it up, but don't fire until I give the word."

"Those coordinates look pretty close to your position, Echo. Over."

"They're smack-dab on top of me, damn it, which is why I don't want you to fire until I say so. Over!"

"Ah, roger that. Wilco. We're standing by. Over."

"This is Echo One, wait one." Waverly lowered the radio. He couldn't see where Tangretti had gone after he'd picked up the Schantz pack. Back behind that smaller dune, he supposed. He picked up the carbine again and sighted on the machine gun nest. It had been firing only intermittently for some minutes now, and he suspected that the enemy gunner probably wasn't exactly sure where the Americans were ... the reason, probably, why more mortar shells hadn't come whistling down on them in the past ten minutes. That could change at any moment though, if the Japanese decided the Americans were still here. Waverly had the uncomfortable feeling, a kind of prickling at the back of his neck, that the Japanese were up to something.

Something that Waverly wouldn't have liked if he'd known what the hell it was.

Glancing back behind him at the beach, he saw Foglio, Davies, and Rand all looking up at him with expectant faces. Forsythe and Kowalski were lying together in the raft.

All they needed now was Tangretti's diversion.

Tangretti had crawled on his stomach along the valley between the dunes until he could climb the southern flank of the smaller, inner sand dune and still keep its bulk between him and the enemy gun. Now he was looking down on the inner lagoon — and on the near shore, completely covered over by camouflage netting. The nearest boats were perhaps twenty-five yards away, probably farther than he could throw the pack, but he wasn't about to try getting any closer.

From here, he would have to sling the pack with a sidearm throw to get it under the net. Not much accuracy that way, but he might get lucky. He checked his watch and waited, counting down the seconds until he could go. He'd promised two minutes, but they ought to be at the beach and ready to go by now.

He could hear the machine gun, pecking away in brief, occasional bursts. At least no one seemed interested in him, crouched there beneath the crest of the dune.

Two minutes. Reaching down, he grasped the T-handle of the igniter through the condom and gave a hard yank.

One ... two ... three...

Smoke spilled from the fuse. He picked up the Schantz pack by its straps and began swinging it around and around like an enormous sling.

...four ... five...

Since the accuracy of a cut fuse like this was always questionable, he wasn't about to hang on to the thing longer than he had to. With a tremendous final spin, he slung the pack over the crest of the dune and down toward the boats. It passed beneath the edge of the net, struck the mud, skipped like a stone into the air…

…seven … eight —

The explosion roared across the inner lagoon and slapped at Tangretti's bare back just as he dropped to the sand. He lay face down, waiting for secondary explosions … but there were none. Rising for a look, he saw that part of the netting had been torn away and several of the poles supporting it had fallen. He couldn't tell if there was any damage to the motorboats at all.

"Shit!"

A rifle crack sounded from nearby, and sand spurted three feet from his head. Twisting around, he looked toward the southeast and saw several khaki-clad figures descending another sand dune fifty yards off — a patrol of Japanese soldiers skirting the southern edge of the inner lagoon.

Snatching up his carbine, Tangretti fired three quick shots, not even taking the time to aim but squeezing them off with the rifle's butt tucked under his arm. Another shot howled over his head. Lurching to his feet, he started running. He didn't know if that patrol had been sent to sneak up on the men at the beach, if they were hunting for him, or if this was just a case of bad timing, but he wasn't going to hang around to find out.

As he ran across the depression between the two dunes, he heard the machine gun firing steady again and assumed they were firing at him. Then he heard the steady, high-pitched *crack-crack-crack* of another carbine.

Scrambling up the notch in the big dune where he and Rand had come through, Tangretti raced along the seaward slope of the dune until he reached Waverly's position.

"What the hell are you doing?" Tangretti snapped, forgetting, for the moment, that he was addressing an officer.

"Somebody had to cover your ass coming out," Waverly said.

"Did the others make it out?"

For answer, Waverly nodded toward the sea. The raft, with three heads in the water around it, was already halfway to the reef.

"Looks like you brought some friends along," Waverly observed.

East, the patrol was spilling across the landscape south of the inner lagoon, five … six men that Tangretti could see, but he was sure there must be others. They wore the pale khaki of army troops, and their rifles bore "toadstickers," the unusually long bayonets used by the Japanese.

Tangretti opened fire, squeezing the trigger as fast as he could. Abruptly, one of the running figures fuzzily visible beyond the muzzle sight of his carbine staggered and fell, and Tangretti stopped firing. Had he just killed a man? Maybe Waverly … but no, Waverly was talking on the radio.

Tangretti leaned into the carbine again and resumed firing. There would be time to think about this later … if there was a later. He kept firing until his carbine ran dry and there were no more loaded .30-caliber magazines. Then he pulled out the pistol and banged away with that, though he knew that the effective range of the .45 wasn't much more than sixty yards or so, even for a marksman.

"Let's pack it up, Gator," Waverly said, punching him in the shoulder. "We can let the big boys take over now."

"What do you —"

His words were cut off by the awesome rumble of an incoming salvo. To sea, the long, gray, gun-studded cliff of a battleship dominated the horizon, orange flashes erupting from her main guns.

"They're going to start inland and work toward us. So let's run!"

Shells exploded in the inner lagoon, against the limestone cliffs, across the sand dunes inland. Tangretti felt the ground lurch beneath his feet as he dropped off the sea wall and onto the sand. Together, he and Waverly raced for the sea, and with every step Tangretti expected the machine gun to open up and cut the two of them down … but the whole world was filled with the roar and detonation of heavy-caliber shells, and they reached the water without a shot being fired. Dropping their weapons, they kept running until the water reached their knees, and then they dove in and started swimming.

The LCP(R) was still waiting for them, just beyond the reef.

CHAPTER 38

Thursday, 12 July 1945
U.S.S. *Gilmer*
Buckner Bay, Okinawa

It took almost three months to finally subdue Okinawa. Not until June 21 had the island at last been declared secure. General Ushijima, the Japanese commander on the island, had committed suicide the next day. Even yet there were stubborn holdouts, Japanese army units organized as guerrillas in the Okinawan hills. It might be years before the last of them were run to earth.

Commander Coffer stretched back behind his paper heavy desk. *Gilmer* was riding at anchor in Buckner Bay — formerly Okinawa's Nakagusuku Wan, but renamed after the American Tenth Army commander mortally wounded by enemy artillery on June 18. The work was piling up, but it would have to wait. Soon, he would leave for Washington, first to begin expediting a request for cold-water gear for the teams, then to take a long-deferred, thirty-days' leave.

He would be returning in time for Olympic, now tentatively scheduled to begin in mid-September.

Even while getting ready to go home, however, the cost of the Okinawa campaign was foremost in his mind. Predictions that Okinawa would be a larger, bloodier reprise of Iwo Jima had proven accurate. Casualties in the Tenth Army had been horrific — 7,613 killed or missing, over 31,800 wounded. Perhaps most horrifying of all had been the kamikaze, the Divine Wind howling out of the sky time after time after time upon the armada encircling the embattled island. Thirty-four American ships had been sunk in those attacks, and 368 damaged. Over 4,900 sailors died when enemy aircraft crashed into their ships, and as many more were wounded.

The grim determination of men who not only were willing to die, but who *wanted* to die, for a chance to kill the enemy was beyond the understanding of most Americans. One type of piloted, rocket-powered glide bomb developed by the Japanese was nicknamed "Baka," the Japanese word for "fool," by the Americans. Stories of fanatic kamikaze pilots and senseless banzai charges and men committing suicide rather than surrendering all reinforced the racist image of the Japanese as somehow subhuman, creatures who did not and could not value human life the way Westerners did.

Coffer didn't share the notion that the Japanese were less than human, but there was no denying that the way they thought about some things — about honor, about duty, about personal responsibility to the community as opposed to self — was radically different than in the West. Two thousand years of civilization, developed throughout most of that time in isolation from the West, had shaped the Japanese mind and soul in ways difficult for non-Japanese to comprehend.

And the war's most visible manifestation of those differences was without doubt the kamikaze. The aircraft came in waves, called *ikusui* — the "floating chrysanthemum" — hundreds of planes flung against the slender barriers of American combat air patrols and radar picket ships in the hope that a few could break through to crash into U.S. ships.

And as many kamikaze pilots as the Americans shot out of the sky, there always seemed to be more to take their place, men — boys, even — with just enough flight training to get airborne and to find their targets. Over two thousand Japanese aircraft, from front-line, modern fighters to antiquated biplanes — had been expended by the Japanese command against the invaders at Okinawa.

Coffer had seen intelligence reports, however, that suggested that well over five thousand aircraft more were still in reserve in the Japanese home islands, awaiting the expected American invasion. If the Japanese had fought so bitterly for Saipan, for Peleliu, for Iwo Jima, for Okinawa … what would their defense of their homeland be like? The price in the blood of Americans already paid at places like Tarawa and Mount Suribachi might well turn out to be insignificant compared to the cost of places with names like Nagoya and Yokohama.

For weeks, now, Coffer had been working with the Mudpac staff, preparing for the UDT's part in Operation Olympic — the invasion of Japan. Since June 6, he had again been the commander of the entire UDT. On that date, Captain Hanrahan had been awarded both the Legion of Merit and the Navy Cross by Admiral Turner and, even better from Hanrahan's point of view, been given command of the battleship *North Carolina*. Until a successor could be found, Coffer was again running the UDT.

Medals. Coffer supposed that Hanrahan deserved those two medals and the recognition and the accolades for his part in the Iwo and Okinawa landings, but somehow the balance of the thing felt wrong. Back in April, Coffer had had to deal with the report of a skirmish fought by members of UDT-21 against Japanese troops on an Okinawa beach — two days *before* the actual landings.

From the way the report had read, the action had involved real Medal-of-Honor stuff, the rescue of two wounded men under fire, the discovery of hidden suicide boats that were then promptly destroyed by shellfire from the U.S.S. *Nevada*, the firefight with Japanese troops. Waverly had put the men involved in for the Navy Cross and Coffer had approved the recommendation; the office of CINCPAC, however, had disallowed the awards on the grounds that the UDT's proper area of operations was *below* the high-tide line, not above it. Coffer thought that there must be some suspicion in the Navy high command that the whole episode had been generated by some frogman's attempt to place one of those damned Welcome Marines signs on the beach.

As a result, the men involved would get the same awards as any other UDT men involved in a swim off a hostile beach: Lieutenant Waverly and Commander Forsythe each would receive the Silver Star, Kowalski, Foglio, Davies, Rand, and Tangretti would receive the Bronze Star.

Personally, Coffer still hated the idea that officers should receive a higher award for the same act of heroism as an enlisted man. Hanrahan's Legion of Merit and Navy Cross only emphasized that particular bit of the military command's class-based favoritism toward officers.

There would be lots more medals to be won in Operation Olympic.

And lots more casualties.

Conservative estimates were already predicting anywhere up to a million Allied casualties in the invasion of the Japanese home islands. One hundred thousand might be killed and wounded alone in the initial invasion of Kyushu. As ever throughout the Pacific campaign, from Kwajalein to Okinawa, the UDTs would be the first to go in to the hostile beaches, recording depths, looking for mines, blowing up beach obstacles. A full thirty Underwater Demolition Teams — three thousand men — were being prepared for the assault on some eighty miles of beaches along the Kyushu coast. After the foretaste experienced in the chilly waters around Iwo Jima and Okinawa, the operational plans called for cold-water training to commence for all teams at Morro Bay and Oceanside, in California, beginning on August 15.

The teams had been fantastically lucky so far. In terms of the relative numbers of men involved, only a handful had been killed or wounded in the Pacific, even when the *Belknap* and *Blessman* casualties were factored in. Coffer doubted that that phenomenal luck would hold, however. The Japanese had learned at Iwo and at Okinawa that allowing the invaders to come ashore before delivering a counterattack was a mistake; in Kyushu, they could be expected to fight bitterly at the water's edge, and even beyond. There were already numerous intelligence reports on Coffer's desk of top-secret Japanese frogman units now being trained ... probably as suicide swimmers to attack Allied ships and landing craft, but part of that preparation must be to meet the UDT personnel sent in to reconnoiter and destroy beach defenses. Throughout the Pacific campaign, despite numerous rumors and several cases of mistaken identity, the men of the UDT had never encountered enemy swimmers.

That would almost certainly change in the upcoming operation, and Coffer was already wondering whether the policy, successful so far, of arming the men with nothing but knives was wise. The use of massive offshore bombardment to cover the reconnaissance and demolition operations might be adequate against machine guns and mortars, but how could you protect the swimmers against *other* swimmers, men who might be armed with explosives or hand grenades and who would be delighted at the opportunity to exchange a life for a life?

Sitting in his office aboard the *Gilmer*, Coffer couldn't help but feel a certain dread, colder than the waters off the Hagushi beaches, that his beloved UDT was going to suffer heavily in this coming campaign.

Whatever happened, he would face it with his men. His return to the helm as CO of the teams was strictly temporary. A new commanding officer for the teams, Captain T. H. Radley, would be arriving soon to take over, and Coffer would again be relegated to his old billet as Mudpac's chief of staff. No matter. His duties hadn't stopped him from a rather intense personal involvement at Iwo. He would see to it that it was the same at Kyushu.

"God help us all," he said quietly aloud to the compartment, empty now but for him. "Operation Olympic is going to make everything else seem tame by comparison."

In the long run, the medals wouldn't matter at all. All that would matter ... all that had *ever* mattered, was the men.

CHAPTER 39

August 1945

At 0245 hours on August 6, a lone B-29 Superfortress long-range bomber detailed from the 509th Composite Group of the Twentieth Air Force rumbled down the length of a runway at Ushi Airfield on the northern tip of Tinian in the Marianas Islands, then roared aloft into the darkness of the early morning sky. Her navigator set course for Japan, fifteen hundred miles away.

The aircraft's name was *Enola Gay*, and she was named after the mother of Colonel Paul W. Tibbets, the plane's commander. On board was Captain William S. Parsons, a naval ordnance expert, who was on the flight to make last-minute technical adjustments to the single, very special device, code-named "Little Boy," slung from the rack in *Enola Gay's* bomb bay. A dull, metallic black in color, Little Boy was ten and a half feet long, twenty-nine inches in diameter, and weighed ninety-seven hundred pounds. Its U-235 gun assembly — unlike the plutonium device code-named Trinity, which had been tested at Alamagordo on July 16 — was untested, and no one was even certain that the thing would work.

At 0815 hours, local time, accompanied by two other Superfortresses carrying observers, photographers, and scientists, the *Enola Gay* approached the Japanese southern port city of Hiroshima. "B-san," as the Japanese civilians called the American bombers, were such familiar sights over Japanese cities during the past few months that the appearance of only three aircraft in the skies overhead was scarcely cause for comment, much less alarm. No doubt they were flying a photo reconnaissance mission over the city, which was an important troop embarkation port and convoy assembly area, as well as being headquarters for the Japanese Second Army.

Tibbets released control of the aircraft to his bombardier, Major Thomas Ferebee, who carefully aligned the crosshairs of the plane's Norden bombsight on a bridge in the center of the city chosen as the aim point. He pressed the button, and the bomb fell free. It required forty-three seconds to fall from an altitude of 31,000 feet. At an altitude of 1,900 feet, it detonated in an air burst, chosen by mission planners who wished to minimize the subsequent radioactive fallout.

Theorists had argued during the bomb's development over whether the "yield," the energy released by the detonation, would be more than the equivalent of one thousand tons of TNT. Highly optimistic estimates suggested that the yield might actually approach five kilotons, a blast approximating that of five thousand tons of TNT. The actual yield was closer to an astonishing twelve and a half kilotons. The blast and the shock wave swept across Hiroshima's center, followed by a searing firestorm. Sixty percent of the city was razed, and the number of deaths was variously estimated — the exact number could never be determined with any accuracy — at anywhere from 78,000 to well over 100,000. Forty-eight thousand buildings were destroyed, and 176,000 people were left homeless. Half-melted pocket watches found in the rubble later pinpointed the instant of the detonation: 8:16 A.M.

The atomic bombing of Hiroshima actually did little to change the Japanese high command's feelings about continuing the war. Early in March, American air tactics had changed drastically, from relatively inaccurate, high-altitude daylight bombing to night attacks using incendiaries, targeting the vast areas of Japanese cities given to construction of paper and wood. On the night of March 9 and 10, 279 Superfortresses had struck Tokyo with 1,650 tons of incendiary bombs; the resultant firestorm had killed between 80,000 and 120,000 people and would ultimately prove to be the single most destructive air attack of the war. The firebombings of the past five months had killed an estimated one million Japanese and left fifteen million homeless.

Most of the Japanese military commanders felt that the atomic bomb was simply another weapon, and one that the Japanese people could endure with the same fortitude with which they'd faced the B-san firebombings. In any case, the Americans could not possibly have more than two or three of the weapons.

The war would continue.

On August 9, the B-29 named *Bock's Car* circled at 30,000 feet above the city of Kokura, waiting for a break in the solid cloud deck for a visual sighting of the aim point. The gods of fortune and weather favored Kokura that day. After waiting for forty-five minutes and making three aborted attack runs, the aircraft commander, Major Charles Sweeney, set course for his secondary target: Nagasaki.

At 1449 hours on August 14 — East Longitude Date — Radio Tokyo broadcast to the world the Emperor's decision to surrender. At that, it was a near thing. A military plot to seize the Emperor and capture his prerecorded address was only narrowly defeated, and a plan to launch waves of kamikaze aircraft at the U.S.S. *Missouri* as she entered Tokyo Bay was averted at the last moment by the quick intervention of Prince Takamatsu.

The argument over whether or not the atomic bombing of two cities was necessary went on until long after the war. Some critics charged that the declaration of war by the Soviet Union against the Japanese on August 8 had more to do with undermining Tokyo's resolve than atomic bombs. The fact remained that over one million men remained under arms in the Japanese home islands, and they had abundant supplies of weapons and ammunition stockpiled against the expected invasion. Over five thousand kamikaze aircraft — twice the number already expended — were hidden throughout the islands in caves and underground hangars. The Japanese were more than willing to continue the fight, at the very least to engage in one final battle on Japanese soil for the honor of the nation. Possibly, those within the Japanese military who discounted the danger of further atomic attacks were right; if Japan was willing to face further firebomb attacks, a few more cities obliterated by atomic bombs would be insignificant. It was the prospect of further firebombings, and the knowledge that the Americans were implacable in their demands for absolute surrender of Japan, that had led Emperor Hirohito to intervene in the high command's deliberations and direct the government to surrender.

For the Americans who'd been planning Operations Olympic and Coronet, however, there could be no doubt that Hiroshima and Nagasaki had saved many hundreds of thousands of lives.

The war, at long last, was over.

CHAPTER 40

Saturday, 18 August 1945
The Crypt of the Shrine of the Immaculate Conception
Catholic University, Washington, D.C.

The guests were still arriving, milling about the echoing stone chamber, searching for their proper seats. Commander Coffer, wearing full dress whites, complete with gloves, sword, and a rack of medals on his left chest that clinked ominously when he made any sudden movement, was standing next to the groom, who was also wearing full dress. Lieutenant Commander Joseph Galloway was an old friend of Coffer's, one of the men who'd helped him launch the UDT in the first place, back in early 1943. Though not a graduate of Fort Pierce, Galloway had long served as the staff liaison between the scattered UDTs in the Pacific, the CDUs in the Atlantic, and the top brass in Washington, a thankless task that had grown ever more murky and complex as the teams had expanded from an original handful to over thirty.

"Nervous, Joe?" Coffer asked with a wry grin.

"Hell, yeah," Galloway said. Then he glanced up sharply at the dome of the Crypt overhead, at the massive columns and ornate carvings, reddened, and lowered his voice. "Uh, yes, sir. Yes, I am a little."

"You and Virginia picked a mighty fine day to get married. The Saturday after VJ day!"

"Well, we didn't know that when we planned it. Lucky coincidence, I guess. I'll sure have a tough time ever forgetting our anniversary!"

Coffer chuckled as he turned to survey the influx of guests. Most of the men were in uniform, of course, and the women were a dazzle of color and finery. The entire city had been going not-so-quietly nuts ever since Wednesday, when word of the Japanese surrender had been made official. Galloway's wedding at Catholic University seemed to be only a small and rather subdued aspect of the much larger, spectacularly joyful celebration.

The wedding had attracted a real cross section of Washington society. Galloway's bride-to-be, Virginia Lewis, was the daughter of a prominent Washington attorney who worked in the office of Secretary of War Stimson, and the guests included Pentagon staff officers as well as a variety of civilians who could count themselves among the capital's political and social elite. A few, like Lieutenant William M. Wallace, looked distinctly uncomfortable and out of place in the throng. Wallace had been one of Coffer's earliest choices for the NCDU and had distinguished himself during the Normandy landings. Now he was back in the States, together with his English bride, Alice, and had a job on Galloway's staff. Wallace had always been a blunt, outspoken man, and Coffer doubted he cared much for either his officer's rank, his staff position, or his present surroundings.

Wallace and his wife had another woman with them, small, dark-haired, and quiet. Veronica Richardson, discharged from the WACs, had come home from England with her seven-month-old son, and Wallace, who had stood in for her father at her wedding, had offered the two of them a place to stay. He even found Veronica a civilian Pentagon job after he'd settled in to his own new post.

That was the way it was in the teams — you looked out for your teammates and their families, through good times and bad.

Unlike Wallace, Lieutenant Commander Alexander Hamilton Forsythe III looked completely at ease in the distinguished company. He moved among the guests with the air of a man accustomed to wealth and power, and even his cane, his noticeable limp, and the rough, raspy voice that lingered after his field tracheotomy on Okinawa didn't seem to bother him much. He had been flown back to the Portsmouth Naval Hospital two weeks after he was wounded at Okinawa, and even now, four months later, he was still on light duty. Word had it that his uncle had a place for him in the Pentagon as soon as he was fully recovered.

Coffer suspected they hadn't heard the last of the commander. Though his career in the teams was probably over, his family connections marked him as a man to watch. Not only was his uncle, like Galloway, on Admiral King's staff, but Forsythe's father had been elected to the House of Representatives last year, and with his Navy record young Forsythe would be a natural to follow in his footsteps.

Wallace approached Coffer and Galloway, his wife on his arm. "Well, well," he said, grinning. "Our young lieutenant commander here looks so scared, I thought he was getting ready to reconnoiter a hot beach somewhere."

"Not quite," Coffer said.

"Don't worry, sir," Wallace said, winking, and he patted Alice's arm. "Marriage doesn't hurt a bit. Quite the contrary, in fact."

"It's not the marriage I'm worried about," Galloway said. He seemed to be having trouble deciding how to manage his white gloves, his hat, and his dress sword, and still leave at least one hand free. "It's the blasted ceremony itself. I'll be glad when this stage production is over!"

"Commander?" Wallace asked. "I know now's not really the time…"

"Aw, go ahead and ask him, Lieutenant," Galloway said. "Now that he knows he doesn't have to invade Japan, he'll probably be willing to do or answer almost anything."

"What is it, Mr. Wallace?"

"Well, I was just wondering if you'd heard anything more about what's going to happen to the teams."

"You're anxious to stay in, I take it?"

"Yes, sir, I am. The way I feel, a man could make his whole career in the UDT."

Coffer noticed the shadow of worry that briefly crossed Alice's face, but ignored it. That, too, was a part of being part of the teams.

"Well, I'm afraid I haven't heard a thing, Lieutenant," Coffer replied. "We'll just have to wait and see."

"Yes, sir. Thank you, sir."

The war was scarcely over, and already the politicians were talking about a major scaling back of the military. All of the young men and women who'd joined "for the duration" would be coming home, of course, but quite a few professional career men were likely to lose their careers, simply because a scaled-back military would not have enough open billets to accommodate them all. Coffer had seen several proposals already calling for the complete elimination of the U.S. Marine Corps, which was seen as superfluous by some. The Army, after all, had conducted amphibious operations in all theaters of the conflict. The controversy was fueled by an ongoing campaign being carried out in the press against Admiral

Turner, who was being blamed for excessive Marine casualties on Iwo Jima.

Needless to say, the Underwater Demolition Teams were on the chopping block as well. Sometimes, the politics of peace were more sordid and less easy to understand than the more forthright tactics of war.

Coffer, of course, planned to fight for the teams. The Navy would never be able to support thirty-some UDTs, but Coffer thought it important that at least a small, core unit of experienced men — officers and petty officers, especially — be maintained. The war just ended would not be the final war in America's history, any more than the so-called war to end all wars of almost thirty years ago. And there were so many promising avenues of research opening up: cold-water diving and rubber suits that would keep a swimmer warm and dry; Lambertson's rebreather apparatus; and a promising invention by a French researcher called SCUBA, for "self-contained underwater breathing apparatus." Some Navy scientists had already proposed the use of tiny one-or-two-man submarines that could carry swimmers long distances under water in complete secrecy. All of those developments promised to take the teams into a whole new world of undersea operations.

If the teams could survive. Coffer had already vowed to do everything in his power to see that they did.

As Wallace and his wife walked back into the Crypt's seating area, Galloway turned to Coffer. "You know, sir, it's going to be an uphill fight. For the teams, I mean."

"I was just thinking about that."

"Push-button warfare, Commander. The wave of the future. Look at what the Bomb did to Hiroshima and Nagasaki. It could be that from now on, it'll be the scientists who fight the wars. Not soldiers. And not us."

"You couldn't be more wrong, Joe. Wonder weapons have their place … but there's always going to be a need to go in to grab the beaches. Or to scout them out first. And that will be done by *men*."

The crowd was settling into an excited silence now; the principals of the ceremony were taking their places. From the massive organ to one side, the first strains of the Wedding March droned forth, filling the Crypt with glory.

"You got the ring?" Galloway asked Coffer.

"Right here. Don't worry. It'll all be over in a moment."

The wedding procession began.

Lieutenant Commander Michael T. Waverly stepped down the ramp of the LCVP and stepped into ankle-deep water. He was keenly aware that he and his men were among the first U.S. Navy personnel to set foot in Japan. He was wearing his khakis — not exactly a full dress uniform, which the occasion seemed to demand, but better, at least, than the usual UDT uniform of swim trunks, mask, and grease.

Behind him came Rand, Tangretti, and a dozen other members of Team Twenty-one, together with an escort of Marines. Everyone was armed; the surrender had caught everybody by surprise, so sudden had been the announcement, and even now, two weeks later, there was a lingering fear that this whole thing could be some sort of an elaborate trap.

The transition to the shores of Japan had been abrupt, too fast to really comprehend. Immediately after word had been received of the Japanese surrender, Teams Eighteen and Twenty-one had been flown to Guam, where they'd been hurriedly briefed, then hustled aboard transports bound for Tokyo Bay. One day after troops had landed to seize Tokyo's airport, Waverly was disembarking from a landing craft to take command of one of the forts defending the entrance to Tokyo Bay. Futsu Saki was located on the eastern shore, almost directly across the waters of the Uraga Suido from the large Japanese port of Yokosuka.

Before the invasion, Waverly had heard, Captain Radley, the new CO of the UDTs, had drawn up a master operations plan for the teams that were to be deployed in the invasion of Japan. The orders ran to 151 mimeographed pages, together with thirty-six charts, maps, and diagrams, a massive document that described in detail meticulous enough even for Waverly the enormously complex meshing of reconnaissance and demolition, of fire support, minesweeping, intelligence gathering, logistics, air support, and fleet movements necessary for the thirty UDTs to carry out their assigned tasks for the landings. In two days after word of the Japanese surrender had reached Okinawa, Radley had rewritten the entire tome, transforming it into a plan, not for invasion, but for occupation. Much remained of the original. Beaches still had to be checked for mines or obstacles ahead of the Marines who would be landing there during the week to come.

Above the beach, Fort Number One loomed above the bay, a mountain of concrete abutments and massive ramparts. A long line of Japanese soldiers and marines stood on the walkway at the top of the beach, silent, impassive, their dark eyes watching the Americans set foot on the soil of their homeland.

Reading their expressions, quite frankly, impossible. Waverly would have understood anger ... or sorrow ... or almost any other visible emotion at all, but all he could see was that dark, waiting watchfulness.

An officer was approaching. Waverly stopped, standing at attention, Rand and the others gathered behind. He could feel the tension growing among the tiny party of Americans. If there was to be a betrayal, an ambush, this would be the perfect time for it.

The officer, in army khakis and wearing a long, slightly curved sword in a black scabbard at his side — Waverly had no idea what the man's rank might be — walked stiffly to within four feet of Waverly and stopped, standing rigidly at attention. For an endless moment, Waverly and the Japanese officer stared into one another's eyes. Abruptly, then, the officer bowed, his torso rigid, his eyes on Waverly's feet. "*Konichiwa*," the man said, straightening.

Waverly's sense of propriety suggested that he should bow as well, that that was what was expected, but his briefing in Guam had insisted that Americans did not bow to Japanese Instead, he snapped to rigid attention and saluted. "*Konichiwa*," he said. "Good afternoon."

The officer returned the salute, then reached for the sword. Waverly stiffened but forced himself to remain impassive. Deftly, the officer unbuckled the sword, and then, bowing again, offered it, scabbard and all, to Waverly. "*Dozo...* "

Waverly hesitated, then reached out and accepted the sword in both hands. It was a beautiful thing, with ivory inlay in the richly ornate handle. "Uh ... *domo arigato*," he said, exhausting nearly all of the Japanese he'd learned since leaving Okinawa.

What a souvenir!

Stiffly, the officer bowed yet a third time. "*Dozo, ishsho ni kite kudasai.*" He then turned, leading the Americans up the hill to the fort.

Following him, Waverly imagined that Forsythe would have wanted to have been here. He wished that Coffer could have been here; if anyone deserved to be part of this parade, it was David Coffer.

Still, he was thrilled and proud to be here himself. It had been a long journey from Saipan, one that had ended, at last, with him receiving a command of his own.

Team Twenty-one. He wondered what the future held in store for them.

Steven V. Tangretti, still feeling a bit out of place in his new chief's khakis, stood at attention behind the railing of one of the gun platforms mounted on the battleship *Missouri's* bridge superstructure, starboard side forward. To his left was Rand; to his right was Commander Waverly. They represented a handful of UDT-21's men invited aboard Admiral Halsey's flagship to witness what was certain to be one of the great historic events of the twentieth century. Below him, on *Missouri's* quarter-deck, the uniforms of dozens of nations ringed the gallery where the drama was to unfold.

Curiously, Tangretti picked out the uniforms of several officers from the Soviet Union, big, stolid, and grim-looking men with medals enough on their chests to serve as ancient coats of mail. Already, with the peace with Japan not even signed, there were rumors and scuttlebutt of problems with the Russians, of Communist takeovers in Eastern Europe, of rather blunt Russian demands for a partition of Japan just as they'd won in occupied Germany and Berlin.

Tangretti couldn't help wondering just where this new peace was going to lead. The Russians had been unlikely allies during the war. Now that the war was over...

He'd heard plenty of rumors, too, about the proposed cuts in the U.S. military now that the war was over, and about the likely elimination of the UDT. The atomic bomb, the American press insisted, had just made conventional warfare obsolete.

Tangretti wasn't too worried, however. The war might be over, but there was still a hell of a lot of work to be done. Eighteen more UDTs had already sailed for Japan; like Eighteen and Twenty-one, they would participate in the dismantling of the Japanese defenses, in Japan itself, and in both Korea and China. And for the future? Well, the teams had proven themselves time after time. Tangretti was pretty sure that the UDT would be around for a long time to come. Whether the enemy proved to be the Russians or someone else, the fact of the atomic bomb did not make specialized units like the teams obsolete. If anything, the threat that the bomb *might* be used made small wars more likely. It could well turn out that, where nations were afraid to unleash the destructive power of atomic bombs in another world war, they might instead resort to little wars.

And without any doubt at all, he knew that the UDT would be there.

His eyes strayed to the Imperial representatives, a delegation of nine, headed by Foreign Minister Shigemitsu Mamoru in rather bizarrely formal top hat and tails, standing at attention opposite a small table. It was still so hard to believe that *this* war was over, that imagining any future war was impossible.

Behind the table, the new Supreme Commander, Allied Powers, Five-Star General of the Army Douglas MacArthur, stood behind a microphone set up for the ceremonies.

"It is my hope," MacArthur was saying, "indeed, the hope of all mankind, that from this solemn occasion a better world shall emerge out of the blood and carnage of the past, a world founded upon faith and understanding, a world dedicated to the dignity of man and the fulfillment of his most cherished wish for freedom, tolerance, and justice…"

He always did have a way with speeches, Tangretti thought. With the end of the war, the bitterness against the brass, largely, had left him, though he retained a wry cynicism about the way things had been run and were being run now. There was the business of Waverly's sword, for instance, the sword the commander of the Japanese fort outside Tokyo Bay had surrendered to him. The American occupation authorities had made him give up the sword and hushed the whole thing over; nothing, *nothing* must detract from the supreme moment when the Japanese representatives surrendered to MacArthur.

The symbolism of a Japanese military authority surrendering his sword to a mere commander of a UDT before the final surrender was official was quite unthinkable!

No matter. The members of Team Twenty-one had already put things in their proper perspective. While working at the docks at Futsu Saki, Tangretti, Rand, Foglio, and Davies had gotten together with a number of the other men and prepared what was known as a demolition banner, erecting it above the docks, facing all incoming ships and troops.

The sign had read, naturally:

WELCOME, MARINES!

EPILOGUE

Thursday, 23 November 1961
Oval Office, the White House

"Gentlemen," the usher announced. "The President of the United States."

They'd been summoned in at last, Tangretti, Waverly, and Galloway ... three officers who'd been involved for some time in the organization of a new and badly needed special operations unit for the United States Navy.

The President, his familiar features fixed in the politician's eternal smile, advanced from behind the desk and extended his hand. He shook hands with Captain Galloway first, then with Waverly, and finally with Tangretti.

"Mr. Tangretti," the President said with his thickest Boston twang. "I've, ah, I've heard a lot about you. As a former Navy man myself, it's good to finally get to meet the man who's been writing so many, ah, unusual ideas about what the Navy should be doing."

"Uh, thank you, Mr. President." Utterly flustered, losing completely the carefully rehearsed speech he'd been carrying in his mind, he could only stammer and say, "I, uh ... I'm afraid I didn't vote for you, sir."

The President's boyish face split into a genuine smile this time, and he laughed. "That's okay, Mr. Tangretti. The problem is, not nearly enough people did!" Turning to his desk, the President picked up a manila folder and thumbed it open. "In any case, this is not a job for politicians. Now, you three have all been involved in the groundwork for creating a

Navy special operations unit. You, Mr. Tangretti, especially, wrote a very interesting report, in which you suggested, ah, rather strongly, as I recall, that this new unit be self-sufficient, with its own means of transport to and from a combat area, that it be trained in various special techniques for insertion and extraction from the battle zone." He found a page of the report and read it briefly. "You mention in particular, deployments by parachute, by small boat, by helicopter, and by midget submarine.

"You go on to suggest, again, rather strongly, that this unit be fully trained in small arms and small unit tactics, that they be allowed to operate far inland and behind enemy lines, rather than being limited to the Navy's normal, blue water purview. Tell me, ah, Mr. Tangretti. Why do you think the Navy needs a unit of this nature?"

Tangretti glanced at Waverly, who gave him a small but unmistakable wink. "Because, Mr. President," he said without hesitation, "there are times when we can't let ourselves be tied down by the rules. What are you going to do, draw a line, like they did in Korea, and say you can't cross that line even when doing so would save lives?"

"Sometimes, Mr. Tangretti, it is necessary for us to draw such lines."

"Maybe. But wouldn't it be nice to have a group that didn't work according to the rules? That could go anywhere, do anything? Besides, the Navy needs a combat element that can project itself ashore, quietly, effectively, and in complete secrecy. That used to be the job of the Marines, but they're established now as their own force, and they have their own agenda, their own equipment and budgetary needs. I would like to see something smaller, supported by the Navy but not dependent on it, that can give the fleet the reach it needs sometimes. Across the high-tide line. Maybe even across international boundaries."

"I see." The President glanced through several more pages, then dropped the folder onto his desk. "You are a persuasive speaker, Mr. Tangretti. I should tell you, however, that Captain Galloway and Captain Waverly have already discussed this with me at length. The idea has been making the rounds up on the Hill too. Senator Forsythe has been pushing it especially hard. I have just signed an order authorizing the formation of a new unit, which will have duties and responsibilities along the lines of what you wrote in your report."

"Thank you, Mr. President!"

"This unit will have, as its proper area of operations, the sea, the air, and the land. The special operations people over in the Pentagon have already put sea, air, and land together into a new acronym: SEALs.

"That will be the name of your new unit."

Tangretti was so excited at the prospect, he almost missed the import of what the President had just said. He had just opened his mouth to say something when the thought registered. He stopped, closed his mouth, and blinked. "Uh … excuse me, sir. *My* new unit?"

"If you want the job. I'm following your recommendation that the men for this new unit be drawn, at least initially, from the ranks of the current members of the Underwater Demolition Teams. And I would like you to head up the unit. It will be your job to work out the training, the equipment, the appropriations, everything the SEALs will need to become the sort of team you've described in your report."

Tangretti felt dizzy. "I … I accept, Mr. President. I'll certainly do my best!"

"I know you will."

The SEALs ... and he was to put the unit together! He wasn't sure, but he had the feeling that the President was already thinking about how the new team could be employed.

Suddenly he couldn't wait to get home to Veronica, to tell her the news.

A NOTE TO THE READER

Dear Reader,
If you have enjoyed this novel enough to leave a review on **Amazon** and **Goodreads**, then we would be truly grateful.
Sapere Books

Sapere Books is an exciting new publisher of brilliant fiction and popular history.

To find out more about our latest releases and our monthly bargain books visit our website:
saperebooks.com

www.ingramcontent.com/pod-product-compliance
Lightning Source LLC
Chambersburg PA
CBHW022233020726
47496CB00004B/883